Praise for Patricia Davids and her novels

"Quaint characters and tender moments
combine in this...sweet tale."
—*RT Book Reviews* on *A Hope Springs Christmas*

"Davids' deep understanding of Amish culture
is evident in the compassionate characters
and beautiful descriptions that enliven her
heartwarming story."
—*RT Book Reviews* on *A Home for Hannah*

"Davids' latest beautifully portrays the Amish
belief that everything happens for a reason,
which helps one focus on the
most important things in life."
—*RT Book Reviews* on *The Christmas Quilt*

"*Military Daddy* [is] a lovingly sweet romance.
This story deftly and evenly covers many subjects,
including alcoholism. Kudos to Patricia Davids."
—*RT Book Reviews*

PATRICIA DAVIDS
His Bundle of Love

&

The Color of Courage

Recycling programs
for this product may
not exist in your area.

LOVE INSPIRED BOOKS

ISBN-13: 978-0-373-65159-7

HIS BUNDLE OF LOVE AND THE COLOR OF COURAGE
Copyright © 2013 by Harlequin Books S.A.

The publisher acknowledges the copyright holder
of the individual works as follows:

HIS BUNDLE OF LOVE
Copyright © 2006 by Patricia MacDonald

THE COLOR OF COURAGE
Copyright © 2007 by Patricia MacDonald

This edition published by arrangement with Love Inspired Books.

® and TM are trademarks of Love Inspired Books, used under license.
Trademarks indicated with ® are registered in the United States Patent
and Trademark Office, the Canadian Trade Marks Office and in other
countries.

www.LoveInspiredBooks.com

Printed in U.S.A.

CONTENTS

Books by Patricia Davids

Love Inspired

His Bundle of Love
Love Thine Enemy
Prodigal Daughter
The Color of Courage
Military Daddy
A Matter of the Heart
A Military Match
A Family for Thanksgiving
*Katie's Redemption
*The Doctor's Blessing
*An Amish Christmas
*The Farmer Next Door
*The Christmas Quilt
*A Home for Hannah
*A Hope Springs Christmas

*Brides of Amish Country

Love Inspired Suspense

A Cloud of Suspicion
Speed Trap

PATRICIA DAVIDS

After thirty-five years as a nurse, Pat has hung up her stethoscope to become a full-time writer. She enjoys spending her new free time visiting her grandchildren, doing some long-overdue yard work and traveling to research her story locations. She resides in Wichita, Kansas. Pat always enjoys hearing from her readers. You can visit her on the web at www.patriciadavids.com.

HIS BUNDLE OF LOVE

And whoever welcomes a little child like this
in my name welcomes me.
—*Matthew* 18:5

For David, who always believed
I could do anything I set my heart on.
And for my mother, Joan.
"Look, Mom! No sleaze!"

Chapter One

"Hey, wait! Mister, you gotta help us!"

Mick O'Callaghan stopped at the sound of the frantic shout. He turned to see a grubby, bearded derelict emerge from the doorway of an abandoned building, one of many that lined the narrow Chicago street. As the man stumbled down the dilapidated steps, Mick recognized Eddy Todd. Eddy, in his stained and tattered overcoat, was a frequent flyer at the Mercy House Shelter where Mick volunteered two days a week.

Staggering up to Mick, Eddy grabbed the front of his brown leather jacket. "Please. You gotta help. She's havin' a baby! I don't know what to do. You gotta help her."

"Take it easy, Eddy. Slow down and tell me what's wrong."

Eddy squinted up at Mick's face, and some of the panic left his watery, gray eyes. "That you, Mick?"

"Yeah, it's me." He kept the old fellow from falling by catching his elbows. The sour odors of an unwashed body and cheap whiskey assaulted Mick. No doubt Eddy had been out panhandling, and some well-meaning Samaritan had given him money for a meal, but he had spent it on a bottle instead.

Eddy regained his balance and tugged at Mick's arm. "Come on. You're a fireman. You can deliver a baby, can't ya?"

Mick cast a doubtful eye at the old tenement. What would a pregnant woman be doing in there? Only broken shards of glass remained in the few windows that weren't boarded over. A section of the roof had collapsed, and debris littered the area. The only signs of life were a few weeds that had sprouted in the sidewalk cracks and struggled to survive in the weak April sunshine. It wasn't the kind of place he wanted to go searching through—especially for an old drunk's hallucinations.

With a gentle tug, Mick tried to coax Eddy away. "Why don't you come down to the mission. Pastor Frank can get you a hot meal. It's meat loaf tonight. You like meat loaf, don't you?"

"Sure, sure, I like meat loaf." Eddy allowed himself to be led for a few steps, then he stopped. "But what about the girl? She shouldn't have her baby in there. It ain't clean, or nothing. Come on, I'll show ya where she is."

Mick studied the building again. What if Eddy wasn't imagining things? He glanced at his watch. Normally, it didn't matter how he spent his days off, but since his mother had moved in for an extended stay after her accident, he tried to make sure she didn't spend much time alone. Tonight was the nurse's night off. Naomi would be leaving in an hour. Perhaps if he hurried, he could check the place out, take Eddy over to the mission and get home before she left.

He turned back to the old man. "I'll take a look, but I want you to stay here," he insisted.

"Sure, sure. I'll stay ri-right here." Eddy nodded, lost his balance and staggered back a step. He wavered on his feet but stayed upright. "You want I should call an ambulance?"

Mick shook his head and hid a smile. "I'll do that if we need one. You just stay put."

Walking carefully up the broken steps, he ducked under crisscrossed boards someone had nailed over the doorway in a vain attempt to keep people out. It took a few moments for his eyes to adjust in the gloomy interior. He faced a long hall with a dozen doors down its length. The first one stood open, and he looked in.

A tattered mattress surrounded by heaps of cardboard boxes lay in one corner. Old clothes, tin cans and trash covered the floor. The place reeked of stale sweat and rancid garbage. As he stepped back, his foot struck an empty bottle of whiskey and sent it rolling across the warped floorboards. Apparently, Eddy had been holed up in there for some time. At least there was no sign of a pregnant woman. Mick turned to leave, but the sound of a low moan stopped him.

It came again, and he moved down the hall to investigate, skirting a pile of broken furniture and fallen ceiling plaster that all but blocked the dark hall. The last door on the left stood open a crack. He hesitated beside it. Four years as a firefighter had taught him caution. Plenty of unsavory characters inhabited these slums, and some of them could be very unpleasant if he'd stumbled onto a meth lab or another equally illegal operation.

Another moan, louder this time, issued from the

room. Someone was in pain. He couldn't ignore that. Standing with his back to the wall, he stretched out his arm and eased open the door. From behind, a hand clamped down on his shoulder, and Mick's breath froze in his chest.

"What ya doin'?" a slurred voice wheezed.

Relief surged through Mick as his heart began beating again. He turned and whispered, "Eddy, you scared the life out of me! Didn't I tell you to stay put?"

"Yeah—yeah, you told me, but she's in here. I found some help," he announced and barged through the door.

Mick followed with more caution. Light poured in from a large, broken window on the back wall. It showed a room surprisingly neat and free of the stench that permeated Eddy's lair. It contained little more than a bare mattress where a young woman with short blond hair lay on her side. She wore a simple black skirt and a pale pink sweater with long sleeves. Her splayed fingers covered her small, rounded belly beneath the sweater. A thin wail escaped her clenched lips. This was definitely not a hallucination.

At the sound of voices, Caitlin Williams lifted her head and sighed in relief. Eddy had managed to bring help. She was sorry she had doubted the old guy. The young man with him crossed the room and dropped to one knee beside her.

"Can you tell me what's wrong?" he asked.

Scared out of her wits but determined not to show it, Caitlin said, "I think my baby's coming."

His fingers closed around her wrist, and he stared at his watch. "How far apart are your contractions?"

"Right on top of each other," she panted, trying to

stifle a groan as another one gripped her. "You a doctor?"

"No, I'm an EMT. Don't worry, I know what to do."

He sounded so calm, so confident. Maybe it would be okay. Peering up at him, she realized with a jolt that she knew him.

She'd seen him at the nearby homeless shelter where she got some of her meals. Only last week, she had watched him playing football with some of the kids there. He'd caught a wobbling pass and staggered toward the makeshift goalposts with half a dozen of them hanging on and trying to pull him down. His muscular frame had made light work of the load, but it was his hearty laughter that had truly drawn her interest. His rugged good looks and dark auburn hair made him easy on the eyes. At the time, she had thought his face was more interesting than handsome. It had character.

"I know you. At the shelter they called you Mickey O."

A warm smile curved his lips and deepened the crinkles at the corners of his bright, blue eyes. "Mick O'Callaghan at your service. And you are?" A vague trace of Irish brogue lilted through his deep baritone voice.

"Caitlin Williams," she supplied through gritted teeth.

"Pleased to meet you." He laid a gentle hand on her stomach. "When is your baby due?"

"Not till—" Pressing her lips together, Caitlin waited for the pains to pass. "August," she finished.

His startled gaze flew to her face, and her fears came rushing back to choke her. "My baby will be okay, won't it?"

"I'll do everything I can." He reached into his pocket and pulled out a cell phone. He flipped open the lid, then muttered, "Not now."

Caitlin saw the worried look in his eyes. "What's wrong?"

"The battery is dead. Eddy?" he called over his shoulder. "I need you to go get that ambulance, now. And hurry!"

"Ri-right, Mick, sure thing. Um…where should I go?"

"Go to Pastor Frank. Tell him Mick O'Callaghan says to call an ambulance, then bring him here. Can you do that?" Taking off his jacket, Mick spread it over Caitlin and tucked it around her shoulders.

Eddy nodded. "Sure, I can do that."

Mick saw the old man stagger as he hurried out the door. Torn between the need to stay with the woman or make sure that help was called he looked at her and said, "Maybe I should go."

She grabbed his arm. "No, stay, please. Eddy can do it. Stay and take care of my baby."

"Okay, I'll stay." He composed his face, determined to keep her calm. He knew a baby born three months early wouldn't survive unless it waited to be born in a hospital.

Please, Heavenly Father, guide me in making the right decisions here.

Her face tightened into a grimace as she curled forward again. "Something's wrong. It hurts."

"You need to breathe through your contractions, like this." He demonstrated. "Come on, breathe, breathe."

"You breathe. I'm going to scream."

She didn't and he admired her control. "Tell you

what, we'll take turns. Every other contraction, I get to scream, and you breathe."

She uncurled and relaxed back onto the mattress. "What have you got to yell about?"

He gave a pointed glance to where she gripped his arm. "You're doing a bit of acupuncture with those fingernails."

She jerked away. "I'm sorry."

"Why don't you hold my hand?" He offered it, but she ignored him and gripped the edge of the mattress instead, and he regretted saying anything.

He had seen this young woman occasionally at Pastor Frank's shelter in the last month. She would show up for the evening meal, but she never stayed long. Like many of the women at Mercy House, she kept to herself. He'd never spoken to her, yet something in her eyes had captured his attention the first time he saw her.

The women who came to Mercy House were mostly single mothers with ragged children in tow or old women alone and without families. Their eyes were dull with hopelessness, desperation and sadness, but life hadn't emptied this girl's eyes—they blazed with defiance.

Up close, their unusual color intrigued him. A light golden brown, they held flecks of green that made them seem to change with the light. They reminded him of the eyes of a cougar he had seen in the zoo. Aloof, watchful, wary. Only now, raw fear lurked in their depths.

Come on, Eddy, don't let me down. Get that ambulance here.

Struggling to hide his concerns, Mick searched for a way to establish a rapport and put her at ease. "Have you got a name picked out for your baby?"

"No. I thought I had plenty of time."

He gave her a wry smile. "I've got names picked out for my kids, and I'm not even married yet."

She arched an eyebrow. "Goody for you."

"A kid's name is important. It's something you should give a lot of thought. Not that you haven't—or wouldn't—I mean," he murmured as he ducked his head.

Caitlin couldn't believe it. This grown man, as big as a house, and probably twenty-five years old was blushing. His neck grew almost as red as his hair. It was sweet, really.

What could she say to someone about to deliver her baby? Things were going to get intimate. Maybe soon. She felt the beginnings of another contraction and reached for his hand. His large fingers engulfed her small ones. Strength and reassurance seemed to flow from him into her, easing her fear. Focusing on his face, she followed his instructions to breathe in and blow out. The pain did seem more bearable.

As the contraction faded, she realized he still held her hand. She pulled away and drew his jacket close, relishing the warmth and comforting scent of leather and masculine cologne. The quiet of the old building pressed in around them.

"So, tell me what names you got picked out," she said at last. "Maybe I'll use one."

He smiled. "For a boy, it'll be William Perry."

"Willie Perry Williams." She tried the name out but shook her head. "Not a chance. Why would you do that to a kid?"

"Are you joking? William 'The Refrigerator' Perry

was the greatest football player in the history of the Chicago Bears."

Her husband had liked football. The thought of Vinnie sent a stab of regret through her heart. He would never see his son or daughter. How she had hoped that he would give up his wild ways once he knew they were having a baby. He hadn't. A high-speed chase while trying to outrun the police ended his life when his car veered off the highway and struck a tree. His death that night had started her down the painful path that led to her current desperate situation.

Within days she had discovered that Vinnie had been gambling away the rent money she worked so hard to earn. The landlord didn't want to hear her sob story. He wanted his money. Three months of unpaid rent was more than she could come up with. She was evicted the day after her husband's funeral. With no money and nowhere to go, she soon found herself living on the streets. The one place she swore she'd never go back to.

She took a close look at her rescuer. Was he the same kind of man? One who would drink and gamble and then lie to his pregnant wife about it? She didn't believe that. Not a guy who liked kids as much as he did.

Managing a little smile, she said, "You don't plan on naming a girl after a football player, do you?"

"No," he answered quietly. "I'll name her after my mother. Elizabeth Anne O'Callaghan."

Amazing! If this guy was any sweeter, he'd rival a candy bar.

Another contraction hit, and his hand found hers. "You got it, that's it. Breathe," he coaxed. "Breathe, breathe. You're doing great."

She curled onto her side and focused on his singsong

voice. With his free hand, he began to rub her lower back in slow circles. Okay, she thought, a sweet guy is a good thing to have around just now.

"Is there someone I can call once we get to the hospital?" he asked. "Family? The baby's father?"

She shook her head. "Vinnie, my husband, he's dead. There's nobody."

"I'm sorry."

She bristled at the pity in his voice. Normally, she would have ignored it, but now she couldn't seem to control the emotions that flared in her.

"I don't need your pity. I've had a little bad luck, that's all." She raised up on her elbow to glare at him. "I'll be on my feet again in no time and a lot better off than I was before."

Holding up one hand, he said, "Chill, lady. I wasn't feeling sorry for you."

"You'd better not. I can take care of myself. And I can take care of my baby, too."

"In here?" He gestured around the room. The broken window let the wind in, and strips of dingy wallpaper peeling from the stained plaster waved in the breeze that carried the smells of mildew and rotting wood.

"Lady, I've seen kids living in places like this covered with rat bites and worse. If you think you can go it alone, you're crazy. There's a system to help if you'll use it."

"Why do you care? You want to name your little girl after your mother, right? You know what I remember about dear old Mom? On my fifth birthday she gave me a Twinkie with a candle in it. Then she left me inside a Dumpster for two days because she was too strung out to remember where she'd put me to keep me quiet while some new boyfriend supplied her habit. Your precious system moved me from one foster home to another when it wasn't giving me back to Mom so she could have another go at me. By the time I was sixteen, I'd figured out living in a back alley was a better deal. Your *system* isn't going to get its hands on my baby. I'll make sure of that."

She squeezed her eyes shut, fighting to hold back a scream as the pain overwhelmed her.

"Okay, you've had it rough," he said gently. "Show me one kid down at the shelter that hasn't. But, if Child Welfare finds out this is where you're living, do you think they're going to let you bring a baby here? I'm just saying stay at a shelter until you find something better. It's not you I'm worried about, it's the baby."

Everyone who'd ever shown her compassion had had their own agenda in mind. Why did she think this guy was any different? Why did she find herself believing he really did care?

"How come you're so concerned about someone else's kid?"

He stared out the broken window for a long moment without speaking, then he looked at her and said, "Maybe because I can't have kids of my own."

She frowned. "I don't get it. What about the names?"

The smile he tried for was edged with sadness. "If I ever marry, I'll adopt children."

"You look healthy to me," she said, giving him the once-over. "What's wrong with you?"

He hesitated, then admitted, "I had a bad case of the mumps when I was a teenager. It left me sterile." He shrugged. "It's just one of those things."

But not a little thing, Caitlin thought as she glimpsed the sadness in his eyes.

"Mick? Mick O'Callaghan?" A shout echoed through the building.

"Last room on the left, Pastor," Mick shouted back.

The sound of someone clambering past the debris in the hall reached them. A moment later, Pastor Frank's bald head appeared in the doorway. "Mick, what are you doing in here? Eddy was raving about you delivering a baby."

His eyes, behind silver wire-rimmed glasses, widened as he caught sight of Caitlin. "For goodness' sake. Are you?"

"Not yet, but we could be. Did you call for an ambulance?"

"I did." The sound of a distant siren followed his words.

Mick turned to her and smiled. "Everything's going to be all right now."

He gripped her hand again. The warmth and strength of his touch made her believe him. He would take care of her and her baby.

Twenty minutes later, two paramedics loaded the stretcher she lay on into the ambulance. Another contraction hit, stronger this time. As she tried to pant through it, the need to push became uncontrollable. One of the paramedics started to close the door, shutting Mick out.

"Wait," she shouted. "He's got to come with me."

She wasn't sure why she needed Mick. Maybe it was because he truly seemed to care—about her, and about her baby.

She stretched her hand out and pleaded, "Please, Mick, we need you."

The two paramedics looked at Mick. The older one said, "Okay, O'Callaghan, come on. We're wasting time." He motioned with his head, and Mick jumped in. Moments later, the ambulance rolled with red lights and siren.

Mick knew he'd be late getting home for sure now. He would have to call once he reached the hospital. The last thing he wanted was to worry his mother. Yet, for some reason he knew he couldn't let Caitlin go through this alone.

She didn't have anyone. He couldn't imagine what that must be like. Besides his mother, he had two sisters, a dozen nephews and nieces and more cousins than he could count. There were enough O'Callaghans in Chicago to fill the upper deck at Wrigley Field, while this destitute young woman was totally alone.

No, God had set his feet on the path that led to Caitlin today. Mick couldn't believe the Lord wanted him to bail out now. Taking her hand, he smiled at her and said, "You got it now. Just breathe."

The siren wailed overhead. Caitlin struggled to block out the sound as she panted through the contraction with Mick coaching her. Why didn't they shut it off? She couldn't concentrate. She needed to hear his voice telling her everything was going to be okay. And she needed to push.

She was pushing by the time the ambulance reached the hospital. Her stretcher was quickly unloaded and wheeled into the building. People came at her from all directions, yelling instructions, asking for information and giving orders she couldn't follow. All she could do was bear down and push a new life into the world as she clung to Mick's hand like a lifeline.

A sudden gush of fluid soaked the stretcher, and her tiny baby slid into the hands of a startled doctor. "We have a girl," he said. Mick lifted Caitlin's head so she could see.

"She's so small." Dread snaked its way into her soul as they whisked her daughter to a table with warming lamps glowing above it.

"Is she okay? Why isn't she crying?" Caitlin tightened her grip on Mick's hand. So many people crowded around the baby that she couldn't see her. She tried to sit up, but a nurse held her back.

"Your baby's being taken care of."

"Just tell me she's okay. Please, someone tell me she's okay." Frantic now, Caitlin struggled to push the nurse aside, but a sudden, sharp pain in her chest halted her.

She tried to draw a breath but couldn't get any air. Something was wrong, terribly wrong. She collapsed back onto the bed as the crushing pain overwhelmed her.

Long minutes later, they wheeled the baby's bed up beside her. Caitlin turned her head and focused on her daughter's small face. For an instant, all her pain faded away.

Her baby was so beautiful—so tiny—so perfect. But she wasn't moving. Someone spoke, but Caitlin couldn't hear them over the roaring in her ears. Then they pushed her baby's bed out the door. Their faces were all so grim.

"Is she dead, Mick?" Caitlin whispered, terrified to hear the answer.

"No," he answered quickly. "They're taking her to

the NICU. It's a special intensive care just for babies. They'll take good care of her there. She's going to be fine."

"Why isn't—she crying?" The pain in her chest made it hard to talk.

"It's because she's so premature," Mick answered. "She has a tube going into her airway to help her breathe, and she can't make any sound with that in."

Caitlin's own breathing had become short, labored panting. A frowning nurse slipped a plastic mask over Caitlin's face and spoke to the doctor. He frowned, too.

Caitlin looked from face to face. She didn't know any of these people. Who would look after her baby?

She gripped Mick's arm, pulling him closer. "Go with her."

He glanced at the E.R. staff, then back to her. "I think I should stay with you."

"I'm fine," she insisted. She forced a smile to her trembling lips. A strange cold was seeping into her bones. "Stay with—Beth. Watch over her for me."

He patted her hand. "Okay. I'll be back soon."

Nodding, she whispered, "Thank you," and watched him hurry out the door.

The nurse beside her claimed her attention. "I need you to tell me your name."

"Caitlin—Williams," she wheezed.

"Are you allergic to any medication? Are you using any street drugs?" Caitlin shook her head at each question the nurse fired at her. The room grew dark around the edges.

So this was what it was like to die. She wanted to cry because she knew what would happen to her daughter now—the same things that had happened to her. It wasn't fair.

"Who is your next of kin?" The nurse continued to insist on answers. Caitlin only wanted to close her eyes and rest, but more people crowded around her, taking her blood pressure, listening to her heart, poking needles in her arm, sticking wires on her chest. They were all frowning.

"Is the man who came in with you the baby's father?" the nurse asked.

"What?" Caitlin tried to focus on the woman's face.

"I said, is that man the baby's father?"

Would Mick see that her daughter was taken care of? She could say he was the father, then he'd have the right to look after her. Would he understand? It didn't matter, she was out of time. She nodded as she whispered, "Yes."

"What is his name?"

"Mick…O'Callaghan." *Don't let her be alone, Mick. Please, take care of her.*

Darkness swooped in and began to pull Caitlin away. She struggled against it. She needed to stay for her baby.

"We're losing her," someone shouted.

Chapter Two

Mick caught up with the baby as they wheeled her into the nearest elevator. Squeezing in beside them, he stared in amazement at Caitlin's daughter. He'd never seen anything so tiny. Her head was no bigger than the palm of his hand; his little finger was thicker than her gangly legs, yet she was so complete. Downy, brown hair covered her head and miniature wrinkles creased her forehead above arching brows. She even had eyelashes! The tiny spikes lay curved against her cheek. Awed by the wonder of this new life, he gazed at her in fascination. Truly, here was one of God's greatest creations.

Her delicate hands flew up and curled around the breathing tube taped in her mouth.

"No, honey, don't pull on that," a nurse chided as she pried the tiny fingers loose. "Hold Daddy's hand instead," she suggested with an encouraging smile.

Hesitantly, almost fearfully, Mick reached for the baby's hand. Her thin fingers gripped his large, blunt one. Her eyes fluttered open. She stared at him and blinked, then her frown deepened into a scowl. An identical, miniature version of her mother's, and Michael Aaron O'Callaghan fell hopelessly in love.

"She looks like her mom," he said, surprised to hear the catch in his voice. He glanced at the woman beside him. "Will she be all right?"

"She has a very good chance, but there is a long road ahead of her, I'm afraid. I'm Dr. Wright. I'm one of the neonatologists on staff here. Her lungs are much too immature to work properly, so she's going to need help. She'll be placed on a ventilator once we reach the unit." As she spoke, she continued rhythmically squeezing a small, gray bag that delivered oxygen to the baby. "Do you have a name for her?"

"Beth," he answered, "or maybe Elizabeth. Her mother can tell you for sure. When can she come and see her?"

"We'll be busy getting Beth admitted and stabilized for the next hour or so. I'd suggest you wait until then to bring Mom in." The elevator doors slid open, and Mick followed them as they wheeled the baby across the hall and into the NICU.

A flurry of activity began as soon as they entered the large room. At first, it seemed like nurses were scurrying in all directions at once, but it quickly became apparent it was a controlled rush as Beth was placed on a larger bed, and hooked to a waiting ventilator. Within minutes, a jungle of wires, IV poles, tubing and oxygen hoses surrounded her.

Glancing around the room, Mick noted with amusement its peculiar mix of Mother Goose and science-fiction technology. Rows of flashing monitors and digital displays shared wall space with giant nursery-rhyme characters above the open beds and incubators. IV poles held bags of fluid, swaying mobiles and colorful toys.

Dr. Wright spoke as she worked. "We need to administer a medication directly into Beth's lungs to help mature them and start some IVs."

Mick interrupted, "What are her chances, honestly?"

"She weighs barely two pounds, and she looks to be about twenty-six weeks gestation, which means she was born fourteen weeks early. Her chances of survival are good if she doesn't develop any serious complications. Only time will tell."

After the excitement of Beth's admission died down, the nurses let Mick sit beside her bed. He couldn't get over how adorable she looked in spite of the tubes and wires. His heart warmed to her as he watched her with a sense of wonder and fascination. After a while, he glanced at the clock surprised to see how late it was. In the rush of events he had forgotten to call home.

"I'd better go and tell your mother how you're doing. I know she's worried."

He took a last look at the little girl whose arrival had generated so much activity. "Goodbye, Beth. Be well," he whispered, knowing he might never see her again. His mother's voice echoed in his mind, and he smiled. He took hold of her tiny hand. "May God grant you many years to live, for sure He must be knowing, the Earth has angels all too few, and heaven's overflowing."

A nurse across the bed smiled at him as she added medication to a bag of IV fluid. "Are you a poet?"

Sheepishly, he grinned. "It's an old Irish blessing, something my mother always says as a kind of birthday wish."

"It's darling. I'll write it out and put it on her bed.

We like to keep personal things by the babies, like toys or photos. Things that help the families connect with their baby."

She reached out and patted his arm. "I'm Sandra Carter. Try not to worry, Irish. She's a fighter, I can tell."

"I hope you're right."

"Hold out your hand." He did and she fastened a hospital wristband around his arm. "You'll need this to get back in."

He fingered the white strip of plastic without comment. He was here under false pretenses, but only because Caitlin had insisted. Still, that didn't quite ease his conscience.

After making his way back to the E.R., he halted on the threshold of the room where he'd left Caitlin. It was empty.

Out at the main desk, Mick spoke to the heavyset woman seated behind it. "Excuse me. Can you tell me where they've taken the woman who just had a baby here?"

"The patient's name?" she asked in a bored voice, continuing to write on the paper in front of her.

"Caitlin Williams."

She laid down her pen, then shuffled through the charts beside her. She located one, flipped it open, then gave him a startled look. "Let me get Dr. Reese to speak with you."

She hoisted her bulk out of the chair and opened a door behind her. "Doctor, there's someone here asking about the Williams woman."

The unease Mick felt intensified when the grave-looking doctor emerged from the doorway. "Are you family?" he asked.

"No. I'm—a friend. Is something wrong?"

"I'm afraid so. Ms. Williams has developed a rare complication of pregnancy called amniotic fluid embolus."

"What does that mean?"

Drawing a deep breath, the doctor continued, "It means during her delivery, some of the amniotic fluid got into her blood stream. Once there, it traveled up through her heart and lodged in her lung preventing her from getting enough oxygen. That stopped her heart."

"She's dead?" Mick struggled to grasp the man's words.

"No," Dr. Reese admitted slowly. "We were able to restart her heart. Ms. Williams is on a ventilator now, but she hasn't regained consciousness. The lack of oxygen can cause profound brain damage, and the embolus can cause uncontrollable bleeding problems. Her condition is extremely serious. She's unlikely to survive."

Unlikely to survive? The phrase echoed inside Mick's head, filling him with a profound sadness. Caitlin was so young. She had a baby who needed her. What would happen to Beth now?

He raked a hand through his hair. "I should have stayed with her. I knew something wasn't right."

"I heard her tell you to go with the baby," the doctor said gently. "These patients often have an overwhelming sense of doom. She knew, and she chose to have you stay with her child. She's a very brave young woman."

"I'm sorry to interrupt," the clerk spoke up. "Doctor, you're needed in room six."

He nodded, then looked at Mick. "I'm sorry we couldn't do more," he said, then hurried away.

"Are you Mick O'Callaghan?" the clerk asked. Mick nodded. The woman pushed several sheets of paper toward him and offered him a pen. "We need you to fill out these forms, and I'll need a copy of your insurance card."

"My insurance card? For what?"

"For your baby."

"No, you don't understand. Beth isn't mine."

"According to Caitlin Williams, she is," the clerk said smugly.

Just then, Sandra and two other NICU nurses rounded the corner and walked past. "Hey, Irish," Sandra said with a bright smile. "I'm glad I ran into you. My shift is over, but I'll be back in the morning. Your daughter's doing fine, but you need to leave us a phone number. We overlooked that detail in the rush of her admission."

She started to leave, but stopped and turned. "Oh, I wrote out your mother's blessing and taped it to Beth's bed. Several other parents have asked for a copy of it. I hope you don't mind." She waved and followed her friends out the door.

"It seems a lot of people think she's your baby," the clerk said with a smirk.

It took a call to his attorney to convince the woman that unless Mick himself had signed the paternity papers, he had no legal responsibility for the child—something Mick suspected she knew already. After that, he called home to make sure his mother was all right. Surprisingly, his mother's friend and part-time nurse Naomi answered the phone.

"It's about time you called," she scolded.

"I know. I had to take someone to the hospital. I'm glad you could stay. I hope it wasn't an inconvenience."

"I can watch my favorite TV shows here as well as at home. Besides, your mother is good company."

"How is she today?"

"Determined to get up and clean house even with her arm in a cast. I knew it was a mistake for that doctor to take her ankle brace off. The woman has less sense than you."

"Keep her down even if you have to sit on her. And tell her I'll be home in a hour or so."

Knowing that his mother wasn't alone was a relief. After hanging up, he went in search of Caitlin. At the medical ICU, a nurse led him to Caitlin's room. He paused in the doorway. A single bed occupied the small room. He stepped next to it and rested his hands on the cold metal rails.

She looked utterly helpless lying with the sheets neatly folded under her arms and her hands at her sides. A thick, white tube protruded from her mouth connecting her to a ventilator. The soft hiss it made as it delivered each breath made it sound as though the machine had a life of its own. Like a mechanical monster, it crouched there controlling her fate. One breath. She still lived. Another breath. She still lived.

Someone had combed her hair. It made her look younger, sweeter. The hard edges of streetwise homelessness didn't show now, only the face of a lovely young woman.

He had promised her that everything would be all right, but he hadn't been able to keep that promise.

The world wasn't full of happy endings; his job, if

not his personal life, had taught him that long ago. Only sometimes, like now, when God's plan was hidden from view, he had trouble accepting things which seemed so unfair. Saddened beyond measure, he turned away knowing he could do nothing except keep her in his prayers.

After taking a cab home, he opened his front door and Nikki, his elderly golden retriever, met him with a wagging tail. Mick stooped to ruffle one silky ear. She licked his hand once then padded back to her bed in front of the fireplace, lay down and watched him across the room with calm, serious eyes. He sank onto the sofa and rubbed his hands over his weary face. The clock on the mantel began to chime midnight. He had to be on duty in less than seven hours. He considered pulling the throw over himself and just sleeping where he was, but decided against it. Instead, he rose to his feet and climbed the stairs with Nikki at his heels.

He glanced down the hall and saw that a light still shone from under his mother's door. He walked to the end of the corridor and rapped lightly on the thick oak panel. At her muffled answer, he eased the door open.

Elizabeth O'Callaghan was sitting up in bed reading by the light of a lamp on the bedside stand. She was dressed in a simple cotton robe of pale blue that matched her sharp eyes behind her bifocals. Her long white hair hung over a thick plaster cast covering her left arm from elbow to wrist, the result of her auto accident. Around her neck she wore a small gold chain and simple gold cross that glinted in the light when she moved.

She once told him that the cross had come all the way from Ireland with her mother. Like her own mother, Elizabeth O'Callaghan had spent her life praying for the less fortunate. And she hadn't stopped with simply praying for them.

After his father's death, Mick's mother had worked to raise her own children and then went on to help other young women who were alone in the world. Mercy House had been her idea. Her work, her heart and soul had started it. With the help of several women and the local pastor, her work still went on. Mick's heart swelled with love and pride when he thought of all she had accomplished. The Lord gave her a strong will, and she used it to help serve Him.

"Hi, Mom. How's the arm feeling?"

"Not too bad." She wiggled her fingers for his benefit.

"Has Naomi gone?"

"She helped me with my bath then I sent her home. I'm better now. I don't need a sitter around the clock. A few more weeks and I'll be able to move back to my own apartment."

"You can move back when your doctor gives you the okay and not before."

"I've put you out long enough. A man your age shouldn't be saddled with caring for a feeble old woman. You should be looking to get saddled with a pretty young woman."

"Where am I going to find one prettier than you?"

She grinned at him, laid her book aside and patted the mattress beside her. "You can't sidetrack me with flattery. I've been waiting up for you. What kept you? Naomi said you had to rush someone to the hospital. Come here and tell me everything."

She sounded like a schoolgirl eager for gossip. He

crossed the room in a few long strides and bent to kiss her cheek. "It's a long story."

"I'm not going anywhere and neither are you until you tell me the whole truth and nothing but the truth, young man." She grasped his arm and tugged until he sat on the bed.

"If you insist."

"I do."

"Okay. I was on my way home from Mercy House when an old bum stopped me to help deliver a baby, but we got the mother to the hospital first, and since the baby weighed only two pounds she had to go to intensive care, and the mother asked me to go with the baby and I did, only while I was gone she told everyone I was the baby's father before she lapsed into a coma. Any questions?"

His mother's eyes were wide with stunned surprise. "About a million. Why don't you start at the top and go more slowly."

He grinned and repeated the story with as many of the details as he knew, stopping often to answer her questions. At the end of his tale, he met her sad, concerned gaze and wished he hadn't shared quite so much.

"This woman really doesn't have anyone we can notify?"

"Not as far as I know. It's the only reason I can think of why she would say I'm the father."

"That poor woman. And that poor little baby. Thank goodness you were there for them. Is there any chance the mother will recover?"

"The doctor didn't think so. I'm not Beth's father but I can't stand thinking of someone so tiny being all alone in the world. Frankly, I'm not sure what to do."

"Why, you do the right thing! And don't be telling your mother that you don't know what that is," she declared. "I raised you better than that."

Mick rose and wished her good-night. On the way back to his room he considered her words. *This time I really don't know what the right thing is. I need Your guidance, Lord. What is it that You want me to do?*

He got ready for bed and lay down, but sleep wouldn't come. Each time he closed his eyes he saw Caitlin's face. He saw her eyes wide with relief when he'd followed Eddy into her room, and he saw them filled with fear for her baby. Such beautiful eyes, closed perhaps forever, yet repeated in miniature, along with her fearsome scowl, in her daughter's tiny face.

He barely knew the woman, but he kept hearing her voice. "Stay with Beth. Watch over her for me." It was the last thing Caitlin had said to him.

Had she sensed that she was dying? Had she been asking him for something more? Was that why she told them he was the father? So her baby girl wouldn't be left alone?

Mick threw back the quilt and sat up on the side of his bed. The light from a full moon cast a glow into the room. Rising, he crossed to the window. Nikki watched him from her spot at the foot of the bed, but she didn't bother to get up.

Pulling the curtains aside, he looked out the second-story window of his home and stared at the shadows of the trees in the park behind his property. It was deserted now, but during the day it would be filled with neighborhood children playing on the swings and slides. On nearby benches, smiling young mothers would follow their play with watchful eyes.

Yet across that park and the railroad yards beyond it, there existed a world those happy children would only know in passing or see on TV. It was a world of intense poverty, where children played in filthy streets and lived in crowded, run-down apartments if they were lucky enough to have a home at all, and where mothers seldom smiled because they worried about where the next meal would come from.

Caitlin came from those streets. If she lived, she'd go back there and take little Beth with her. But if Caitlin died, where would her child go? Into foster care until she was old enough to run away and end up like her mother? Or would she be one of the lucky ones playing in a park like this?

He let the curtain fall back into place. None of the children in the park would ever be his. Facing that fact was more painful tonight than it had ever been. Perhaps because, for a moment, when Beth had grasped his finger and gazed up at him, he had known what it felt like to be a father.

He raked his fingers through his hair. He wasn't responsible for Caitlin or her child, yet somehow the two of them had captured a piece of his heart. He felt connected to them. It wasn't right that they were alone. They needed someone to care about them. They needed him. Before he could change his mind, he crossed the room to the closet where he pulled on a gray wool cable-knit sweater, a pair of jeans and his sneakers, then he headed out the door.

A fine mist fell as he drove down the dark streets. The swish-swish of his wiper blades was almost mesmerizing. Twenty minutes later, he pulled into the parking lot of the hospital. Wondering if he was being a fool, he hurried out of the rain and through the emergency room doors.

At the NICU he showed his wristband, and a nurse answered his questions. Beth was doing as well as could be expected. She invited him in, but he declined. He needed to see Caitlin.

When he entered the ICU and reached her room, he hesitated at the door. What did he hope to accomplish here? Maybe nothing. He pulled a chair up beside her bed. Reaching through the rail, he took hold of her hand.

"Caitlin, it's Mick," he said softly, and gave her hand a gentle squeeze. Glancing at the array of machines and blinking lights around her, he sighed. He didn't know if she could hear him. But if she could, he wanted her to know that she wasn't alone. He began to talk about her baby.

"We're calling her Beth for now. She weighs only two pounds. I know that doesn't sound like much, but she really is a cute, little thing. She looks like you, I think—except kind of scrawny. She has brown hair with a touch of red," he added and smiled. "I don't suppose you're part Irish, are you?"

His words died away in the dimness of the room, and only the sound of the ventilator continued. One breath. One breath.

What should he say? What would a young mother clinging to life want to know about her child? What would he want to know if it were him? His grip on her hand tightened.

"Your baby is doing fine. The nurses are great. They really seem to care about her. One of them called her a fighter. I guess that means she's going to take after you."

He studied the small hand he held in his large one.

Her fingers were long and delicate, but some of her nails were short and ragged. Did she chew them? He knew so little about her, yet she had entrusted him with her baby.

"Girl, do you have any idea how much trouble you've caused me? I don't know why you told them I was the baby's father, unless you thought you weren't going to make it. But I'm not her father, although—well, although I wish I were. She needs her mother—she needs you. You've got to hold on."

He couldn't think of anything else to say. He bowed his head and sought comfort for himself and for her in the words he knew so well. "Our Father, Who art in heaven…"

Lost in a strange darkness, Caitlin searched for a way out. She had to find her baby. She didn't want her daughter to know the terrible, gut-wrenching fear of being left alone—of wondering what she had done that was so bad her own mother would leave her. That was the one promise Caitlin meant to keep. No, she wouldn't leave her baby—not ever.

Pain came again, deep inside her chest. She cried out, but no sound formed in her mouth. Perhaps it was her heart breaking because she missed her baby so. She tried to move her arms but she couldn't. Something or someone held her eyes closed.

A faint voice called her name, and Caitlin struggled to listen. Her baby was fine, the voice said. Had she really heard those words? Joy filled her.

She listened closely. She knew this voice. It was a man's voice. He was praying. The sound of his deep, caring voice saying those simple words brought a sense of comfort unlike anything she had never known.

Then the pain struck again and she began to choke. Somewhere, a shrill alarm sounded.

Chapter Three

Mick paced the confines of the small waiting room outside the intensive care unit where he'd been ushered, and prayed as the minutes ticked by. Was Caitlin's life slipping away beyond those doors? What would become of Beth? Why didn't anyone come and tell him what was going on? Finally, twenty agonizing minutes later, a young doctor appeared. He didn't look encouraging. Mick prepared himself to hear the worst.

"How is she?"

"Stabilized at the moment. She had some bleeding from her lungs. We've managed to control it for now."

"Thank God." Relief caused Mick's tired muscles to betray him, and he sank into one of the blue tweed chairs in the room.

"If it doesn't reoccur—she has a chance."

Mick looked up. "You don't sound very sure of that."

"Her condition is critical. It's best not to hold out false hopes."

"Can I see her?"

"For a few minutes," the young doctor conceded.

In the unit, Mick paused outside Caitlin's door. What was he doing here? Why was he getting involved?

Because she didn't have anyone else.

Stepping up to her bed, he leaned down and whispered, "Don't worry, Sleeping Beauty. I'll see that they take good care of you, and of Beth. You aren't alone. God is with you."

He pressed her hand but got no response. He studied her quiet, pale face. He had called her Sleeping Beauty, and the name seemed to fit. Her heart-shaped face with its prominent cheekbones and expressive flyaway eyebrows coupled with her short hair gave her an almost elfin appearance. What was it about her that drew him so? Was it only because she was alone that he felt this intense desire to take care of her? Somehow, he knew it was more than that.

Crossing to the door, he glanced back. Caitlin's chest rose and fell slightly in time with the soft hiss of the ventilator. One breath. One breath.

"Rest easy. I'll watch over little Beth for you."

As soon as he said the words a deep sense of satisfaction filled him. This was right. This was what he was meant to do.

After leaving Caitlin, he went to see her baby. Beth lay on her side snuggled in a soft cloth nest covered with tiny red and blue hearts. The ventilator tubing and IV lines were neatly organized now, but a daunting array of machines surrounded her bed. Glancing around the unit he saw a number of other parents who like himself had been drawn here in the middle of the night. Most of them stood by beds looking uncertain, their faces a curious mixture of hope and fear, pride and pity.

He pulled up a stool and sat beside Beth. His heart

went out to her. She was so little and so alone in the world.

One of her hands moved up to curl around the tube in her mouth, and her brow furrowed in a frown. Gently, he uncurled her fingers and gave her his thumb to grip instead. "You're not really alone," he whispered. "You've got the good Lord and me on your side."

For the longest time, he stared at her tiny face. Each feature so perfect and so new. That she lived at all was nothing short of amazing.

"It's amazing, isn't it?"

The words mirrored his own thoughts so closely that he wasn't sure he'd really heard them. He glanced up and saw a woman seated in a rocker holding a baby on the other side of Beth's bed. She looked old to be a new mother. Her short, dark hair was streaked with gray at the temples and crow's-feet gathered at the corners of her eyes, but she was dressed in a hospital gown beneath a yellow print robe.

"I'm sorry. Did you say something?" he asked feeling bemused, or maybe just sleep deprived.

"I said, it's amazing. They're so perfectly formed even at such an early age."

He nodded. "Yes. I never knew." His throat closed and tears pricked at his eyes. He struggled to regain control and after a moment, he pointed with his chin. "Is yours a boy or a girl?"

Her smile held an odd, sad quality. "I have a little boy." She lifted the blanket so he could see the baby's face. The features of a child with Down syndrome were unmistakable.

"He has a lot of hair," Mick said, trying to find something kind to say.

She ran her fingers through the baby's long hair. "Yes, he does. It's so very soft," she said almost to herself.

The baby began to fuss. She snuggled him closer and patted him until he hushed. She looked at Mick and smiled. "I wanted to thank you for the lovely saying on your daughter's bed."

Mick glanced at the foot of Beth's bed. His Irish blessing had been written in green ink and surrounded by little green shamrocks drawn on a plain white card and taped to the clear Plexiglas panel. "It's something my mother says."

"It helped me so much."

Smiling gently, he said, "I'm glad."

She tucked her son's hand back inside the blanket. "When I first saw my son—first realized what was wrong with him, I thought it would have been better if he had gone to be with the angels—" Her voice cracked. She blinked back tears when she looked at Mick. "Isn't that terrible?"

Mick found himself at a loss as to how to answer her, but the nurse had come back to the bedside. She dropped an arm around the woman and gave her a quick hug.

"No, it isn't terrible. We can't help the way we feel. Disappointment, fear, sadness—they're all feelings that catch us by surprise when something goes wrong."

"I do love him, you know. It's just that we've waited so long for a child. I'm almost forty. He was going to be our only one," her voice trailed into silence.

A moment later she patted the nurse's arm. "You've all been wonderful. Thank you. And you." She looked at Mick. "Your mother's saying pointed out to me that God knows what He's doing. My son wasn't meant to be an angel in heaven. He was meant to be an angel here on Earth, like your little girl."

Gazing at Beth's frail form, surrounded by everything modern medicine offered, he could only pray the woman was right.

"You look like death warmed over."

Mick closed the door of his locker and cast Woody an exasperated glance. "Thanks. I could say the same about you."

Towering a head taller than Mick, Woody Mills, a Kansas farm boy turned Chicago firefighter and a close friend, grinned. He pulled his cowboy hat off and ran a hand through a blond crew cut that closely resembled the stubble of the wheat fields he'd left behind. "Tough night?"

Mick nodded. "I never made it to bed."

He wasn't looking forward to staying up another twenty-four hours. Maybe they'd have a quiet shift, and he could grab a few hours in the sack.

"Woody!" They both turned at the sound of the shout. Their watch commander, Captain Mitchell, appeared in the open doorway. "Ziggy needs help in the kitchen. Give him a hand."

Mick groaned, and Woody laughed. "That's right, Mick'O. It's Ziggy's week to cook. So guess what we're having?"

Mick leaned his head against the locker. "Spaghetti. Why can't he cook something—anything—else? He knows I hate spaghetti."

"Then it'll be a good week to go on a diet. Besides, the rest of us like it, so you lose." Still chuckling, Woody left the room.

The gong sounded suddenly and Mick raced for his gear along with the other men. He never found the time that day for a nap or for a plate of spaghetti. Two structure fires kept the company out for most of his shift. It was late the following morning when he found the time to call the hospital to check on Caitlin and the baby.

Caitlin's condition was unchanged, but the news about Beth was less encouraging. She was requiring higher oxygen and higher ventilator pressures, and she'd developed a heart murmur.

"Her murmur is due to a PDA," Dr. Wright explained to Mick over the phone. "It's a condition that often occurs in very premature infants. Before a baby is born very little blood goes to the lungs. As the blood is pumped out of the heart, it passes through a small opening called the ductus arteriosus and goes back to the placenta for oxygen. After a baby is born, this artery closes naturally, and blood flows to the lungs. But in many premature infants, it doesn't close and that's a problem. We can treat her with medication, but if that fails, she'll need surgery."

"Isn't surgery risky for such a small baby?"

"PDA ligation is a routine procedure, but let's not get ahead of ourselves. It may close after the drug is given. I'm optimistic but this is one of the complications I mentioned. I'll keep you informed. Also, our social worker needs to talk to you about signing paternity papers."

It was the perfect opening to admit that he wasn't Beth's father. Only, he didn't take it.

Inside the odd darkness, Caitlin drifted all alone. Sometimes it was as dark as midnight, other times it grew vaguely light, like the morning sky before the sun rose, but never light enough to let her see her surroundings. Voices spoke to her, telling her to open her eyes or move her fingers. She tried, but nothing happened. When the voices stopped, she was alone again.

It was pleasant here. No pain, no hunger, no cold; none of the things she'd come to expect in life. The urge to remain here was overwhelming, but she couldn't stay. She had to find her baby. Once she found her baby she'd never be alone ever again. She would always have someone to love and be loved by in return.

At times, a man's voice came. Deep and low, mellow as the notes of a song, it pulled Caitlin away from the darkness. He spoke to her now, and she knew he was watching over her little girl. Her baby wasn't lost at all.

The voice told her all kinds of things—how much the baby weighed and how cute she was. Sometimes the voice spoke about people Caitlin didn't know, but that didn't matter. Sometimes, he spoke about God, and how much God loved her. He spoke about having faith in the face of terrible things. His voice was like a rope that she held on to in the darkness. If she didn't let go, she could follow the sound and find her way out.

Now his voice was saying goodbye and she hated knowing that he was going away. She felt safe when he was near.

Something soft and warm touched her cheek gently. The fog grew light and pale around her. She opened her eyes and the image of a man with deep auburn hair and a kind face swam into focus for an instant, then the fog closed over her again.

"She opened her eyes!" Excited, Mick stared at Caitlin and prayed he hadn't imagined it.

"What did you say?" The nurse, who'd just entered the room, looked at him in surprise.

"She opened her eyes! She looked at me."

It'd been five days since Caitlin had slipped into a coma, and for the last two days Mick had divided his waking hours between sitting with Beth, whose condition was slowly worsening, and sitting with Caitlin. This was the first sign of any spontaneous movement from her.

"Caitlin, open your eyes," the nurse coaxed. Nothing.

Mick leaned close to Caitlin's ear. "Come on, Sleeping Beauty. I know you're in there. Give me a sign."

Again nothing. The nurse pinched the skin on the back of Caitlin's hand, then lifted her eyelid. Turning to him the nurse asked, "What were you doing when she moved?"

A flush heated Mick's face. "I was getting ready to leave, and I kissed her cheek," he admitted, feeling foolish.

Giving him a sad smile, the nurse touched his arm. "Sometimes we see the things we want to see, even if they're not really there. How is her baby doing?"

Mick glanced at Caitlin's still form and motioned with his head. The nurse followed him from the room. Once outside, he raked a hand through his hair and said, "Beth isn't good. Her heart hasn't responded to the medication they've given her. It looks like she'll need surgery."

"I'm sorry to hear that."

"Are you Mr. O'Callaghan?" Mick turned to see an overweight man with thin gray hair standing in the hall. His ill-fitting, dark blue jacket hung open displaying a wrinkled white shirt stained with a dribble of coffee. He held a scuffed black briefcase in one hand.

"Yes, I'm O'Callaghan," Mick answered.

"I'm glad I finally caught up with you. I'm Lloyd Winston, the social worker for the NICU."

"What can I do for you?"

Mr. Winston glanced at the nurse, then said, "Why don't you come to my office. We can speak in private there."

Mick held out a hand. "Lead the way."

"Have you got a minute to help me change this bed?"

"Sure."

Caitlin heard voices clearly this time—they were right beside her. Cool hands touched her body. She struggled to open her eyes, and for a moment, the blurred forms of two women came into view. Abruptly, they pulled her onto her side, and the movement sent waves of dizziness and pain crashing through her.

"Isn't she the saddest case?"

"No kidding."

"I heard the baby might not make it."

"I heard that, too. Hand me the lotion."

One of them smeared cold liquid across Caitlin's back. Were they talking about her baby? She fought to concentrate.

"My cousin had a little boy that was born prematurely. He's five now, but he's blind and deaf. She feeds him through a tube in his stomach, and he takes round-the-clock care."

"That's awful."

"It's awful to see my cousin tied her whole life to a child who's so damaged that he can't even smile at her.

At five, he's hard to move and lift to change his diapers. Think what it's going to be like when he's twenty-five."

My baby's not damaged. She's perfect. Caitlin wanted to shout at them. She wanted to cover her ears with her hands, but her arms were deadweights.

From the moment she suspected she was pregnant, she had wanted a little girl. Her daughter was going to grow up to run and laugh and give her mother a dozen hugs a day. They would have each other forever. Caitlin would never leave her baby hungry, or hurting, or scared and alone in the dark the way she had been treated as a child.

Without warning, Caitlin was rolled to her other side. Her joints and muscles cried out in protest and nausea churned in her stomach. She moaned, but no sound escaped her. Tears formed at the corners of her eyes.

"It's time for her to stay on her left side. Can you help me change the sheets on that patient in room eight?"

The sound of their voices faded away, and Caitlin was alone again, but she was glad they were gone. She didn't want to hear about a child who was deaf and blind. She had to find her own baby.

She concentrated on opening her eyes. Bit by bit, her eyelids lifted and a room came into focus. There was dark blue tiled floor and wallpaper with lines of deep blue flowers running up a pale blue background. It was a room she'd never seen before. She tried, but she simply couldn't keep her eyes open and the room faded away.

Lloyd Winston's office turned out to be on the same floor as the NICU, and the office was as untidy as the man himself. His desk and file cabinets were piled high with books, forms and folders. Empty foam cups overflowed from the trash can. He cleared off a portion of the desk by moving its contents to a stack on the floor, then sat down. Mick took a seat and waited for him to speak.

Flipping open his briefcase, Winston pulled out a file. "I understand you haven't signed the paternity papers for your daughter. Do you realize that until you do, you're not legally the baby's parent?"

"I understand that," Mick answered. "The situation with Caitlin and myself is a bit—well—unusual." Mick watched the man's confusion grow as he explained how he and Caitlin had met. When he finished, Winston leaned back and pressed his fingertips together over his ample paunch.

"You'd like me to believe that after meeting you for the first time, out of the blue, a woman, who may or may not think she's dying, names you as her baby's father?" His tone held more than a hint of disbelief.

"That's what happened."

Winston leaned forward and stared at Mick intently. "I know that taking on the responsibility of caring for a critically ill infant can be very daunting. It's understandable that you're reluctant to admit to being the child's father."

Mick leveled his gaze at the overstuffed social worker. "I'm a firefighter. Walking into a burning building is daunting. Trust me. Beth is not my biological child."

The man's eyes widened at Mick's tone. "I see. This certainly complicates things. Dr. Wright tells me the child needs surgery. I'll have to get a court order to make her a ward of the state right away."

Mick frowned. "She has a mother. She doesn't need to be made a ward of the state."

"Ms. Williams's condition prevents her from giving consent for any procedure, and I understand her recovery is doubtful. Since she's incapacitated and you are not any relation to the child, the state must assume care."

"For how long?"

"I beg your pardon?"

"How long will Beth be a ward of the state?"

"Until we can locate a relative. Which we might have done by now if you had come forward with the truth sooner."

"What if you can't locate anyone?"

"If we don't, she'll remain a ward of the state and go into foster care when she leaves here."

A knock sounded at the door, and a nurse from the NICU looked in. "Mr. O'Callaghan, you're wanted in the unit."

Mick shoved out of his chair. "Is something wrong with Beth?" Fear sent his heart hammering wildly.

"I'm afraid so," she said. "Please come with me."

Chapter Four

Mick rushed into the NICU. A crowd surrounded Beth's bed. The monitor above it alarmed as the blip of her heart rate barely moved across the screen. He stopped a nurse hurrying past him, glad to see it was Sandra Carter. "What's wrong?"

"Doctor, the father is here," she said.

"Good." The man in green scrubs looked at Mick. "X-rays show your daughter has suffered a collapsed lung and the air trapped inside her chest is putting pressure on her heart."

Sick with fear and powerless to help, Mick couldn't take his eyes off Beth's pale, gray color. She wasn't moving.

Someone touched his shoulder. Glancing over, he saw Lloyd Winston standing beside him. "They'll do everything they can," he said gently.

"Prep her, then we'll get a chest tube in," the doctor barked orders before turning to Mick. "I understand you have some medical background. Do you know what we're doing?"

Mick nodded. "You're going to put a tube in her chest

and suck the air out so her lung can reexpand. Will she be all right?"

"I believe so." Dr. Myers opened a small plastic pack and pulled out a surgical gown. Quickly, he donned it as Sandra poured dark brown liquid antiseptic over the skin on Beth's chest. "Have X-ray standing by, and give her a dose of fentanyl for the pain," he instructed.

"Yes, Doctor. Her oxygen saturation is forty."

"Gloves! Where are my gloves?" he snapped.

"Right here." Another nurse peeled open a package. He pulled them on.

Beside Mick, Lloyd Winston spoke. "You don't have to watch this. We can wait outside," he offered.

"No, I'm fine," Mick answered. How long had her heart rate and oxygen levels been this low? Five minutes? Longer? How much time did she have left before she suffered brain damage? Was it already too late?

As the doctor worked, Mick's gaze stayed glued to the monitor. After what seemed like an eternity, Beth's heart rate climbed to eighty, then one hundred. Slowly, the color of her skin changed from gray, to mottled blue then to a pale pink. One little leg kicked feebly under the drape, and Mick sagged with relief. "Thank You, Lord."

Sandra glanced at Mick and frowned. "Hey, we don't do adults in here. Someone get Dad a chair."

"I'm all right." Mike tried to wave aside her concern.

"No, you're not. You're white as a sheet. Lloyd, take him out to the waiting room."

"I want to stay," Mick protested. What if her other lung collapsed? She could die, he knew it.

"I know you want to stay," Sandra said, "but this isn't something you need to watch. She's not feeling the pain, I promise you that."

"You'll come and get me if…things get worse." Mick stared into her eyes. She nodded and he knew she understood what he was asking.

In the waiting area, he paced back and forth. Ten steps across, ten steps back. The same blue tweed chairs as in the adult ICU sat against the walls. It seemed that all he did anymore was wait—with fear grinding in his gut while doctors and nurses tried to save first Caitlin, and now Beth again.

Please, Lord, let Beth be okay. She's so little. Hold her in Your hands and keep her safe.

Lloyd sat and watched Mick. "Can I get you something?"

"If you have a prayer to spare for her, that wouldn't come amiss."

"Certainly. I have one for her and one for you, as well. I've seen a lot a babies get chest tubes. It isn't as serious as you think."

Mick knew better. It was deadly serious, but he couldn't find the words to tell a stranger that he feared Beth might die. Some of what he was feeling must have shown on his face.

"It's okay to be scared," Lloyd Winston said.

Mick sank into a chair beside the social worker. "I know. How do you deal with this kind of pain every day?"

"You said you're a firefighter? Don't tell me you haven't seen some bad things yourself."

Dropping his head to stare at his clenched hands, Mick nodded. He'd seen his share of terrible things— things a man couldn't unsee. There were days when he wanted to quit. If not for the Lord's grace, he might have.

"I expect it's the same for both of us," Winston continued. "We got into our lines of work to make a difference. We stay because, not every day, but some days we do make a difference in people's lives."

Mick nodded, surprised at how well the man understood him. He'd made a snap judgment about Lloyd Winston, thinking the man was an overworked bureaucrat who didn't care. He was wrong. It was evident that Lloyd cared a lot.

Mick's smile faded. "What will happen if Beth doesn't make it? If she dies—what will happen?"

"Usually, the body remains here until the family chooses a mortuary, but in this case, she'll be taken to the city morgue. If no one claims the body after three or four months they'll bury her. The city provides plots for unclaimed bodies."

"What'll happen if she lives, but her mother doesn't?"

"As I said, she'll be placed in foster care."

"No." Mick heard the word, but almost didn't believe he had said it. Was he really considering such a deception?

"I'm sorry, I don't understand." Winston stared at him.

"Beth isn't going into foster care. I know her mother wouldn't want that." *Is this what You want, Lord?*

Was he losing his mind? Saying that Beth was his child was a lie. But Mick couldn't hand her over to strangers—whether she lived or died. Wasn't this what Caitlin wanted? For him to take care of her child if she couldn't? He was adopting Beth with her mother's blessing. His troubled conscience grew quiet.

"I'll sign the paternity papers."

Winston left and returned a few minutes later. Mick

took the form and stared at the blank line on the bottom. Signing it would give the child of a stranger his name. Legally, Beth would become his responsibility forever. It would be up to him to make a home for her, to see that she got to school on time for the first day of kindergarten, to see that she had the money to go to college. He'd become responsible for medical bills that could leave him in debt until he was an old man. If she died today, he would plan her funeral.

Was this right? Was it truly what God wanted of him? If he didn't do this, could he live with himself? Could he walk away and go on with his life knowing he had let Caitlin down? He knew that he couldn't.

I'm sorry for this lie, Lord, but I believe in my heart that this is what You are asking of me. Please help me to do the right thing. Bending forward, he scrawled his name on the line.

"Mick, you can come in now." Sandra stood in the doorway.

He leaped to his feet. "Is she okay?"

"She's stable. Come and see for yourself."

He followed her into the nursery. A clear tube stained with droplets of blood protruded from Beth's right side and led to a plastic box below her bed. In its chambers, a column of water bubbled freely.

"It looks weird," Sandra said, "but it doesn't hurt her."

Beth was alive, that was all that mattered to Mick. *Thank You, God. Make me worthy of this gift.*

He slipped a tentative finger beneath the baby's limp hand. She lay pale and quiet, making no move to grip his finger as she'd done before. Sandra pulled a tall stool over beside the bed, and Mick nodded his thanks. Sitting down, he tilted his face to gaze at his baby.

His baby. His daughter. A warm glow replaced the chill in the center of his chest. She belonged to him, legally, if not by blood. How often had he wondered what it would be like? Wondered if he could love an adopted child the same as his own flesh and blood? Now he knew. He'd come to love Beth the first moment she had frowned at him. He loved the way she wrinkled her brow, and he loved her long, delicate fingers. He loved the way she kicked her feet over the edge of her bunting, and the way she fussed until someone changed her diaper when she was wet. He couldn't imagine loving any child more.

As he sat watching her and trying to imagine a future together he saw Beth's face contort into a grimace. She stiffened her arms, holding them out straight. Her whole body twitched. He looked for help. "Sandra, something's wrong."

She came quickly to the bedside. She took hold of the baby's arm, but it continued to jerk. "Let me get the doctor."

She returned with Dr. Myers. "How long?" he asked, watching the baby intently.

"A minute now," Sandra replied.

"You're right. Looks like a seizure. Let's get an EEG and give her a loading dose of phenobarbital. I'll write the orders."

Mick caught the doctor's arm before he could turn away. "What would cause her to have a seizure?"

"I can't say for sure. We'll have to do some tests. We'll let you know the results as soon as we get them."

Mick stayed with Beth for another hour, then he left

the NICU and made his way down to the adult intensive care unit where he waited to be allowed in to see
Caitlin. Her nurse for the evening gave him the first encouraging news he'd had since the day Beth was born.
Caitlin was assisting the ventilator at times by breathing on her own.

"Does this mean she's waking up?"

The nurse shook her head. "Unfortunately, no. Patients in a coma can often breathe without a vent."

"I see." And he did. If Caitlin came off of the ventilator but didn't wake up, she might live in a vegetative
state for years.

He opened Caitlin's door and stepped into the dimly
lit room. She lay on her side facing the window. Beyond
the dark panes of glass, the lights of the city glowed
brightly, and traffic streamed by on the streets below.
Cars filled with people who had homes and families
waiting. Everyone had somewhere to go. Everyone except the woman on the bed.

What he knew of her life had been filled with pain.
Had she ever known a safe night in the arms of someone she loved? Would she have a chance for any of
those things, or would she live out her life caught between waking and dying, kept alive by tube feedings
and overworked nurses?

Pulling up a chair, he sat beside her and took her
hand. "I had to make a choice today, Caitlin. I signed
paternity papers. Beth is now legally my child. Our
child, I guess. As strange as this sounds, in my heart I
feel sure it's what you wanted. It's the only way I can
look after her."

He watched the ventilator for a while, but he couldn't

tell if it was breathing for her or if she was breathing by herself.

"I'd like to tell you that things are going well for her, but the truth is, she's in a lot of trouble. It was touch and go all day today."

Tears pricked his eyes, and his throat closed around the words he didn't want to say. "I don't know if she's going to make it, Caitlin. And I don't know how I'm going to face it if she doesn't. I love her already—I do."

He wiped his eyes with the back of one hand and drew a shaky breath. "I have to believe she's going to be okay. I have faith, and I've prayed more in the past few days than in any time in my life."

He leaned forward and brushed his knuckles down the soft skin of her cheek. "Lady, you have no idea of the mess you started. I'm not even sure how I'm going to explain this to my family. Frankly, they're going to think I'm certifiable."

"You did what?"

"That can't be legal, can it?"

Mick listened to the protests and objections of his older sisters as they sat at the oak table in his kitchen three days later. He knew they would react this way. That was why he'd called them together, to get the protests over with all at once. Then maybe he could get some sleep.

Beth's lung was healing, but an EEG confirmed she was having seizures. The doctors had started her on a drug called phenobarbital to control them. Soon after that, she had gone to surgery to close her patent ductus arteriosus, and Mick had spent agonizing hours in the surgical waiting room with Pastor Frank and Lloyd Winston at his side for support.

The surgery had gone well, and Beth's condition had finally stabilized enough for Mick to feel that he could spend some time at home. Thank goodness his mother was better and didn't require his constant care. The last few days had seemed longer than a month. He was bone tired, but he needed to get this meeting over with.

"What about this child's real father? Don't you think he has something to say about this?" Mary demanded, crossing her arms over her ample bosom and rattling the lid of a dainty teapot that sat in the center of the table.

Mary was the oldest, and he expected the most opposition from her. He'd often joked that he'd been born with three mothers instead of one. Alice, the sister closest to him in age, was his senior by twelve years. His mother sat at the table with them but she remained quiet.

Mick said, "According to Caitlin the baby's father is dead. She told me when we first met that there isn't anyone."

Mary's frown deepened. "Even so, I can't see why you think you need to be the child's parent. Did you even consider the financial obligation you're taking on? You'll have to support this child until she's eighteen even if her mother recovers."

"I know that."

Mary's lips pressed into a thin line. "And if her mother doesn't recover? Do you think you can raise a child alone?"

"Yes, I do," he answered with more confidence than he felt. He'd asked himself these questions and more over the past several days. He might not be the best parent in the world, but he intended to give it his best shot.

He looked at each of his sisters in turn. "She's a tiny, helpless baby—so tiny I could hold her in one hand, and she doesn't have a soul in the world to care for her. No one should have to go through the things she is going through alone."

"Will she…will she be right?" Alice asked.

"What do you mean?" he asked.

"Children like this—aren't they—sometimes mentally challenged?"

Mary looked at him with pity. "Oh, Mick, what have you gotten yourself into?"

He wanted to ignore their questions. He knew the possibilities, but it didn't change the way he felt. Beth was his, for better or for worse.

"It's too soon to tell if she will have disabilities," he said. "Tests show she had a small bleed in her brain. A Grade Two, they called it. Some babies do have problems after that, but some do fine. We can only hope and pray she'll be healthy, but it doesn't matter."

"Of course it matters!" Mary's tone was incredulous. "Did her mother use drugs? Is she addicted? Has she been tested for AIDS?"

Mick tried to curb his annoyance. Couldn't they accept that Beth was simply a baby in need of love and affection?

His mother held up her hand. "Hush, girls, and leave him alone. You two don't know how lucky you are to have had healthy babies. No child comes with a guarantee. Only God knows what we will have to face. I've been willing to trust Him all my life and so does Mickey. It's something both of you would do well to try."

He took a deep breath. "If I can't do anything else for

her—even if she doesn't make it—I can see that she's not alone in this life."

Mary's gaze fell before his. "But signing paternity papers seems so extreme."

"It was the only way," he said.

Alice lightly clapped her hands. "Great speech. Just the right touch of a plea for maternal understanding. How long did you practice?"

"I think what Mickey is doing is wonderful." His mother rose to his defense. "It's not like he's totally clueless around children. Why, he babysits your kids often enough."

Mary gave a huff. "Watching the kids for an hour or two is not like raising them. And what about your job? You can't simply take off for the next few months."

"I can use the vacation time I've got coming, and I can afford to take off a few more weeks if I have to."

"And when this baby comes home from the hospital? Who's going to watch her when you go to work? You can't expect Mom to take on the job at her age."

"I'm not expecting any of you to take care of Beth. I'll arrange for day care like the rest of the world does."

"You don't always have to be the hero, Mick," Alice said quietly.

"I'm not trying to be a hero here."

"Are you sure?" Mary asked. "First you follow in Dad's footsteps in the same job that got him killed. And no offense, Mom, but then, Mick insists on moving you in with him after the accident. As great as that is, Mick, I think you're putting your own life on hold. You were only eight when Dad died, but you were determined to be the man of the family."

Mick rose from the table with the pretext of refilling his coffee cup. He'd become the man of the family because, with his dying breath, his father told him he had to.

"My life isn't on hold, and Mom is welcome to stay here as long as she wants."

"Because you promised Dad you'd always look after her," Mary stated.

He whirled around, barely noticing the hot coffee that sloshed over his hand. "Leave Dad out of this!"

"Please, children, don't fight," Elizabeth pleaded.

Mick stuck his stinging knuckles under the tap and turned on the cold water. "Mom is here because we *all* decided it was the best solution. As for my work—I like being a firefighter. It's my life, Mary. Just because I didn't choose a nine-to-five job like your boring businessman husband doesn't mean it's a waste. Money isn't everything."

"As usual, I see you don't intend to listen to anything I have to say. If you wanted my advice, you would have asked for it instead of telling me after the fact. Mother, I hope you can talk some sense into him."

Biting back his retort, Mick turned around. "I'm sorry, Mary. I don't want to argue. I do want your support in this."

"And I can't give it. A child needs a mother and a father. You've got no business trying to raise one by yourself." She rose and headed out the back door, letting it slam behind her.

"You shouldn't have said that about Rodger," Elizabeth chided.

"Oh, pooh." Alice waved her mother's objection aside. "He *is* boring and Mary was the first one to notice."

"No, Mom is right." Mick dried his hands. "I let Mary get under my skin, and then I say something that makes her mad."

"Mary was born mad," Elizabeth added quietly.

Mick and Alice turned to stare at her in astonishment.

After glancing from one to the other, she straightened. "Well, it's true. It's the red hair."

Mick laughed. "My hair's red. Do you say that about me?"

Alice snorted. "Mom has never said an unkind word about you from the day you were born. Frankly, it irked me. Nobody's that perfect."

"Mom doesn't know the half of it," he retorted.

Elizabeth grinned at him. "Don't be too sure about that."

"No," Alice said, "you, little brother, are too good for your own good."

"Would you rather I lie, drink, steal and swear? That's not a very Christian attitude."

"What I'd like is to see you go a little wild once in a while. Skip church on Sunday. The place won't fall down."

"Alice!" Clearly appalled, Elizabeth gaped at her daughter. "Just because you don't go to church on a regular basis is no reason to tempt Mickey to give it up."

Rolling her eyes, Alice asked, "Are you tempted?" When he shook his head, she turned to her mother and spread her hands. "See? All I'm saying is that he needs to have a little fun in his life. He's way too serious."

She rose and crossed the room to stand in front of him. "If you're determined to do this, fine. Just make sure you're doing it because *you* want this, and not because you think this is what Dad would want you to do. Otherwise, much as I hate to say it, I'm with Mary on this."

"Good news, Mick." At the NICU the following morning, Sandra came across the room to greet him. "We pulled Beth's chest tube today. She's doing fine."

"That is good news."

"Would you like to hold her?" Sandra asked.

Joy leaped in his heart. "Of course I would."

Then, just as quickly, his elation took a dive, tempered by a heavy dose of dread. "Are you sure it's okay?"

Smiling, Sandra patted his arm. "I'll be here to keep an eye on her. Have you heard of kangaroo care?"

He shook his head.

"It's where we let parents hold their babies skin-to-skin. We'll lay her on your bare chest and cover her with a blanket. Your body heat will keep her warm, and the sound of your heartbeat will soothe her. Want to try it?"

"Sure."

"Good. We'll be able to do this once a day if she tolerates it, but moving her is rather complicated and that's the stressful part. We ask that you hold her for at least an hour. Do you have that much time today?"

"You bet."

At the bedside, he saw Beth lying curled on her side with both hands tucked under her chin.

"Hey, sweet pea. I get to hold you today. Isn't that great?"

Beth's eyes fluttered at the sound of his voice, and she yawned. Chuckling, Sandra said, "I don't think she's suitably impressed with you."

Sandra indicated a recliner beside the bed. "Okay, Mick, take your shirt off."

He pulled his T-shirt off over his head. Feeling a bit self-conscious, he sat in the chair, still as a fire hydrant, while the nurses transferred Beth. The scary part came when they unhooked her from the vent. Alarms sounded until Sandra laid the baby on his chest, and reconnected her to the machine.

His large hand covered Beth's entire back and held her still as she squirmed in her new environment. She was light as a feather against him. He could barely take in the rush of emotions that filled him. Sandra laid a warm blanket over the two of them, and Beth proceeded to make herself comfortable. She wiggled against his skin, her tiny fingers grasping handfuls of his chest hair.

She felt wonderful, amazing. So real and so precious. A tiny, warm body pressed against his heart. It was everything he had ever imagined it would be and more. He wanted to hold on to this marvelous moment forever. Did Beth hear his heartbeat? Did she draw comfort from the sound? Did she remember the sound of her mother's beating heart?

An intense sadness settled over him, dulling his happiness.

He looked up at Sandra, hovering close by. "It should be her mother holding her for the first time."

"At least she has you. Some children never know a loving touch their entire lives even when they have two parents."

Caitlin opened her eyes to see sunshine streaming in through a wide window that framed a blue sky and fluffy white clouds. Her nose itched. She raised her hand to scratch it then stopped, startled. A padded board and a loop of clear tubing were taped to her hand. Swallowing painfully, she discovered a tube in her mouth.

Bits and pieces of a half-remembered dream danced at the edge of her mind. A deep voice telling her everything would be all right, the wailing of a siren, someone saying, "It's a girl," other voices saying, "blind and deaf."

She tried but nothing settled into place, and her head began to pound. She moved a hand to her belly, seeking the lump that sometimes stirred and kicked. She found only flatness. Had she lost the baby? Cold fear settled in her chest.

The sound of a door opening came from behind her. A moment later, a young woman in a nurse's uniform came around the bed. She stopped short, and her eyes widened in surprise as she met Caitlin's gaze.

"Well, hello. It's nice to see you awake. In fact, it's quite a shock." Taking a small light from her pocket, she leaned over the bed rail and shined it in Caitlin's eyes, checking first one, then the other. Putting the light away she slipped her hand beneath Caitlin's and said, "Squeeze my hand."

Caitlin did, and the woman's smile widened. Gingerly, Caitlin touched the tube in her mouth.

The nurse nodded. "You're on a ventilator, that's why you can't talk. It's been helping you breathe, but I don't think you'll need it much longer. I know you have a lot of questions. Let me get something for you to write on."

Something to write on? No, that wouldn't do. They'd find out how stupid she was. They'd laugh at her. They always did.

The nurse started to turn away, but Caitlin grabbed

her. Fearfully, she patted her now flat stomach and waited with dread crawling inside her.

The woman smiled in understanding and grasped Caitlin's hand. "Your baby is here in the hospital, and she's being well taken care of, so don't you worry. We have to concentrate on getting you well enough to go and see her. Okay?"

Caitlin relaxed in heartfelt relief. Her baby was here. She had a little girl, and she would be able to see her. Everything was fine. Just like the voice had promised.

The nurse returned followed by a short, bald man in a white coat. "Welcome back to the world, young woman," the doctor said. "Do you remember what happened?"

Caitlin shook her head, ignoring the pen and paper the nurse laid on the bed.

"I'm not surprised. You've been in a coma. We'd just about given up hope that you'd wake up." Like the nurse, he used a small light to check Caitlin's eyes.

"Mick never gave up hope," the nurse said. "He's been in to see you nearly every day. You're lucky to have a guy like that. Every minute he isn't with you, he's upstairs with your baby. He has the makings of a great dad."

Caitlin frowned as she tried to make sense of the woman's chatter, but the doctor drew her attention when he asked her to follow the movement of the light, then to move her hands and her feet. At last, he straightened. "I'm going to remove the tube in your throat. If you have any questions, go ahead and write them down." He indicated the pad beside her.

Caitlin shook her head. Any questions she had could wait until she could speak for herself.

Caitlin winced as they peeled the tape off her face. When the doctor pulled out the tube, she choked and gasped for air. The nurse put a mask over her face. Quickly, her breathing became easier.

The doctor straightened, and stuffed his stethoscope in his pocket. "Your throat will be sore for a few days, and you'll be hoarse. Let us know if you have any trouble breathing."

"Thanks," Caitlin managed to croak.

"Start her out on ice chips, then sips of clear liquids. Let me know how she does."

"Yes, Doctor." The nurse disappeared out the door.

He patted Caitlin's shoulder. "You're a very lucky woman."

She didn't feel lucky. She felt like a lab rat who'd tested a new poison and found it hadn't quite killed her.

The nurse came back with a foam cup and offered Caitlin a plastic spoon full of ice. Taking it gratefully, she held the cold moistness in her dry mouth, letting it melt and spread to every corner before she chanced swallowing. It was as painful as she expected but the ice felt so wonderful on her dry tongue that she took a second spoonful eagerly.

"This is so exciting," the nurse said. "I just phoned Mick. He's on his way—he'll be here shortly."

Waiting until every bit of the marvelous ice had melted, Caitlin swallowed her second spoonful, grimacing at the discomfort. "Who's Mick?" she managed to croak.

The woman's eyes widened. "You don't remember him?"

Caitlin shook her head, puzzled by the woman's obvious surprise. Pointing to the ice, she asked, "Can I have more?"

The nurse gave her another spoonful. "Are you positive you don't remember Mick O'Callaghan? Think carefully."

"No. Who is he?"

"Your baby's father."

Caitlin choked on her piece of ice.

Chapter Five

"I'm telling you, I don't know anybody by that name." Caitlin tried to hide her exhaustion. Her throat burned from her efforts to talk. She knew her own name; she even knew who the president was, but she didn't know anyone named Mick. So, why was some guy pretending to be her baby's daddy?

The doctor jotted a note on her chart. "Amnesia isn't unusual after a trauma such as you've experienced, but it's usually limited to the time directly preceding the event. The fact that you can't remember a specific person is somewhat worrisome."

"No kidding," she croaked.

"It's best not to try and force your memory. You've been in a coma for ten days. For now, you need rest."

"Ten days?" Caitlin stared at him, aghast. She'd been asleep for ten whole days? How was that even possible? Her daughter had been alone all this time. Who'd been taking care of her? She grabbed his arm. "I've got to see my baby."

"I'm sorry, but you can't get up yet. You've been very ill." The doctor gently removed her hand.

"I want to see my daughter. Let me out of this thing." She shook the bed rails.

"Your baby is being taken care of. If your vital signs remain stable, we'll talk about letting you visit the NICU tomorrow."

Caitlin stared at him. "What's that?"

"NICU stands for neonatal intensive care unit."

Blinding pain stabbed through Caitlin's head. "Intensive care? What's wrong with her?"

"Your baby is very premature. She needs special care to help her breathe and stay warm."

"I've got to see her." Again, she tried to sit up.

The doctor stopped her. "Not today."

"Please?" She hated pleading.

"Perhaps tomorrow," the nurse said.

Caitlin looked down and smoothed the sheet with her free hand, then leaned back and closed her eyes. She wasn't strong enough to fight both of them. Let them think she'd given up. "Okay. I guess I am kind of tired."

The doctor patted her shoulder. "I'm sure you are. Get some rest. Tomorrow will come soon enough."

After a moment, she heard the door close, but the faint sound of movement told her the nurse had remained. She waited. Lying quietly in bed, sleep pulled at her, but she fought it. What if she didn't wake up the next time she drifted off?

Long minutes stretched by until at last Caitlin heard the door open and close. She chanced a peek. The room was empty.

Studying the bed rails, she couldn't find a way to lower them, so she scooted to the foot of the bed. Slipping out the end, she stood and clutched the footboard.

The room spun and tumbled around her like clothes in a Laundromat dryer.

"What do you think you're doing?"

Startled, Caitlin looked up to see a tall man with auburn hair and a deep scowl on his face standing in the doorway. The movement cost her what little balance she had, and she pitched forward.

She would have hit the floor if he hadn't been so quick. Instead, she felt herself swept up and cradled in arms that were as strong as they were gentle.

"Easy does it. You're okay, I've got you."

She kept her eyes closed to shut out the sight of the spinning room as the last of her strength drained away. She knew that voice. It haunted her dreams.

Mick stared at the pale slip of a woman in his arms. Her full lashes, tipped with burnished gold lay fanned against her high-boned cheeks. They fluttered for a moment, then lay still. An ugly, red mark left by the tape that had held her ventilator tubing marred her fair skin.

Sleeping Beauty was awake. He was glad for Caitlin's recovery, but his dreams and plans for Beth had died a quick death when he got the phone call. Oh, he intended to remain a part of her life—a big part. But just how much depended on the woman he held.

Caitlin stirred in his arms, and he noticed the thinness of her body beneath his hands. She felt delicate and fragile. During the past week and a half, she had lost weight she didn't have to spare. The thought roused feelings of pity. How had someone so small and exquisite survived in the harsh, violent world of Chicago's slums?

And how could she take care of Beth in that same brutal environment? The thought of what might happen to them sent chills down his spine. He'd seen enough worst-case scenarios to know the odds were stacked against them.

Caitlin gathered her strength as she rested for a moment with her cheek pressed against the crisp material of the man's shirt. It held a clean, fresh smell, but beneath that scent was a deeper more disturbing one—a masculine essence.

"Next time wait until someone is here to help before you get up." Deep, mellow and scolding, the voice from her dreams rumbled up from the chest beneath her ear. She chanced opening her eyes. The face above her was handsome except for the frown etched between his deep blue eyes. Handsome and vaguely familiar. She stared at him feeling both puzzled and disturbed.

"Mick, what on earth happened?" The surprised question came from the nurse who hurried into the room. "Is she hurt?"

"I don't think so."

"Let's get her back into bed. What was she trying to do?"

"I haven't the faintest idea."

Caitlin's dizziness eased, but her pounding headache didn't. Still, she kept her gaze fastened on the face of the man who laid her gently on the bed. So this was Mick, the guy claiming to be her baby's father. There was something familiar about him—but she couldn't put her finger on it.

The nurse checked Caitlin's IV, then wrapped a blood pressure cuff around her other arm. "I had hoped that seeing you might jar her memory."

"Stop talking about me like I'm not here." Caitlin eyed the man beside the bed. He rubbed his hands on the sides of his jeans then thrust them into his front pockets and avoided looking at her. Why was he saying he was her baby's father? What did he want?

The nurse seemed satisfied with Caitlin's blood pressure. She folded the cuff and tucked it in its holder above the bed.

"Betty, could I talk to Caitlin alone?" Mick asked.

"Of course. I'll be right outside if you need me." The nurse flashed him a sympathetic smile, patted his arm and left.

So he was on a first-name basis with the nurses. The knowledge made Caitlin uneasy. What was his angle? She waited until the door closed. Arching one eyebrow, she said, "Okay, Mick—jar me."

He pulled a chair up and sat beside the bed. Clasping his hands together, he stared at them for a long second, then met her gaze. "What's the last thing you remember?"

She tried to concentrate, but her headache pounded away inside her skull. Trying to remember only made it worse. She struggled to keep her face bland. It never paid to let others see your weakness. "I remember thinking I was in labor."

"You called out and Eddy came."

"That's right," she admitted slowly. "He said he'd get help, but I had my doubts."

A small grin lifted the corner of his lips. "I guess we both underestimated him."

It was his smile that triggered her memory. Oh, yes, she knew him now. She had sketched him once, tried to capture his powerful body and his gentle manner that was so at odds with his size. She had caught that unique quality with limited success. Maybe because gentleness was something she knew little about. "I've seen you at one of the shelters."

"I try to get over to Mercy House once or twice a week."

"Eddy brought you to my room, and you stayed with me until the ambulance got there. You came with me. The siren was so loud. What happened after that?"

"You had your baby in the emergency room."

"I don't remember," she whispered.

"You told me to go with her when they took her to the nursery, and I did. Apparently, before you passed out, you told them I was the baby's father."

Caitlin resisted the urge to believe him. "Why would I do that?"

"The doctor said that women who have an embolus like you did—they know something is wrong. If you thought you were dying, maybe you didn't have anyone else who could take care of her."

He was telling the truth. Somehow she knew it, but she couldn't remember. What kind of mother forgets the birth of her own child?

No! She couldn't think like that. She was going to be a good mother. Sitting up, she ignored the pain and dizziness that came back as she swung her legs over the edge of the bed. "I have to see her."

"Whoa!" He grasped her shoulders. "You almost wound up on the floor the last time you tried this."

She struck his arm away. "Get your hands off me."

"Hey, I'm trying to help. Do you *want* to fall on your face?" His voice rose in response to hers.

"What I want is for you to get away from me," she shouted.

The door opened and the nurse entered, followed closely by the doctor who had examined Caitlin earlier.

"Oh, no you don't," the nurse chided. She quickly slipped her arms under Caitlin's legs, lifted them back onto the bed and pulled up the rail, killing Caitlin's hopes.

Angry and frustrated by her own helplessness, Caitlin shook the bed rails again. "Put this thing down! You can't keep me away from my baby!"

The doctor spoke up. "Ms. Williams, you must calm down."

Mick listened to the outburst that followed in stunned disbelief. Sleeping Beauty was awake, but this was no princess. And she wasn't behaving the way he had imagined Beth's mother would act. He should have known better. The woman had spent her life on the streets. Why had he expected something different?

The doctor grabbed Caitlin's swinging arms and held them still. "Nurse, give her ten milligrams of Valium IV, *stat*."

"No!" Caitlin's voice rose to a shriek. The fight drained out of her. "No drugs. Please—I'll be good. I will. Only, no drugs," she pleaded.

Her gaze fastened on Mick. Those wide, beautiful, tawny-gold eyes begged for his help again, he knew it without her saying a word. How did she do it? When her defenses were up, he couldn't read a thing in her eyes, but now they spoke volumes, like the time he'd found her in labor.

Mick laid a hand on the doctor's shoulder. "Sedating her won't be necessary."

Releasing his grip on her now limp hands, the doctor

straightened. Caitlin remained quiet. Staring at Mick, she nodded slightly then closed her eyes in defeat.

"Outbursts like this can't be tolerated," the doctor began.

Mick spoke up. "Don't worry, it won't happen again. Will it, Caitlin?"

Her eyes snapped open and for a moment, defiance glared out at him, but it quickly disappeared. "No, it won't happen again," she answered meekly.

What a chameleon she was. He almost laughed. Instead, he said, "Ms. Williams is obviously distraught over her desire to see her daughter. I'm sure she would rest better if she could see her baby, even for a few minutes. I could take her."

Rubbing his arm where Caitlin had landed a blow, the doctor considered the request. "I'm not insensitive to her concern, and she certainly appears stronger than I expected. I'll have one of the nurses accompany you. But just for a brief visit, then she comes directly back here."

"Understood," Mick agreed. Caitlin remained silent. Did she have enough strength to tolerate the trip? Perhaps it wasn't wise to risk taking her to the NICU.

Suddenly, her hand shot out and gripped the doctor's arm. "Thank you," she whispered hoarsely. Her eyes brimmed with unshed tears as her gaze fastened on his face.

The doctor patted her hand. "You win this round, but don't expect to win every one. I pack a mean left hook, myself."

A slight smile trembled on her lips as she nodded.

With Betty's help, Mick swaddled Caitlin in a blanket and carefully lifted her into a wheelchair, then with the two of them managing the IV pole and pumps, they made the trip down the hall to the elevators. He watched with renewed concern as Caitlin slumped lower in the chair when the elevator door closed. He touched her shoulder. "Are you okay?"

Caitlin battled the nausea threatening to overwhelm her as the elevator rose, but she straightened at Mick's touch and managed to answer, "Sure."

If she admitted to anything different, showed any sign of weakness, she knew he'd take her back to her room, and she wouldn't see her baby. Her head alternated between piercing pain and reeling dizziness. If she had tried to walk she never would have made it.

He rattled on about the NICU, but she couldn't listen. It was all she could do to keep from falling out of the wheelchair.

The bell chimed for their floor and the doors parted. "This is it," Mick announced.

Anticipation lent Caitlin added strength. Her baby was here.

Mick maneuvered her through a set of wide doors. A young couple stood washing their hands at a large sink. Mick waited until they were finished, then he pushed Caitlin up to the sink. He patted a sign on the wall beside her.

"The directions for working the sinks and for washing your hands are right here. You have to do this every time you visit. I'll let them know you're here." He stepped over to a sliding glass window and spoke with a woman seated at a desk behind it.

Caitlin stared at the gibberish on the wall. Now what? She searched for a way around her problem. There was always a way. Leaning back, she turned her friendliest smile on the nurse waiting beside her and held out her arm with its IV board. "I can't get this wet, can I?"

"It says to use the germicidal foam. Let me help you."

"Thanks." Caitlin waited while the woman applied a white foam that looked like whipping cream and smelled like alcohol.

Mick came back at that moment. "Let me get scrubbed, then we can go in."

Caitlin watched closely. She could remember how to do just about anything if she saw it done once. He pulled a small package from a holder on the wall. Opening it, he used a funny little stick to clean under his nails, then he scrubbed up to his elbows with a brush. He kept glancing at a clock over the sink. After three minutes, he rinsed and dried off with paper towels. She could remember that.

Betty held the door open as Mick pushed Caitlin through and said, "I'll wait downstairs until you're done. Give me a call when she's ready to come back."

He agreed then maneuvered Caitlin's wheelchair into a large room, and her heart began to race. At last, she was going to see her baby. But in the room lined with babies in beds and incubators, Caitlin suddenly realized she didn't know which baby was hers.

She had no idea what her daughter looked like. She wouldn't know her own child! They could show her anyone's baby, and she would have to believe them.

A nurse came across the room and stopped beside Mick. "Is this Beth's mother?"

"Yes," Mick said, "Caitlin, this is Sandra, Beth's primary nurse."

Bewildered, Caitlin glanced from one to the other. "Who's Beth?"

The nurse frowned slightly and looked at Mick. He knelt beside Caitlin. "Beth is your baby's name."

"You named her? Who gave you that right? Where is she?"

"She's down here." The nurse led the way, and Mick pushed Caitlin's wheelchair down the length of the room.

Caitlin stared at the infants in the beds as she passed them. Some were tiny, smaller than any babies she'd ever seen. Black, white, crying, sleeping, there had to be thirty of them here, at least. A mother seated in a rocker was smiling at the child she held. A couple waited as a nurse opened the front of an incubator and carefully lifted their baby out, trailing a tangle of cords. Monitors lined the walls above the beds. An alarm sounded somewhere, then another and a nurse hurried past them to a bed at the far end of the unit.

Mick stopped beside a flat bed with clear plastic sides and a warming lamp glowing overhead.

"This is your daughter," the nurse said, opening the side of the bed. Mick edged the wheelchair closer.

Shock, disbelief and confusion swirled through Caitlin as she stared at the tiny infant on the bed in front of her. She was so small!

The baby lay on her back with her scrawny arms folded against her chest, and her hands resting beside her cheeks. A white bandage covered most of her right side. Wires ran from small patches on her chest and legs. Thick tape across her cheeks held a breathing tube in her mouth. Clear tubing tied into her shriveled umbilical cord led to IV pumps beside the bed. Her long legs looked like they belonged on a frog. She didn't look anything like Caitlin had imagined she would.

Had she caused this? She didn't smoke, didn't do drugs. She'd tried to eat right, but the stuff at the soup kitchens wasn't always that healthy. Once, she'd even shoplifted a bottle of vitamins. If only she'd gone to the free clinic again and gotten another checkup, maybe they would have prevented this. What if it was her fault, and now her baby was suffering because of it?

Caitlin waited to feel joy, happiness, love—all the things she had known she would feel when she first saw her baby—all the things she wanted desperately to feel.

Instead, she felt guilt and grief. In the dreams she had cherished for months when she was cold and hungry and alone, she had imagined a plump, sweet-smelling baby she could hold close to her heart. Nothing like this.

Caitlin looked up at the nurse. "Are you sure this is my baby?" she asked, then cringed. How stupid did that sound? What mother wouldn't know her own child?

The nurse smiled. "I'm sure she's yours. We put an identification band on her right away. Both you and Mick have one with the same number on it. See? Has she changed a lot since she was born?"

"I never saw her. At least, I don't remember if I did."

They were waiting for her to say something else, Caitlin sensed it. But what could she say when there was nothing but emptiness and sorrow inside. Was this the way her own mother had felt? *Please, don't let that be true.*

She managed a smile, but she felt as if her face would crack. "Will she be okay?"

"We're doing everything we can. She has a good chance."

A good chance. To live? That meant there was a chance she could die. Coldness settled over Caitlin and she shivered. An alarm sounded. She looked at the monitors, but she couldn't tell anything from the glowing numbers.

Mick touched her arm. "It's another baby."

When Sandra left to answer the alarm, he pulled up a chair and sat beside Caitlin. "I know she's tiny, but she's really cute, don't you think? Her hair looks like it may be red. She weighs one pound, twelve ounces today."

Caitlin couldn't listen to him. Why didn't he shut up? His babbling made her headache pound harder than ever. She wanted to concentrate on the baby—her baby. The tiny face swam out of focus, and Caitlin realized tears had filled her eyes.

"You can touch her," Mick offered.

"She's so little. What if I hurt her?"

"You won't."

Cautiously, Caitlin extended her hand and lightly stroked the baby's downy hair. Moving her fingertips to a miniature arm, Caitlin marveled at the softness of her baby's skin as she stroked its length. The baby jerked once and kicked out with her legs. Her tiny face screwed up, and she began to cry, but no sound came from her. Caitlin snatched her hand away. "What's the matter with her?"

Mick stood and cupped his hands across the baby, quieting her with soft words. He looked down at Caitlin. "Don't stroke her, just hold her like this. My little girl likes to be contained. Her skin is too thin and sensitive to stroke."

Caitlin's fright turned to anger as she listened to his lecture. He didn't have any right to be here. Maybe she had asked for his help once, but he had no business saying the baby was his.

Sandra came back to the bedside. "Very good, Mick. You're reading her signals."

"Signal? I don't understand." Caitlin glanced at her in confusion.

"Preemies have their own type of language. Body language, really. We have some wonderful handouts that explain all about it. Mick's been doing his homework. I wish all of our fathers took as much interest in their babies as he does."

"There's still a lot I don't know," he admitted. "I did pick up some books on parenting in the NICU. You can borrow them if you'd like," he offered Caitlin.

"Sure." She wouldn't admit to *him* that she couldn't read. Reading didn't make a good parent. Only love did that. Her stabbing headache made it hard to concentrate. She fingered the loose, white plastic band on her arm. Here was the only proof she had that this tiny person belonged to her and she couldn't even read it.

Nothing seemed real. Maybe if she held her baby this void she felt would fill with something—anything.

She turned to the nurse. "I want to hold her."

Sandra shook her head. "I'm sorry, Mick has already held her today. Tomorrow you can."

Mick had held her. Mick had named her. Mick, Mick, Mick. Caitlin wanted to scream. This man, this stranger, was stealing her baby. His touch, his voice gave her daughter the comfort her mother should give her. The nurse smiled at him like he belonged here. Caitlin couldn't bear to watch a moment longer.

"Take me back to my room."

"Oh, Ms. Williams, that doesn't mean that you can't stay and visit with her." The nurse laid a hand on Caitlin's shoulder, but Caitlin shrugged it off.

"I want to go back, now!"

"But you've barely touched her," Mick said. He took Caitlin's hand and laid it on the baby, covering it with his own. "Hold her like this with your hands cupped around her. It makes her feel safe."

The baby squirmed. Maybe she didn't want her mother touching her. Why would she? Her mother was a stranger. None of this was right. He was making it all wrong.

"Let go of me!" Caitlin jerked away from him, but her armband caught on something. A shrill alarm pierced the air.

Panic and fear crashed over her. "What did I do?"

Chapter Six

"I need some help," Sandra yelled. Within seconds, two other nurses were at the bedside. One of them pulled Caitlin away from the bed.

"What's wrong? What did I do?"

"You pulled out a line that was in an artery. We have to stop the bleeding."

"I didn't mean to. It must have caught on my armband. Is she okay?" Caitlin looked from face to face, desperately wanting to be reassured, but everyone was intent on the baby. No one answered her.

"Please, is she okay?"

Mick took her hand. "We need to let them work."

Caitlin focused on his stern face. "It was an accident."

"I know."

"I wouldn't hurt my baby. I wouldn't." Yet, she had, just by touching her.

Sandra spoke to Mick, "I'm afraid you'll have to step out."

"Sure." He turned Caitlin's wheelchair toward the door.

"No, wait! Let me stay." Caitlin couldn't bear to leave. She needed to know her baby was okay.

"We're in their way. We have to give them room to work." He spoke quietly, but his tone brooked no arguments.

Caitlin swallowed her protests and allowed him to wheel her away. She slumped in the chair and covered her face with her hands. A vast weariness pressed down on her, leaving her to feel strangely disconnected. Nothing was the way she had dreamed it would be. Nothing was right.

Mick pushed Caitlin out into the waiting room. He tried not to feel resentment toward the woman seated in front of him. It had been an accident, he knew that, but Beth was so small. He and the nurses always took special care with her lines.

Sitting on one of the chairs, he folded his hands on his knees. "They'll let us know when we can come back in. Sandra's really good about that."

"I want to go to my room." Caitlin's voice was flat, emotionless.

"What happened was partially my fault." He laid a hand on her shoulder in an effort to comfort her, but she flinched away from him.

"Take me to my room." Her words were little more than a strained whisper.

"Sure." He pushed her back to the ICU, managing both her wheelchair and IV pumps with difficulty.

Several nurses stood at the desk chatting, but Betty hurried forward with a bright smile when she caught sight of them. "What'd you think? Is she as cute as Mick is always telling us?"

Caitlin didn't say anything. She sat unmoving with

her head bowed. Mick caught Betty's eye. "I think we overdid it."

Betty shot him a puzzled look, but took her cue from him. She patted Caitlin's arm. "You look exhausted. Let's get you back into bed." She beckoned to the other nurses. They wheeled Caitlin into her room and closed the door.

A few minutes later, Betty came out.

"How is she?" he asked.

"Withdrawn, but physically fine as far as I can tell. What happened?"

"She accidentally pulled out Beth's arterial line."

"Oh, my. Is the baby okay?"

"I think so. I don't understand it."

"What?"

"Caitlin. She didn't seem happy to see the baby. She seemed more shocked than anything, although I explained what she would see when I took her there. She seemed so remote, so cold. It wasn't how I expected a mother to act."

"Maybe she was frightened," Betty offered. "And rightly so. A baby as premature as hers can be a scary sight."

"Shouldn't a mother be attached to her baby no matter how tiny it is? Isn't that how it works?"

"Honestly? Not for everyone. Especially mothers of premature babies. They're afraid the child will die and they shy away from the pain they think they'll feel. Given time they come to love their baby as much as any mother does. But sometimes—well—not every woman is cut out to be a loving mother."

The door to Caitlin's room opened as the other nurses came out. One of them closed it behind her, but not before Mick caught a glimpse of Caitlin. Pale and still, she lay curled on her side.

Betty gave Mick a sympathetic pat on the arm. "Give her some time. She's been through a terrible ordeal."

Inside the room, Caitlin blinked rapidly to hold back her tears. Crying never did any good. It only showed others your weakness. She'd heard the nurse tell Mick some women weren't cut out to be mothers. They had been talking about her. She should have resented their judgment, but she didn't. They were right.

She wanted it to be different. She wanted a baby to love and cherish. Instead, her child cried at her touch and quieted at the touch of a stranger. As tiny as she was, did Beth know that her mother would hurt her?

Caitlin never wanted to hurt anyone. Okay, maybe Vinnie after she discovered he'd stolen every cent she had managed to save. After she found out how he'd lied to her. But he was already dead and nothing could hurt him. She was the one left to suffer for his deeds.

She turned over and faced the wall, determined to ignore the pain of Vinnie's betrayal as well as her fierce headache. If only she had stayed asleep, then her baby would still be safe. How was she? Would anyone let her know?

Closing her eyes, Caitlin waited for sleep to come. She welcomed the thought now. There was no pain in sleep, no fears. Maybe she'd never wake up again. Maybe that would be best.

Was that why her own mother had sought to stay in a drug-induced stupor? For the first time in her life, Caitlin felt the stirrings of sympathy and understanding for the woman who had caused her so much pain.

* * *

The room lay shrouded in darkness when Caitlin awoke. Sleep hadn't sent her back into the gray world where she had existed before. Instead, she had to face what she had done. Her headache had lessened, but it was still there, promising to mushroom again if she moved her head. A rustling sound came from behind her. She knew who was there. She'd known the moment she opened her eyes. "How is she?"

Please, please let her be all right.

"She's doing okay, now," Mick answered. "They've given her a transfusion."

Caitlin whipped her head around. "Isn't that dangerous?" She'd been right about the headache.

"There's a very small risk, but they didn't have much choice. Look, I'm sorry about what happened. You weren't up to it. I should have listened to your doctor."

Caitlin turned back to face the wall. It was easier to talk if she didn't have to see him. In the darkness, his voice seemed more like the voice in her dreams, the one who had promised her everything was going to be all right. Only that had turned out to be a lie, too. She bit her lip to stop its trembling. "I didn't mean to hurt her."

"I know. There's so much stuff to be careful of. You weren't used to it. Tomorrow will be better, less overwhelming. If she's doing well, you can hold her."

What if she did something else, something worse? Torn between the need to hold her baby and her deep-seated fear of harming her, Caitlin made a decision that broke her heart. "I won't see her tomorrow."

An uncomfortable silence filled the room.

"Well, as soon as you're feeling better," Mick said.

She ignored him. Why didn't he leave? Why couldn't she open her mouth and send him away?

Because she wanted him to stay. He was a link to her child. And maybe she wanted him to stay because she felt something different when he was near. She felt safe. It was a feeling she didn't dare trust. "You named her Beth, right?"

"Elizabeth Anne, actually, but everyone calls her Beth."

"After your mother?"

"Yes. When she was born, you said, 'Go with Beth.'"

"I don't remember."

"I didn't know what else to call her. 'Hey You' seemed a little impersonal."

She smiled slightly. His voice was so beautiful—deep, expressive, soothing. Just the sound of it made her headache better. No wonder the baby responded so well to him.

"Elizabeth Anne," she tried the name on her tongue. It sounded regal. It was a big name for such a tiny person. "I guess it's as good a name as any," she conceded.

The silence lengthened. She waited for him to make some excuse and leave. She'd spent so much of her life alone. Funny that she dreaded it still. At least her baby hadn't been alone. Mick had been there for her. She began to remember bits of things he'd said and done when Eddy brought him to her room.

Caitlin tried to swallow the lump that pressed up in her throat. She wanted to thank him, but she couldn't find words to express the way his voice—his very presence had given her an anchor when she'd been so lost.

She closed her eyes and struggled to shut away the feelings this man aroused in her—feelings of caring and tenderness, feelings that threatened to overwhelm her only because she was still so weak. She didn't need an anchor now, and she didn't need him. She needed to be strong. Only the strong survived on the streets. She couldn't afford to depend on anybody but herself.

In the past, she had depended on others, but they always let her down. She wouldn't forget that fact. Not after her mother—not after Vinnie. Everybody had an angle, only some were harder to figure out than others.

She drew a deep breath, then turned over to face him. "What are you getting out of this?"

His eyes widened at her tone. "I don't understand."

"You've got nothing better to do than hang out at the hospital with a woman in a coma and someone else's kid?"

"Beth is a very special child."

Caitlin resented the determined pride she heard in his voice—something that she should feel, but didn't. Maybe she wasn't cut out to be a mother. She certainly hadn't had a role model to follow. "You can't have kids, right?"

"That's true."

"So you thought you'd take mine?"

A frown creased his forehead. "It's not like that."

"Oh, yeah? Well, what was it like—exactly? You've been telling people you're her father. That's a lie."

"You're the one who said it." His tone grew defensive.

"So you tell me."

"Look, there are some things we need to discuss, but I don't think now is the time. You're getting upset."

"No kidding!" She turned away again. "You're giving me a headache. Take a hike, why don't you?"

Even as she spoke, she hoped he'd ignore her words, hoped desperately that he would see through her act and stay. She was so tired of being alone.

Mick stared at her back in the dim light from the window. He didn't know if he wanted to shake her or gather her in his arms and comfort her. Maybe both. One moment she was like a lost child, the next minute she was a sharp-tongued shrew. Which person was the real Caitlin?

"You're tired," he said. "We'll talk later."

"Whatever."

Opening the door, he paused and cast one last glance at the rigid figure on the bed. He heard a muffled sob and saw her wipe at her eyes. Softly, he closed the door and left.

The next day, Mick stood in the deserted street and stared at the crumbling facade of the abandoned building where he'd first found Caitlin. The boards that once crisscrossed the door lay on the sidewalk where the ambulance crew had tossed them in their hurry to get their gurney inside; otherwise, nothing had changed. This was the last place he had any hope of finding out something about Caitlin.

Pastor Frank knew nothing of Caitlin's history. Like a lot of the homeless, she came and went at the shelter with barely a word.

With a little more digging, he'd found a small newspaper article about the death of Vincent Williams. A visit to Harley's Diner, the place Vinnie was accused of robbing, yielded only the information that Caitlin had worked there, but that she had been fired after the incident. He was able to track down where she lived from their records, but the landlord of the run-down apartments would only say that Caitlin had been evicted the same week her husband died. The man didn't know and didn't care where she went. As far as Mick could tell, after that Caitlin had ended up here.

Inside the old building it was cool, dark and smelled of mold where the rain had dripped in from the sagging roof. He passed Eddy's room and glanced in. It was empty.

After making his way around the debris in the hall, Mick opened the door to Caitlin's room and stepped inside. The same mattress lay in the corner. Three cardboard boxes sat beside the bed and a few clothes hung from nails in the wall.

Dropping to one knee beside the mattress, he noticed a small black purse tucked between two boxes. He picked it up and dumped out the contents onto the bed.

A gray vinyl wallet held six dollars and eighteen cents, but no ID and no pictures. A tube of lipstick and three books of matches were the only other things in the purse. All of the matchbooks were from the Harley's Diner where Caitlin had worked busing tables and washing dishes.

Mick turned his attention to the boxes. The first one contained a few cans of food. The next one held some clothes, and nothing else. The last carton said Sunkist Oranges. Did she like oranges or had the box simply been handy? He opened the lid.

A baby blanket lay on top. Neatly folded, the downy soft square was covered in pastel-colored hearts and teddy bears. A second blanket, white and trimmed with yellow lace, lay under the first one. He set them carefully aside. Next he drew out a pink sleeper and small pair of white knit booties with tiny blue bows and laid them on the blankets.

Caitlin had obviously wanted her baby. Except Mick knew wanting a child wasn't enough. Perhaps Beth's premature birth had been a blessing in disguise. The Lord moved in mysterious ways. Now she would never live in this dump. She'd never be homeless or hungry or cold. Now she had Mick O'Callaghan to look after her.

The rest of the box held only papers. He took a closer look. They were sketches.

Rising, he carried them to the window and sat on the sill. One by one, he held the drawings up to the light.

Eddy stooping to pet a scrawny cat. A thin woman clutching a small child in her arms. Pastor Frank holding a cup to the lips of a frail, elderly woman. Somehow, the strokes of the pencil had captured the warmth in Eddy's gesture, the fear on the face of the young mother and the gratitude in the old woman's eyes.

He leafed through several more sketches; they were mostly of children—kids from the shelter and from the streets. Then the next drawing stopped him cold. He was looking at himself.

He had a football in his hands and three small defenders were putting a stop to his run by hanging on to his legs. The details in the picture were incredible. She had captured the boys' determined expressions perfectly, but the gentle look of happiness on his own face surprised him the most.

He thought back to that day. He had glimpsed Caitlin in the shadow of the building watching the game, but he didn't remember seeing her with a drawing pad. He stared down at the sketches in amazement. Could she have drawn these detailed images from memory?

He looked through over a hundred sketches that Caitlin had drawn. At the bottom of the box, he found a single photograph bent in half. Picking it up, he unfolded the picture and gazed at a small blond girl standing beside a young woman with dark hair. The child was Caitlin, he was sure of it. Was the tired-looking woman with a cigarette dangling from her lips Caitlin's mother? The white line of the folded picture separated the mother and child, perhaps just as her mother's addiction had separated them in real life.

A scraping noise reached him, and Mick's head snapped up. Something heavy was being dragged down the hallway. A moment later, the door swung wide, and an overcoat-clad figure backed into the room, muttering loudly. "Ya stupid piece a junk. I should a left ya for the garbage truck."

"Eddy, what in the world are you doing?"

The old man spun around, his eyes wide and startled. "Sheesh, Mick, ya scared the livin' daylights out of me."

"Sorry. Can I give you a hand with that?" Mick offered, leaving his place on the windowsill after he replaced the photo and the sketches in the box.

Eddy's face brightened and a nearly toothless grin appeared. "Look what I found fer Caitlin." He pulled an ancient, enormous baby carriage through the doorway.

"Pastor Frank told me she had a baby girl. She don't have no place to keep a baby in here, so I got her this. Pastor Frank said I was a real hero for gettin' her help that day. He said without me, her baby woulda died fer sure. Ain't that somethin'? I mean—him sayin' I was a hero?"

"It's nothing but the truth, Eddy."

"You—you think I was a hero, too?"

Mick patted the small man's shoulder. "I know you were the hero that day."

Eddy's smile faded, and his face grew somber. "I ain't never amounted to nothin' in my whole life. Not like you, bein' a fireman and all. I been a drunk and a bum…since I was born, I reckon, but I did somethin' right for once, didn't I?"

"You sure did."

Eddy wiped at his eyes with the back of his dirty, tattered sleeve. "What are you doin' here?"

Mick glanced around the dingy room with its peeling plaster and sagging ceiling. "Caitlin is pretty sick. I was hoping to find out if she had any family or friends, anyone I can notify."

Eddy scratched his head. "Not that I know of." He pushed the baby carriage across the room. The thing bobbed and wobbled on a bent front wheel.

"How about the baby's father? Did she ever tell you anything about him or his family?" Mick probed.

"Yeah. Let me think."

Mick waited impatiently. "It's important, Eddy."

"Oh, I know. She said he was a case of bad judgment."

"That's it?"

"She ain't much for talkin'."

"Take a look at these sketches and see if you recognize anyone who might be a friend of hers."

Eddy took them and held them out at arm's length. "I don't see so good anymore, Mick."

Battling back his frustration, Mick nodded and took the drawings from him. "Okay, Eddy. Thanks for your help."

"Pastor Frank said the baby's gonna be in the hospital a long time on account of her being so small. That true?"

"Yes, she only weighs about two pounds. It's going to take her a few months to get big enough to go home."

"Do ya—do ya think I could come and see her? Like a visitor, I mean? I'd like to do that."

Mick looked at Eddy's grubby clothes and at his beard with wine stains and bits of food clinging in it. The smell of his unwashed body was overpowering, yet his face held such hopeful longing. How could Mick tell him no without crushing the pride that Eddy had found for the first time in his life?

"She's too tiny to have visitors yet," he said gently.

"Oh." The hope on Eddy's face drained away. Looking down, he brushed at the front of his clothes. "Sure, I understand."

Mick couldn't let the man think he wasn't good enough to see the baby whose life he had helped save. "But she's getting bigger and stronger every day."

Eddy looked up. "She is?"

"I'll tell you what. You check in with Pastor Frank. When she's big enough to have visitors, he can bring you to see her."

"Honest? You mean it? Ah, Mick—" Eddy's voice broke, and he turned away to busy himself straightening up the leaning pram.

After a moment, he said, "I clean up pretty good, Mick. You'll see. She won't be ashamed of me."

Mick blinked back the tears that threatened his own eyes. "How could she be ashamed of the guy who saved her life?"

Mick gathered up Caitlin's things. A sketch fluttered to the floor and he bent to pick it up. It was a portrait

Caitlin had drawn of herself. Her pixielike face and wide eyes stared back at him, but like Caitlin herself, the sketch gave him no answers.

He had to admit that holding her in his arms had stirred his protective instincts and made him aware of her as a woman, but who was she really? He'd invented a persona for her when she'd been unconscious, he realized, and now he was disturbed to discover it didn't fit her at all.

Where was the vulnerable, desperate woman he'd taken to the hospital? The woman he'd begun to care about? He wasn't comfortable with the Caitlin who had emerged yesterday. Her refusal to see the baby again disturbed him deeply.

There were unfit parents in the world, he knew that. In his line of work he'd met men and women who neglected and abused their children. He simply didn't want to believe Caitlin was one of them. Even if she was the best mother in the world, she didn't have a job or a place to live. She couldn't take care of herself let alone a baby. She needed his help. She needed him.

The doctor listened to Caitlin's chest, checked her eyes, peered down her throat, had her squeeze his hands and finally hit her knees with a little, red rubber hammer. Without comment, he took the chart from the end of her bed and leafed through it.

He gave her a pointed look over the top of his glasses then snapped the chart shut. "You're making a remarkable recovery. A week ago, I wouldn't have believed it was possible. How would you like to move to the maternity floor? You'll be closer to the NICU."

"I'd like that." Caitlin struggled to keep her elation

from showing. She'd be closer to her daughter. Closer, but not close enough to cause any more problems.

"Good. If you keep up this progress, I'll have to let you go home in a few days."

Caitlin twisted the edge of the covers in her hands. Home? Where would that be? A crowded shelter or maybe the building where Mick had found her? Some choice. Neither one was a fit place to take a newborn.

If only Beth had waited until August to be born. Caitlin had planned to earn enough money selling her sketches to tourists down on the Navy Pier over the summer months to be able to afford a place to live. She'd made a few bucks in the past two months, but not many people wanted to sit for portraits when the cold north wind was whipping off the lake.

No matter, she'd manage somehow—she always had—but she hadn't had a baby to look after. How was she going to pay the hospital bills, or find a job or someone to look after the baby while she worked? She forced those fears to the back of her mind. She couldn't dwell on them or she'd go crazy.

"Feeling hungry?" the doctor asked.

She shrugged. "I could eat."

Turning to the nurse, he said, "Betty, pull that IV and start her on a general diet."

"Yes, doctor."

After he left, Betty said, "This is great. Now you'll be right down the hall from the NICU. Let me get you a menu. You can choose something for dinner tonight besides Jell-O."

There didn't seem to be any end to the things they wanted her to read in this place. If she wasn't careful, they'd discover the truth. She hated the way people treated her when they found out. She hated being stupid.

"I don't see how you expect me to read anything without my glasses." It was her oldest line.

Betty's eyes widened in surprise. "I didn't know you wore any. Maybe they're in the things that came from E.R. with you." She opened the closet and began searching through a large, white plastic bag marked with the hospital's logo. "They don't seem to be here. Are you sure you had them with you?"

"I was unconscious, remember?"

"Why don't I give Mick a call? Maybe he has them."

"No! I mean, don't bother. I'll manage."

"Perhaps I can read you the choices and mark them for you. Will that work?"

"Whatever." Caitlin stared at the window. She didn't like acting this way, but she had discovered early on that if people didn't like her, they left her alone. When she was alone, she didn't have to watch what she said or did.

"It's no trouble. Let me take your IV out. The sooner that's done, the sooner you can move out of here."

Caitlin held up her arm. "Knock yourself out."

Two hours later, Betty helped her out of a wheelchair and into her new bed on the maternity floor. As she watched the woman prepare to leave, Caitlin realized that she would miss the cheerful, little nurse. Betty had been nothing but kind even when Caitlin had been deliberately rude. As the nurse maneuvered the empty chair toward the door, Caitlin called out, "Hey, Betty." She looked back and Caitlin managed a smile. "Thanks. For everything."

Betty grinned, then surprised Caitlin by crossing the room and enfolding her in a quick hug. "Good luck, honey. I'll keep you in my prayers," she said, and then she hurried out the door.

Caitlin tried to swallow past the lump that rose in her throat. She wasn't used to people being kind to her.

Somewhere down the hall a baby was crying. But not her baby. Her baby was barely clinging to life. Every time she heard that sound, she'd be reminded of what she didn't have. Of what she had missed out on.

A new nurse came and took Caitlin's temperature and checked her pulse, then offered to take her down to the nursery. Panic exploded through Caitlin. What if she did something else that hurt the baby? "No. I—I want take a nap. I've got a headache."

It sounded lame, but it was no lie—the pain behind Caitlin's eyes never let up. The nurse gave her a puzzled look but didn't push the issue. After the woman left, Caitlin stared at the wall as thoughts of her daughter ran around and around in her mind. As the shadows of evening lengthened, Caitlin's feelings of inadequacy and guilt grew. Beth needed a breathing machine, and IVs. She was hooked to wires of every kind. She needed doctors and nurses with her now, not a mother who had failed at everything in life. Not a mother who couldn't even keep her safe until the right time to be born.

Caitlin's throat tightened at the thought and she began to sob. Turning over, she muffled the sound in her pillow.

If only Mick were here. She longed to hear his voice telling her that everything would be okay. She pressed her palms to her aching temples. Why should she crave the comfort of a man she barely knew? She didn't need anyone to take care of her. She had always taken care of herself. Always!

Confused, frightened and weary, Caitlin stayed in her room and slept fitfully as the night slowly crawled by. Her breakfast tray arrived, but it sat untouched on her bedside table until someone came and took it away.

Occasionally, a nurse came to check her temperature and her pulse or with an offer to take her to the NICU. Caitlin ignored them, and for the most part, they went away. The more persistent ones she brushed off with rude remarks. They left too, and that was what Caitlin wanted. She wanted to be left alone.

Mick snapped his locker shut and glanced at the clock. Twenty-three hours and thirty minutes until he could see Beth and Caitlin again. It was his first day back on the job since he'd signed paternity papers. Already he missed visiting Beth, but at least Caitlin would be with her.

When he had called the hospital yesterday afternoon he'd been informed that Caitlin had been moved to a floor adjacent to the neonatal unit. He heard the news with mixed emotions. He was happy Caitlin was improving, but where did that leave him?

Woody stopped and leaned on the locker next to him. "Is it true?" his friend demanded.

"Is what true?"

"That you had a baby and that she's really sick?"

"Who told you?"

"Captain Mitchell let it slip. So, it is true! Why didn't you tell me? What's wrong with her?"

"She's premature—she only weighs two pounds. She's doing okay now, but it was touch and go for a while. She'll be in the hospital for several months."

Woody punched Mick's shoulder. "You dog! I didn't

even know you were seeing anyone. So, who's the mother?"

Mick rubbed his arm. "I'm not sure that's any of your business."

"I'm your best buddy. You can tell me anything. Do I keep secrets from you?"

"Sometimes I wish you would."

Mick debated whether he should explain that Beth wasn't really his child. And what could he say about Caitlin?

"Is she a fox?" His friend probed for more information.

"She's pretty, if that's what you mean. Her name is Caitlin Williams. We met first at Pastor Frank's place."

Woody's disbelief was almost comical. "Then she's definitely not a fox. The only fox in the church I went to as a kid was the dead one on the collar of the old dame that sat in the pew in front of me."

Mick shook his head. "There is a lot more to church than checking out the girls. Are you still cruising the art galleries looking to pick up classy chicks?"

Woody grabbed Mick's arm and cast a quick look around. "Hey, watch it, will you? I'd never live it down if these guys found out."

"Being an art lover isn't a crime."

"Yeah, right. The only art that's appreciated around here is the picture of the swimsuit model on Ziggy's calendar. These guys wouldn't know the difference between a Picasso and a piccolo."

"Your secret is safe with me."

"It had better be. And speaking of secrets, tell me more about this woman. I didn't know you were dating anyone."

"We were never exactly together." He shook his head. "It's a long story."

"In other words, it's none of my business."

"It's not that." Taking a deep breath, Mick said, "It's that she's decided she doesn't want me involved. She doesn't want my help. Have you ever met a woman who makes you feel like you don't know which side is up?"

"Often. It's what they do."

Mick grinned. "No, this is something more. I really care about this woman, but I can't figure her out."

"No one can figure out women."

"You're being a big help."

"Mick, you can't make her let you into her life unless you take her to court and get a custody agreement to share the kid. How many of those relationships turn out friendly? Either she's still interested in you or she isn't. Decide how far you're willing to go before you're in over your head."

Wasn't he already in over his head? Mick crossed his arms and leaned back against his locker. "I know I can't risk driving Caitlin away and losing Beth, too."

It was a little after one o'clock in the morning, and Caitlin had been in her new room for nearly two days before she faced the fact that she couldn't make herself stay away from Beth any longer. Gathering her courage, she walked down the hall to the NICU.

Her legs felt like rubber, but she forced herself to go on. How long would this weakness plague her? Out on the streets, weakness made a person an easy target. She'd learned the hard way that she had to look strong even if she wasn't.

She scrubbed her hands and arms as she had seen

Mick do, then showed her ID band to the unit clerk.
The woman opened the door and Caitlin walked into
the nursery. A gray-haired nurse came up to her with a
bright smile and asked, "Can I help you?"

"I'm Caitlin Williams. I'd like to see my daughter."

"Ah, you're little Beth's mother. It's nice to meet
you. I'm Phyllis, and I'm her nurse tonight. She's doing
very well."

The nurse led the way to Beth's bedside. Once there,
she lowered the Plexiglas panel and pulled up a chair
so Caitlin could sit down. Beth lay on her side in a U-
shaped roll that kept her arms and legs tucked close to
her body.

"Has anyone explained our equipment to you?" Phyllis asked.

Caitlin shook her head. She still couldn't get over
how small and how totally helpless her baby looked.

"Okay, I'll explain it all, but you only need to remember one thing."

Caitlin's gaze flew to the nurse's face. "What's that?"

The woman smiled warmly. "All of this equipment
belongs to the hospital, but Beth belongs to you. Our
job is to take care of her until she's ready to go home,
but we can't replace you. Your job is to love her."

Caitlin bit her lip and nodded. It sounded so simple.

The nurse patted her arm. "Good. This machine is a
ventilator, and it's helping her breathe. You and I breathe
twenty-one percent oxygen in the air around us. Beth is
getting thirty-two percent oxygen. The monitors tell us
her heart rate, how fast she's breathing, and how well
she's using the oxygen we're giving her. It will also tell
us if she needs more."

She indicated the small clear tubes taped to the baby's stomach. "These are her IV lines. One is in an artery in her umbilical cord and the other one goes into a vein."

"The first time I was here, I pulled one of them out," Caitlin admitted.

"Yes, I know." The nurse laid a hand on Caitlin's shoulder. "It was a very unfortunate accident. In the twenty years I've been working in this NICU, it's only happened a few times."

Surprised, Caitlin glanced up. "You mean someone else did it, too?"

"Yes, and they were just as scared as you were. I know things seem overwhelming, but try not to focus on the equipment. Focus on your baby. Talk to her. She's heard your voice all these months, and she'll know it now. She knows your smell and your touch. Really, she does. Babies are amazing people. Now, I'll leave you two alone." The nurse started to move away.

"Can't you stay?" Caitlin called after her, frightened at the idea of being left alone with her baby.

"I have other babies to take care of. I'll be right over here." She indicated an incubator down the aisle. "Just sing out if you need something."

Caitlin nodded, but couldn't quell her sense of fear. She stared at her baby. Now what?

Chapter Seven

Caitlin stared at her daughter. Talk to her about what? Beth stretched in her sleep and stuck one foot in the air. Carefully, Caitlin reached for it. Five tiny toes spread wide apart then curled tight as she touched them. Leaning closer, Caitlin saw the baby's second toe was longer than her big one.

She's got my feet!

"Beth with the funny toes is mine," Caitlin whispered.

A sudden flood of emotion took her breath away. It tightened her chest until she could barely breathe. Her baby's foot was warm and real in her hand. For the first time, she felt connected to her child. The rolling, kicking, belly-heaving lump had turned into a person with feet like her mother's.

A profound sense of wonder grew into a joy unlike anything she had ever experienced. Suddenly, she had to know everything about her child. She studied Beth's thin legs and knobby knees. She had Vinnie's knees.

"Well, if you had to get something of your dad, his knees aren't such a bad thing."

Pity for Vinnie skirted the edge of Caitlin's happiness. How could something so wonderful have come from something so wrong?

The baby stirred and captured Caitlin's attention once more. The diaper, small as it was, almost swallowed her. Her arms were as lanky as her legs. And was that hair on her back? It was! Fine, downy hair covered the baby's shoulders.

"You look like a cross between a monkey and a frog, you poor little thing."

The tape that held the ventilator tubing in place hid part of the baby's face, but Caitlin intently studied the rest. She saw a small pointed chin and flyaway eyebrows, and wrinkles on a wide forehead. Her soft cap of hair held a hint of red just as Mick had said.

Sitting motionless, gently clutching her daughter's foot, Caitlin's gaze poured over every inch of her baby. Wonder, fear and a deep happiness stirred inside her. This was her daughter—her child for a lifetime. The knowledge made her want to shout with joy. For the first time in years, she felt maybe God was on her side after all.

If You're listening, God, thanks for saving my baby.

Her elation faded and doubts pressed in. How would she take care of such a small and frail person? Would she repeat the mistakes that Dotty, her own mother, had made?

Dotty hadn't been able to care for herself, let alone a child. Caitlin lost count of the times her mother tried to get straight. Each and every time, Caitlin hoped and prayed and promised God anything if only He would help her mother stay off drugs. Each and every time her mother failed, Caitlin knew it had somehow been her fault. She hadn't been good enough. She wasn't smart enough, or quiet enough, or neat enough.

After she had been taken away from her mother, she went through a string of foster homes. There were a few bad homes, but there had been more good ones— ones with people who cared about her, and whom she cared about in return. The best one had been the Martin family. She lived with them for almost the whole year when she was eight.

The Martin family took her in and treated her like she was somebody special. They went to church and took Caitlin with them. They prayed together and they talked about loving each other and loving God. Caitlin found it odd at first, but after a while it began to comfort her, knowing that God was looking out for folks.

But in the end He didn't let her stay with the Martins, either. No matter how hard she prayed, she was still sent away. Once more she went back to Dotty during one of her sober, repentant spells. If God heard any of Caitlin's prayers after that, He didn't show it.

Dotty claimed to want and love Caitlin, and maybe she did, until life became too difficult, until her cravings for drugs pushed aside her need to be a mother. Then Caitlin was neglected and forgotten again.

It wasn't long before Caitlin understood that her mother was never getting straight, and she knew that God didn't care.

So, Caitlin stopped caring about being good, or neat or smart. Surviving became her goal. She never allowed herself to depend on anyone ever again. Not until Vinnie had she let another person get close. And what a fool she had been over him.

Oh, he was good—she gave him credit for that. He

was as smooth a liar as she had ever met, and she had met some great ones. He'd studied her and found a weakness she hadn't even known she possessed. He made her feel needed.

He had pursued her with a single-mindedness she mistook for love, but she refused to follow in her mother's footsteps. She insisted on getting married. To her surprise, Vinnie agreed. Things were good at first, but it wasn't long before he started to stray.

Afterward, he made a great show of being sorry and begging her to forgive him. The sad part was that she did. She believed him when he said he was paying the rent and putting the meager paycheck she earned into a savings account. She signed them over to him every Friday evening without hesitation.

Then, one Friday night, it wasn't enough. That night Vinnie robbed the diner where she washed dishes and he died in a car chase with the police.

Now, she didn't have money or a place to live. She didn't have a job or much hope of finding one, but she had a baby.

A beautiful, baby girl. She had someone to love and cherish—someone who would love her in return. She touched Beth's cheek with her fingertips. The baby opened her eyes and blinked. Caitlin smiled and leaned toward her.

"Hello, Beth," she said softly. "We haven't really met, yet. I'm your mother."

Phyllis stopped by again. "Would you like to hold her?"

"Could I?" Excitement sent Caitlin's pulse racing. "I'll be real careful."

"I know you will. Let me get someone else to help."

"What do I do?"

"Just relax and enjoy her."

Caitlin tried, but she was so nervous her hands shook as two nurses transferred the baby from the bed and laid her on Caitlin's chest. At the feel of her baby's small, warm body next to hers, Caitlin's heart expanded with a wealth of emotion so overwhelming it stunned her. She laid her cheek against Beth's head and longed to curl around her, to draw her even closer and hold her so tight that nothing could ever hurt her again.

Caitlin's whole world narrowed to the child she held. Her very own wonderful, wonderful child.

She had no idea how long she held Beth. It wasn't until the nurse came back and asked her if she was tired that Caitlin realized she was.

"A little," she admitted after glancing at the clock and seeing it was almost five in the morning. She was tired, but content for the first time in a long, long while.

They moved Beth back to the open unit and Caitlin's sense of helplessness returned. She could hold her child, but Beth needed nurses and machines. Caitlin rose stiffly from the rocker.

"Let me call your nurse and have her take you back to your room," Phyllis offered.

"No, I can manage."

"Are you sure?"

Caitlin nodded. She had to regain her strength, and she couldn't do it by letting others take care of her.

"All right." Phyllis turned away, then paused and looked back at Caitlin. "I meant to ask you earlier if you were planning to nurse her?"

Caitlin frowned. "I wanted to, but I can't now, can I?"

The nurse's smile was indulgent. "Of course you can.

I'll get you a pump and show you how to use it. You'll need to start pumping every three to four hours. If you do that, your milk should come in again. It'll take a while, and you'll have to be faithful about pumping, but when Beth is ready to start feedings, you should have something to give her. We'll store what you pump in our freezer. That way, we can have milk for her even when you can't be here.

"Mother's milk is the best thing for her. It's easiest for her to digest, and it has antibodies that will help her fight off infections. She'll have to be a lot bigger and off the ventilator before she can actually try to nurse, but she'll get there."

Suddenly, Caitlin's feelings of helplessness eased as she realized this was something that no one else could do for her child—not Mick, not the nurses, no one. Mother's milk was best and it was something only she could provide. Elation filled her. "I'll do whatever it takes."

"Good. I'll get you a kit."

The nurse left, and Caitlin smiled as she tucked Beth's foot back inside the roll. A small arm shot up and waved in the air in response. Caitlin grasped the hand and felt tiny fingers clutch hers in return. Waves of warmth flooded Caitlin's heart. Her baby did need her, and somehow, she would find a way to take care of them both.

Mick left the firehouse as soon as his shift was over and drove straight to the hospital. Fortunately, it had been a quiet shift, and he'd managed to get a few hours of sleep. Now he had forty-eight hours until he had to be back on duty and he planned to spend a lot of that with Beth, and hopefully Caitlin.

At the NICU, he was pleased to see that Beth had Sandra as a nurse again. It made him feel like he had a friend taking care of Beth.

"How's she doing?" he asked, pulling a stool close to the bedside.

"Hey, Irish. We've missed you around here."

"I had to go back to work."

"I understand. Beth is doing well. She even gained a little weight. About a quarter of an ounce."

"How did Caitlin do?"

Sandra's smile faded. She turned away and began to straighten some papers on the bedside stand. "Ms. Williams didn't come in when I was here yesterday."

Mick frowned. "She didn't? I was told she was moved to the maternity floor. Isn't that just down the hall from here?"

"Yes, it is."

"And Caitlin didn't visit at all? Maybe she isn't feeling well. I should go check on her."

"I heard in report that she's being released the day after tomorrow."

"That soon?"

Sandra eyed him intently. "You didn't know? I assumed she was going home with you."

Mick avoided her gaze. He didn't want to get into a lengthy explanation. "Caitlin and I aren't together."

"I'm relieved to hear it."

"Why?"

"You don't seem like the kind of guy who'd put up with a person like her."

"I don't know what you mean."

"She's been pretty rude to some of the staff."

"I know she's got a mouth on her."

"Well, her nurses offered to bring her in several times, but she flatly refused to come. Apparently, she was none too nice about it."

"She refused to see Beth? In the ICU we had to all but tie her to the bed to keep her from coming here."

"We have to be concerned when a mother shows signs of detachment from her infant. If Ms. Williams doesn't begin to visit regularly, we'll have to inform our social worker."

"I don't know what to say." Mick cupped his hands carefully around Beth's body. She squirmed a little, then lay still. She was so adorable. He knew he'd never tire of watching her.

Sandra covered Mick's hands with her own. "Beth is such a little darling. It's good to know that she has at least one attentive parent. I've seen a lot of fathers go through here, but I've rarely seen one as loving and as devoted as you."

"My—don't you two look cozy."

Mick's head snapped around. Caitlin stood a few feet away watching them with narrowed eyes. If anything, she looked even paler than the last time he'd seen her. Dark circles under her eyes made her face look pinched and worn.

Sandra removed her hands from Mick's. "Good morning, Ms. Williams. It's nice to see you."

Mick stood and offered Caitlin the stool. "I just came in to say good morning to Beth, and Sandra was kind enough to update me on her condition."

"How sweet. Maybe she'd like to update me, too."

"Of course." Sandra's smile was cool. "Beth gained

a small amount of weight, about a quarter of an ounce, and her oxygen is at twenty-seven percent."

Caitlin sat down and gently took one of Beth's hands in her own. "That's less than when I was in earlier."

Puzzled, Mick glanced from Sandra to Caitlin and back. "Sandra, I thought you said Caitlin hadn't been in?"

"I guess I was mistaken."

Caitlin gave her a pointed look. "I guess you were."

"I didn't see you yesterday or the day before, and I wasn't told in report that you'd been in." With that, she left the bedside.

Caitlin watched her go. "That woman doesn't like me."

"But she's very good with Beth."

"I guess that's what matters, isn't it?"

The scent of Mick's crisp aftershave soothed Caitlin's headache. Everything about him was soothing. His voice, how he cared for Beth. She had to remind herself that he wasn't for the likes of her. He'd be interested in smart women, someone like Sandra. Not someone too stupid to read.

She should concentrate on Beth, not her feelings for Mick. Her baby was the one who was important. They had missed too much time together already. He was a distraction she couldn't afford. It would be better if he left before she found herself hoping for something more from him.

She said, "Thanks for stopping by, but don't let us keep you."

Mick shifted from one foot to the other beside the bed. Caitlin gave him a dismissive glance. "What?"

"There are some things we need to talk about."

With an exasperated sigh, Caitlin swung around on the stool to face him. The sudden movement sent dizziness sweeping through her, but she managed to stay upright with a tight grip on the bed.

"Mick, thanks for getting me to the hospital and for watching over the baby while I was out of it, but I'm fine now. You can go. You've done your job like a good little Boy Scout."

He glanced around the unit, then leaned close to her. "It isn't that simple."

She leaned away from him, away from the desire to rest her aching head against his strong chest the way she had when he held her in his arms. "It is that simple. I'm her mother. You're just some guy who happened by. Thanks for the help, but we'll be fine on our own now. I think it would be best if you didn't come around anymore."

"Why?"

For a lot of reasons that she couldn't say aloud. She didn't want to feel this longing that possessed her whenever he was near. She didn't want to hear the voice that wove its way through her dreams with whispered words of reassurance and caring and made her believe that everything would be okay.

He wasn't part of her life. He donated a few hours of his time each week to play with the kids at the homeless shelter—he didn't live there. He didn't belong to the world that Caitlin struggled to survive in. He was a fantasy, a fairy tale, a glimpse of the kind of life she could only dream about.

Sandra came back to the bedside with a new bag of IV fluids and began to change the old one. Caitlin addressed her. "Is it true that only a parent can decide who's allowed to visit a baby in here?"

"Yes, that's true," Sandra answered.

Caitlin indicated Mick with a jerk of her head. "I don't want him in here anymore."

Obviously puzzled, Sandra glanced from one to the other.

"Caitlin, please," Mick pleaded. "Let's talk about this in private."

"There's nothing to talk about."

Sandra laid down the bag and tubing. "I can't keep Mick from seeing Beth. A father has the same legal rights that a mother does, whether they are married or not."

"He's not her father."

"I was told—"

"I don't care what you were told." Caitlin's headache mushroomed and her dizziness worsened. She saw Mick's eyes narrow as he stared at her. She couldn't let him see how weak she was. She summoned up the strength to glare at him and keep her voice level. "I'm telling you he's not her father."

"Sandra, can you excuse us?" Mick spoke quietly, his gaze never wavering from Caitlin's face.

"I'm afraid not. I'm going to have to ask you to take this outside the unit. The relationship between you two is not my concern, but Beth's welfare is. Babies are very susceptible to our emotions, and I won't allow you to upset my patient."

Glancing at the woman's set face, Caitlin felt a grudging measure of respect for her. "Fine. Whatever."

Caitlin stood, and Mick's hand quickly closed around her elbow to help steady her. For a moment, a surge of something she couldn't define raced through her blood at the warmth of his touch. If only she could lean on him.

Don't do it. He'll just let you down when you don't expect it. Hadn't she learned anything? No one was going to take care of Caitlin, except Caitlin. She twisted away from him, and keeping her back straight, she walked out of the unit and down the hall to her room. Once inside, she sank gratefully onto the side of her bed. The simple walk had left her exhausted.

"Are you all right?" he asked.

"I'm fine," she lied. "I don't know why you're still hanging around. What part of *go away* don't you get?"

"I wanted to make sure you were okay."

"Save your pity for the kids at the shelter. Beth and I are going to be fine on our own." She was so tired. If only he would go. She didn't want to say things that would hurt him.

Mick shoved his hands into his pockets and turned away, but he didn't leave. He crossed the room to stare out the window. Something was eating at him, she could tell by the tense set of his shoulders. After a moment, he turned to face her.

"It isn't pity that I feel for Beth. I've grown to love her. The kind of love a father has for his child. I don't know how else to tell you this except to say it flat out. When Beth needed surgery and it looked like you weren't going to recover, I signed paternity papers. Beth is legally my daughter."

Chapter Eight

Caitlin shot to her feet, anger lending her a surge of strength. "You can't take her away! She's mine! She's my baby!"

"Calm down." Mick seemed unfazed by her outburst.

"Don't tell me to calm down!"

"Yelling isn't going to help anything. Let me explain."

"Oh, I already know what's going down. You're trying to steal Beth from me."

He regarded her with a steady gaze. "I'm not trying to steal anything. I'm trying to do what's best for her."

"*I'm* what's best for her," Caitlin shouted, advancing toward him. "*I'm* her mother, and *I* can take care of her."

"How?"

His quiet question drove the fight out of Caitlin and left her reeling. She backed away until her trembling legs touched the bed. She sank onto the edge of the mattress.

She didn't know how. Looking down, she saw her hands were shaking. She clutched them together until her knuckles grew white in an attempt to hold them still.

"By the time Beth leaves this hospital her bill will be close to two hundred thousand dollars. Do you have it stuffed in a sock somewhere, because I didn't find it in your purse or your boxes?"

He'd looked through her things, through her sketches and her few pitiful possessions. She felt sick inside. "You had no right to do that."

"I was trying to locate some family or friends."

"I told you, there isn't anyone. I'm all she has. I'm all she needs."

"Caitlin, no one should have to live the way you were living. I want to help. I've put Beth on my insurance. Her care here will be covered, all but a few thousand dollars. I'll take care of that."

"I don't want your money."

"It's not for you, it's for Beth."

Caitlin stared at him a long time without speaking. He met her gaze without flinching. Was he sincere? People she trusted had fooled her in the past. She watched his face closely. "What are you getting out of this?"

"I get to know that Beth isn't going to be destitute, that she isn't going to be living in a shelter, or a slum, or worse."

"I don't need your help." Her defiance was an act she prayed he couldn't see through.

"That's not the way I see it." He leaned a hip against the windowsill and folded his arms. "According to her doctor, Beth will be here for at least another two months. If, by the time she's ready to be discharged, you have a job and a decent place to live, I won't do anything except provide support payments. I'd like to think we can work out a schedule for visitation."

And if she didn't have those things? Fear, cold and

deadly, crawled over Caitlin. Her stomach clenched in a painful spasm, and bile rose to the back of her throat. He couldn't take her baby from her, could he?

"You aren't her father. There's some kind of test that'll prove it."

"You mean a paternity test? One can't be done without my consent. I've signed a legal paternity paper. I can even produce witnesses from the E.R. who'll swear that *you* said I'm her father."

"I'll say I lied."

Mick watched with concern as the color drained from her face. He was going about this all wrong, but the woman knew how to push his buttons. She couldn't take care of Beth without help. He had to make her understand that.

"Social services won't let you take a baby back to the squalor you were living in. I can provide everything she needs."

"I see you've thought this through." She managed to hold her head up, and he admired her control, but she couldn't stop the quiver in her lower lip.

"I'm serious about seeing that Beth is well taken care of. I love her like she was my own child."

"And this is how you show it? By threatening to take her from her mother?"

"I'm not threatening you. I want to give Beth a decent life. She would have died if she had been born out there. You barely survived. Is that what you want for her?"

"No." She pressed a hand to her trembling lips.

Suddenly she wavered, and he crossed the room in three long strides to reach out and steady her. He'd been too hard on her. He should have found an easier way to make her see that she had to accept his help. "Are you okay?"

"I'm going to be sick." She bent forward.

Mick held on to her, preventing her from tumbling off the bed. Bracing her against his side, he reached for the call light. "Easy," he coaxed. "I'll get you some help."

When her spasms passed, he helped her sit up and lie back in bed. Her face resembled white marble with pale blue veins the only color in it. He was ready to rush out into the hall and grab the first nurse he saw when Caitlin's eyes fluttered open.

Slowly, she focused on his face. "I messed up your shoes."

"I think maybe I deserved it."

"You did." She closed her eyes again.

"I'm sorry I upset you. We can talk about this later."

Her eyes snapped open, and her gaze bored into his. "There's nothing to talk about. She's my child, not yours."

The intercom on the wall over the bed clicked on. Someone said, "May I help you?"

"Yes," he answered. "Miss Williams has just been sick. Could you send a nurse in?"

"Someone will be right there" came the clipped reply.

Caitlin turned her face away from him. Stubborn, irrational, pathetic—every word fit the pale young woman in front of him, but the image that stuck in his mind was that of a wounded lioness snarling in defense of her cub. Maybe it was the color of her eyes or the fierce determination beneath her words. Whatever it was, he knew he would have a fight on his hands unless he could convince her to accept his help.

He waited in awkward silence for the promised help and breathed a sigh of relief when a nurse finally entered the room. He stepped back from the bed. "I'll wait outside."

Caitlin made no comment, and he left the room with the sinking feeling that he had failed miserably at presenting his case. Instead, he was afraid he had left exactly the opposite impression.

After locating a public restroom, he cleaned his shoes as best he could then returned to wait outside Caitlin's door. It opened at last, and the nurse came out. He moved to pass her, but her arm shot out blocking his way.

"I'm sorry. Ms. Williams has requested that you not be allowed back in."

Caitlin obviously wasn't willing to listen to reason.

"All right, I'll leave," he told the waiting nurse. "Do you have something I can write a note on?" He took her pen and notepad and wrote out exactly what he intended to do. He offered to help Caitlin find a job and a place to stay. His only aim was to help her get back on her feet.

Caitlin listened to the muffled voices outside her door. If only he would go away. She never wanted to see his face again. In the dark interior of the crumbling building where she had labored in pain, Mick had appeared like a movie hero. His voice had been soothing and calm, his hands had been strong and gentle. She had dared to trust him because there hadn't been anyone else. Now, he could take away the only good thing that had ever come into her life. An overwhelming sense of betrayal brought a fresh rush of tears to her eyes.

Dashing them away with both hands she vowed they would be the last ones she ever shed over Mick

O'Callaghan. She had to be strong now—strong enough to keep her baby. When the time came, she and Beth would disappear before Mick could stop them. The first thing she had to do was to get out of this hospital.

The door opened, and the nurse came back into the room. "Has he gone?" Caitlin asked.

"Yes. He wanted you to have this." She held out a note.

After a second of hesitation, Caitlin took it. Opening the folded piece of paper, she stared at the dark, bold lines marching across the page and desperately wished they made sense to her the way they made sense to everyone else. Crumpling the message, she tossed it toward the trash can. It didn't matter what he had to say. She wouldn't let him or anyone else take her baby. Ever!

Caitlin waited, but the anger she hoped would burn away the memory of Mick's deep, soothing voice didn't materialize. The ache of his betrayal remained, but she couldn't hate him.

Beneath the pain caused by his words, she saw the truth in what he said. He only wanted what was best for Beth. Maybe she couldn't take care of her baby.

No, she wouldn't accept that. Flinging aside the covers, she forced her weary body out of bed. "I'm going to the nursery."

The nurse moved to help. "Are you sure you want to get up?"

The room swam around Caitlin, and she clutched the side of the bed to steady herself. "I'm fine. Really."

She even managed a smile. She couldn't allow anyone to see how sick she was. She had to get dismissed from this place.

"Excuse me, but are you Ms. Williams?"

Caitlin turned to find a man in an ill-fitting suit standing in the doorway.

"I'm Caitlin Williams," she answered.

The man seemed distracted as he searched through papers in the folder he held. His face brightened when he located what he was looking for. "I'm Lloyd Winston, the social worker for this unit."

On a scale of one to ten, that statement dropped the man to a quick zero in her books. Had Mick already set the ball in motion to get custody of Beth? She tried to hide her sudden fear.

He closed the file and smiled at Caitlin. "I see here in your doctor's note that he plans to dismiss you tomorrow. I understand that you are currently without a place to live. Tell me, where do you plan to go once you're discharged?"

"Out of here."

"That's your only plan? Well, perhaps I can help. Let me see what shelters have openings."

Mick maneuvered his SUV through the Saturday afternoon traffic with less than his usual care. He was furious.

Lord, help me. I know I shouldn't pass judgment on Caitlin, but she is deliberately making things harder.

She had been dismissed from the hospital, and the only information he could get was that she had gone to a shelter. Apparently, she'd asked Winston not to disclose which one.

Cutting sharply in front of another car, Mick ignored the irate honking behind him and took the off-ramp. Ten minutes later he pulled up in front of his home.

His mother and Naomi stood at the curb pulling

shopping bags from the trunk of a gray sedan. The women smiled when they caught sight of him.

"You're just in time. Make yourself useful." His mother held out a bag. He took it, picked up another then followed the women into the house.

Once inside, he placed his bags on the kitchen counter. Naomi began putting the contents away. "We haven't seen much of you lately, Mick."

"I've been at the hospital a lot. Did you miss me?"

She chuckled and batted his arm. "Of course I didn't, but your mother did."

"Nonsense, Naomi, I'm a big girl. I can spend a few hours without someone hovering over me. How's the baby doing?"

"Better. Dr. Wright said she'll begin trying small feedings tomorrow. It's definitely a step in the right direction."

His mother nodded. "Good. And how's the baby's mother?"

"She's a royal pain." He glanced at her. "Sorry."

Elizabeth gazed at him for a long moment. "I'm surprised to hear you admit as much. For a while I thought you were developing an infatuation for her."

He looked away from her intense scrutiny as he shifted uneasily. "It's not like that. It's just that she needs so much help, but she won't admit it."

Naomi shut the cupboard door with a crack. "Maybe it's because her house isn't on fire."

He looked at her sharply. "What do you mean?"

"It seems to me that you're way too eager to dash in and try to save her."

"And that's a bad thing?"

"Of course, it isn't," his mother interjected.

"Unless the person you're trying to save knows the house isn't burning," Naomi added.

"You think she doesn't want my help because she doesn't believe she needs it?"

Naomi leaned against the counter and crossed her arms over her thin chest. "Look at it from the poor girl's point of view. She asked for your help when she was in labor, didn't she? And she accepted the help you offered?"

"Yes."

"If you're right, and she named you as her baby's father only when she thought she was going to die, it stands to reason that now that she's recovered, she feels that she doesn't need your help anymore. I think you should respect her wishes. You can't force people to accept help if they don't want it."

"But she's destitute. How is she going to take care of Beth if she doesn't have a job or a place to live?"

"Surely she has family or friends she can stay with?" Elizabeth suggested.

"Not that I could locate."

"Did you ask her?" Naomi demanded.

"Sort of," he admitted slowly.

"And did you give her a chance to answer, or did you charge ahead with your plans for her 'rescue'?" With both hands she made quotation marks in the air.

"Maybe I was a little forceful, but I care about Beth."

His mother moved to cup his cheek with her free hand. "You're a very caring man. I'm sorry things didn't work out the way you hoped."

"I can't let Caitlin take Beth and vanish."

"Wait a minute." Elizabeth held up one hand. "Caring for a child who's alone in the world is one thing, but getting involved in a custody dispute is a whole different kettle of fish."

"My choices are do nothing and let Caitlin disappear into those stinking slums with a helpless baby, or I make sure that doesn't happen. God put me in Beth's life for a reason. I'm not turning my back on her."

He rose and headed for the front door, more disappointed than he cared to admit.

She caught his arm and stopped him. "Mick, you can't save every destitute child you see."

"I can save Beth. She's going to be part of my life. Why is it so hard for everyone to accept that God wants me to care for this child?"

Elizabeth pulled her hand away. "It may be what the good Lord wants. But I think you need to be very sure this isn't just about what Mick O'Callaghan wants."

Caitlin stood and listened to the hawk-faced matron in charge of the women's dorm at the Lexington Street Shelter.

"Your bed is the last one on the left. There's no smoking and no drinking. Keep a close eye on your valuables—we're not responsible if anything gets stolen. There are twenty-two women and children on this floor and one bathroom, so don't hog it. We provide two meals a day. Breakfast is at 7:00 a.m. sharp. Supper is at six. If you're late, we don't hold anything for you. Any questions?" She folded her arms and waited.

Caitlin shook her head. "I've stayed here before. I know the rules." She stared down the long, narrow room. She'd stayed here once during the coldest nights of winter when she had been sixteen, scared and out of food. It wasn't a pleasant memory.

This time, she wouldn't be leaving after a few meals of thin soup and a break in the weather. The hospital social worker had arranged for her stay here so that she could be near a phone in case Beth's doctor needed to contact her. It had been the closest shelter with room to take her on such short notice.

She moved down the crowded room lined with narrow beds toward the one the matron had indicated. The place reeked of unwashed bodies. A worn-looking woman rocked and hummed to a little girl of about three. The child was whining that she was hungry. Loud snoring came from beneath a heap of blankets on a bed in the middle of the room while a teenage girl paced the small space in front of the room's only window with her arms clasped tightly around herself.

Caitlin sat on the thin, blue-striped mattress of the last cot and looked around. She was alone again no matter how crowded the room was. Leaning down, she slid a plastic bag with her few belongings underneath the bed. The crackle and rustle of papers made her frown.

The nurses at the NICU had made sure that she had plenty of information when she was discharged—all of it in writing. Neat little brochures on colored paper that were useless to her. She had wanted to ask questions, but the staff had been so busy with admissions that she had simply been handed the papers and hustled out the door.

A harsh, racking cough interrupted the soft humming of the young mother. After a few moments, she began to sing in a trembling and off-key voice. "Hush little baby, don't say a word. Mama's gonna buy you a mockingbird."

She didn't seem to know the rest of the song because

she repeated the same lines over and over again. Lying on her side, Caitlin faced the wall and listened to the senseless song.

"Hush little baby, don't say a word."

Was Beth crying now? Did she miss her mother's touch, her voice? Would the nurses pay as much attention to her now that they were busy?

A hollow place had formed in Caitlin's heart when she walked out the hospital doors without her daughter. It grew now into a vast emptiness that ached like a gnawing hunger. She missed her baby—missed the smell of her and the feel of her. She had left her baby behind. It didn't matter that she hadn't had a choice.

Maybe Mick would be with Beth tonight. He did care about her, Caitlin knew that. Yesterday, she had been scared and angry. That made her determined to prove that she could care for Beth by herself. But now, miles away, Caitlin could only hope Mick would ignore her angry words and stay with the baby. Beth didn't deserve to be alone. No child did.

How many times had Caitlin huddled, cold and hungry, while her mother was gone for days on end? Back then, Caitlin had dreamed that her father would somehow find her and take her away with him. The man in Caitlin's imagination had been a man like Mick— tall and strong, and sure of what was right. But no one ever came.

Mick claimed he wanted to be a father to Beth, but for how long? How long before he couldn't find the time for a kid who wasn't really his? Life had a way of dulling even the best of intentions. She didn't want Beth wishing for some imaginary daddy, or worse yet, pining for someone real who never came around.

Caitlin would be all that Beth needed. If Beth had a mother who loved her and cared for her, she wouldn't miss having a dad.

Closing her eyes, Caitlin tried to shut out the sounds and the smells around her and recall Beth's face. She pictured her tiny hands and feet. She pictured the way Beth's mouth widened into an O when she yawned, the way her eyebrows arched perfectly in the center.

Caitlin's fingers itched for her pencils and drawing pad. If only she could put the pictures in her head down on paper, then maybe she wouldn't feel so alone. She'd have something of Beth to keep beside her.

But she didn't have her sketchbook anymore. Her sketches, her baby's clothes, everything that she owned had been left behind in the building where Mick found her. Someday she would make her way back there, but she held little hope of finding her things undisturbed.

The next morning Caitlin rose from a fitful, nightmare-haunted sleep where she searched through garbage cans and dark alleys for a baby she could hear crying but couldn't find. At breakfast, she forced down a bowl of lukewarm oatmeal before she gathered her few possessions and walked the long miles back to the hospital.

At the nursery, she went directly to Beth's bed. Only when she saw for herself that Beth was okay did Caitlin relax. She touched her daughter's hand and gazed at her beautiful face. "Morning, jelly bean. I told you I'd be back."

"Jelly bean—that's cute."

Caitlin looked up to see Mick standing a few feet away. Her foolish heart took an unexpected leap of joy, and she almost smiled before she remembered to be angry with him.

He moved to the bedside. "The nickname fits her. She's little and she's sweet."

Caitlin turned her attention to the baby, determined to ignore him. "What do you want?"

"I won't stay long," he said. "I just wanted to apologize for upsetting you. I was wrong."

"No kidding."

"Look—" his exasperation came through in his voice "—I want you to know I'm sorry for trying to strong-arm you. You don't want my help, that's fine. Where you go and what you do is none of my business. My concern is for Beth. I'm only going to ask you for one thing."

She slanted a look at him. "What?"

"While she is in the hospital, I'd like to continue to visit her."

"You're asking my permission?"

He thrust his hands in his pockets and looked down. "Yes. You're her mother, and I'm just some guy who happened by."

Caitlin mulled over his change of heart and wondered what had prompted it. Did this mean he wasn't going to try and take Beth away from her? She was almost afraid to believe him. "And what if I say no?"

He leveled his gaze at her. "I'll respect your wishes."

She studied his face and saw the uncertainty in his eyes, saw the tenseness in the set of his shoulders. He was waiting for her to tell him to get lost.

But he wasn't just some guy who had happened by. She hadn't dreamed the voice she had heard in the darkness. It had been his voice. And he'd stayed with Beth when the baby needed someone the most. He'd given his mother's name to the child of a total stranger. Some guy passing by didn't do all of those things—only someone who truly cared about Beth.

Doubts clamored inside Caitlin's head warning her not to trust him, but faced with his kindness and sincerity, she chose to ignore them. "I guess it would be okay."

Hope brightened his eyes. "Thank you. This means a lot."

Caitlin turned her attention back to the baby and prayed she hadn't just made the biggest mistake of her life. "I'm doing it for her, because I can't be here as much now."

"I understand. Now that I'm back at work, I won't be able to be here as often as I'd like, either. Look, I don't know where you're staying, but if you ever need a ride here or anything, just say the word."

"I take the bus." She didn't want to admit to him that she couldn't even afford bus fare. "Getting here at night is hård. If you could spend time with her then, that would be nice."

If he came at night, she wouldn't have to see him. She wouldn't have to pretend she didn't long to hear his voice or to feel the touch of his hand.

Her grudging permission sent a wave of relief through Mick. He sat next to her and struggled to separate the feelings running through him. It was more than happiness at getting to see Beth again. A lot of it had to do with seeing Caitlin.

He liked being near this woman, he liked the sound of her voice, the way the light changed the color of her eyes. He liked the soft curve of her ears and the way she tucked her hair back when she was nervous.

An alarm sounded and he scanned the array of monitors to see which one it was. Beth's nurse reached up to silence the one that monitored the oxygen level of her blood. It was then he noticed how much oxygen she was getting.

"She's up to fifty percent," he said. "She hasn't been that high before."

"Hasn't she? Let me check her chart." He waited impatiently for her to confirm what he already knew. "You're right," she said. "I'll let Dr. Wright know."

"What is it? What's wrong?" Caitlin demanded. Her hand closed on Mick's shoulder in a death grip. He covered it with his own in a gesture of comfort as they waited for the doctor.

Dr. Wright came to the bedside and quickly checked the baby over. "She is needing more oxygen and her heart rate is up as well. That has me a bit worried. She may be getting sick."

"But how could she get sick in here?" Caitlin asked, clearly worried and perplexed.

"Babies like Beth have a very poor immune system. No matter how careful we are, we can't prevent every illness. We'll draw some blood work and that will tell us more."

"But she'll be okay, won't she?" Mick asked. The pounding of his heart was so loud he thought he might not be able to hear the doctor's answer.

Please, Lord, Beth has been through so much already. Isn't it time she caught a break?

Dr. Wright smiled. "If her blood work shows any signs of infection, we'll start her on antibiotics. Unfortunately, this isn't all that unusual. Remember, Beth has a long road ahead of her. We have to take it one day at a time."

Caitlin noticed then that Mick's hand covered hers where it rested on his shoulder. She pulled away from him, but she missed the comfort of his touch.

After the doctor left the bedside, Caitlin cupped her hands around Beth the way Mick had shown her the first time she saw her daughter. Mick had taught her so much. Sudden tears stung Caitlin's eyes and her throat tightened as regrets welled up out of nowhere. She wasn't surprised that he noticed.

"Caitlin, what's wrong?"

"It was so hard at first."

"What was hard?" he asked gently.

"All of it. Knowing you named her, knowing you held her first. I resented the way you seemed so at ease with her while I was scared to even touch her. It was like she didn't even need me."

"You're her mother, of course she needs you."

"The first time I came in here, I didn't even know which baby was mine. What kind of mother doesn't know her own child?"

"Maybe one who was unconscious for days, one who almost died? Don't beat yourself up over the things you can't change."

"I'll always feel I missed the most important moment of her life—and of mine."

She couldn't believe she was telling him these things. Yet looking into his bright blue eyes filled with compassion and understanding, she knew that there was something about this man that drew out a part of herself that she had never wanted to share with anyone else. His voice, his touch, they made her feel something that she had been missing her whole life. He made her feel safe.

She looked away, afraid he would read in her eyes just how much she longed for the comfort of his touch.

Mick reached across the space between them and placed the tips of his fingers under her chin. Gently but firmly, he turned her face back to his. "You did miss out on something special. You have a right to feel cheated. But what's important is how you go on after life hands you a raw deal. Remember that God never gives us more than we can bear."

"The Guy has got way too much confidence in me."

Mick smiled. "No, I don't think so."

"You really believe that stuff? About God, I mean."

"I really do."

"Well, I don't. He's never given me an even break."

"He gave you Beth."

"Yes, He did. I can't believe how much I love her."

"That's the same way God loves you. It's hard to have faith, I know. But once you find it, once you realize how much God loves you, then all things are bearable. Don't look for God with your eyes, Caitlin. Look for Him with your heart."

"You make it sound so simple."

"It is."

She wanted so badly to believe him, but instead she shook her head. "Maybe God loves you, but He doesn't love me."

Chapter Nine

A few days later, Caitlin stifled a groan, picked up her spoon and stirred the thin oatmeal in the orange plastic bowl in front of her. She forced herself to swallow a bite.

Between the chills and the sweats and her aching body, all she wanted to do was sleep, but her rest had been fitful at best. The shelter was noisy even at night with so many women packed into one room, and her bed, the one closest to the only bathroom, guaranteed she heard the gurgling and clanking pipes every time it was used.

She took another bite of her unappetizing fare and almost gagged. Oatmeal wasn't her favorite food even when her stomach wasn't doing flip-flops. She forced down a third spoonful. She had to keep up her strength so that she could be with her daughter.

Beth wasn't doing well. She'd had another seizure and had been started on another round of antibiotics. It seemed like she took one step forward and fell back two. The last few days had been really rough.

Sometimes, Caitlin wondered if it was wrong to put

Beth through so much pain. She wondered if it wouldn't have been better if… *If she hadn't lived.*

The terrible thought tormented her each time Beth underwent yet another round of painful tests—each time she watched sobs rack her daughter's tiny body when she was poked for blood or another IV. Because Beth was still on the ventilator, she couldn't make any sounds. Somehow, the silence of her crying made it all the more gut-wrenching to watch, and Caitlin's burden of guilt grew heavier.

If this is Your plan, God, it stinks.

Mick had faith. It was plain for all to see, and Caitlin was moved by his devotion, but she couldn't find it in her heart to accept a God who would let a tiny baby suffer.

Mick entered the nursery late that afternoon and made his way to Beth's bedside. Sandra, seated in a rocker across the aisle, fed a chubby infant with thick black hair. Arching one eyebrow, she said, "I'd say good afternoon, but from the looks of you, I'd guess it hasn't been."

"Do I look that bad?"

"Worse. Bad day at work?"

"Yeah, bad three days. I took an extra shift so one of the guys could spend some time with his family on Memorial Day. I forgot how much I hate working holiday weekends."

He sank onto a stool and gently took Beth's hand in his. His heart lightened as her fingers closed over his in a soft grip. Just seeing her made the whole crazy world seem better. He hadn't been in for four days and now that he was, he couldn't believe he'd stayed away so long.

At his last meeting with Caitlin, he'd had a glimpse of just how much she loved Beth. He had begun to think that he'd been wrong about her. Maybe she could get on her feet and take care of Beth, too. He prayed often about what he should do. Still, the answers he sought continued to elude him.

Stepping out of the role of a father was proving to be harder than he had expected. So was not seeing Caitlin. For some reason, she had taken to haunting his dreams at night.

"Want to talk about it?"

For a second, he thought Sandra was asking about his nocturnal visions, but before he blurted out his confession, he realized she was asking about his job.

"No, not really," he answered with a shake of his head. He didn't talk about the car wrecks and the bad fires, the ones with lives lost. For now, he wanted to put his job out of his mind and concentrate on the little wonder in front of him. "How's my girl doing?"

"About the same today. We've stopped her feedings again."

Mick pinned Sandra with a steady stare. "This isn't usual, is it?"

"Every baby is different. There is no 'usual.'"

He turned his attention to Beth. Her color didn't seem right. He glanced at her oxygen reading and was relieved to see it was normal. Maybe he was being paranoid. Three days and nights of pulling bleeding people out of mangled cars up on the Eisenhower Expressway and taking bodies out of smoldering houses tended to make a guy feel that nothing turned out right. Beth was going to be fine. He had to believe that. "Is Caitlin here?" he asked.

"You just missed her."

Something in Sandra's voice made him glance sharply at her.

"What's wrong?"

"The staff has noticed a change in Caitlin's behavior."

Mick sent her a tired, amused smile. "What? She's turned sweet all of a sudden?"

Sandra grinned at his teasing. "That *would* be a change." Her smile faded. After tucking her charge in, she pulled her rocker over beside Mick. "Have you seen her lately?"

Mick stared at Sandra's concerned face. "No. Not for several days. Caitlin and I agreed it would be best to divide our time so that Beth usually had one of us here. Caitlin comes in the daytime, I come in the evenings when I'm not working."

"Caitlin has been here every day, I'll give her that, but she has started coming in later and not staying as long. One nurse reported that she thought Caitlin was strung out. She could barely keep her eyes open. She slept in the chair beside the baby for most of the time she was here."

Mick found himself coming to Caitlin's defense. "Maybe she's just tired. It's got to be hard getting here every day. Have you suggested she take a day off and get some rest?"

"Of course we suggested that."

"And?"

"And you know Caitlin. She didn't take the suggestion well. She said she was fine in a tone that sounded more like 'Mind your own business.'"

"Maybe I should talk to her."

"There's something else. Several of the mothers in the unit have reported that they have had money taken from their purses."

"And you think Caitlin had something to do with it?"

Sandra nodded at the baby across the way. "Both mothers have babies near this bed, and both of them were here the same time Caitlin was. Does Caitlin use?"

"You mean drugs? No."

"Are you sure?"

Was he? Caitlin had grown up a street kid. Drug use was common among them, he'd seen it often enough. Even if she hated the fact that her own mother had been an addict it didn't mean that Caitlin didn't have the same dependency.

Sandra must have read the doubt in his eyes. "Caitlin's behavior hasn't been sterling at the best of times, but this change makes us very suspicious. Having a sick baby is a terrible strain on any mother. Many of them feel tremendous guilt."

"What will you do?"

"We've already done it. When Caitlin came in today, we had security take her to the lab for a drug test."

"She consented to that?"

"She was…how shall I put it…very verbal in expressing her opinion of us, but she went."

"When will you have the results?"

"Tomorrow afternoon at the latest. But, Mick, her results will be confidential. I'm stretching it just telling you that we're having her tested. We won't be able to tell you the results, one way or the other."

He tightened his grip on Beth's hand. "What will happen if Caitlin's drug test is positive?"

"If she is using, she won't be taking Beth home."

Caitlin didn't know how much longer she could keep walking four miles twice a day. Instead of getting strong she seemed to be getting weaker. Today she hadn't been able to drag herself out of bed until almost noon.

She braced herself before she entered the nursery. Would her drug-test results be back or would she be subjected to another day of frigid stares and barely concealed dislike by the staff? She looked forward to the apologies they would have to give her when her results showed she was clean. A person couldn't act a little tired without some snoopy nurse jumping to wild conclusions.

In the nursery, Dr. Wright stood beside Beth's bed. For a moment, their images swam in front of Caitlin's eyes, and she grabbed the back of a nearby chair to steady herself. When she looked up, the doctor was staring at her intently.

Caitlin straightened and moved within a foot of the woman. "I'm clean, right?" she demanded.

The doctor had the grace to look shamefaced. "Yes. I'm sorry we had to put you through that, but Beth is our primary concern."

Caitlin scanned the faces of the nurses around the unit who were watching with undisguised curiosity. "Did you hear that? I'm clean."

The women quickly busied themselves with other tasks, but Caitlin was satisfied that they all knew they had misjudged her.

Dr. Wright laid a hand on Caitlin's arm. "There's something else we need to discuss."

Caitlin's elation died a quick death. "What?"

"Your lab work showed a high bacteria count in your milk. Have you been running a fever or having chills?"

"I'm a little tired, that's all."

"I'm afraid it's more than that. If you are sick, you shouldn't be visiting the baby. You can make her sick just by touching her. And we can't be giving her your milk. We'll have to discard what you've brought in." She took the small bottle from Caitlin's hand and tossed it in the trash. "I'm sure all of this was explained in the handouts we gave you when you went home. Do you have a doctor you can see?"

Caitlin shook her head.

"I'll write you a prescription for some medication. I want you to take it as directed and I'm afraid you'll have to wait forty-eight hours before coming in to see the baby again."

Dr. Wright scribbled something on a small square of paper and placed it in Caitlin's hand. Her fingers closed around it, but nothing registered except that she had hurt Beth again. Suddenly, she had to get away. Surging to her feet, she pulled away from the doctor's steadying hand. Somehow, she stumbled out of the nursery and down the hall to the elevators. Gasping for air, she leaned against the wall as she waited for the doors to open.

How could she have been so stupid? She had tried to ignore her own illness, and she had made Beth sick. The elevator doors slid open and Caitlin stepped in. Thankfully it was empty. As the doors closed, she wished they would stay shut forever. If only she could be trapped in here. Then she couldn't harm her baby.

Her ignorance had caused Beth to be stuck with needles countless times. The information was in the colorful pieces of paper Caitlin had been sent home with—only she was too stupid to be able to read them.

The elevator didn't keep her trapped, instead, it opened at the main lobby where people were coming and going as if nothing were wrong. With weary steps, Caitlin made her way out the main door. The gloom of the overcast evening had deepened into a premature darkness and rain had begun to fall. Without a thought, she walked out into the cold mist.

Mick pulled into the hospital parking lot and turned off his engine. A thin drizzle had begun to fall earlier, and it continued lightly but steadily into the evening. Through the speckled windshield he spied Caitlin leaving the building. She was late tonight.

She didn't even have a jacket on, he noted, only a thin sweater. Hunching her shoulders, she left the protection of the hospital entrance and stepped out into the rain walking toward the bus stop. She'd be drenched in no time if she intended to wait at the curb in this stuff. Didn't she have any sense? He had half a mind to drag her into his car and keep her dry until the bus came by. Glancing down the street, he saw the bus turn the corner, and he realized that wouldn't be necessary.

Stepping out of his vehicle, he made a dash across the parking lot and stopped under the cover of the hospital's wide portico. He wanted to spend an hour or so with Beth before he called it a night. He cast one last glance at Caitlin. The bus stopped and opened its doors, but she walked past as if she didn't see it. What in the world was she up to now?

Sandra's suggestion that Caitlin had been strung out during her last visit sprang to his mind. He didn't want to believe it, but Sandra's concern had him almost convinced. If Caitlin was using drugs he had to know. He had to have proof. Unsure of exactly what he intended to do, he stepped out into the rain and began to follow her.

The bus belched a cloud of dark smoke as it pulled away, and the sound of Caitlin's harsh coughing reached Mick as the roar of the engine faded away. She wrapped her arms around herself as though she were chilled, but she never raised her head as she made her way across the street and continued down the dark sidewalk.

The streetlamps made pools of silvery liquid light in the rain, but Mick avoided them as he followed Caitlin. He didn't want to be spotted if she looked back. After a few blocks, the lights grew fewer.

He followed discreetly, trying not to attract attention. After a while, he realized no one cared. The few people he met hurried past with their heads down, or they hunched beneath umbrellas or newspapers held up to shield them from the drizzle.

After nearly two miles, the sidewalk became busier, and Mick closed the distance between himself and Caitlin as she continued into a district known for its unsavory activities. If she was looking for an easy place to score drugs, she was headed in the right direction.

He moved past the peep shows, novelty shops, bars and adult bookstores without a second glance. He was afraid of losing sight of Caitlin.

Up ahead of him, she slowed her steps then stopped. She sank onto an empty bench near the street corner and slumped forward with her head bowed. Mick stopped as well. Turning, he pretended to gaze at the jewelry displayed in a brightly lit pawnshop window while he covertly glanced toward Caitlin. What was she waiting for? Was she meeting someone? A dealer, maybe? Mick started to move closer when a gray car with a dented fender pulled to a halt at the curb in front of the bench.

The driver leaned across the seat and rolled the window down. "Hey, baby! You wanna party?"

Caitlin raised her head to stare at the man. Suddenly, Mick thought he'd be sick. His hands balled into fists. Was that how she had survived on the streets? He didn't even want to think about the answer. He started toward her.

"Get lost, creep!" At the sound of her sarcastic voice, Mick skidded to a halt.

Caitlin stood and walked on, pulling her thin sweater tight once more. The rain plastered her hair to her bowed head. Mick had never felt more ashamed of himself than he did at that moment.

At the corner, she turned and headed down Lexington. It was then that Mick thought he knew where she was going. The Lexington Street Shelter was about six blocks farther on. Had she been walking all this way to see the baby every day?

She paused at the side of an old brick building and reached out a hand to steady herself. Without warning, she crumpled to the pavement.

Mick broke into a run. Darting across the rain-filled street, he dodged a taxi and almost bowled over a man waiting at the crosswalk. Ignoring the indignant shout behind him, he raced to the fallen woman and dropped to his knees beside her. Her eyes fluttered open as he lifted her by the shoulders. "Caitlin, are you all right? Caitlin, answer me!"

"Mick? What are you doing here?"

"Never mind that. Are you okay?"

"I think so." She raised a trembling hand to the back of her head and winced. Lowering her hand, she stared at the blood smeared across her palm. "Or maybe not."

"Let me see."

"It's nothing."

"I'll be the judge of that." Easing her head forward, Mick probed her scalp with hands that were less than steady. He located a knot, but it was too dark to see the damage.

"You've got a goose egg. It doesn't feel like a bad wound, but I can't tell for sure. Can you stand?"

"I think so." She made an effort to rise.

He helped her up and steadied her once she gained her feet. She bowed her head and leaned heavily against him. He wrapped his arms around her and held her close. The feeling of her safe in his arms brought a rush of gratitude.

Thank You, God, for prompting me to follow her.

The trembling woman he held was so slight that he thought a single gust of Chicago's notorious wind might blow her away. She lifted her face to gaze at him. Possessed with the need to keep her safe, Mick bent his head and covered her trembling lips with a gentle kiss. For a second, she seemed to melt against him and it felt so wonderfully right. Then she stiffened and pushed away.

Pulling back, Mick stared into her eyes now wide with surprise. She bit the corner of her lip and looked away. A tremor shook her slender body.

"We need to get you out of this rain." Mick took a firm grip on her elbow as he led the way out of the alley and back toward the busy street. Within minutes he had flagged down a cab.

Caitlin gave the cabby the address of the shelter, then lapsed into silence in the backseat. Mick pulled off his jacket and tucked it around her. It was damp, but it still retained some of his body heat and he didn't have anything else to offer. He considered putting his arm around her, but thought better of it. The kiss had been a mistake. While she hadn't protested his embrace, she had clearly been surprised by it and perhaps even a little frightened. Adding to her fright was the last thing he wanted.

When the taxi pulled up to the curb in front of the shelter Caitlin handed him his jacket. "Thanks, Mick."

She opened the door and stepped out, but he was close behind her. After telling the driver to wait, Mick took her arm and hustled her toward the door of the building.

Once inside, he halted in the lobby lit by a single bulb in a bare socket in the ceiling. The place was packed with men and women sitting and lying around the perimeter of the room. The rank smells of unkempt bodies and dirty, wet clothes laced the thick air.

Ignoring the squalor around him, Mick took Caitlin by the shoulders. "Let me have a look at your head. I'm not going to leave you here if you should be in an emergency room."

Wordlessly, she turned around. Her meekness sent a small jolt of worry through him. Once he was satisfied it wasn't a deep cut he pulled her around and took a closer look at her eyes. Her skin that should have been cold from the damp rain was hot to his touch.

"I'm fine, Mick, don't fret." Her voice, so timid and soft, sent alarm bells ringing in his mind. This wasn't right. It wasn't the Caitlin he knew.

"You don't look fine. You look like a drowned cat. What you need is a hot bath, dry clothes and a filling meal," Mick stated firmly.

"That's just what I'll do, Mick. You don't have to hang around."

"Ha!" said a woman seated on the floor of the lobby. "They ain't got a tub here, only a drizzling shower and the water ain't never hot."

Mick frowned. "You've got to be kidding." Glancing around at the ragged men and women lining the room, he knew she wasn't. Not all of the shelters in town were as well-equipped or as well-funded as Mercy House.

"She can't get nothin' to eat, neither. They done served the last meal, and the kitchen ain't open again till morning."

Suddenly, the pieces began to fall into place. Caitlin wasn't using drugs, she was exhausted and undernourished.

"Mick, I'll be fine. I'll go right to bed. All I need is a little sleep." Even as she spoke, Caitlin's knees buckled and she would have fallen if he hadn't scooped her up.

"You aren't fine, and you aren't staying here." He and the nurses had misjudged Caitlin badly. Her only crime was that she didn't know how to ask for help. He turned and carried her toward the door.

"Where you takin' her?" the woman called after him.

"To my place. I'll bring her back when she's able to take care of herself."

"They won't hold her bed. If she ain't in it by ten, they'll give it to somebody else."

"Let them!" The door closed behind him with a bang.

Chapter Ten

The taxi driver cast Mick a puzzled look when he deposited Caitlin in the backseat and climbed in beside
her, but didn't make any comment. As the cab pulled
away, Caitlin's head lolled to Mick's shoulder, and this
time he didn't hesitate to drape an arm around her and
pull her close.

"I don't want to go home with you," Caitlin said. A
shiver coursed through her.

"I'm not giving you a choice." Mick glanced at her,
but her eyes were closed, and she missed the amusement that curved his lips into a smile. He was relieved
to hear some defiance creeping back into her voice. She
attempted to sit up, but Mick pressed her back against
his chest. It felt right to hold her close. For now, it was
enough to know that she was safe.

All too soon, the cab pulled to a stop in front of
Mick's home. He paid the driver, then gently lifted Caitlin from the car.

"I can walk," she protested weakly.

"So can I," Mick countered.

"I mean, you don't have to carry me."

"I want to."

"Oh."

That silenced her, or maybe she was simply too exhausted to put up more of an argument. On the porch, he set her feet down long enough to locate his keys and unlock the door, but he kept a firm grip on her with one arm. When the door swung open, he scooped her up and carried her inside.

Nikki gave a woof of a greeting from her spot by the fireplace. Mick lowered Caitlin to the sofa. With a quick tug, he pulled the worn, fuzzy throw emblazoned with the Chicago Bears logo from the back of the couch and swaddled it around her. Nikki rose and ventured across the room.

"You have a dog?"

Mick didn't understand the wistful tone that filled Caitlin's voice.

"This is Nikki. She won't hurt you."

Wagging her tail in greeting, Nikki sat down and promptly laid her head on Caitlin's lap. One of Caitlin's hands crept out from between the folds of the blanket to stroke the dog's head. "She's beautiful."

Mick patted the dog's side with a quick thump. "She's a good old girl. She wouldn't hurt a flea. I'm sure she'd hold the door open for a burglar and then lick his face just to show him how happy she was for the company."

Why was he standing here babbling about the dog? The woman on his sofa looked ready to keel over. He frowned. "When was the last time you had something to eat?"

"I don't know."

"Today? Yesterday?"

She didn't answer. He turned and headed for the

kitchen. He searched through the cabinets until he located a box of instant soup. It would be fast and it would warm her up. He poured the powdered broth and tiny noodles into a thick white mug then put the kettle on to boil. When the kettle began to whistle, he filled the cup, cooled it with an ice cube and carefully carried it in to Caitlin.

She was where he'd left her, only her head was lying back against the sofa. The fingers of one hand were still threaded through the long fur of Nikki's ear, and the dog watched her with adoring eyes. Nikki shifted her gaze to Mick as he came into the room, but she didn't move until he nudged her aside with his knee. Gently, Mick laid a hand on Caitlin's shoulder. "Wake up."

"Go away," she said without opening her eyes.

"No. Come on, sit up a minute."

"I said, go away."

"And I said, no."

She peeked out from under one lid. "You're a mean man."

"I know, but I have my good points."

"Name one."

"I've got a cup of hot soup here."

Both her eyes shot open. "That would be a good point."

"Think you can drink this before it gets cold?"

She reached out with both hands. "Even if I have to fight the dog for it."

Mick chuckled, but he didn't miss how her hands shook before they closed around the mug. "Don't worry, Nikki is a picky eater. I'm afraid instant chicken noodle soup is beneath her notice."

Caitlin took a tentative sip, then a longer one. With

a murmur of appreciation, she licked her lips as she clutched the mug close to her chest and bent her face to inhale the fragrant steam. "Her loss. This is good."

"I'm glad you like it."

"It's fantastic," she murmured as she raised the cup to her lips and took another sip. She gripped that mug like it was the last meal she was ever going to get. He could make sure that it wasn't, and he could see that she had a decent place to live, as well.

He had plenty of room here. He practically rattled around in this big, old house when he was home—which wasn't all that often. Somehow, he'd convince her to stay here. He owed her that much for his unjust suspicions. She wasn't going to get back on her feet staying at that run-down shelter. She needed help. He intended to see that she got it. "I'm going to let my mom know you're here."

"I already know." He looked up to see his mother descending the stairs. "I heard voices and came to see what was going on."

She crossed the room, took a seat beside Caitlin, and held out her hand. "Hello. I'm Elizabeth O'Callaghan. You must be Caitlin."

Caitlin nodded as she took the offered hand. "My daughter is named after you."

"I know. I'm quite flattered. My dear, you are soaking wet. Mick, why don't you run a bath for our guest."

He smiled. "That was next on my list."

"I don't want to be any trouble."

Caitlin's feeble protest caused his mother to grin. "It's no trouble at all. I'll find something you can change into. Don't just stand there, Mick. Get a move on."

Caitlin giggled. "So this is where he gets it."

Elizabeth gave her a puzzled look. "Gets what?"

"His tendency to boss people around."

Mick chuckled as he followed his mother up the stairs. He called over his shoulder. "You might think I'm bossy, but you have just met the master."

After adjusting the temperature of the water pouring into the ancient claw-footed tub that occupied the house's only bathroom, Mick straightened. His young nieces always insisted on a tub full of bubbles with their baths. Would Caitlin like that? If she hadn't had anything but lukewarm washups at the shelter since she was dismissed from the hospital, he was pretty sure she might.

Turning, he surveyed the room. The last time Mary's kids had slept over, he had picked up a box of bubble bath at their insistence. He finally discovered the slightly battered box under the sink. He shook out a bit of the powder under the running water and a few bubbles began to form. It didn't seem like enough. With a shrug, he emptied the rest of the box in the tub and headed downstairs to get Caitlin.

She was asleep again. The empty soup cup dangled precariously from one hand while her other hand lay on Nikki's head where the dog had curled up on the sofa beside her.

"Get down, mutt," he grumbled softly. Nikki ignored him as usual. Mick bent and scooped Caitlin up in his arms.

Her eyes fluttered open. "You kiss nice."

He didn't know how to respond to that so he said, "Your bath is ready."

He started up the stairs and noticed how pleasant it was to carry this woman in his arms.

"I don't need a bath," she grumbled.

"Would it be ungentlemanly of me to say, yes, you do?"

Her tired eyes settled into a frown. "I don't stink."

"I never said you did."

"You said—"

"I said you need a bath. You've been soaked to the skin and chilled to boot, and a hot bath is exactly what you need."

"Okay. But I don't stink."

"No, you don't," he agreed, and hoped she didn't notice the amusement in his voice. He pushed open the bathroom door and stopped.

"Awesome!" she said in amazement.

Mounds of foam filled the tub and lazy sheets of it slid over the side to pool on the floor. Quickly, he deposited her on the toilet seat and turned off the water, feeling like a first-class nitwit.

"I thought you'd like a bubble bath. It's just Mr. Bubble—that's all I had. My niece left it here. I know my sisters used to use some kind of scented foamy stuff that smelled like lilacs or gardenias or some such flower." He realized he was babbling like an idiot and stopped talking.

"This is just like in the movies. I always wanted to do this."

He frowned at her. "You've never taken a bubble bath?"

"Not that I remember."

She didn't seem to realize how pathetic that simple statement sounded. What a hard, bare life she had lived. He rubbed his palms on the sides of his jeans. "Well then, I'm sure you'll like it. Just don't fall asleep and drown. I'll wait outside the door and you can hand me your clothes. I'll toss them in the washer for you."

She cast a suspicious look in his direction.

"Don't worry, dear," his mother came in behind him. "I have a robe you can wear. Go on, Mick. Shoo."

He retreated and closed the door.

A few moments later, it opened a crack and his mother dangled Caitlin's clothes out by one hand. He took them and beat a strategic withdrawal to the laundry room in the basement. He tossed her skirt and hose into the washer, but paused as he stared at the sweater in his hands. A few drops of blood speckled one shoulder.

It was frighteningly easy to imagine Beth living a life with Caitlin, and he shuddered at the thought of what she would endure if that happened. Caitlin deserved his help. Because if she didn't get it, Beth might be with her the next time she waited in the lobby of a crowded shelter to find out if there would be a bed for the night. And if there wasn't room, Beth would sleep with her mother in a doorway, or alley, or on a grate to keep from freezing to death in the winter.

No, Beth wasn't going to live like that. He would make sure of it. He started to toss the sweater in with the rest of the load, but a piece of paper fell out of one of the pockets and landed at his feet. He made a quick search of both pockets, but he didn't find anything else.

Bending down, he picked up the paper and smoothed out the small, damp note. With a muttered oath, he hurried back upstairs. He knocked on the bathroom door and didn't get any answer. "Caitlin, I need to talk to you."

"Just a moment," his mother answered.

He heard the sound of the shower curtain sliding on the rod, then his mother called out, "You can come in."

He pushed open the door. The gray-and-white-striped shower curtain hid most of Caitlin. All he could see was her head as she leaned against the back of the tub. His mother sat on a small vanity stool beside her. Caitlin opened her eyes and smiled sweetly.

"This is totally awesome." She lifted her palm filled with a small mountain of suds and blew. Bubbles danced through the air. "Can you imagine being able to do this every day?"

Having soap and hot water was something he never gave a second thought to, but with a simple question, she changed all of that. He held out the note. "I found this in your sweater pocket."

"What is it?" She frowned at the paper as if she'd never seen it before.

"Caitlin, this is a prescription for antibiotics for you written by Dr. Wright."

All at once, huge tears began to stream down her face. Alarmed, Mick said, "What's wrong?"

"I never meant to hurt her. I'm so sorry." With that, she broke into hysterical sobs.

"It's all right." The force of her uncontrolled weeping was so unlike the tough and resourceful woman he knew that he began to fear she would do herself physical harm.

"Let me handle this," Elizabeth said as she pushed him out the door and closed it in his face.

Finally, his mother called for him to come in. He opened the door and saw Caitlin wrapped in a long, thick robe and slumped against his mother on the edge of the tub. Elizabeth held her awkwardly with her one good arm.

"Can you carry her to the spare bedroom, son?"

"Of course." He slid his arms around Caitlin and lifted her easily. In the bedroom, he sat down on the edge of the bed where he held her and rocked her and murmured words of comfort until the storm of her weeping abated. She kept repeating that she was sorry. Sorry for what, he couldn't make out.

He looked at his mother, hovering beside him and said, "She's on the verge of exhaustion. This can't be good for her."

"She needed sleep more than anything else, but we can't put her to bed in a damp robe. I'm not sure I can get her into one of my nightgowns by myself."

Gently, he laid Caitlin down on top of the coverlet and went to his room. From his chest of drawers, he pulled out a button-down pajama top that would have to suffice for a nightgown and returned to her room. He paused beside his mother in indecision. "Can you manage this?"

"Yes, this will work. I'll call if I need you." She took his shirt.

He was sitting on the side of the bed when his mother joined him a short time later.

"She's more than exhausted, Mick. The woman is sick."

"I know." He held out the crumpled prescription.

"Has she been seeing the baby?"

"Every day. I'm guessing that's why Beth is sick, too."

He picked up the phone and dialed the number for the NICU.

"This is Mick O'Callaghan," he said tersely when the unit clerk answered. "I need to speak with Dr. Wright, immediately."

A knocking sound woke Caitlin from a pleasant dream. She opened her eyes and stared at an unfamiliar room with walls painted a delicate shade of rose. Across from her, white curtains billowed from an open window. Beyond she could see the branches of a huge tree silhouetted against a blue sky. Beside the window, a large purple toy cat stared at her from a rocking chair. Another knock sounded. It came from behind her. She turned over and winced. Every part of her body ached.

A door opened and Mick peeked around it. He stepped into the room looking uncertain and wonderfully handsome. "How are you feeling?"

"Kinda…confused."

"I'm not surprised. You've been asleep for thirty hours."

He crossed the room in three strides. She flinched when his hand shot toward her, and he froze. "I'm not going to hurt you. I only want to make sure your fever's down. May I?" Slowly, he extended his hand and touched her forehead.

She remembered now, she remembered everything— the doctor telling her that her milk had made Beth sick, Mick's rescue, meeting his mother. He had brought her to his home. What else had been real and not part of a dream? Had he really kissed her?

Embarrassment flooded her, but she couldn't help thinking about kissing him again.

"I'm fine." She turned away from his hand.

"You're better, but not fine. Look, I've got to get to

work. I won't be back until tomorrow morning. Mom is here and my number is on a pad by the phone in the kitchen if you need anything. Make yourself at home. Fix yourself whatever you'd like to eat. I'd like you to consider staying here for a while. My mother will be here as well."

"How come a guy your age still lives with his mother?"

He laughed. "I don't normally. Mom was injured in a car accident two months ago. I'm sure you saw the cast on her arm."

"Yeah, I wondered about that."

"Her doctor didn't want her staying alone. My sisters both have jobs that require them to travel. I work one day and get two days off. Having Mom stay with me seemed like the best solution. She has a nurse that comes in while I'm gone. You won't be expected to take care of her if that's what you're worried about."

"I wasn't thinking about that. I'd like to repay your kindness, but I'm not sure I can stay here."

"It's only until you're well. You don't have to make a decision today. Just tell me you'll think about it."

Soft bed, clean sheets, a room to herself—or back to the shelter—oh, hard choice! "Okay, I'll think about it."

He nodded then started to leave the room, but as he opened the door, he turned back. "Oh, I left your medicine on the bathroom sink. Dr. Wright said to take one pill morning, noon and night. Your pump is in there, too."

He looked down, and Caitlin saw his dog wiggle past him into the room. She trotted over to the bed with her tail wagging and pressed a cold, wet nose into Caitlin's hand.

Caitlin pulled her hand away and crossed her arms, then turned to stare out the window. She didn't want Mick to see the tears that threatened once more. "I don't need a pump."

"Sure you do."

"Didn't the good doctor tell you my milk is what's been making Beth sick?"

He didn't answer her, but a moment later, she heard him pull a chair next to the bed. "Caitlin, look at me."

She couldn't. She couldn't let him see how much it hurt to fail at the one thing she wanted so desperately to do for her baby. Gentle fingers cupped her chin and pulled her face toward him. She couldn't look him in the eye, so she fastened her gaze on the top button of his dark blue shirt.

"Dr. Wright told me it was possible that the infection you have may—*may*—" he emphasized the word again "—have made Beth sick. But she also said babies who are on formula, even babies that haven't been fed, can have the same problem."

She looked into his eyes. "Honest?"

"Honest."

"But they threw my milk out."

"I know." He pulled her close and wrapped his arms around her, and she rested her cheek against his shoulder. His touch said without words that he understood how much that had hurt.

"Once you're better, you can start saving your milk again. As soon as Beth is ready, they'll give it to her."

"What if it makes her sick again?"

"It won't."

She straightened, pulling away from him. "But if it does?"

"Then we'll cross that bridge when we come to it. The main thing now is to get you well. There's plenty of food in the kitchen. You need to eat and put some flesh on your bones." He tweaked her nose. "You're way too skinny."

She sniffed once and rubbed her nose with the back of her hand. "I'm not skinny."

"You're skinny, skinny, skinny."

She tried to hold back her smile, but lost the battle. "You're a mean man."

"As I pointed out before, I have my good points."

"I don't see any soup, so I guess you'll have to name one."

"I kiss nice. You said so yourself."

Before she could think of a comeback, he rose and left the room, closing the door behind him. Nikki put one paw on the bed and whined for attention. Caitlin reached out to pet the dog.

"If I said that, I was delirious." Maybe she had been, but it was the truth.

Tossing the covers aside, she sat up on the side of the bed and glanced down at the green-and-white-striped pajama top that more than covered her. She vaguely remembered Mick's mother putting it on her. A soft warmth stole over her at the memory. These people were gentle and kind. She wasn't exactly sure what to make of them.

She stood and felt the hem of his shirt drop to her knees. Grinning, she raised her arms and flapped the sleeves dangling a good six inches past the end of her hands. The door opened after a gentle knock. Caitlin paused in midflap as Mick looked in again.

"I almost forgot—" Whatever he started to say dissolved into a hearty laugh.

She dropped her arms to her sides and scowled at him.

He held up one hand. "I'm sorry. It's just that it's a pretty silly getup."

She planted her hands on her hips. "It's your shirt, not mine. If anyone here has bad taste in sleepwear, it's you."

He flushed. "I came back to tell you my mother left a few things for you to wear. They're in the closet along with your clothes. She said to keep what you like, she doesn't wear any of them anymore."

He hesitated a moment, as if he intended to say something else, but instead he closed the door. Caitlin waited, but this time the door stayed shut.

His kindness to her was something she didn't quite know how to deal with. He was kind to everyone, she reminded herself. He was kind to the kids at the shelter, to scared women in labor and even to old bums. The feel of Mick's strong arms holding her might tempt her to believe it had been something more, but she wasn't stupid. Besides, he was way out of her league. A man like him could have the pick of any number of women. Smart women, women with class. Not someone like her.

Out of curiosity, she crossed the room and opened the closet. A plush pink bathrobe hung from a hook on the back of the door. She fingered its softness. A half dozen outfits hung from hangers on a wooden rod. One was the black skirt and pink sweater she'd been wearing for weeks. She pushed it aside. "If I never wear this again, it'll be too soon."

Instead, she reached for a pair of raspberry red

sweats that looked like they might fit. When she pulled the top off the hanger, she noticed it still had a price tag attached. She checked the others. They all did.

Caitlin looked at the dog sitting at her side. "Keep what I want because his mom doesn't wear them anymore? One or both of them are very poor liars."

Nikki whined and gave a small woof.

"I'll take that to mean you agree."

Looking for her shoes, Caitlin spied a familiar orange crate on the floor. With a glad cry, she dropped to her knees.

"My baby clothes, my sketchbooks, it's all here." She lifted the baby blanket from the box and held it to her cheek. Mick had saved her things. There was no way she would ever be able to thank him. Sitting back on her heels with a happy smile, she lovingly replaced the blanket. There was no way she was going to lose them again. Jumping up, she pulled off a pink-striped pillowcase from the pillow on the bed and stuffed her treasures and new clothes inside.

Her stomach growled, reminding her that she hadn't had anything to eat except broth for the past two days. She dressed in the soft sweats, then with pillowcase in hand, she opened the door of the room and stepped out into a narrow hall. The dog slipped past her, and Caitlin followed the animal downstairs.

Nikki made a beeline for the kitchen. She stopped in front of the refrigerator and raised a paw to scratch at the door.

"My thoughts exactly," Caitlin agreed. Pulling open the fridge door, she stared in amazement at the food that crammed the shelves. "Awesome!" She looked at the dog. "He did say to fix myself anything I wanted, didn't he?"

Nikki answered her with a short, sharp bark.

"That was a definite yes." Caitlin reached in, pushed aside a bag of oranges, a jug of milk and a carton of eggs to pull out a round pan. "I don't know about you, but I want some of this pie."

She made a quick check of the cabinet drawers, located a fork, then plopped on a chair at the table. The first giant bite of whipped topping and chocolate cream pie straight from the pan was the best thing she had ever tasted. The second bite was every bit as good. Only when the pan was half-empty did she pause long enough to take a closer look at her surroundings.

It was hard to imagine having all this space and not having to share it with somebody. She ran a hand over the smooth surface of the table. She'd never eaten off anything so fine, not even when she'd been in some of her good foster homes.

A delicate teapot sat in the center of the table. Her eyes widened as she reached for it and turned it over. She had learned a thing or two about good junk in her years of scrounging in garbage cans and Dumpster diving for food and stuff to sell.

"Do you see this?" she asked the dog in astonishment. "This little green crown means this is valuable. I could get twenty, maybe twenty-five bucks easy for it at a pawnshop."

"Nikki is smart for a dog, but I don't think she can read labels." Elizabeth stood in the kitchen doorway dressed in a pale blue robe and slippers.

Caitlin flushed with embarrassment and looked down. She couldn't read either—she was no smarter than the dog. Replacing the teapot with care, she said, "I wasn't going to steal it."

Elizabeth came to the table and laid a hand on Caitlin's shoulder. "It never occurred to me that you might. But if you like it, you're welcome to have it."

"No, thanks. I'm not much of tea drinker."

"Maybe that's because you've never had someone make you a *good* cup of tea. Sit there and I'll fix you some Earl Grey with honey and cream. I promise you'll love it." She headed to the stove and picked up the kettle.

Caitlin jumped up. "Let me do that."

Elizabeth shook her head. "No, I can fix tea one-handed. Naomi will be here any minute. She'll spend the day fussing over me and scolding me. This may be the only chance I get to do something for myself. Please, sit down."

"Okay. If you're sure." Caitlin sank into her chair again. "I'd like to do something to repay you for these clothes."

"Your clothes? I don't understand."

"Mick said you wanted me to have these because they didn't fit you. Only you forgot to take the price tags off."

Elizabeth gave a bark of laughter. "It wasn't me. I can't believe my son went shopping for women's clothes. What else did he buy?"

"I have them right here." She touched the pillowcase with one foot.

"Wonderful. You can show me what he bought later this morning. When we've finished our tea I'll give you a tour of the house. Would you like that?"

"If you think Mick won't mind."

"Of course he won't. Besides, if you plan on staying for a while, you'll need to find your way around. Do you plan on staying?"

"I don't know. It feels kind of weird living in someone else's house as an adult."

"I have to agree with that. It was wonderful of Mick to let me stay here after my accident, but I do miss my own space. I thought the pillowcase meant you were on your way out."

"No. I just don't want to lose my stuff again. I was really lucky to get it back this time."

Elizabeth's eyes filled with understanding and sympathy. "It must be difficult to keep the things you love living on the streets."

Caitlin shrugged. "People will steal anything of value. You can't blame them. Some of them have nothing. They don't know any other way to survive."

"It's the sad truth. Keep your things close if it makes you feel better and keep the pillowcase. I never did like that pattern, anyway."

"Thanks."

"Good. Now, the plan is tea and a tour. I have to warn you, Mickey is not a great housekeeper. Dust bunnies abound under his furniture. Once I have two good hands again, I'm going to make a clean sweep of things."

Caitlin brightened. Here was a way she could repay some of their kindness. "I've got two good hands. Show me where the broom is and I'll get rid of them for you."

"You've been sick. Mickey would skin me alive if he knew I'd put you to work your first day out of bed."

"We won't tell him. If he's like most men, he'll never notice that the place has been cleaned."

Elizabeth pressed her one good hand to her lips and chuckled. "My dear, I do believe I'm going to enjoy having you around."

Mick pulled into his drive the next morning, turned the engine off and remained sitting behind the wheel. Was she still here, or had she taken off? He shouldn't be surprised if she had. He couldn't believe how much he wanted her to stay.

He walked around to the front, picked up the morning copy of the *Tribune* from the steps and quietly let himself into the house. Nikki wasn't in her usual place, and that gave him his first bit of hope.

He checked the kitchen. No Caitlin and no dog. He stopped at the foot of the stairs and called out. Only silence greeted him. Where was everyone?

He climbed the stairs and after knocking twice, he opened the door to the guest room. It was empty, the bed neatly made. He checked the closet. The clothes he'd bought and all her things were gone.

Chapter Eleven

Mick struck the closet doorjamb with the heel of his hand in frustration. He wanted her to be here. He wanted her to stay more than he cared to admit. She was sick, broke and alone in the world. She needed his help, but every time he tried to give it, she threw it back in his face. Why did he keep trying?

He knew Beth was part of it, but it was more than his attachment to the baby that drew him to Caitlin. Caitlin was like a song in his head that wouldn't go away. The more he tried to ignore it, the more he found himself humming the same tune over and over. His attraction to her didn't make sense. They had almost nothing in common. She didn't even share his faith.

The sound of a dog barking followed by a burst of girlish laughter reached him through the open window. He rushed to look out. Caitlin lay stretched out in his hammock in the backyard. One bare foot hung over the side, and she swung herself back and forth with an occasional push. She held one of Nikki's favorite toys and laughed at the dog's antics as Nikki bounced up and down waiting for her to throw the ball.

Mick's heart gave a leap of joy that he couldn't ignore or explain away. She was here.

He sank onto the chair beside the window, knocking aside the stuffed cat. Reaching down, he picked up his niece's toy and stared blankly into its glass eyes. If it started talking he wouldn't be as surprised as he was by the realization that he was falling in love with the woman outside.

When had it happened? He certainly hadn't been looking for a relationship, had he?

Caitlin's laughter rang out again and drew his gaze. Nikki was trying to crawl into the hammock and was making a serious attempt to lavish doggie kisses on Caitlin's face. His Sleeping Beauty was awake, and she was even more beautiful in the bright light of day.

Her giggles eased the doubts clambering in Mick's mind. He'd rarely seen her smile, and this was the first time he could recall hearing her laugh. It felt good to see her happy. Perhaps that was why God had brought her into his life.

Her life had held little happiness, but he'd never heard her complain. Instead, she faced it with a belligerent determination and a resilience he could only admire. Was it any wonder that he was attracted to her?

So what are you going to do about it, Mick'O?

He didn't have a clue. No, that wasn't quite true. He knew one thing for sure. He wouldn't do anything to hurt her. She had been hurt far too much already. For now, she was safe and happy, and he didn't want to jeopardize that. Caitlin was as wary as a feral cat and just as likely to disappear unless he could gain her trust.

Mick put the purple cat back on the window ledge.

He had a lot of soul-searching ahead of him. *Please, Lord, show me what I need to do to help her.*

He left the spare bedroom and went downstairs to the back door. From there, he watched Caitlin playing with Nikki until the dog spotted him and came loping toward him. Caitlin picked up a stuffed pillowcase from beside the hammock and followed.

"You're home," she said with a smile that turned his heart upside down.

"I am. Any problems while I was gone?"

"Not a one. Nikki and I had a great time, didn't we, girl?"

"I'm glad. You look better. How are you feeling?"

"Less like a drowned cat all the time."

"Good. Where is my mom?"

"Naomi took her shopping. They should be back in an hour or two. Your mom had a list of things she thinks I need."

"Does that mean you're planning to stick around? I thought maybe you were on your way out." He pointed to the bag she carried.

"It's just my stuff. I don't want to lose it again."

"I think it would be safe up in your room."

"I guess it would. I'm just not used to leaving my stuff unguarded, that's all."

"If that's the way you feel, I've got a duffel bag that might work better than a pillowcase."

"That would be great. Thanks."

"So, you do plan to stay."

"I'm not an idiot. This is better than any shelter. It'll do until I find a place of my own. Besides, Nikki needs someone to play with when you're gone. Don't you, girl?" She leaned down to pat the dog.

It was the answer he wanted and his heart took flight.

Straightening, she threw a punch at his midsection. "Right now, I'm starved. I hope you can cook because I hate cooking. Besides, I'm no good at it, and all the pie is gone."

He'd never seen her this accommodating. He'd half expected a bitter battle just to get her to spend another night here. "I don't cook much myself, but I guess we'll get by."

"Fast food is fine if you want to treat me to Mickey D's. Hey, I can eat at Mickey O's or Mickey D's."

Surprised, he gaped at her. "Was that a joke?"

She frowned. "Yes. It wasn't that bad."

"Not at all. Sometimes, I'm a little slow after I've been at work for twenty-four hours. How about some bacon and eggs?"

"Sounds great. I can make the tea. Did you know you should always warm the pot first? I like the orange kind better than the Earl stuff, but please don't tell your mother I said that."

Bemused, he said, "Do you think if Prince Charming had known that Sleeping Beauty had a multiple-personality disorder he would have kissed her anyway?"

"Huh?"

"Never mind." He held the door open. "After you."

She flounced past him into the house. He followed her to the kitchen and watched as she put the kettle on then slid into a chair at the table. She ran a hand through her short hair. "You got a nice place here. It's kind of big for one guy, isn't it?"

He pulled the eggs and bacon from the fridge and carried them to the stove. "A little, but it suits me.

There's always plenty of room when my family comes to visit."

"Your mom is really sweet. I'm not sure if I should ask, but what happened to your dad?"

"He died when I was eight. He was a fireman, too. How about your parents?"

"Mom OD'd a few years ago. I don't know who my dad was."

"Any brothers or sisters?"

"Nope. I always wanted a sister, though."

"Great! I'll give you one of mine. I've got two."

"Was that who helped you buy my clothes? Did you know you forgot to take the tags off?"

He sent her a sheepish glance. "I guess I was too worried about getting them into the closet without waking you."

"Why say they belonged to your mother?"

"Because I thought you might refuse them if you thought they were from me. I don't know if anyone has mentioned this, but you can be stubborn at times."

She shrugged one shoulder. "I need clothes, and these fit pretty good," she acknowledged, rubbing a hand down her denim-clad thigh.

"I see that. I was afraid the jeans would be too small."

"How'd you know what size to get?"

He propped one hand on his hip. "Having sisters gives one a sense of fashion, darling. Actually, I took your skirt with me and let the saleslady make an educated guess."

"Be sure and tell your mom that. I think she was worried that you knew how to buy women's clothes."

"I think I'll let her wonder about that one."

Her giggle did his heart good. "How do you like your eggs?" he asked.

"Cooked, but not burnt."

He turned to the stove. "Cooked, but not burnt it is. In fact, hand me some mild cheddar, not the sharp, and some Tabasco sauce from the fridge. I'll make you Mickey O's famous Scrambled Eggs O'Callaghan."

When she didn't answer, he turned back. A frown had replaced her smile. "What's the matter?"

She jumped to her feet. "Get it yourself, what am I, your servant? Anyway, I-I've got to go to the bathroom." She fled from the room.

"I guess you do," he said to the empty air.

The eggs and bacon and tea were ready by the time she came back. He set a plate in front of her, then sat down, bowed his head and said grace. Caitlin didn't participate, but sat quietly until he finished. She ate, but she remained subdued. She answered his questions with monosyllables and none of his jokes brought back her smile.

"Are you feeling okay?" he asked at last.

"I'm fine. Thanks for breakfast." Her voice held a sharp edge to it. She carried her plate to the sink.

"I can clean up," Mick offered, wondering how he had offended her.

"No, I do my part."

"Would you like to go to the hospital when you're done?"

She spun toward him. "Oh, yes."

He nodded. "Let me grab a quick shower, and we can go."

"Don't you need to get some sleep?"

"I was able to grab a few winks at work. I thought

I'd take you to the hospital and let you spend some time with Beth while I came home and pulled in a few more z's."

"That would be great." Caitlin paused, then added. "Your job is a tough one, you must love it."

It blew him away that this woman could see how he felt about his work when his sisters, who knew him so much better, still didn't understand.

"I think it's the calling God chose for me. I can't imagine doing anything else. Of course, my family thinks I'm nuts."

"But you said your dad was a fireman."

Mick nodded and stared at his plate. "He died on the job."

"I'm sorry."

He nodded without looking up. "I was eight, but I remember it vividly—the men at the door, my mother's weeping, the race to the hospital, the smell of charred flesh in the burn unit."

She slipped onto the chair beside him and covered his hand with her own. "Did you get to see him before he died?"

"I did."

"Was it terrible?"

"His face wasn't burnt. One of his arms was covered in a thick bandage. They had a kind of tent over the rest of him. He was conscious, and he said he wasn't in much pain. I think the hardest part was my mother's crying. For him, too. He told me I would be the man of the house and that he expected me to take care of her. I didn't have the slightest idea how I could do that, but he made me promise, and I did."

"That wasn't fair."

He looked at her then. Her eyes were full of sympathy, as if she knew what that vow had cost him. "Maybe it wasn't, but I did my best to keep that promise. He died the next day. I never wanted to be anything except just like him."

"Well, you are. You're a fireman."

"I don't mean the job. I wanted to be the same kind of man he was. He was the best dad a kid could have. He always had time for me. We played catch, we went fishing, we took in the ball games—he was always there for me. I wanted to be the same kind of father. But it didn't work out that way." Mick voiced the death of his dreams in a matter-of-fact tone that bore little resemblance to the state of shock that he had been in when he endured his doctor's explanations of sterility.

Sterile—the word changed his life. It made him less than a man, and he knew then that he would never be like his father. In time, he came to grips with the knowledge, even learned to accept it as God's will.

"But you can adopt, right?" Caitlin asked.

How many times had he heard that platitude from his family? He forced a smile and nodded. "Sure, I can always adopt."

"Your mother never remarried?"

"No, she never did." He was glad to change the subject.

"How did she take it when you decided to be a firefighter?"

"My sisters didn't understand, but Mom was proud of me. The fact that I wanted to be like him made her very happy."

"That was lucky."

"Lucky? Why?"

"Because it turned out to be a job you love."

He nodded and gave her a small smile. "You're right. I could have done it to please her and then been miserable."

"Did you?"

"Do it to make her happy? Maybe."

"Are you still trying to make her happy?"

He frowned. "What do you mean?"

"Taking me in, naming Beth after her, taking responsibility for a baby that isn't yours."

He studied her face a long moment. "Caitlin, I try to live my life the way I think God wants me to live it. Do you know what that means?"

"Kind of. But I don't believe in all that stuff."

"What do you believe in?"

"Not much. Life stinks and then you die. That's it."

"That doesn't leave much room for hope, or love or kindness."

"Sometimes that stuff comes along, but you can't count on it. If you do, people let you down. I count on me and no one else."

"You can count on God, Caitlin. He loves you no matter what you think. And you can count on me. Please believe that."

"Aren't we going to the hospital?"

It was obvious she wanted to change the subject. "Sure. As soon as I wash up."

In the bathroom upstairs, he braced his hands on the sink and stared into the mirror. He rarely talked about his father, but it was easy to talk to Caitlin. She had endured a childhood far tougher than his, and maybe that created a bond between them. She was a homeless waif, but he saw the potential for so much more in her.

A frown creased the brow of his reflection in the mirror. He had told her a great deal about himself, but she had shared almost nothing about herself. She was willing to accept a place to live but he sensed that she still didn't trust him.

Would she learn to? Perhaps if he gave her enough time. If she didn't, he stood to lose more than the growing affection he felt toward her. He stood to lose both her and Beth.

Caitlin stood beside Beth's bed and waited. The baby lay on her back with her arms limp at her sides. Sandra listened to her with a stethoscope.

"How is she?" Caitlin asked when Sandra pulled the instrument from her ears.

"About the same, except she's up to sixty percent on her oxygen."

"Her color doesn't look so good. What does Dr. Wright say about it?"

"She says we need to keep a close eye on her, but we're doing everything we need to do. This happens sometimes when these little babies get sick."

"Can I hold her?"

Sandra laid a hand on Caitlin's shoulder. "I don't think it would be a good idea. She hasn't tolerated much today."

Caitlin nodded. She would do whatever the nurses and doctors thought was best. She'd learned her lesson. Guilt, she found, was harder to get rid of than head lice.

"You're looking more rested," Sandra said.

"Thanks, I feel better."

Pulling a chair close, Sandra sat beside Caitlin. Two other nurses who often took care of Beth came over and stood behind her. Caitlin tensed. What was going on now?

Sandra reached out and covered Caitlin's hand with her own. "We want to apologize."

"For what?"

"I think you and I got off to a bad start. Mick told me how sick you've been, and how you'd been walking all the way from the Lexington Street Shelter—"

"Sometimes Mick talks too much."

"In this case, I don't think so. As nurses, we should have noticed you were sick. You and I weren't on friendly terms and that led me to believe the worst about you. I'm sorry."

"I'm sorry, too," one of the women behind Sandra added.

"So am I," the other one chimed in.

Caitlin met Sandra's gaze. "It wasn't your fault. I should have told someone I wasn't feeling well. If I had, Beth wouldn't have gotten this sick."

"It wasn't entirely your fault. We take part of the blame. Anyway, we wanted you to know how sorry we are."

Caitlin swallowed the lump that formed in her throat. These women had taken care of her baby day and night for weeks. She resented them for being the ones Beth needed. Sometimes, she even felt that they were trying to replace her as Beth's mother, but the truth was, without them Beth wouldn't be alive.

"If you have any questions, about anything, please know that we'll be glad to answer them," Sandra continued. "Our job is to see that Beth goes home with you as soon as she can."

Caitlin nodded but didn't trust herself to speak. It

seemed that all she wanted to do anymore was cry. She wasn't used to people being nice to her.

The nurses left to attend to other babies, and Caitlin drew her chair closer to Beth's bed. She kept one eye on the baby's oxygen saturation monitor. A drop in that number was often the first clue that Beth wasn't tolerating touch or sounds near her.

"Hey, jelly bean, how are you? I'm sorry I haven't been in, but I've been sick myself. I sure missed you." Caitlin grasped Beth's hand but it remained limp.

"I know you don't feel good. Mick says hello. He wanted to come up—I could tell—but he said he thought we needed some time together—just you and me.

"I'm staying at his place with him and his mom. He's got a big house with a yard right beside a park, and he's got a dog."

He had all the things that Caitlin had dreamed of having. All the things she wanted to give Beth.

"The place you and I get won't be fancy, but it'll be decent, and I'm going to tell you every day how much I love you. So, you have to get better."

Sitting back in the chair, Caitlin was content to watch Beth sleep and study her face. She was so beautiful. Caitlin had heard that mothers always thought their own kids were the cutest, even the ones who had ugly kids, but until now, she hadn't understood how that was possible. Beth was beautiful in so many special ways. Suddenly, Caitlin had to sketch her.

After telling Sandra that she would be back, Caitlin went to the parent's check-in room and pulled the duffel bag Mick had given her from one of the tall, narrow lockers. She unpacked her sketchbook then stuffed the bag in again. Back at Beth's bed, Caitlin flipped her drawing pad open and began to transfer her baby's most beautiful features to paper.

First she sketched Beth's fingers, the long, delicate way they lay cupped on the bed. Then her pencil mapped out the faint frown lines on Beth's brow and the gentle arch of her eyebrows. Soon a picture of her baby's face emerged, but at the mouth, Caitlin paused. She'd never seen Beth's mouth without the ventilator tube and the thick mustache of tape that held the tube in place.

Smiling at her daughter, Caitlin said, "I guess that part of you will have to stay a mystery." Reluctantly, she added a small part of the equipment that was so alien and yet so much a part of her child.

"You draw beautifully."

Caitlin looked up to find a young woman standing at her shoulder. "Thanks. It helps having a pretty model."

"Are you a professional artist?"

"Not hardly."

"You could be. I've often admired the poem she has on her bed. It helps me keep faith that my little boy will get better." The woman pointed to the card with green shamrocks around its border.

Caitlin had noticed the card the first time she had come to visit, and she had wondered what it said, but she couldn't bring herself to ask. Instead, she said, "Which one is yours?"

"Jacob is in the last bed on this aisle. He weighed almost the same as your daughter when he was born."

"Is he doing okay?"

"Pretty good. He got off his ventilator today. It's the second time they've tried him off. Last time, he went a day before he had to go back on."

"That's good. Beth has never been off hers."

"She will. Well, I'd better go. It's time to feed him. I like to hold him when he gets fed even if it's just by tube. It's not like I can do much more for him yet."

"I know what you mean." Their gazes met and Caitlin nodded. She knew about feeling useless, about not being able to do a single thing that would ease her baby's way. She recognized that same emotion in this mother's eyes.

"I'll let you get back to your drawing," the woman said and walked to her child's bed. Caitlin watched as the nurse moved Jacob to his mother's arms and attached a syringe with milk in it to his stomach tube. The look on his mother's face was pure happiness as she held him close.

Glancing around the unit, Caitlin realized she wasn't the only mother riding the emotional roller coaster of having a baby in the NICU. Some mothers were proudly showing their infants to visitors, one sat silently staring into an incubator and a few others leaned over the sides of their children's open units to try and be close to their babies. Nurses moved between the beds with a smile or a word for the parents, who like Caitlin, were learning to take one day at a time, and to measure success in a few ounces of weight gained.

Later, when Jacob's mother was leaving, she stopped beside Caitlin again. "I know it's a lot to ask, but could you sketch a portrait of my baby? I'd be happy to pay you for it."

"I don't know. You can take pictures in here, I've seen people with cameras."

"I know. We've taken lots of them, but your drawings...I don't know...they're so soft." She reached down and touched the page Caitlin was working on. "All that's here is your baby. In a photograph, all the equipment, all their stuff, it's always in the picture."

Caitlin turned over the idea in her mind. She could use the money, but somehow, it didn't seem right to take advantage of a mother with a sick child. "I'll think about it," she said.

"If you decide that you want to, I'll let Jacob's nurse know that you have my permission."

"Good point."

The woman smiled and leaned closer. "They are sticklers, aren't they? I know their hearts are in the right place, but sometimes, I have to wonder whose baby he is—mine or theirs?"

"Let me get this straight." Woody moved a chess piece, then leaned back in the black leather chair beside the game table in his apartment. His stark white walls held numerous landscapes done in watercolors and oils in every size. "You aren't the father of this baby. But instead of letting Caitlin go her own way, you keep tabs on her and wind up taking her home with you."

"She was sick and walking all the way from the Lexington Street Shelter to the hospital." Mick studied the board and made his move. His heart wasn't in the game. He was here because Woody was the one person he could talk to who wouldn't judge or offer unwanted advice.

"I get that part." Woody moved a knight to block Mick's next play. "Wow! No wonder you didn't tell me the whole story when I asked. Now that she's better, why is she still staying with you and your mom?"

Mick reassessed his strategy and moved his queen.

"She doesn't have anywhere to go. She's homeless, re-member?"

"So you are going to take care of both of them. Mother and child. A ready-made family."

"I didn't plan it that way."

"I know that. You never look more than four moves ahead when you play this game, why should your life be any different?"

"Now you make me sound like a fool."

"Not a fool, Mick. Just a guy who leads with his heart instead of his brain." He countered Mick's move. "Check and mate."

Mick studied the board. Woody was right. About the game and about Mick's tendency to follow his heart. He sat back and looked at his friend. "What would you do in my shoes?"

"Buy a bigger pair. Your boots are two sizes smaller than mine."

"You know what I mean." Mick reached down and moved the chess pieces back to their starting positions.

Woody began to line his up as well. "I can't help you with this mess, buddy. If the child was yours, I'd say you have every right to be part of her life. But this? I know you thought you were doing the right thing, but I'm not so sure. I guess you'll have to find out what it is that you really want and then go from there. If you like this woman as much as you say, get to know her better. If she can take care of Beth, give her some room. If she can't—you've got to do what's best for the kid. You and I have both seen the downside of situations like that."

"I know we have."

"And what's the most common thing friends and

neighbors say when we find a neglected or abused kid in a home?"

"They say 'I knew something was wrong.' Or 'I wish I'd done something sooner.'"

"Don't let that be you, Mick'O. Don't let that be you."

The next morning, Mick looked up from the potatoes he was peeling at the kitchen sink. "Mind if I ask you a personal question?"

"Shoot," Caitlin answered.

"Do you like celery in your stew or will it be okay if I just add potatoes and carrots?"

She looked up from the sketch she was working on and cocked an eyebrow. "That's your idea of a personal question?"

"You don't think like or dislike of celery is personal?"

"Not hardly."

He carried his pan of stew makings to the stove, then faced her. "Okay, a personal question. Where did you learn to draw like that?" He indicated the sketch pad on the table in front of her. A remarkably detailed picture of Nikki asleep on the kitchen tiles was taking shape.

"I sort of picked it up."

"You're good. I thought you might have had professional training or art courses in school."

"No." Caitlin flipped the paper over and began another series of quick strokes with her pencil. "In school, I was always in trouble for doodling instead of doing my work."

"Surely one of your teachers recognized your talent?"

"Nope."

"I can't believe that."

"Maybe it was because my teachers were my main subjects." She held up the pad. It was a picture of him, but with a carrot for a nose and celery stalks for teeth in a wide-mouthed grin.

Mick chuckled. "I can see where that might have gotten you in trouble." He glanced at his watch. "Did you remember to take your medicine?"

She pulled the vial from her pocket and shook it. "Yup." Suddenly she looked serious. "Mick, why are you doing this?"

He turned back to the stove and set the fire to a low flame before he glanced at her again. "Because I like stew, and it's one of few things I can cook well."

"I don't mean the food. Why are you letting me stay here? I can't figure out your angle."

"Do I have to have an angle?"

"Does a rat have a tail?"

"Only if it's a four-legged one."

"True." She laid the pencil down and stared at him. "I don't know what you expect in return, but I'm not *that* kind of girl."

He straightened in astonishment. "I never thought you were. Do you honestly think I'm the kind of man who'd demand something like *that* in exchange for a place to stay?"

She gathered her sketches, picked up her duffel bag and stood. "Nobody gets something for nothing. I just wanted to be up front about it."

Nikki scrambled to her feet, and her nails made clicking sounds on the tile as she followed Caitlin from the room.

Mick rubbed a hand across his jaw. Maybe having

Caitlin stay wasn't as good an idea as it had seemed. He had tried getting to know her better, but just when he thought she was opening up, she blindsided him with something that pushed him away.

He noticed that she had left her medicine on the table. He started to call after her, but thought better of it. Tucking the pills in his shirt pocket, he listened to her running up the stairs. Was she running away from him?

Lord, what is it going to take to make that woman start trusting me? I really could use some help here.

Chapter Twelve

Caitlin pounded up the stairs and hurried into her room. "I can't believe I said that!" She dropped onto the bed and turned her head to stare at the dog that had followed her. "I can't even *believe* I said that."

She flopped backward on the bed and covered her face with her hands. "This is totally humiliating."

She'd ruined everything with her big mouth. He'd toss her out for sure now that she'd insulted him. And to think she had wondered if he might be interested in her. Interested, ha! Mick might be interested in a bright woman like Sandra, but not a dummy like Caitlin Williams.

Nikki laid her head on the bed and whined.

"Did you see his face? If I'd asked him to cook you for supper, I don't think he could have looked more stunned."

She pushed the dog's nose aside. "I had a right to say something, didn't I? Now we can both relax."

No, if Mick wasn't outright insulted, he was probably laughing about the very idea right now.

Caitlin sprang to her feet and paced the floor. She

didn't have to wait for Mick to ask her to leave or to laugh at her. She'd leave now. There were plenty of places she could go. Only, if she left, she'd have to walk right past him downstairs and there was no way she wanted to do that.

It was either go down and face him or toss her bag out the window and escape. Right now, jumping from a second-story window held a certain appeal. She sat down on the edge of the bed and waited.

An hour later a knock at the door caused her heart to leap in her chest. Emotionally, she braced herself. She'd been thrown out on the street more than once. She'd survive. Taking a deep breath, she said, "Come in."

It wasn't Mick, but his mother who looked in. "Caitlin, Mick wanted me to give you these and to tell you that dinner is almost ready."

She held out the vial of pills Caitlin had left on the table. Caitlin took them from her outstretched hand.

"Did he say anything else?"

"Not really, why?"

"I thought maybe he'd want me to leave now."

"Why would you think that?"

"I said something to him that I shouldn't have."

"I see. Do you want to tell me about it?"

"No. I think it's best that I find somewhere else to stay."

Elizabeth stepped inside the room. "Are you unhappy here? Have we done something to offend you?"

"No. You've been super to me." Caitlin pulled the purple cat into a close embrace.

"Then why do you want to leave?"

Caitlin shrugged, but couldn't meet her gaze. "I like living on my own, that's all."

"Do you like it? I mean, do you really?"

"Sure."

Elizabeth sat down beside her. "Caitlin, dear, you are a poor liar. I don't think you like being alone, but for some reason you believe you don't deserve anything better."

Caitlin bit the corner of her lip. "That's not true."

"How right you are. You deserve *much better*. And your daughter deserves better. I want you to stay. Mick wants you to stay. Right now, the thing he wants most in the world is to see that your little girl doesn't end up living a hand-to-mouth existence in some slum. He believes the only way to guarantee that is by helping you."

"I can take care of myself."

"In time, I firmly believe you can, but do you want your daughter living the way you've had to live until that day comes along?"

Caitlin swallowed hard at the prospect. "No."

"I didn't think so. Whatever your feelings are for Mick or for myself, Beth is really the important one, isn't she?"

Why did she have to make so much sense? Caitlin searched Elizabeth's face and felt her affection and respect for the woman deepen.

"Please say you'll stay," Elizabeth coaxed.

"Okay. But only until I can get a place of my own."

"Good. That's all we're asking. Once you find a job you can pay Mick back if you feel you must."

"I will."

"You can start by coming down and pretending to like the way he cooks."

"It's not that bad."

"You must be kidding?"

"It's better than eating out of a garbage can."

Elizabeth's smile slipped a little. "I shall simply have to take your word on that. Now, come on. The food is getting cold."

Once seated at the kitchen table, Caitlin cast a covert glance at Mick. He didn't look angry. Relief made her realize how hungry she was. She picked up a piece of bread and took a quick bite. Looking up, she saw that Mick and Elizabeth were watching her. He had one hand on his mother's injured shoulder. Both he and Elizabeth extended a hand toward Caitlin.

"What?" she mumbled.

"We'd like to give thanks," Mick said.

"That's fine." She took another bite.

Mick seemed to choke back a laugh, but quickly composed his face. "Please join us. We all have things to be thankful for."

Caitlin wiped her fingers on her jeans and joined hands with them. Mick's hand was large and warm. His mother's hand was soft and dainty.

Mick bowed his head. "Dear Lord, bless this food before us. As we gather here, make us ever mindful of Your presence in our lives and grateful for the gifts You have bestowed upon us."

Caitlin listened to his words and heard the deep sincerity in his voice. She never realized that people who got three squares a day might be as thankful for their food as people who had to hustle for it. Mick had a way of mixing up her ideas of how the world worked. He was unlike anyone she'd ever met. It was no wonder she found him so attractive.

He had come into her life at a time when she and Beth needed help the most. His kindness and concern were as foreign to her as bubble baths. In the depths of her heart she realized that his quiet strength came from his deep belief in God. For once in her life she was on the receiving end of goodness from people who asked for nothing in return. Maybe Mick was right, maybe God did care what happened to Caitlin Williams.

When Mick finished saying grace, Caitlin added a hearty "Amen."

During the meal that followed, she didn't find a thing wrong with Mick's cooking. His mother kept up a running conversation that covered the lulls in both Mick's and Caitlin's contributions.

"Do you cook, Caitlin?" Elizabeth asked as she pushed a chunk of fatty meat to the side of her plate.

"Enough to get by. Burgers and stuff like that."

His mother cast a cheeky grin at Mick then leaned toward Caitlin. "I have a great Italian cookbook that you can borrow. Spaghetti is an easy dish to fix and Mick goes on and on about the kind he gets at work."

Caitlin stirred her stew. Following a simple recipe was one more thing she couldn't do without knowing how to read. How stupid had she been to think Mick might be interested in someone like her?

In the past she might have made some rude comment to change the subject, but she found she didn't want to hurt Elizabeth's feelings. Mick seemed to sense her discomfort.

"I've had all the spaghetti I can stand at the firehouse this week. At home, burgers would be fine if you'd like to cook. Please don't think we mean to have you slaving in the kitchen."

Grateful for his intervention, she met his gaze. "How do you like your hamburgers?"

"Cooked, but not burnt."

Seeing his grin as he tossed her own words back at her erased the last of her doubt. He wasn't angry with her. Her heart lightened. She liked him, she liked him more than was good for her, but she couldn't seem to help it. She would be the perfect houseguest from now on. Anything to make him happy.

Over the next week, Caitlin was drawn into the lives of Mick and Elizabeth. She discovered that Elizabeth had founded Mercy House and still worked to keep it running by raising money and finding volunteers. Mick worked his days at the firehouse and on his days off he helped out at Mercy House and drove Caitlin to spend time with Beth.

Slowly, the strangeness of living in a real house with a real family faded and Caitlin began to feel that she belonged. Her affection for both Mick and his mother deepened daily.

One evening, Caitlin sat curled up on the sofa with Nikki while his mother shared the other end. Mick lounged in his favorite chair. They all laughed at the latest sitcom on TV.

Was this truly how people lived, Caitlin wondered? Did families laugh together in the evening? Did they bow their heads and say grace before meals? Looking around, Caitlin knew this was the kind of life she wanted for Beth. Only, how could she ever provide it?

When the nightly news came on, Elizabeth excused herself and headed up to bed. After the sports report, Mick clicked off the TV. "I think it's time we got some sleep."

"Mick, I haven't thanked you for everything you've

done for me, and especially for what you've done for Beth."

"There's no need to thank me."

"But there is. Without you, neither one of us would have had a chance. I've never met anyone like you."

He shrugged. "You don't hang out at enough fire stations. Guys like me are a dime a dozen there."

"No, I don't think so."

"Okay, I'm one in a million, but it's still past your bedtime." He tipped his head toward the stairs.

Caitlin stared at her hands. "Do you believe God grants us special gifts?"

"Every time I see Beth, I know I'm face-to-face with one."

She nodded. "Whatever God wants from me He can have as long as she is okay."

"Caitlin, God doesn't make deals."

"Then what does He want?"

"He wants us to love Him above all else and for us to love each other. We have to open our hearts and trust in His will. We do it by letting go. By giving up thinking that we're in charge of our lives and realizing that He's in charge."

"How do *you* do it?"

Mick chuckled. "Not very well at times. I'm no saint. I struggle with my temper. I get impatient with people."

Mick might not be a saint, but Caitlin knew he was a good, decent man. The fact that Mick O'Callaghan had come into her life was the closest thing to a miracle that she had ever seen.

He might be able to shrug off her thanks, but it didn't lessen her gratitude.

"Go on," he said. "Hit the sack."

She nodded and did as he asked.

Once in bed, sleep eluded Caitlin. Turning over, she flipped her pillow searching for a cool place and kicked aside the sheets. Mick O'Callaghan was a good man—a genuinely good man. Everything she learned about him only made him that much more special. He was an easy man to love.

She sat bolt upright in bed.

She was in love with him. She hadn't wanted to, hadn't planned to, but here in the darkness she saw the truth. She was in love with Mick O'Callaghan.

"Are we ready for the big moment?" Dr. Wright asked, standing beside Caitlin's chair.

"I am *so* ready," Caitlin replied. She waited with Mick beside Beth's bed in the NICU. Beth was being taken off her ventilator for the first time in her young life.

"Okay, let's do it," the doctor said with a happy smile.

With the help of a nurse and a respiratory therapist, she removed Beth's breathing tube, and Caitlin heard her baby cry for the very first time. Tears sprang to her eyes at the sound of that weak, hoarse, pitifully tiny wail. It was the most beautiful sound she'd ever heard.

A hand closed over hers, and she looked over to see Mick smiling at her in understanding.

"That a girl," Dr. Wright coaxed the baby, "tell us all about it. What do you think, Mommy? Isn't she cute without all that tape on her face?"

"I think she's gorgeous," Caitlin managed to say through the emotion that threatened to choke her.

The doctor quickly adjusted a thick, stiff tubing with small prongs that fit into Beth's nose. Velcro straps attached to a colorful stocking cap held the tubing in place.

"This awkward-looking thing is called C-PAP," Dr. Wright explained. "It blows oxygen in under low pressure and that makes it easier for her to breathe, but from now on, every breath she takes is on her own."

When the doctor left the bedside, Caitlin glanced at Mick. He was grinning like an idiot. He touched the tubing in Beth's nose and said, "It looks like she's wearing the face guard of a football helmet."

"If you're thinking she'll be the next linebacker for the Bears, you can forget it."

He chuckled. "I can't believe how big she's getting. Even her cheeks are getting chubby."

"Well, she weighs a pound more than when she was born. She's three pounds and two ounces now."

Mick leaned closer. "You know, I think she has your mouth."

"Do you?"

His gaze rested on Caitlin's lips until she grew uncomfortable with his scrutiny. The atmosphere between the two of them had been strained in the last week. Oh, he had been as kind and as considerate as ever, but often she'd seen him staring at her intently. She was desperately afraid that he would discover just how much she had come to care for him.

She reached to hold Beth's foot. "She has her dad's knobby knees," she said to change the subject.

"Hey. My knees aren't—"

Caitlin's glance flew to his face. He looked stunned. Slowly, the joy faded from his face. He sent Caitlin a rueful smile. "I forgot for a second that she isn't really mine."

"Mick, I…" She what? Caitlin had no idea what to say.

He stood suddenly. "Well, I've got to run."

"I thought you were going to stay?"

"I can't. I have something I have to take care of. I'll pick you up out front at four o'clock."

"Okay." She managed a smile.

He leaned down and dropped a kiss on Beth's head and quickly left the unit. Watching him, Caitlin bit the inside corner of her lip. A man like Mick would make a wonderful father. A jerk like Vinnie didn't deserve to have a dog, let alone a daughter as beautiful as Beth. There had been a time in Caitlin's life when she would have given anything to know who her father was, to be able to see him just once. Vinnie wasn't much, but Beth should know who he was; not knowing, always wondering and dreaming, it was no good.

Someday Beth would want to know what her father had been like—if she looked like him, if she had his eyes or his smile.

Caitlin picked up her sketch pad and began to draw Vinnie as she remembered him, concentrating on the good times they had had together. She could see that Beth would have this much.

When she finished her second sketch of Vinnie, she flipped the page and began a drawing of Beth without her ventilator tube to add to the growing number of pictures she had compiled of the baby's days in the hospital. A nurse came to the bedside and began to take Beth's temperature. Finishing that, she picked up the stethoscope and placed it on the baby's chest. Quickly, Caitlin added the nurse's hand holding the stethoscope to her picture. After all, Beth had needed lots of helping hands to get her this far.

"What do you have there?"

Caitlin looked up to see Dr. Wright peering over her shoulder. "It's okay if I draw, isn't it? I can put it away."

"Of course it's okay. I'm simply admiring your work. Why, it's wonderful. Ladies, come look at this."

A group of nurses gathered beside Caitlin's chair. She heard compliments and exclamations of delight exchanged all around her, and she grew embarrassed at being the center of attention.

"Do you ever sell any?" someone asked.

"Sometimes I sell portraits over at the Navy Pier," Caitlin admitted.

"Really? How much do you charge?"

"Do you have a studio?"

The questions came faster than she could answer them.

"I'd love to have a portrait of Beth," Dr. Wright said. "She's been such a special little girl."

"I can do that." Caitlin flipped back through the pages until she came to one with Dr. Wright leaning over Beth to examine her. Carefully, she pulled the sketch from the book and handed it to the doctor.

"My goodness, you certainly flatter me," the woman said beaming. "I don't usually look this good after a night on call. Why is it that I've never noticed you sketching before?"

"Mostly, I draw when I'm at home."

"From memory? You can draw a detailed picture like this solely from memory?"

"Things I see just sort of stick in my head."

"What an extraordinary talent." Dr. Wright stared

at the picture she held, then looked at Caitlin as if she had never truly seen her before. "How much do I owe you for this?"

"Nothing."

"Nonsense. You can't give it away for free."

"Sure I can. You've done more than enough for Beth and me. I'm not going to charge you for a little picture."

"Very well, I'll accept this one, but the rest I insist on paying for."

"The rest?"

"I've been wanting to get some new pictures for my office walls." She held up the sketch. "This would be perfect in a light blue mat with a silver frame."

"A grouping of three would be nice," one nurse suggested.

"I know—three of Beth, one on the vent, one when she's bigger and one when she's ready to go home."

"What a neat idea."

Like traffic on a busy street, their chatter flowed around Caitlin. She couldn't believe all the enthusiasm for her work.

"How soon could you have six more done?" Dr. Wright asked.

It took a minute for Caitlin to find her voice. "Six?"

"I have two walls that I'd like to put groups on. How much do you charge?"

Dr. Wright wanted to display her pictures on the walls of her office. Her pictures!

A doctor wouldn't want the kind of quick portraits that Caitlin did down on the pier. She would want ones with a lot of detail. The other women seemed interested, too. Maybe some of them would buy her work. But how much should she charge? If she named a price too high, they wouldn't want them.

She settled on a price that was twice as high as she usually charged down on Dock Street.

"Oh, no," Dr. Wright said quickly, and Caitlin's hopes fell. "I've purchased original works in galleries, and I'm not going to allow you to give these away." She then named a price that made Caitlin's jaw drop. It was five times what she had suggested.

"Which babies would you like me to sketch?" Caitlin managed to ask.

"That's a good question. Beth, of course, but who else?"

"You'll need to get permission from the parents," a nurse reminded her.

"I don't imagine that will be hard, not once they see what a wonderful job Ms. Williams does."

Caitlin cleared her throat. "Little Jacob, down on the end, his mother asked me to do a sketch of him."

"Excellent. See, what did I tell you?"

Dr. Wright's brows drew together in a slight frown. "I don't want to monopolize your time. I know you come here to be with your daughter, and I don't want to detract from that."

For that much money, Caitlin would draw standing on her head in a corner while she visited Beth. "No problem, Doc. I'm here every day, anyway. I can't always hold her, so I can draw while she's asleep."

"If you're sure you don't mind?"

"I don't. It'll be good to have something to keep me busy." And something to put money in her pocket— more money than she would have made in a month washing dishes at Harley's—and simply for doing something she loved. God was surely smiling on her today.

Dr. Wright stood. "Great. Let me show this sketch to some of the other parents and see if they'll give their permission to have you draw their children. And let me get you an advance for the ones I've ordered in case you need to get more supplies. Would fifty dollars cover your expenses?"

Caitlin stared at her in astonishment. "Sure."

"Okay, good. I'll be right back with it."

"Ms. Williams, do you think you could do a portrait of my two children?" a short, dark-haired nurse asked. "They aren't babies, they're two and five. It would make a perfect birthday gift for their grandmother."

Bemused, Caitlin smiled and nodded. "I'm sure we can work something out."

She would be earning her own money. Mick was going to be so proud of her.

Chapter Thirteen

As promised, Mick pulled up to the front of the hospital at four o'clock and spied Caitlin waiting on a bench out front. She waved and hurried toward him. His spirits soared at the sight of her. Her smile was like sunshine. It warmed him all the way to his toes. Since she had moved into his home, he couldn't ever remember being happier.

She was grinning from ear to ear as she threw her duffel bag on the floor and climbed in beside him.

"You'll never guess what happened." Excitement electrified her voice and sparkled in her eyes.

"Okay, I won't try. What?"

"They want to buy my artwork!" With a squeal of delight, she threw her arms around his neck. "I can't believe it."

"Whoa!" He returned her enthusiastic hug. "Slow down and tell me what you're talking about."

She pulled back a fraction, still grinning. "Dr. Wright saw me sketching Beth, and she wants to buy some of my prints to hang in her office. She's going to pay me for them. She even gave me an advance."

Her announcement stunned him. She was earning her own money. But not enough to live on, of course. No, she still needed his help. "That's terrific. I told you someone would recognize your talent."

Suddenly, he realized how close her face was—how close her lips were. He shifted his gaze to her eyes— her wonderful, beautiful eyes. The pace of his heart accelerated and the excitement changed, deepening into something different. She sensed it, too. With a sheepish grin, she moved away and settled herself on her side of the car, taking her time about buckling her seat belt.

"How's Beth?" he asked.

"Dr. Wright said she might be able to do without the C-PAP in a few days. Course, she'll still be on oxygen for a while. Where are we going?" she asked as he pulled out into the street.

"I have one more stop to make."

"Where?"

"Mercy House."

"Oh."

The flat tone of her voice caused him to look at her sharply. "Is something wrong?"

"No," she said at last.

Mick glanced at her frequently as he drove into a section of town where abandoned buildings grew more frequent between run-down homes and boarded-up businesses. She didn't speak, and he wondered what he had done or said to upset her.

He pulled to a stop in front of a renovated three-story clapboard house with a wide porch across its front. A tall sign in the sparse grass beside the broad steps read Mercy House Shelter for Women and Children. The sign was somewhat misleading as the soup kitchen that oc-

cupied the spacious basement served anyone who came
to the door, but the bedrooms in the house were given
over to housing women who found themselves and their
children without a place to live.

Stepping out of his SUV, Mick went to the back and
opened the hatch. Caitlin stood on the sidewalk staring
at the house. "Give me a hand, will you?" he asked. She
joined him, and he handed her a small cardboard box,
then he grabbed a bigger one for himself.

The front door of the shelter opened and an elderly
man came down the steps toward them. He wore a beige
polo shirt that was tucked into brown polyester pants
belted high on his waist letting a good three inches of
his pale blue socks show above scuffed black loafers.

"Hi ya, Mick," he called. Stopping beside Caitlin,
the fellow took the box from her unresisting grip with
hands that trembled faintly. "You shouldn't be liftin'
stuff," he scolded.

Caitlin's eyebrows flew up. "Eddy?"

A wide, tooth-gapped grin appeared on his face.
"Yup. Told ya I cleaned up pretty good, didn't I, Mick?"

"Yes, you did," Mick agreed. He never would have
recognized the man without his tattered overcoat, thick
gray beard and long hair if he hadn't spoken.

"How's that baby?" Eddy asked.

"She's doing better," Caitlin answered. "Eddy, you
look great."

"Nah, I don't, but thanks anyway. I'm gettin' some
help with my drinkin' and Pastor Frank, he gave me a
job here." His skinny chest puffed out. "I'm his right-
hand man, now."

Pastor Frank appeared in the doorway. "You certainly are, Eddy. I don't know how I managed without you."

Mick nodded toward the box he held. "The guys at the station donated some clothing. Where do you want these?"

"Bring them into the living room, and I'll let the ladies know that they're here. It's good of you to help us like this, my boy."

Smiling, the pastor came down the steps and extended his hand toward Caitlin. "And you must be the young woman I've heard so much about."

"Caitlin Williams," she replied as she took his hand.

"I'm glad to hear your daughter is doing better. Mick's been keeping me informed. He thinks the world of your little girl, but then, he thinks the world of all children. I've never known anyone with quite the gift he has for making them happy."

The man took Caitlin by the elbow and walked up the steps beside her. "Welcome to Mercy House. I'm sorry I couldn't offer you a place here when Mick first called, but we've been full to the rafters. It's sad how many women and children have no place to go." He held open the door and waited for Caitlin to proceed.

Caitlin didn't answer him. She glanced back at Mick, but he was talking to Eddy. She bit the corner of her lip and walked inside with a sinking feeling.

"Caitlin, would you excuse us?" Pastor Frank asked. At her nod, he turned to Mick. "Could I see you in my office for a moment?"

Mick followed the pastor into his office. Frank moved to his chair at the small, scarred oak desk that along with a large gray filing cabinet was the only furnishing in the Spartan room. "I've known you since you were five, Mick. Your mother is a dear friend. Obviously, your intentions are good, but are you going about this in the right way?"

"I don't know what you mean."

"I have room for Caitlin now. Don't you think it would be better if she were living here?"

"She's fine at my place. There isn't any need for her to move in here."

"How much longer will your mother be staying with you? Now that she's better, I know she's anxious to get back to her own home and to her friends."

"I thought she'd stay until Beth was out of the hospital. Has she told you she wants to leave?"

"Not in so many words, but surely you must see that having Caitlin living with you is putting your mother in a difficult spot? She can't leave the two of you there alone."

"I didn't intend to offer Caitlin a place to live, but now that I have, I won't go back on my word. I want to protect this woman—to see that she and her baby don't slip through the cracks and end up as two more lost souls in a city that already has far too many."

Mick moved to stare out the window at the children playing in the backyard. "Caitlin's mother was an addict and she never knew her father. She's a throwaway kid. You see them every day—you know what they're like. They don't trust anyone. She'd rather starve in a back alley than ask for help because she doesn't believe she needs it or deserves it. She's learning to trust, maybe for the first time in her life. I won't do anything to destroy that. She needs someone to take care of her."

"She isn't a child. What she needs isn't someone to take care of her. She needs to be able to take care of herself. Give her the tools to do that, show her that you believe she can, and you will have helped her more than any amount of free room and board ever will."

Mick pondered the pastor's words. If Caitlin could manage on her own what would it mean for him? He hated considering the idea. He wanted both of them in his life.

Frank picked up his pen and began to scribble notes on a pad. "I'll do what I can to find her a job. Does she have any technical training? Has she expressed an interest in going to school to learn a trade?"

"No, but you should see her artwork. She has a rare gift."

"That's something. Talk to her—find out if there's anything she'd like to do. I'll work on locating a place for her and the baby to live. This may take some time. Is she going to be okay with that?"

"I'll see that she is."

Caitlin leaned against the living room wall and watched the office door as she worried her lower lip between her teeth. They were talking about her in there, she was sure of it. Did Mick intend to leave her here? He wouldn't do that without telling her first, would he?

She bit down on the nail of her index finger and tore the corner of it. Who was she kidding? Her own mother had put her in a Dumpster and forgotten about her. Why should anyone else care what happened to her?

Maybe this was what God wanted from her? Mick had talked about trusting God's will. Maybe God wanted her to give up her nice place in exchange for Beth getting better? If that were the case, she'd do it and not complain.

She had money in her pocket and a chance to earn

more. She was better off than she had been in a long time. She looked around the room. This wouldn't be a bad place to stay.

The office door opened and Mick came out. He smiled at her and her heart tripped into double time. Man, she had it bad for him. All he had to do was smile at her and she was willing to forgive him anything. Even if he left her here she wouldn't hold it against him.

He stopped in front of her. "Ready to go? I don't know about you, but I'm starving. Let's get something to eat on the way home."

A ton of tension drained out of her. She realized she was biting her fingernail and quickly tucked that hand under her arm. "That would be great."

Later, with a burger in one hand and a box of hot, crispy fries balancing on her lap, Caitlin asked the question that had been turning itself over and over in her mind. "Did you ask Pastor Frank if I could stay at Mercy House?"

"Is that what you want to do?"

She shrugged. "Not really." She wanted to stay with Mick forever, but that wasn't going to happen. She was lucky to have stayed this long.

Mick gave her a sidelong glance. "We've never talked about what you would like to do—for a job, I mean."

"I'll take whatever I can get."

"Still, you must have something that you're interested in. You're such a talented artist. Have you thought about going back to school to study art?"

She paused with her burger halfway to her mouth. Back to school? There was a joke.

"No. Drawing is a hobby. I can make a few extra

bucks on the side with it, but I need something full-time to pay the bills."

"Pastor Frank is willing to try and find you a place of your own. When you're ready, that is. There isn't any rush, and I mean that. He can help find you work, too. He does it all the time for the women who come to the shelter."

Pastor Frank would send her to job interviews where she would have to fill out applications.

"I can get my own job, thank you. I haven't started looking because Beth has been so sick."

"I understand. Like I said, there isn't any hurry."

"No, she's better, and it's time I got busy."

"You can start with the paper when we get home. Something might jump out at you."

Sure, she thought, like the one or two words that she recognized in print. "I'll start tomorrow."

"But I'm on duty tomorrow."

"So?"

"Nothing, I guess, but I thought maybe I could drive you to some job interviews."

"I can take the bus."

"It would be easier if you'd wait until I could take you."

"Mick, I can manage."

"I'd like to help."

"And I'd like to be able to eat a burger without you thinking you need to wipe my face between bites," she snapped, and turned to stare out the window.

He was dense as pavement. She hated acting like this, but she would have to find her own job. She couldn't let Mick or anyone else discover that she couldn't read.

"I'm sorry," he said after a long silence.

"Forget it."

"No, you're right. I tend to forget that you aren't helpless."

She twisted around in the seat to face him. "I can't forget it. Not ever! I'm the one who has to hold down a job and take care of Beth."

"Caitlin, I'll always be here if you need something."

"You don't get it, do you? You've got your own life. Beth and I, we can't be waiting for you to find time for us. I've seen it happen more than I care to tell. A guy gets involved with a girl, he likes her, likes her kid, but it isn't his kid and sooner or later, he stops coming around."

"I won't be that way."

"Maybe not," she conceded. "But I can't take that chance. It's hard for me to say thanks and the truth is, I'll never be able to repay you for the help you've given me, but I have to be able to survive on my own."

"Life is about more than surviving."

She looked away. "Not for some of us. Not for me."

"Caitlin, I can't let Beth lead that kind of life."

"You don't have a choice."

"You forget, I'm her legal father."

She hadn't forgotten, but until now, she had assumed that he wouldn't press the issue. Did he still think that he could take Beth away from her? Cold fear gripped her heart. "Is that a threat?"

Mick turned the car into his driveway and stopped. He shut off the engine, then looked at her. "Of course not. It's only that I want life to be about more than surviving for you and Beth. You deserve more, Caitlin. You deserve a life of comfort and security with someone who cares about you."

"Until that comes along, I'll manage by myself."

He stared at her, and she could see the struggle going on inside of him. "If things were different for us—"

"But they're not. I don't need you feeling sorry for me."

"You're wrong. I don't feel sorry for you. I admire you, very much. I care about you."

"I care for you, too, Mick, and for your mother. You've both been very kind to me. But now that I'm well, I need to stop depending on you and start taking care of myself."

"But I want to take care of you. I'm saying this all wrong."

He covered her hands with his and her heart raced. She tried to read his eyes, but she didn't trust what she saw there.

"Caitlin, I care about you deeply. You know that I love Beth like she was my own flesh and blood. I'll be a good father to her. I guess what I'm trying to say is that I want to marry you."

She didn't know how to respond. She longed to tell him of her love, but she knew she wasn't worthy of him. Once he discovered her secret he would be as ashamed of her as Vinnie had been. She'd never be able to go out to eat with him and his friends because she couldn't read a menu. She wouldn't be able to read bedtime stories to Beth, or write a birthday card to his mother. Mick deserved better.

He loved Beth. He was willing to marry Beth's mother to keep her safe. He was so noble. It was almost more than Caitlin could bear.

"Thank you, but no. Taking care of people is what you do. I understand that. But this isn't the way. I won't pretend that your offer isn't tempting. It is. Only, not for the right reasons."

"You'd never have to worry about food or a place to sleep ever again. Beth would have a mother and a father to look after her. What better reason is there?"

"Love for a child isn't enough. I wish it were."

He looked so bewildered. She opened her car door and turned away to keep her face hidden from him. She knew there was little hope that she didn't look like a woman whose heart had just been broken.

Chapter Fourteen

Early the next morning, Caitlin stood at the curb and waited for the bus with her duffel bag slung over one shoulder. After tossing and turning for much of the night, she didn't see that she had any choice. She had to get out of Mick's life. She couldn't face him day after day loving him the way she did.

Both Mick and Elizabeth had still been asleep when Caitlin let herself out of the house. She hated sneaking away, but she knew she couldn't face them and not break down. She'd call as soon as she got settled. She could handle a phone conversation, but looking Mick in the face when she said goodbye was more than she could take.

At last, the bus pulled up in front of her. When the tall door slid open, she hesitated. No one got off and there wasn't anyone else waiting to get on.

The stout woman driving asked, "Well? Are you coming?"

Caitlin chewed the corner of her lip for a second. "Is this the bus to Grand?"

"If that's what it says on the front, honey, then it must be. Are you getting on, or not?"

Struggling to hide the shame that burned like acid in the pit of her stomach, Caitlin climbed the steps and dropped her fare in the slot. She found a seat and gazed out the window, taking note of the houses and landscape along the route. Once she got to Grand Avenue, she'd be able to find her way around. She knew that area. Finding her way back would be the tricky part. Street names didn't mean anything unless they were numbers. Numbers she knew.

When the bus reached an area she was familiar with, Caitlin got off and walked the remaining blocks to the Mercy House. Relief flooded her when she spied Eddy working in the front yard. She walked over to where he was weeding a small flower bed.

"Hi, Eddy."

The old man looked up, peering over the rim of a pair of glasses missing an earpiece. "Caitlin, is that you? How's that baby doin'?"

"She's getting better."

"I'm glad to hear it. I pray for her every day. What are you doin' here?"

"I'm here to stay for a while."

"I'm sorry, Caitlin. We don't have a room for you."

"What? Are you sure?"

"I'm real sure. Pastor Frank thought you was gonna be stayin' with Mick for a while. Last night a lady with four little kids came and Pastor Frank gave them the last room. I'm sure sorry about that. You want to check with Pastor Frank?"

"No." Her hopes fell. So much for her great plan. "I guess I can stay with Mick a while longer. I was just hoping to get out from under his feet, that's all. Maybe you can help me with something else."

"What kinda help can an old, crazy fella like me give you?"

"I need a job."

His brow wrinkled even more. "I don't know of any work."

"I do. I've got the want ads with me." Caitlin handed him the paper.

Looking puzzled, he said, "I still don't understand."

Caitlin glanced around to make sure no one could overhear her, then leaned closer. "I need your help because…because I can't read."

"That ain't a crime."

"I never said it was."

"You're actin' like it is what with this whisperin' an' all."

Straightening, Caitlin regretted sharing her secret. "I don't like other people knowing how stupid I am."

"You ain't stupid."

"It'll look that way when I can't fill out a job application. I need to find work before Beth comes home. I have to be able to support us."

"Pastor Frank can help. You're not the only woman who has trouble reading."

"Pastor Frank might tell Mick. I don't want him to know. He'll think I can't take care of Beth. But I can. I just need to get a job."

"Okay, calm down. What can I do?"

Caitlin led Eddy to a small bench in the yard. She sat down and handed him the paper. "Read these ads and help me find a job that I can do. I'll do anything if it means being able to keep Beth."

"Okay, sure, but what are you gonna do when you have to fill out their forms and such?"

"That's why I need you to come with me. If they want me to fill out an application, I'll ask if I can take it home. If they say yes, I'll bring it outside, and you can fill it out for me. If they say no, I'll find some way to sneak one out to you. I've got to have a job. Will you help me?"

He patted her arm. "Sure, I'll help. You was always nice to me."

"Thanks, Eddy. You don't know what this means to me."

Two weeks later, Caitlin looked up from her sketching to smile at Beth sleeping soundly inside her incubator. It was wonderful to see her making progress after all that had happened. Each day, Caitlin discovered something new about her daughter. Beth liked to sleep on her left side. She woke up hollering, but she calmed down as soon as someone spoke to her. She even seemed to like her mother's off-key singing.

Studying her baby's sweet face, Caitlin wondered if her own mother had ever watched her sleep this way. Had Dotty seen anything beautiful in her, or had she only seen a burden?

Pity for the woman who would never know her granddaughter welled up in Caitlin, and some of the anger she harbored toward her mother crumbled away.

Maybe this is what Mick means when he talks about forgiving those that have sinned against us.

Shaking off her somber thoughts, Caitlin concentrated on Beth once more. She needed only a small amount of oxygen and she was tolerating tube feedings of milk and sucking on a pacifier. Twice a day, Caitlin gave her small amounts of milk from a bottle. Beth slurped it down. If nothing else went wrong, she would be big enough to be discharged in a few weeks. But to where?

Caitlin was still staying at Mick's, but things were tense between them. She'd been avoiding him because, sooner or later, her guard was bound to slip, and he'd see that she was in love with him.

In spite of Eddy's help, Caitlin hadn't been able to find work. The money from the sales of her sketches was adding up, but it wouldn't be enough to last more than a few weeks even if she found a cheap place to live.

Beth's monitor beeped loudly. Caitlin looked up expecting the usual false alarm. Beth had become a whiz at getting her toes or fingers tangled in her lead wires and pulling them loose. This time it wasn't a false alarm; Beth's heart rate had slowed to less than eighty.

Caitlin sprang to her feet. "Sandra, something's wrong!"

The nurse came quickly. She opened one of the round portholes, stuck her hand in and began to rub the baby's back, but her gaze stayed focused on the monitor. When Beth's heart rate began climbing, Sandra looked in at Beth and asked, "Are you trying to scare your mother?"

"If she is, she's doing a fine job. What's wrong?"

"It looks like she had an apnea spell. It means she forgot to breathe. It's common in premature babies, but it can also be a sign of a seizure. Did you notice her yawning or twitching or doing anything unusual?"

"No."

"Then it may have been simple apnea. Preemies have nervous systems that are immature and sometimes, especially when they're sleeping, they simply stop breathing. If it lasts long enough, their heart rate slows down, too."

"Babies die from that, don't they?"

"You're thinking about SIDS—sudden infant death syndrome. It isn't the same thing, but premature babies are more at risk for developing SIDS. I'll let the doctors know about this. They may want to do a few more tests."

"Like what?"

"Like checking her blood to see if the level of her seizure medication is right. It has to be adjusted as she gets bigger otherwise she'll outgrow her dose."

"If it's this apnea stuff, what will they do?"

"We usually start them on a drug called caffeine. It's the same thing you get in coffee or soda. Coffee keeps you awake and gives you a lift. This does the same thing for Beth. It will help keep her breathing when she does fall asleep. Most babies grow out of these spells before they go home."

"What if they don't?"

"In that case, they stay on the caffeine and they go home on a monitor that will alarm if their heart rate or their breathing gets too slow."

"I'd feel better having a monitor. How do I get one?"

Sandra patted Caitlin's arm. "You're getting ahead of yourself. If Beth needs one, the doctors will arrange for it. If she doesn't, you'll have to treat her like a regular baby."

"I'm not sure I can."

"I know, but it'll get easier. How would you like to try nursing her this time?"

"Really? That would be fantastic! Only, I don't know

what to do. I mean…I've never actually…well…she's never…you know, nursed from me."

Sandra smiled. "I think together we can find a way to manage. But I don't want you to expect too much this first time. It will be new for Beth, too. Lots of premature babies don't know what to do right off the bat. They can learn, we have ways to help, but don't be too disappointed if she doesn't latch on right away. I'll get a pillow for you, and I'll show you how to get ready for her."

Sandra pulled the curtain around the cubicle to give them some privacy.

A few minutes later, Mick entered the nursery and made his way toward Beth's spot hoping that he wasn't too late for the afternoon feeding. Beth was still being limited to only short times out of her incubator, and he didn't want to miss a chance to hold her. He saw that the curtain was drawn around her bed and wondered why. The sound of a giggle reached him and he listened intently.

"She's getting it all over her face." It was Caitlin's voice, and she was clearly amused.

"Just stroke down on her lips until she opens her mouth wide, then shove it in." Sandra's voice followed. She, too, sounded as if she were struggling not to laugh.

"I think she's got it."

"I don't think so, but she's trying," Sandra answered.

"Wow! I feel that."

Sandra laughed. "Okay, that is a positive sign."

"She's doing it." Caitlin's voice was full of joy.

Mick knew he should leave, but his feet were rooted to the spot. Bands of love, pride and happiness tangled around his heart and squeezed. Caitlin had worked so hard to be a successful nursing mother. The two of them deserved this special time together.

Sandra said, "I'll be back in a few minutes to check on you. Call if you need anything."

Mick took his cue and left the room before they knew he was listening in. Fifteen minutes later, he came in again and saw the curtain was open. Caitlin held Beth in the crook of her arm. A soft light shone in her eyes and a happy smile curved her lips. "Mick, I'm glad you're here."

He smiled back feeling foolishly proud as he settled into a chair beside her.

During the past weeks, Caitlin had been avoiding him. Using the excuse of job hunting, she had been gone from the house for long hours if he was home. Whenever he tried to bring up how he felt about her, she practically ran out of the room. He tried to remember not to push, but it got harder every day.

Sandra came back to the bedside. "There are some people in the waiting room who would like to see both of you."

Caitlin looked curious. "Who is it?"

"They said they were friends of yours. One of them is a pastor."

"It must be Pastor Frank," Caitlin said. "It's fine if he comes in."

A few minutes later, Caitlin looked up and smiled. "Eddy! What a surprise. Come in."

"Are you sure it's okay?"

"Of course it is. Come and meet Beth." She raised the baby higher in the crook of her elbow. "Eddy, meet Elizabeth Anne Williams. Beth, this is the fellow who saved us both by getting the ambulance the day you were born."

Eddy propped his trembling hands on his thighs as he leaned forward. "Sheesh! I ain't never seen a baby so small."

"She's a lot bigger now than when she was born," Mick said, hiding his hurt and disappointment. Caitlin had called her Elizabeth Anne Williams, not O'Callaghan. He shouldn't have expected Caitlin to think of Beth as bearing his name. Legally she did, but not in her mother's eyes.

"Sheesh," Eddy said again, clearly in awe.

"Sit down," Caitlin patted the chair beside her. "Would you like to hold her?"

Eddy straightened and waved his hands. "Oh, no. She's too little. I might drop her or something. Maybe when she's bigger—and walkin'. I got a present for her down at Mercy House."

"You didn't have to get us anything."

"I know. It ain't much, but you'll be needin' it."

"What is it?"

"I ain't gonna tell ya, but when you take this cutie to yer new home, it'll be waitin'."

Caitlin sent Mick a questioning look. He shook his head. He had no idea what Eddy was talking about.

"What do you mean, my new home?" she asked.

"Oh, I wasn't supposed to say nothin'. Pastor Frank was gonna tell ya himself. I guess I'd better go and let him come in. She's real cute, honey. Thanks for lettin' me see her." He gave a short nod, sniffed once, wiped at his eye then fled from the room.

A few minutes later, the pastor joined them. He grinned at Caitlin and the baby. "My, she is a tiny one.

Babies never cease to amaze me. What a wonderful way God chose to start people."

He took the seat beside Caitlin. "I have some good news, but I think Eddy spoiled my surprise. I've found an apartment for you. It's not much, only two rooms over a garage, but it's sound, and it's close to the hospital. And the first three months rent will be free."

"A place of our own, for real? How?" She looked at Mick.

"It wasn't me." He listened to Pastor Frank's news with a sinking heart. It often took the man months to find homes for the women at his shelter. Mick had expected Caitlin would be with him for weeks yet. Certainly until after the baby came home. He didn't want her leaving. Not now—not ever. He wanted to see her bright and beautiful face every day.

"The Lord moves in mysterious ways," Pastor Frank continued. "Out of the blue I received a call from one of my parishioners about having a place for someone. It was too small for the women at the shelter who all have several children and the two elderly women with us couldn't manage the stairs. But it seemed perfect for you. The place is empty now. You can move in right away. It even has some furniture."

"A place of our own," Caitlin tried to infuse some joy into her voice. It was what she wanted only she wasn't ready to leave Mick.

Sandra came to stand beside Caitlin's chair. "It's time for Beth to go back in her bed. We don't want her wasting her calories keeping warm. We want her to use them to grow."

"But Mick hasn't gotten to hold her," Caitlin protested.

"I'll hold her tomorrow," he said. "Let her sleep now."

She tried to read his face, but she couldn't tell what he was thinking. Was he sad to know she would be leaving, or relieved to get rid of her?

Pastor Frank excused himself and left. Mick walked with him out of the unit. Caitlin let Sandra put Beth back to bed, then she left as well.

Mick was waiting by his SUV in the hospital parking lot. He held open the door for her. Climbing in, she tried again to find out what he was thinking. "Pastor Frank didn't waste any time getting me a place."

"No, he didn't." Mick shut her door and walked around. He seemed angry. She waited until he got in and started the engine.

"It sounds like a nice place," she ventured.

"It sounds small."

"Compared to your place, maybe. But for just Beth and me, it sounds okay."

"We'll see."

"What does that mean?"

"I'm not going to let you and Beth move into some dump."

"Did I hear you right? You aren't going to *let* me? What makes you think that *you* can tell me what to do?"

"Don't get your hackles up. I didn't mean it like that."

"And just how did you mean it?"

"All I meant was that I want to check the place out."

"You want to check out the place *I'm* going to live? Why?"

"You know why."

"I want to hear you say it." Angry now, she didn't try to hide the fact.

"All right! Because it might not be the kind of place

you should take a baby who has spent the last two months in a hospital."

"I can't believe you think I'd let her stay in a place that wasn't okay."

"Let me see," he said, sarcasm cutting deep through his voice. "Oh, like the place I found you in! Now that was okay, wasn't it?"

"I didn't have a choice then. I was working on getting a decent place, only Beth came too soon."

"There will always be problems that come up. I just don't see how you can take care of her by yourself."

She turned away from him and stared out the window. She had to be strong. Now more than ever. She couldn't let her feelings for Mick blind her to what he could do. She drew in a deep, steadying breath. "Beth and I will be fine without your help."

He gave an exasperated sigh. "I know you love her, but love won't put food on the table, it won't pay the rent. Beth needs a father. I intend to be there for her. I grew up without a father, and so did you. You know what it's like. Why won't you let me take care of both of you?"

She jerked around to face him. "Yes, I grew up without a father, but I barely missed him because I never knew who he was. You know who I did miss? I missed my mother! I missed her every time she was too strung out to get out of bed while I went hungry because there wasn't any food. I missed her every time she left me alone and didn't come home for days. All I ever wanted was for her to love me. Me! Not the stuff she shot up her arm." Her voice broke, but she struggled to keep control.

"All I ever wanted was for my mother to love me

the way that I love Beth. She's all I need, and I'm all she needs. Beth was never yours. I'm sorry you can't accept that."

"She isn't my blood, but she's mine in my heart. I don't want to fight, Caitlin."

She didn't either, but she couldn't let him think that he could run her life. He had the power to take her child away if she failed to live up to the standards he set. She hardened her heart. Keeping Beth was all that mattered. She stared straight ahead and kept her voice level when she said, "Beth isn't some fantasy replacement for the children you can't have."

"That's not fair!"

She cringed at the pain she had inflicted, but there was no way to call the words back. Instead, she said, "Life ain't fair, Mick'O. I'm surprised you hadn't noticed. I'm going back inside and stay with Beth a while longer."

She reached for the handle and pushed open the door. He didn't try to stop her.

"Go home, Mick. I can find my own way from now on. You know, I'm looking forward to being out on my own again." It was, without a doubt, the biggest lie she had ever uttered.

Mick didn't answer. He simply stared at her. She couldn't bear the pain in his face. She closed the door and walked away.

It was barely a week later when a timid knock came from the front door of Caitlin's new home. She dropped the curtain rod she was hanging and hurried to open it. Maybe it was Mick.

It wasn't. His mother stood on the stoop. She held a

large shopping bag in her hand. Her other arm remained in a sling, but the cast was gone. Caitlin stared in surprise at her unexpected guest.

Elizabeth smiled and wiggled two fingers in an awkward wave. "Hi. I hope you don't mind my dropping by. I was out shopping, and I saw the cutest baby clothes. I couldn't resist. I hope you don't mind."

"Ah—no, I don't mind at all. Come in."

"Thanks, but I have a few more bags in the cab." She pushed the one she held into Caitlin's hands and hurried down the steps. She returned with bag after bag until Caitlin wondered if the woman had been knocking over infant stores across the city and was trying to get rid of the stolen goods. As she set the last bag on the counter, Caitlin wondered if the gesture had been Mick's idea. She couldn't bring herself to ask.

Elizabeth looked around, and said, "My gracious sakes! What is that monstrosity?"

"I think it's called a pram. It's a present from a friend."

"It's a gigantic, black leather baby buggy with crooked wheels." She moved closer to examine it. "This thing must be a hundred years old. I don't think I've ever seen one except in movies. What are you going to do with it?"

"I'm going to use it as a baby bed."

"You're joking."

"I know a girl whose baby slept in the bottom drawer of her dresser. Why couldn't a baby buggy work as well?"

"I guess it could." Elizabeth bent to examine the pram then wrinkled her nose. "Thank goodness the baby isn't coming home yet. This is going to take some work to get it clean."

Looking instantly contrite, she straightened and said, "I'm sorry. That sounded heartless. I'm sure you wish your little girl were home no matter what. How is she doing?"

"Great, except that she still forgets to breathe sometimes. She's on a drug to help that, and she's still on one to control her seizures, but she's gaining weight. I nurse her three times a day now. If she keeps gaining, she'll get to move out of her incubator in a few more days."

"I'm glad. You've been very brave in the face of all that has happened."

Caitlin shook her head. "No, I'm not. I worry every minute that something else will go wrong."

"That's only natural. It's a mother thing." Moving around the apartment, Elizabeth picked up Caitlin's sketchbook from the stained-and-scarred coffee table. "May I?" At Caitlin's nod, she leafed through the book. "These are wonderful. Mick told me you're an artist and that you are selling some of your work."

"Lately, every grandparent with a baby in the nursery wants to buy a portrait. Dr. Wright has even talked to a guy who owns a gallery. He's gonna take a look at my stuff."

"That's great."

"Maybe, maybe not. I don't want to get my hopes up. How is Mick?" she asked, hoping she didn't sound too eager for information.

"Actually, I haven't seen much of him. I got my cast off two days ago, and I'm moving back into my own apartment. I've been busy setting things to rights there. I'm sure he's been busy with work."

Too busy to come to the hospital. Caitlin knew because she spent every day there, herself. He'd promised that he would always be there for Beth, but this was how Caitlin knew it would turn out. He was getting on with his life. Only, she hadn't expected it to hurt this much.

Elizabeth moved a step closer and laid a hand on Caitlin's shoulder. "I'd really like to keep in touch with you."

"I'd like that, too."

"Well, since I'm here, why don't I take you out to lunch?"

"You don't have to do that."

"Nonsense. You have to eat, don't you? I tell you what. In exchange for a meal, you can bring your young knees over to my apartment and take a broom to the dust buffalo under my bed and sofa. You'd be doing me a big favor."

"I thought they were dust bunnies."

"They've been growing since I've been at Mick's. Please say you'll come and tackle them for a crippled, old woman."

"Since you put it that way, sure."

"Excellent. I told the cabby to wait in case you said yes. I can't wait to show you my little place. I have quite a teapot collection that I think you'll like. That reminds me. Do you have a teapot? If not, I shall make you a present of one of mine. Good tea requires a good pot to brew in."

Caitlin smiled as she followed Elizabeth down the steps. Besides the fact that she truly liked Mick's mother, it would be easy now to find out how he was doing. She missed him more than she had ever thought possible.

* * *

It was after two in the morning when Mick entered the NICU and made his way to the incubator where Beth lay sleeping. Propped on her side, she held both fists close to her face like a tiny boxer getting ready to take on all comers. She was a fighter like her mother, and he thanked God for that. Life wasn't going to be easy for her.

He draped one arm on the top of her box and leaned in close, but he didn't speak, didn't open the porthole to caress her tiny head as he longed to do. She needed her sleep. She was doing so well now that the past months seemed like a fading nightmare. How many times had she cheated death while he paced in the waiting room? He had come to hate the sight of those blue tweed chairs. He'd never buy anything that color.

An alarm sounded a few beds down the aisle, and a nurse walked by to silence it. There was still a hustle in the nursery, but it was more muted at night. Perhaps it was the dimmed lights that kept everyone talking more quietly and slowed the frantic pace. He'd taken to visiting Beth in the small hours of the morning since Caitlin had moved out of his house.

Without her presence, he found it hard to sleep. Instead of tossing and turning in his lonely bed he came here. Here he didn't miss her scent—her vibrancy—the sound of her voice. Here he came to watch over Beth while she slept.

Each day, Beth grew stronger. And each day the child he thought of as his own slipped further away from him. He had to let her go. Just as he had let her mother go.

Knowing that Caitlin didn't want him in her life was tearing him apart. She wanted to live her own life. He understood that, even respected it, but the love he felt wasn't fading now that they were apart. Would it ever? How could he face a lifetime without Caitlin and Beth?

Lord, grant me Your wisdom and guidance. Please. Because I don't know what to do.

Chapter Fifteen

"These are your going-home instructions. Do you have any questions?" A nurse Caitlin hadn't met before handed her a sheet of paper. Caitlin took it and stared at it trying to calm her fears. How could she possibly do this? How could she care for Beth without doctors and nurses there around the clock? What if there was something important in this paper?

Tell her. Tell her you can't read.

She opened her mouth to confess, but the words stuck in her throat. Would they let her take Beth home if they knew how stupid she was? The fear of losing her baby always lurked in the back of her mind. If they thought she couldn't take care of Beth, would they give her to Mick, instead?

She glanced at the car seat by her feet. Beth slept quietly, looking utterly adorable in a pink, frilly dress with a matching band around her head. No, Caitlin decided, she couldn't risk it. As soon as she had a chance, she'd take the paper and have Eddy look at it.

Caitlin forced a smile. "It all seems pretty clear."

"Good. Here are the prescriptions for Beth's medications. Take them to the pharmacy of your choice."

"But I'll still give her the same amounts, right?"

"That's right. Her caffeine is ten milligrams, that's one cc in the morning, and her phenobarbital is eight milligrams, two cc's at night. I've put several small oral medication syringes in this bag."

Caitlin nodded. She knew how to give the medications. She'd watched closely as Sandra had shown her how to draw two cc's of liquid from the round bottle and one cc from the oval bottle. Both medicines were red liquids, but she knew the round bottle was the drug that would control Beth's seizures and the oval bottle was the drug that would keep Beth from having apnea. "The pharmacy will give me the same medicines, right?"

"Yes, they'll be the same as what Beth was taking here. Do you have any questions about the home monitor?"

"No, the guy who set it up explained everything. I've had my CPR training. I know all the emergency numbers."

Dr. Wright came into the nursery just then followed by a small man in a sharply tailored, dark blue suit. Caitlin shook the hand that Dr. Wright held out.

"I wish you the best of luck, Ms. Williams. Before you go, let me introduce you to someone. This is Karl Wiltshire. Karl, this is the young woman I've been telling you about, Caitlin Williams."

"Ms. Williams, I've been looking forward to meeting you. I've been admiring some of your work in Dr. Wright's office. You have a remarkable talent."

"Thanks." Caitlin still felt embarrassed by the attention her work seemed to be getting.

The man held out a business card. "I own a gallery downtown. I'd be interested in displaying some of your work."

He smiled at Beth. "I can see that you're going to be busy for a while, but I'd like to get together with you. Would next Friday be too soon?"

Stunned, Caitlin took his card. Her work in a gallery? The idea blew her away. "Um, no. Next Friday will be fine."

"Excellent. Let's say ten o'clock?"

"Great. Would it be okay if I brought the baby?"

"Of course. Bring what you think is your best work and we'll discuss it." With that, he shook Caitlin's hand again and followed Dr. Wright out of the unit.

"Well," the nurse said, "I guess that's everything."

Caitlin tucked Mr. Wiltshire's business card in the bag with Beth's things. Looking through the bag, she realized something was missing. "I don't see Beth's card. It has green shamrocks on it."

"You mean her Irish blessing. I think it's still on her crib. I'll get it for you."

A few moments later, she returned with the card in her hand. She read it aloud. "'May God grant you many years to live, for sure He must be knowing, the Earth has angels all too few, and heaven's overflowing.' Isn't that beautiful?"

"It's perfect." Tears pricked the back of Caitlin's eyes. Reaching out, she took the card from the woman's hand. Mick had chosen these words for Beth on the day she was born, and Caitlin would cherish them forever.

The nurse said, "I'm surprised Mick isn't here."

"He's been working a lot, I guess. He hasn't been able to come and see her lately."

"Except at night."

Caitlin frowned. "What do you mean?"

"I usually work the night shift. I'm covering for a nurse who is sick this morning. I've gotten used to seeing Mick here in the wee hours."

Caitlin blinked hard. Mick had been to see Beth, but he hadn't come to see Beth's mother. That hurt, although she knew it shouldn't. Did he still worry that she wouldn't be able to take care of Beth by herself?

Beth was going to be the only priority in Caitlin's life from now on. She would stop mooning over Mick O'Callaghan. She would stop missing him. Maybe someday, she'd even stop dreaming about him.

Slipping the strap of Beth's monitor over her shoulder, Caitlin picked up the car seat. "Please tell everyone I said thank you."

"Good luck, and don't be afraid to call us with questions."

Glancing around the unit once more, a sense of loss settled over Caitlin. Strangely enough, she was going to miss this place. She looked down at her baby and smiled. "Let's go home, jelly bean."

The cabdriver waited for them while Caitlin took Beth's prescriptions into a nearby pharmacy. She hurried, knowing the meter was still running. She had some money, but none to waste.

In the pharmacy, the woman behind the counter handed Caitlin the drugs in a small white paper sack. It wasn't until she and Beth were back in the cab that Caitlin opened it and looked in. There were two identical oval, amber plastic bottles.

Caitlin stared at them in dismay. At the hospital, the seizure medication had been in a round bottle. Her heart hammered with panic. How was she going to tell them apart? She took a deep breath and tried to remain calm. She'd find a way to manage. She always found a way.

A few minutes later, the cab pulled up to the small apartment that she and Beth were going to call home. Caitlin leaned forward to pay the driver. "Could you help me carry some things in?"

"Sure. No problem," he replied.

Caitlin took one bottle of medication from the package and let it slip to the floor. Then she unbuckled Beth's car seat and lifted the baby out of the cab. "I'll take her if you can get her monitor and the diaper bag."

Caitlin was halfway up the outside stairs that led to her new home when the driver called out, "Hey, you forgot some medicine here."

She turned back frowning. "I don't think so. What is it?"

He peered at the bottle. "It says Caffeine Ci—something."

She sagged with relief. "Oh, yes, it's mine. It must have fallen out of my bag."

"Good thing I saw it." He tucked it in his shirt pocket, then lifted the diaper bag and the monitor from the cab.

Once inside the apartment, Caitlin set the bottle with Beth's seizure medication on the kitchen counter. She'd mark it with something that would let her tell the medicines apart right away. She set Beth's car seat on the floor beside the couch.

The driver carried in the diaper bag and Beth's VCR-sized monitor. "Where do you want these?"

"Anywhere is fine."

"Oops, she's spitting up," he said, pointing to Beth. "My youngest one was always doing that."

Caitlin took the diaper bag from him, and he moved aside as she found a cloth to wipe Beth's face. When she looked up, he was standing by the kitchen counter reading the bottle he held.

"I'll take that," she said.

"Oh, sure." He handed it to her. "What's it for, if you don't mind my asking?"

"She has apnea. The caffeine helps her to keep breathing."

"Wow. And the Pheno stuff?"

"It controls her seizures."

"Seizures? The poor kid." His voice held an edge of pity that annoyed Caitlin.

"The doctors think she'll outgrow them."

"That's good. Well, I'd better get going. Good luck to you both," he said.

Caitlin showed him to the door and closed it behind him, then she stared at the bottle in her hand. She had found a way this time, but it might not be so easy the next time. Not being able to read hadn't meant much when she only had herself to worry about. Street smarts had mattered more than the things she'd learned in school, but now she had Beth to think of.

Someday Beth would go to school, and she'd want her mother to help with homework and stuff. Caitlin bit down on her fingernail as she stared at her sleeping daughter.

Could she lie and fool her own daughter the way she had fooled others? She didn't want to, but she didn't want Beth to be ashamed of her, either.

Carrying the bottle in her hand to the kitchen, she set it on top of the refrigerator. She found a small rubber band in a drawer and put it over the neck of the bottle on the counter. It would be easy to tell them apart now. Next time she had them filled, she'd ask the pharmacy for two different kinds of bottles.

She crossed the room and sat down on the brown floral sofa that had come with the apartment and stared at her baby, still sleeping peacefully. The quiet of the small place surrounded them. They were home. She had her baby with her now and forever.

Beth stirred and began to fuss. Happily, Caitlin picked her up and began to nurse her. This was how she had always known it would be. Silently, Caitlin thanked God for the beautiful child He had given her.

Mick helped loop the long fire hose back onto the sides of the truck. He pushed back his helmet and wiped the sweat and soot from his forehead with the back of his coat sleeve. Woody secured his end then turned to Mick. "Our shift ended forty minutes ago."

The small kitchen fire had produced a lot of smoke, but most of the home was still intact. The family stood huddled together on the sidewalk, thankful it hadn't been worse.

Mick looked over his shoulder at his friend. "Don't tell me you're complaining about overtime."

"Not me. I can always find ways to spend it. Now that we're off, what are your plans for the next few days?"

"A hot shower, some breakfast and then I'm going to see Caitlin and Beth."

"You've waited—what? A whole week?"

"I wanted to give them time to get used to being in a new place, but I need to see how they're doing."

"Mick, they're doing fine."

"I know they're fine. I'm the basketcase. How am I going to convince Caitlin that I'm in love with her? She thinks I'm only interested in Beth."

The "fantasy replacement" for the child he couldn't have. Her comment had hurt, but in a way, it had been true—to start with. Only so much had changed since the day Beth was born. He had changed. He needed both of them in his life.

Woody slapped Mick's shoulder and pushed him toward the cab of the truck. "First, let's get back to the station and out of this gear, and then we can discuss your love life. The main thing is, don't rush her. Take it slow and easy. Be a friend."

On the ride back to the firehouse, Mick pondered Woody's advice. It made sense. Slow and easy, that would be the plan.

Please, Lord, let me prove to Caitlin that I love her. That I want us to be a family.

He'd show her he could be a dependable friend before anything else. She would be hard to convince. She was stubbornly independent. She had a little money now from her drawings, but that wouldn't last long. Soon she'd see that she needed him and he'd be there for her.

After showering and getting dressed in Levi's and a blue plaid cotton shirt, Mick pulled a small bag from the top shelf of his locker. Inside was a plush pink bunny that played a child's prayer when its paws were squeezed. Today he would simply say that he had stopped by to see Beth and give her a welcome-home present. Caitlin would believe that.

Beth wouldn't quit crying. Caitlin paced the floor of her small apartment, switching the baby from one weary arm to the other. It was almost eight in the morning, and Beth had been crying since before midnight. Caitlin's feelings of frustration and inadequacy had long since given way to pure exhaustion.

"What's wrong? Tell me what you want," she pleaded, knowing she had already tried everything. "I've fed you and changed you and rocked you. What else do you need?"

Even the warm bath and wrapping Beth tightly had failed to calm her for more than a few minutes. Nothing worked.

Caitlin was due at the Wiltshire Gallery at ten o'clock. She had less than two hours to get presentable and get downtown. Having the gallery accept her work was so important. Why did Beth have to choose this night to have a case of colic? "Hush, baby, please."

Beth arched her back and flailed her arms as her cries continued. The last bit of Caitlin's patience vaporized. Crossing to the bedroom, she laid the baby abruptly in her oversized buggy. "Well, just cry then! I don't care!"

Shutting the door with a bang, Caitlin dropped onto the sagging sofa, pressed her hands over her ears and battled the need to burst into tears herself.

She waited, watching the hands of the clock tick slowly around. Five minutes. After ten minutes, she gave up. Dragging herself off the sofa, she returned to the bedroom. Beth's cries had subsided to ragged sobs and pitiful whimpering. She turned her tiny face toward Caitlin, her wide-eyed expression a picture of panic and fear.

Consumed with guilt, Caitlin scooped her up and

held her close. "I'm sorry, I'm sorry. I'm a terrible mother, only I just don't know what else to do."

A knock sounded at the front door and Beth began crying loudly once more.

Now what? Carrying her screaming child, Caitlin yanked open the door, then sagged with relief. "Mick. Oh, I'm so glad to see you."

"What's wrong?" His concern was her undoing.

A sob escaped her. "I don't know." She thrust the baby toward him. "She just keeps crying and crying. I've done everything I can think of."

Taking the baby from her, he balanced Beth in one arm and draped his free arm over Caitlin's shoulders. "Okay. It's going to be all right. Babies get fussy sometimes."

"Not like this."

He led her to the sofa and sat beside her. "When did this start?"

"I don't know. The day before yesterday, I think. She started having high heart-rate alarms on her monitor."

"But no apnea?"

"No, and she won't eat. Maybe there's something wrong with my milk again."

Caitlin watched anxiously as Mick laid the baby in his lap and checked her over. Laying two fingers on the inside of Beth's elbow, he checked her pulse as Caitlin had learned to do.

"Did you give her any caffeine this morning?"

"No, not for the past two days. Her pulse was too high. I count it every time just like they showed me at the hospital."

"She doesn't feel warm, I don't think she has a fever, but her pulse is way too fast."

"What should I do?"

"I think we had better get her in to see a doctor."

"You think she's sick? I thought she was just having colic." Guilt and remorse rose like bile in her throat. She should have taken her to the doctor last night. Instead, she had let her baby suffer for hours.

"I'll take you to the E.R. Bring her medicine, they'll want to know what she's on."

Trying desperately to stave off a wave of panic, Caitlin gathered Beth's things and followed Mick down to his car. He fastened the baby's car seat into the center of the rear seat, and Caitlin got in beside her daughter. Beth continued to cry as Mick drove. It broke Caitlin's heart not to be able to pick her up. Suddenly, the baby's crying became a choking gurgle. She stiffened and arched as her face twisted into a grimace.

"Mick, she's having a seizure."

"Is she breathing?"

"Yes. What do I do?" *Please God, help her.*

"Just make sure she's breathing," Mick said.

After nearly a minute, Beth stopped arching and went limp. The color of her face paled and slowly took on a blue tinge. Leaning her cheek close to the baby's nose confirmed Caitlin's worst fears. She fumbled with the straps of the car seat. "She's not breathing now."

"We're almost there."

"I'm starting CPR. God, please help me do this!" Pulling Beth to her lap, Caitlin bent and covered her daughter's mouth and nose with her own mouth and delivered two small puffs of air. Beth's chest rose and fell and Caitlin knew she had done it right. She continued to deliver puffs of air until Beth suddenly drew in a breath of her own and let out a cry.

"Thank You, Lord." Mick's voice wavered with emotion.

Seconds later, the car skidded to a stop in front of the hospital's E.R. He jumped out and jerked open Caitlin's door. "I'll take her."

Caitlin handed Beth to him and followed close behind as he hurried through the hospital doors. His tense explanation to the clerk on duty got them ushered quickly into a room. A nurse took Beth and laid her in the center of a large cot.

Caitlin pressed a hand to her trembling lips. Beth looked so small and helpless. A doctor entered the room and began to examine Beth. He asked question after question. Mick stood silently behind Caitlin with his hands on her shoulders. She was so thankful that he was there.

When the doctor was done with his examination, he gave the nurse instructions for lab work and then suggested to Caitlin that she might like to step out while they drew blood.

"No, I've seen her stuck before. I want to stay."

"I'll stay as well," Mick said.

Together they helped to hold Beth still while a man from the lab stuck her arm. When it was all over, Caitlin picked up her sobbing baby and held her close.

The nurse indicated a chair. "You might as well be seated. It'll be a while before the test results come back."

Nodding, Caitlin sat down and Mick took a seat beside her. The nurse held out a clipboard. "We'll need some paperwork filled out."

Mick reached for Beth. "I'll hold her while you do it."

"No, she needs me right now." Caitlin glared at the nurse. "Can't that wait? Can't you see how upset she is?"

With an apologetic look to the nurse, Mick took the clipboard from her. "I'll fill it out."

"All right, just be sure and have Mom sign it."

The nurse left the room and Caitlin avoided Mick's gaze as she concentrated on calming Beth. After a few minutes of silence, she said, "Good ol' Mick to the rescue, again. Do you have some kind of radar that lets you know when I'm in trouble?"

"I only stopped by to give Beth a homecoming present and to see how you were doing."

"We were doing fine until last night." She knew she sounded defensive, but once again he had proven that he knew Beth better than she did. It irked her that she had needed his help, even as she admitted to herself that she had never been happier to see anyone when she had opened her door.

"Thanks for bringing us to the hospital. You don't have to stay if you're busy."

"I'm not busy." He finished filling out the form, then leaning forward, he clasped his hands together and waited in silence.

Thirty minutes later, the doctor walked in. He was frowning as he stared at the papers in his hand. "I understand that Beth was sent home on phenobarbital and also on caffeine, is that right?"

"That's right," Caitlin answered. Something was wrong, she knew it by the way he wouldn't meet her gaze.

He looked at Mick. "You're listed as the father, but I see you have a different address."

"Caitlin and I don't live together."

The doctor stared hard at Caitlin. "Do you have Beth's medication with you?"

Caitlin fought down the need to take Beth and run. She had done everything just as the nurses in the NICU had told her to. She hadn't done anything wrong. She pulled them from her bag and held them out.

"I've been giving them just like I was taught." Caitlin drew a quick, deep breath. She was suffocating in the small room. The walls pressed in closer and closer. Mick and the doctor were staring at her intently.

The doctor walked to the cart in the corner of the room. After a moment, he turned around and held out both bottles and two syringes. "Show me how you've been giving them. Let's let Dad hold Beth for a minute."

Caitlin licked her dry lips. "I can hold her."

Mick rose and took Beth from her arms. "Show the doctor how you've been giving Beth her medicine."

The doctor knew. Caitlin didn't know how, but she was sure of it. Was it possible she had mixed up the medicines? She had been so careful to keep them apart. She took the bottles from him with hands that trembled. Looking down, she saw neither one had a rubber band on it.

"Draw up the phenobarbital first," the doctor suggested.

Which was which? What should she do? She looked from the doctor to Mick. Now he would see how stupid she was.

"I can't," she admitted in anguish.

"Why not?" the doctor asked gently.

"I had it marked. You took the rubber band off. I know it was the right one. It was, wasn't it? The rubber band was on her seizure medicine. It was two cc's every night in a little bit of milk so she'd take it all before I fed her, and the apnea medicine was one cc in the morning. I had it right. I know I did. Only, maybe—maybe the cabdriver mixed them up." Panic choked her. What had she done?

"Let me see." Mick took the bottles from her limp hand. "This one is phenobarbital and this one is caffeine. What do you mean the cabdriver mixed them up?"

A strange calm settled over Caitlin. The life she had dreamed of with her daughter disappeared before her the way the winds scattered the morning mist that rose from the lake. She had nothing left to lose.

"I pretended to leave one in his cab and when he asked if it was mine, I had him read the label. He had the caffeine in his hand so I knew I had her seizure medicine. I put it down on the counter. He must have switched them. I thought it was such a good plan."

"I don't understand," Mick looked more confused than ever.

"I—I can't read. But I would never hurt, Beth. Never."

"You wouldn't hurt her? You've been giving her the wrong doses of medicine. This is phenobarbital! You could have killed her!"

The anger and loathing in his eyes was painful to see. Beth whimpered and Caitlin reached for her, but Mick turned away and hushed the baby, murmuring words of comfort as he held her close. Caitlin stared at his back. She didn't blame him. Mick would never let anything hurt Beth.

She'd been crazy to think that she could raise Beth. She was no better than her own mother. Dotty had her drugs to blame. Caitlin couldn't blame anyone or anything but herself. Beth would be better off with Mick. He would never hurt her.

The door opened beside Caitlin as the nurse came in, and in a moment of agony unlike anything she had ever faced, Caitlin knew what she had to do. She had to give up her baby. She had to go where she could never, ever hurt Beth or Mick again.

One last glimpse of Beth's face was all she wanted. Only Mick held her close and Caitlin couldn't see her. Tears blurred her vision and tightened her throat.

God, please forgive me.

Quietly, she turned away and slipped out of the room.

Chapter Sixteen

The doctor scrawled on Beth's chart then handed it to the nurse. "I'm going to admit the child for observation overnight. It's a simple matter to get her phenobarbital level back up, but the caffeine will have to wear off on its own. She'll need to be on a monitor until her heart rate is more normal."

The nurse left the room and the doctor spoke to Mick. "You'll be able to stay with her tonight."

Mick nodded, too angry and upset to speak. How could Caitlin have taken such a chance with Beth's health? He glanced around, but Caitlin had left the room.

The doctor laid a hand on Mick's arm. "I take it you didn't know she couldn't read?"

He shook his head. "I had no idea. How did you know?"

"I didn't. The nurse suspected something when the baby's mother became belligerent about filling out the paperwork. We see it more than you'd think. When your daughter's lab reports came back, I knew either the pharmacy had filled the prescriptions incorrectly, or it had been given incorrectly. That's why I asked to see the bottles. She had a rubber band around one. I was pretty sure then. When I took that off, she couldn't tell the bottles apart. Somehow, she must have marked the wrong one."

Beth whimpered and Mick gently bounced her until she quieted. "Caitlin loves Beth. She'd never knowingly hurt her. I don't understand why she didn't tell me."

"Fear, I imagine."

"Of what?"

"Fear of ridicule, shame, the reasons are often deep-seated and difficult for the illiterate person to define. Many of them become incredibly skillful at hiding the truth even from family members."

The door opened and the nurse looked in. "The peds floor has a bed ready now. I'll take you upstairs."

"Did you tell her mother that Beth is being admitted?" Mick asked.

"I looked for her, but I couldn't find her."

He shouldn't have yelled at her. Of course, she hadn't meant to hurt Beth. "Did anyone see where she went?"

"No, but I've sent someone to look for her. Beth needs to be on a monitor. We shouldn't delay."

Reluctantly, Mick agreed. In the room where Beth would spend the night, he impatiently answered the staff's questions and glanced frequently toward the door, but Caitlin never appeared. Where was she?

When Beth fell asleep at last, he went searching for Caitlin himself. What did she think she was going to accomplish by ducking out like this? Maybe he had re-acted badly, but surely she knew he didn't believe she would intentionally hurt Beth.

It didn't matter how independent Caitlin wanted to

be, she would have to accept the fact that he was going to be a part of their lives from now on—a big part of it.

Why on earth hadn't she told him the truth? Why hadn't she asked for his help? He would have given it gladly. She had no right to jeopardize Beth's health for nothing more than her pride. When she did show up, he intended to give her a piece of his mind. Making a mistake was one thing, but this juvenile behavior of running away from her problems had to stop.

So she couldn't read—big deal. All she had to do was to say so. But no, she was too pigheaded for that. Now that he knew, he could remember a dozen times in the past when he should have suspected something. Maybe he could understand that her pride had prevented her from telling others, but why hadn't she trusted him? He loved her.

He dropped his gaze to stare at the floor. He loved her, but he had never told her that—he had kept his secrets, too.

As the hours dragged by and she didn't come in, he began to worry. A cold fear started to uncoil inside him.

She had looked so scared in the E.R. Like a jerk, he had yelled at her, and her face had gone white. Something in her beautiful eyes changed, and she had looked so remote. Wrapped up in his own concerns for Beth, he hadn't recognized what he saw until now. It had been hopelessness.

Tears blurred Caitlin's vision as she ran down the sidewalk. It didn't matter where she went. She only wanted to get away—away from the look on Mick's face—away from the knowledge that she had almost killed Beth. She ran until pain clenched her side in a tight grip and her breath came in short ragged gasps.

Anguish, guilt and regret choked her. She had abandoned her baby. Love for her daughter almost made her turn around, but then she remembered Beth's face twisted in pain as spasms jerked her little body. She had done that to her baby. Her ignorance had done that.

Desperately, she wished that she had trusted Mick enough to tell him the truth. Instead, she saw his angry face and heard his voice as he shouted, "You could have killed her."

The pain in her side made her slow down, but she kept moving. If she stopped putting one foot in front of the other, she would sink into a heap of despair.

This is for the best. I can't take care of her.

She would only end up hurting Beth again. She saw that now. Leaving Beth with Mick was the right thing to do. Beth would be safe with him.

The gray world around her gradually turned into darkness as night fell and still Caitlin walked, turning this way and that, down streets whose names she couldn't read, past stores whose signs she didn't understand.

Beth would be okay. Mick would look after her. He could give her a life of security and love.

Cars streaked past Caitlin as she plodded on, but she barely noticed. Slowly, towering buildings replaced the houses along the streets. There were people around her now, laughing, calling out for cabs, hurrying past with cell phones pressed to their ears or shopping bags clutched tightly in their hands. No one noticed her. Funny how easily she had slipped back into being another invisible street person.

That thought made her pause. She had spent years rarely making eye contact with anyone, surviving on the fringes of society and sometimes wondering if she really existed at all. Going back to that kind of life would be unbearable after Mick and after Beth. Never seeing Beth again, never holding her close, that would be unbearable, too.

Ahead of Caitlin rose the white, ornate pylons of the Michigan Avenue Bridge. Across the bridge, the lights of Chicago's Magnificent Mile stretched like a glittering chasm of glass and steel, a world in which she had no part. Below her, curving along the edge of the river lay Wacker Drive and farther on, Lower Wacker Drive. In her early days on the streets, she had lived by staying warm, huddled in a cardboard box on the grates on Lower Wacker with dozens of other street people. They had taught her how to survive. Only now, surviving wasn't enough. Mick had made her believe that.

Fog drifted in ghostly curtains across the bridge as if drawn along by the flow of the water beneath it. Caitlin kept to the walkway until she reached the center of the bridge. There she leaned on the rail and stared at the dark, churning water below her. A lifetime without her baby—without Mick—what was it worth?

Down there was an end to her pain and grief. She wouldn't have to face a lifetime of missing Beth and missing Mick, of knowing how badly she had failed both of them. Her hands tightened on the rail. It would be so easy to close her eyes and take a simple step over the side into nothingness.

Caitlin raised her face to the night sky. Suddenly filled with anger, she shouted, "Is this Your great plan, God? Well, it stinks! Do You hear me? It stinks!"

She sank to her knees by the rail. Tears streamed unheeded down her cheeks. Everything she loved was lost.

With her face pressed against the cold railing, Caitlin watched the inky water swirl below the bridge. One easy step and it would all be over. She closed her eyes and pictured her baby cradled in Mick's gentle arms.

"Beth, I never meant to hurt you," she whispered. "Mick will keep you safe. He's so strong. Only—I don't want you to grow up thinking that I never loved you, because I love you with all my heart."

Who will tell her that if you kill yourself?

The thought came from deep within her heart. From the place Mick had once told her she could find God. Caitlin rubbed the tears from her eyes to clear her vision. Slumped against the railing, she drew her knees up and wrapped her arms around them to ward off the chill of the night.

Is this what You wanted, God? For me to give up Beth so she'd be safe and loved? If that's so, then I guess this is okay because that's all I want, too. Honest. Only how can I live without her? I give up, Lord. Please, help me. I can't do this alone.

Slowly, a sense of calm and peace grew inside her, pushing away the chill with a feeling of warmth. Whatever He wanted, it wasn't for her to end her life here.

Pulling herself to her feet, Caitlin walked off the bridge with unsteady steps, but she kept walking.

Hours later, on the verge of exhaustion, she sank into a corner of an alley a few streets back from West Madison. Wrapping her arms around her drawn-up knees, she rested her head on them and tried to sleep, but she couldn't. Her grief and pain were impossible to ignore.

Please, Lord. Give me the strength to go on.

Beth would grow up happy and loved with Mick as her father, but wouldn't she always wonder why her mother had abandoned her? Caitlin couldn't add that burden to her child's life. Someday, when Beth was old enough, someone needed to explain it to her. Besides Mick, there was only one person Caitlin thought might understand.

What Beth might someday think about her was more important than what anyone had ever thought of her in the past. She wanted to be someone Beth would be proud of. To do that, she had to become something better than what she was. And she couldn't do it alone. *Help me, God. Show me the way.*

When the sun rose at last, Caitlin tilted her head back to stare at the strip of blue sky overhead and a new sense of determination filled her. She had lost everything that was important, but she wouldn't be ashamed anymore. God had shown her that.

She rose stiffly to her feet. Although she had been to the area only once before, she knew she could find the way. When she judged it to be late enough, she made her way to the apartment building on the corner. She passed a group of boys playing stickball in the street and wondered if Mick had ever played ball like that. Maybe he would teach Beth how, someday.

Caitlin realized she would never watch her daughter at play, never see her take her first steps, never hear her first words. Sadness, sharp as a knife, cut through her, but she walked on. She couldn't go another hour without knowing how Beth was.

Inside the lobby, tastefully decorated in shades of gray and muted blues, she gathered her newfound courage close and pressed the elevator button.

On the fifth floor, she made her way to apartment 516. Overwhelmed by the temptation to turn and run away, she knocked quickly before she could change her mind. The door opened before she was ready. Elizabeth O'Callaghan's face took on a look of absolute shock.

"Caitlin, what on earth are you doing here? My dear, everyone was so worried about you. Mick is simply frantic. Are you all right?"

"How's Beth?" Her words came out in a husky whisper because she couldn't talk around the lump in her throat.

"She's fine. She went home from the hospital this morning."

It was the news she needed to hear. Nothing else mattered. Relief left her weak and shaking.

Elizabeth grasped Caitlin's elbow. "Come inside and sit down. You look as pale as a sheet."

Caitlin shook her head. "I won't impose on you. I just had to know she was all right. I came here because I want you to tell Beth when she's old enough to understand that…"

Words failed her as she struggled to hold back her tears. "Tell her that I loved her with all my heart, but I couldn't take care of her. Tell her I left *because* I loved her. And tell Mick…tell him…"

"Tell him yourself." His voice came from behind her, and she froze.

Chapter Seventeen

Caitlin couldn't move, couldn't speak, as pain crashed like a tidal wave through her. She didn't dare turn around. *Please, Lord, I'm not strong enough for this.*

She kept her eyes down. If Mick had Beth—if she saw her baby girl just once—she'd never be able to leave her again.

She forced her wooden legs to start walking toward the stairs at the end of the hall.

"Running again, Caitlin?" he called after her. "I thought you said you loved her?"

Her feet stopped even as her mind screamed for her to keep going. She tilted her head back to stare at the ceiling. "What do you want from me, Mick?"

"I want answers."

"I don't have any."

"I need to know why you abandoned your child. Why?"

Abruptly, anger at Mick replaced her desire to flee. If he wanted answers, then she'd give him what he wanted to hear.

"Because I couldn't do it, okay?" she shouted.

"You were right all along. I couldn't take care of her. I couldn't be a mother. I couldn't manage because I'm too stupid to learn how to read."

"You aren't stupid." His voice was right behind her.

"I am. You said it yourself. I could have killed her." Tears slipped unheeded down her cheeks.

She took a deep breath and steadied her voice. "Anyway, she's better off with you. You'll give her a good life. A life with a real home and clothes that don't come from a thrift store. She'll have all the things I'd never be able to afford."

"That's a lie, and you know it. This isn't about things. I deserve to hear the truth."

Stunned by the pain in his voice, she spun around. Just as she feared, Beth lay snuggled in the crook of his arm. Caitlin pressed a hand to her lips to hold back a sob.

Her baby. She was so beautiful—more beautiful even than Caitlin remembered, and her heart swelled with painful happiness and pride.

"How could you walk out on her?" he demanded. "How could a mother do that?"

Caitlin closed her eyes. Suddenly, weary beyond words, she knew he wouldn't go until she admitted the bitter truth.

"I did it for her—to keep her safe. May God forgive me."

"I don't understand."

He didn't. She had to make him understand. She struggled to find the words. "I hurt her, Mick."

"I know you didn't mean to."

"My mother never meant to hurt me, but she did. So many times! And I forgave her every time. I believed her each time she said she'd change—but she never did. Listening to her say how sorry she was didn't erase any of the pain. It didn't ease my hunger when she spent money on dope instead of food. It didn't make the slaps and punches less painful when I wouldn't sell drugs for her pimp of a boyfriend. Then one day, I just ran out of forgiveness, and I started to hate her."

Caitlin raised her face, her gaze drawn to her sweet baby. "I didn't want that for Beth."

With her heart in broken pieces, she looked away. "I couldn't take care of her any more than my mom could take care of me. Maybe the reasons are different, but that doesn't matter. Yesterday in the E.R., when I heard myself stammering the same excuses—I was sorry—I didn't mean it—I'll do better—I realized I was just like her. That's why I left. So I'd never hurt Beth again. I know you love her. I know she'll always be safe with you."

Looking up at Mick, a ghost of a smile crossed her face. "God must truly love you, Mick O'Callaghan. He's given you the greatest gift."

Mick studied Caitlin's pain-filled, tear-streaked face. Slowly his anger and confusion faded. Whatever he had expected, it hadn't been this. Compassion welled up in him. As a child, she had suffered what no child ever should. Now she was willing to suffer even more to spare her daughter the same fate.

Like the two women who came before King Solomon, the true mother had been willing to give up her child rather than see him harmed. Mick felt humbled in the face of Caitlin's sacrifice.

Lord, make me worthy of this woman.

He loved her. He understood what she had done and

what it had cost her. Even if she didn't love him, he couldn't separate her from Beth. He needed both of them in his life. But how could he convince Caitlin of that when she believed he only wanted her child?

He glanced from Caitlin to Beth—his daughter in every sense of the word except one—and his heart ached for what he knew he must do. There was only one way he could prove to Caitlin that he believed in her, that he forgave her.

Forgive my arrogance and my pride, Lord. Grant me Your wisdom. I've never needed it as much as I need it now.

"Caitlin, you are not your mother," he said gently. "Everything you did—even leaving—was because you wanted what was best for Beth. No one can love Beth more than that. She doesn't need things. She needs her mother's love—your love."

Startled, Caitlin's gaze flew to his face. Had she heard right? Was he offering her a chance to gain back everything she had thrown away? "What are you saying?"

"I'm saying that Beth needs her mother, and I think her mother needs Beth even more."

A powerful joy unfolded in Caitlin. With trembling hands, she took Beth from him and drew her close. The sweet fragrance of her baby was her undoing. She broke into gut-wrenching sobs. "I'm so sorry, Beth. I'll never leave you again. Never! Never! Thank You, God. Thank You."

Elizabeth held her door open wide and Mick helped Caitlin to the sofa. It was several long minutes until she regained a measure of control. When she was able to stop crying, she kissed Beth's face, then looked at him. "I don't know what to say. I don't have words to tell you how much this means to me. How can you forgive me for what I did?"

Choking back the lump that filled his throat, he said, "I know you love Beth, and I knew you would come back."

"I came back to make sure she was okay, not to take her away from you. Only to tell her why I had to leave, and to tell her that I always loved her. I just need to get my head on straight, first."

He tilted his. "It doesn't look crooked to me."

She smiled, but quickly looked down. He lifted her chin with one finger. Fear and indecision gathered in her bright eyes. "What if I can't do it? What if I *am* like my mother?"

"You're not."

"I think I'm scared."

"I know. So am I."

"You? Of what?"

"The same things you are. That I'll make a lousy parent, that I'll be too strict, or too lenient. That she'll run into the street when I'm not looking, or that she'll break my heart when some guy wants to marry her. It scares me to death, but I know that God loves her and she is always in His tender care."

"Yes." Caitlin gripped his hand and squeezed. "I believe that, now. He was never far away. I just wasn't looking with my heart."

Early on a Sunday morning two weeks later, Mick stood in his own kitchen trying to find a pot holder. "It's coming, it's coming. Take it easy," he said in a harried voice.

Beth was screaming in her bouncy chair on the kitchen table. Nikki whined in sympathy and got in Mick's way as he hurried to fix her formula. He pulled the bottle from the pan and checked the temperature by shaking a few drops onto his wrist. It was almost warm enough. He put the bottle back in the water and turned off the heat. Grasping the handle of the pan on the stove with his shirttail, he turned and headed for the sink but stumbled over the dog. He lost his grip on the pan of hot water and it crashed to the floor. The bottle of milk went rolling under the table.

Nikki dashed after it. Proudly, she came back to sit in front of him. The bottle swayed from the nipple clenched in her mouth.

Two nights of getting up every three hours to feed Beth had worn him to a nub. *Please, let Caitlin get here soon.*

"Give me that!" Exasperated, he yanked the bottle away from the dog, but the nipple stayed firmly in her teeth, and milk sprayed from the topless container in a wide arch that hit Beth, the table and the kitchen wall.

After a moment of stunned silence, Beth's wailing skyrocketed, Nikki dropped her prize to lap up the spilled milk, and the doorbell rang.

In a daze, Mick stared at the disaster. The doorbell chimed again. He lifted Beth from her chair, wiped her dripping face on his sleeve and carried the still-screaming baby with him to the front door. His hope that it might not be Caitlin died swiftly when he pulled open the door and saw her.

His heart jumped into double time. The words *I love you madly* hovered on his lips, but he held them back. This wasn't the right moment.

"Perfect timing!" he growled. "Now you get to see my inept attempt at being a parent."

"Hello, to you, too, Mick. And how's my little precious girl? Did you miss me?" Caitlin plucked the wet baby from his arms, relieved him of the empty bottle and marched toward the kitchen. At the doorway, she halted. "Oh, my!"

She looked back at Mick and burst into laughter.

With the sound of her adorable mirth still ringing in his ears, Mick retreated to the living room and sank into his chair. It was there that she joined him ten minutes later. Beth, clean and dressed in fresh clothes, sucked contentedly on a pacifier.

He gave Caitlin a rueful grin. "I'm *so* glad you're home. I had no idea what I was getting myself into when I said I'd watch her for two days. How did your show go?"

Her smile was beautiful to see. It warmed him all the way to the bottom of his heart.

"It went well. I sold enough prints to keep Beth in disposable diapers for—oh—at least a month."

"We missed you."

"I missed you, too. Was it really bad?"

"I don't know how you find time to do portraits and take care of her. You amaze me."

"Thanks, Mick. That means a lot." She paused as if she wanted to say more, but rose instead. "I'd better get going."

"There isn't any rush." He racked his mind for something else to say, for some way to keep her close a little longer.

"Beth and I'll be late for church if I don't get going.

Your mother's expecting me to help with the nursery today."

"Send the cab away. I can give you a ride to church."

Her face brightened. "I'd like that. If you don't mind?"

"Not at all. I'll be ready in two minutes. What do you think of Pastor Frank's little church?"

"Everyone at the Westside Christian Church has been wonderful. You can really feel God's grace in the way people care about each other there. I've been so blessed, and a lot of it is due to you, Mick."

"You found the Lord in your own heart, Caitlin."

"I know He was there all along, but you're the one who helped me to understand that. I don't know how I'll ever be able to repay that gift. You're a very special person."

Mick felt the heat rise to his face and knew he was blushing. "Have lunch with me after church, and I'll consider us even."

Was it too soon to let her know he had grown more than fond of her? He didn't want to press her or scare her off. He waited with his heart pounding in his throat for her answer.

"I have a better idea. I've invited your mother over for lunch. Why don't you join us? I've been learning to cook some new things. I'm making spaghetti today."

Mick blinked twice. His smile slipped a little.

Caitlin gave him a puzzled look. "You don't have to come if you don't want to."

"I want to," he answered quickly. Gazing at her, his heart grew light at the sight of the soft smile on her face.

Thank You, Lord, for bringing this woman into my

life. This time, I'm not going to lose her so please for-give this little white lie.

"The fact is," he said, "I love spaghetti."

Epilogue

Caitlin lifted Beth in her car seat from the back of a cab. Now seven months old, her tiny premature daughter had grown into a happy baby with a sweet smile and chubby arms and legs. The pediatrician's scale showed she was definitely making up for her slow start. Caitlin asked the driver to wait, then turned to see Mick sprinting down the steps of his house toward her. Her heart did this crazy flip-flop whenever she saw him. How much longer could she hide the fact?

She was head over heels in love with the guy, and he continued to act like a perfect gentleman. But sometimes she was sure he saw her as more than a friend, and Beth's mother. But if she were wrong, she might jeopardize the easy relationship they shared. For Beth's sake, she didn't want that to happen. Then yesterday something occurred that gave her renewed hope.

Mick reached her side in a few long strides. "Let me give you a hand." His voice seemed more breathless than the short trip to the curb warranted.

"Thanks." She handed him the baby's carrier and

tried to stay calm as she walked ahead of him up to the house.

"What time will you be back?" he asked, holding the door.

"I meet with my reading tutor until noon, then I'm working at the gallery until four-thirty, so let's say five. Will that be a problem?"

"Not at all. You know I'll keep Beth any chance I get. How's the new job going?" He set Beth's carrier on the floor.

"It's great. I put my nose in the air and pretend I know more about art than the people who come in to buy it. Most of them can't resist a piece if a snob tells them it's a steal."

"I can just see it. By the way, have I told you how proud I am that you are learning to read?" he asked quietly.

She looked up to find him staring at her intently. A flush heated her cheeks. "You are?"

"Yes, I am. That took a lot of courage."

Looking to her child asleep at her feet, Caitlin said, "No, it didn't. Not after what happened to Beth."

From outside, the cab honked once. "I guess you'd better get going," Mick said.

"In a minute. Woody came into the gallery yesterday. He told me something interesting."

"Oh, yeah?"

"I mentioned you were coming over for dinner Friday, and he said as long as I didn't feed you spaghetti I'd be safe."

"Woody has a big mouth."

"I've fixed you spaghetti a dozen times in the past few months. You've never complained once."

"Well—I—I like it the way you fix it."

"You do?" She smiled to herself. Yes, there was definitely hope for her. "Guess I'd better run."

He caught her arm as she turned away. "Aren't you forgetting something?"

His touch sent a tingling spiral of warmth through her. Her gaze moved from his hand to his face. "What?" she managed to ask in a husky whisper.

"A goodbye kiss—for Beth."

"She's asleep. I don't want to wake her." The tingling grew stronger. He pulled her closer.

"I could save one for her. For later," he suggested.

"Yeah…that's…a good idea." Caitlin didn't care that they weren't making any sense because as soon as his lips touched hers, she only wanted to keep on kissing him. Her arms circled his neck. All the joy she had kept hidden in her heart bubbled to the surface leaving her giddy with happiness.

The cab honked again, and Mick broke the kiss. Caitlin pressed her cheek against his chest and was thrilled with the feel of his strong arms around her.

"Whoa!" he said between deep breaths.

"If you say you're sorry, I'll hit you," she threatened.

He chuckled and kissed the top of her head. "Sorry? No, sorry wasn't what came to mind."

"Well, it should be!"

"Why should I be sorry?" Concern filled his voice.

"Because you took so long to do this!"

"Honey, I wasn't sure how you felt. I didn't want to rush you into anything that you weren't ready for. You've had so many big changes in your life."

She pulled back and gazed into his eyes. "I love you,

Mick O'Callaghan. I love you. I've been waiting months to tell you that."

"I love you, too. More than you'll ever know. I love you the way the night sky loves the stars. The way the sun—"

"Shut up and kiss me again."

He did, and quite thoroughly.

When they broke apart, he stroked her cheek with his knuckles, then slipped his hand behind the nape of her neck and pulled her close until his forehead touched hers. "Will you marry me?"

"Yes."

"No hesitation?"

"God brought you into my life so that we could be together as a family. Who am I to argue with a plan that good?"

"I don't deserve you, but I'm going to spend the rest of my life trying to make you happy."

"You do that without even trying."

Vaguely, she heard the cab honking. Mick held her out at arm's length. "Your driver is getting impatient."

She nodded in resignation. "I'm going to be late for class." In her carrier, Beth began to fuss.

"You could skip today," he offered.

Oh, how she wanted to. At one time, she would have, but Caitlin shook her head. "And set a bad example for our daughter? I don't think so."

"Say that again."

She wrinkled her brow. "I don't think so?"

"No, the part where you said 'our daughter.'"

Caitlin grinned, happier than she ever remembered being. "*Our daughter* is awake and if you don't have her bottle ready in two minutes or less, she'll scream the house down." As if on cue, Beth's crying rose in volume.

He let go of Caitlin and lifted the baby from her carrier. "She's a lot like her mother in that respect," he said with a knowing smile. Taking Caitlin by the elbow, he walked her to the door. "Tonight, you and I are going to have a long talk."

"Talk? I had more kissing in mind."

"Okay, a little of that, too." He gave her a quick peck, then a gentle push toward the street.

Reluctantly, Caitlin climbed into the cab. As it pulled away, she rolled down the window and blew a kiss toward the two people she loved more than anything in the world and gave thanks to God for the blessing He had showered upon her.

Mick's shout reached her as the cab turned the corner and she sank back onto the seat with a contented smile. She met the driver's eyes in the rearview mirror and sighed. "Wasn't that the most beautiful thing you ever heard?"

"I missed it, lady. What did he say?"

"He said 'Hurry home. We'll be waiting for you.'"

* * * * *

Dear Reader,

I hope you enjoyed *His Bundle of Love.* This was my first published novel. The story is one dear to my heart since I spent many years as a registered nurse in a neonatal intensive care unit much like the one where little Beth spent her first months. The drama, pain and joys of my work were sometimes difficult to put into words, but I wanted to portray Caitlin in a realistic light. Her feelings of guilt and helplessness are something many mothers experience when their baby is born prematurely.

While our nurses and doctors work tirelessly to save each child that comes to us, we also know that ultimately their fate is in God's hands. It is His strength that makes our work possible.

Also like Caitlin, there are people secretly coping with illiteracy. Sometimes it is because of learning difficulties as a child or because of language barriers, but shame and fear of ridicule often lead these people to live without the joy of reading the Bible, a restaurant menu, a good romance or a simple story to their grandchildren. I hope my portrayal of Caitlin's struggles has given you new insight into this growing problem.

Patricia Davids

THE COLOR OF COURAGE

A man's heart plans his way,
But the Lord directs his steps.
—*Proverbs* 16:9

To Joshua.
You're the best grandson in the world, honey.
Now get those grades up!
And to all the men and women serving
in the United States military.
Please accept my thanks and my humble gratitude.

Prologue

"Lindsey...I need you...to do this."

Standing beside her brother's hospital bed, Sergeant Lindsey Mandel fought back tears. She held his hand though she knew he couldn't feel it. "Danny, what if it doesn't work out?"

"You'll make it work...I know you will." He spoke quickly because he could only talk when the ventilator keeping him alive breathed out.

She brushed her hand over his close-shaven head. He was six years older than she was, thirty-one to her twenty-five. Today, he looked decades older than when she had seen him three months ago. "Don't give up, Danny. You can still get better."

A wry smile twisted his lips. "Who are you...kidding?" What might have been a chuckle turned into a cough and an alarm sounded from the monitor above his bed.

Frightened, Lindsey glanced to Danny's wife, Abigail, sitting on the other side of the bed. Behind her, the door to the room opened and a nurse in green scrubs looked in. The beeping stopped and Abigail waved the woman away. "It's all right. He just needs to stop talking for a while."

Admiring her sister-in-law's calm, Lindsey willed herself to relax. Abigail rose, moved to Lindsey's side and asked, "Why don't we go grab a cup of coffee?"

"Good idea…. Get her…out of here…for a while."

Abigail leaned down and kissed his forehead. "You just want us to leave so you can flirt with the cute nurses."

"Rats…you found…me out." He closed his eyes.

Lindsey leaned down to kiss him, too. "I'll be back," she promised.

He nodded, but his eyes remained closed. He looked so weary. When she turned to go, she heard him say, "I'm proud of you…First Sergeant…Mandel."

A heavy band of emotion squeezed her heart. "I'm proud of you, too, Master Sergeant Mandel."

"Don't spend…your whole leave…in this hospital."

"I'll spend my leave anywhere I choose," she retorted.

A fleeting smile crossed his face. "Headstrong… as ever."

"Because you raised me that way. Stop talking and rest."

Outside of his room, Lindsey paused as several men in uniform walked past, pushing others in wheelchairs. Everywhere she looked, the halls of Walter Reed hospital bustled with activity. Walking silently beside Abigail to a small waiting room, Lindsey waited until her sister-in-law filled two cups from the vending machine. Dressed in a pair of rumpled beige slacks and a wrinkled mauve shirt with her dark hair pulled back haphazardly into a silver clip, Abigail looked worn to the bone.

"The coffee isn't good, but I've had worse." She handed one to Lindsey.

Lindsey stirred a packet of creamer into the piping brew. "I can't believe Danny wants me to take Dakota away. He loves that horse. He's given up, hasn't he?"

Initially, her brother's will to live in spite of his injuries had helped Lindsey cope, but the unfairness of it all weighed on her.

Abigail gestured toward the red vinyl chairs lining the wall. "Why don't we sit down. I don't think he has given up. He's just coming to terms with the reality of the situation. The shrapnel severed his spine. He's a quadriplegic. After three months of therapy, he knows he isn't going to get much better."

"But there's still hope."

"The doctors think, with work, he'll be able to breathe on his own, but he'll never ride again. Yes, he loves that horse. That's why he wants you to take Dakota back to Fort Riley with you."

"Danny has lost so much already. It doesn't seem right to take Dakota away, too."

"Look around you, Lindsey. Most of the men and women who are patients here were wounded in action. Do you know what the majority of them say they want? To stay in the service. To get back to their units. Danny knows he can never go back, but he needs to do something positive. He feels he can do that by donating Dakota to your unit. You have no idea how excited he was when he heard about your transfer into the mounted color guard last year."

"Danny tried to transfer into the Third Infantry a number of times. The Old Guard has a mounted unit. Why not donate Dakota to them? That way Dakota would still be in Washington, D.C., and Danny could go and see him when he's better."

"I thought about that, but the Old Guard only takes black, gray or white horses. Your unit takes bays."

Brown horses with black manes and tails and minimal white markings were the traditional mounts of the Seventh Cavalry, the regiment Lindsey's unit portrayed at Fort Riley, Kansas. Dakota wouldn't be excluded for that reason, but less than half of the horses brought to the fort passed the intensive training requirements.

"What if he isn't suitable for us? Then what?"

"He's just got to be, Lindsey. Please, make this work. It would mean so much to Danny. He desperately needs something to look forward to, or else—or else I'm afraid to think about what could happen."

Chapter One

Leaning forward in the saddle, Lindsey patted Dakota's neck and tried to quell her nervousness. "This is it, boy. This is your final test. You have to get this right."

The dark brown gelding responded by tossing his head and pulling at the reins as if to show her that he was eager to get down to business. She couldn't help but smile.

Running a hand down her mount's sleek, muscular neck, she found the calmness she needed. She drew a deep, cleansing breath. The cool breeze carried the smell of dust, fallen leaves and the earthy scent of horses. Looking over the fence to the hills rising just beyond the road, she saw the golden-hued stone buildings of old Fort Riley where they stood nestled between oaks, elms and sycamores bearing the first touches of fall colors. Dakota pulled impatiently at the reins again.

"Okay, I'm the one stalling," she admitted. "I just want this so badly—for you and me, but mostly for Danny."

Each week her brother called for updates about Dakota's training, offering advice and pointers that she didn't really need but accepted anyway. Today, he would be waiting impatiently for her call. She intended to give him good news.

Reaching down, she checked that her saber and rifle would slide easily out of their scabbard and boot. The reproduction models of the 1860s U.S. Cavalry equipment were spotless after her careful preparations that morning. Even the brass buttons of her blue wool cavalry jacket gleamed brightly in the late-morning sun. She was as ready as she could get.

Be with us today, Lord, for Danny's sake.

At the touch of her heels, Dakota bounded forward. Together, they sailed over a series of low jumps, then slid to a halt and whirled back at the end of the field. On the return run, Lindsey drew her saber and headed into a series of poles topped with red and white balloons. As Dakota wove in and out, she slashed left and right, breaking as many as she could. He didn't even flinch at the loud pops or the swish of the sword cutting close beside him.

Four men on horseback waited for her at the end of the course. She slowed to a trot. Each man drew his saber and held it over his head with the tip pointing backward. One by one she struck their swords with her own as she passed close behind them, making the steel weapons ring with bell-like tones.

Sheathing her saber, she drew her pistols. Digging her heels into her mount's sides, she headed into the jumps again, this time blasting the balloons with her revolvers. Dakota raced on without faltering until they cleared the last hurdle. Only one maneuver remained.

Holstering her guns, she pulled the horse to a sliding stop and dismounted. Drawing her carbine rifle from its boot, she gave a low command, lifted Dakota's foreleg and pulled his head around. "Throwing the Horse" was the hardest movement for the young gelding to perform. Many horses refused the command.

To her relief, Dakota knelt, then lay down and rolled onto his side without hesitation.

"Stay down," she ordered. Stretching out behind his back, Lindsey rested her rifle on his shoulder and fired off three rounds. They were only blanks, but the sharp reports were as loud as if they had been real bullets. Dakota jerked slightly at the sound of the first discharge, but remained quietly on his side, providing lifesaving cover for his rider as cavalry horses have been trained to do through the ages.

As the echoes of the last shot died away, Lindsey rose to her feet and gave the command to stand. After scrambling to his feet, Dakota shook himself and waited patiently for her to remount. She wanted to throw her arms around his neck and hug him, but not now, not yet.

"Good boy, you were perfect. Just perfect," she murmured as she swung up into the saddle. She knew she was grinning like a fool, but she couldn't help it. After only three months of training, Dakota had proved himself worthy of a place in the elite Commanding General's Mounted Color Guard at Fort Riley. Danny would be so proud.

She returned to the end of the field, where other members of her unit sat on their horses. Beside the men, Captain Jeffery Watson, her unit commander, stood with his arms crossed and a faint frown on his face. Stopping in front of him, Lindsey saluted smartly.

"Well done, Sergeant Mandel."

"Thank you, sir."

The other men in her unit gathered around. "You looked fine out there." Private Avery Barnes was the next to offer his opinion. The dark-haired Boston native pushed his cap back to smile at her with a roguish grin.

"She always looks good. It was Dakota who looked great," drawled Corporal Shane Ross as he leaned over and patted the horse's neck. It was no secret the tall blond Texan was fond of all the four-legged members of the unit. He took as much pride in their skill as he did in the abilities of the horses' human partners.

"So, does this mean Dakota is in?" the third soldier queried. Private Lee Gillis, the newest enlisted member of the mounted color guard was watching their captain closely.

Captain Watson reached out to rub Dakota's cheek. "I will admit that I was worried when I learned that Dakota belonged to your brother, Sergeant."

Lindsey gave him a puzzled look. "May I ask why?"

"The last thing I wanted to do was to tell a wounded veteran that his horse wasn't suitable for our unit. Thanks to your hard work, I won't have to do that. I think Dakota makes a fine addition to our stable."

She nearly melted with relief as the men around her grinned and offered their congratulations. "Thank you, sir. I know I speak for my brother when I say that it is an honor to have Dakota accepted."

Crossing his arms again, the captain allowed a smile to soften his stern features. "As the icing on this cake, I wanted you all to know that I just received word from the Joint Task Force-Armed Forces Inaugural Committee that the Commanding General's Mounted Color Guard had been invited to participate in the upcoming Presidential Inauguration parade."

A cheer of excitement went up from the men. Lindsey grinned at their enthusiasm, "That's wonderful news, sir. Will Dakota be going, too?"

"Dakota has earned his place. And, of course, as the highest ranking non-commissioned officer, you will be the U.S. flag bearer for our unit. I'm sure you'll want to ride Dakota for that, but if you prefer another mount, I'll understand."

"Oh, no, I'll be riding Dakota." Wait until she told Danny. He would burst his buttons with pride.

"I've decided to include Dakota in Saturday's performance. Can he handle the crowd at a Kansas State football game?"

"I know he can, sir."

"Good. That will be all, Sergeant. Dismiss the detail." Captain Watson stepped back from the horses.

Lindsey saluted, dismissed the men and then let the overwhelming happiness sink in. Being asked to participate in the Inaugural parade was an incredible honor. She might be the one bearing the flag, but she would be carrying it for her brother. Giddy with delight, she headed for the stables. This was one phone call she couldn't wait to make.

Early Saturday afternoon, Brian Cutter walked along the edge of the Kansas State University football field in Manhattan, Kansas, leaning heavily on his cane. Halftime activities for the first home game of the year were well underway. The energetic shouts of cheerleaders dressed in purple and white, the noise from thousands of fans and the blare of the band was almost deafening. But Brian had his eye on a group of halftime performers who seemed unfazed by the clamor.

Beneath the goalposts at the north end of the field, six horses stood quietly waiting for their riders. The matching bays all sported dark blue blankets and Mc-Clellan Cavalry saddles.

He had watched them being unloaded behind the stadium and something in the third horse's gait had caught his attention. The gelding's walk wasn't quite right. Maybe it was nothing more than a bruise from the trailer ride, but he wanted to make sure the horse's rider was aware of what he'd seen. Until the horse was examined, it shouldn't be ridden.

The riders were out now and preparing to mount. Brian tried to hurry, but his bad leg was aching again. He didn't need a weatherman to tell him a cold front was moving in. Sharp pain shot through his hip and forced him to rely more heavily on his cane, making him feel much older than his thirty-two years. He arrived at the temporary picket line just as a young woman dressed in Civil War military garb was checking her saddle and girth.

"Excuse me, miss. I need a word with you." Brian knew he sounded curt and short of breath. She turned her attention on him and whatever he had intended to say flew out of his mind the way a yearling bolts out the barn door and into a summertime pasture.

She was a stunning woman. Even dressed in men's clothing did little to hide her feminine figure. The round, flat-topped soldier's cap with its short bill sat atop a mass of thick, auburn curls, but it was her eyes that captured his attention. An unusual color of silver green, they reminded him of the springtime quaking aspen near his Montana childhood home. A sprinkling of freckles dusted her cheeks and nose. Her lips were full and parted in a sweet smile.

"Yes?" she prompted. Something in her wide smile reminded him of Emily.

He pushed the ridiculous idea aside. His deceased wife and this woman didn't look alike at all.

The female soldier glanced to where the other members of the group were forming up. "You said you needed a word with me? I'm about to go on. Can you make it quick?" Her tone was polite but dismissive. He found himself irritated with her attitude.

"Your horse is lame. You shouldn't be riding him until someone looks at his right front leg."

She frowned, as if deciding whether or not to take him seriously. "Dakota seems fine to me."

To her credit, she walked around the animal and ran her hand down the horse's leg, then led him a few steps to observe him before giving Brian a frosty smile. "I don't see a problem."

"I saw it when he got off the trailer."

She swung up into the saddle with ease. Looking down at him, she managed a smile that wasn't quite polite. "We just finished a fifteen-minute warm-up. He's fine, honest. I'm sorry, but my men are waiting on me."

"You're doing the animal a disservice. You should pull him out of this exhibition until he can be examined."

"Thank you for your concern, but I know this horse better than anyone. If he were having trouble, I'd be the first to notice."

He stepped forward and laid a hand on the horse's bridle. "I'm a vet. I get paid to notice when an animal isn't moving right."

From the corner of her eye, Lindsey saw that several of the support men from her unit who weren't riding had begun to move toward her. If this guy didn't back off, he might find himself in a lot of trouble. A scene was the last thing she wanted. A big part of the CGMCG's mission was public relations.

"That may be true, but you aren't our vet. Thank you for your concern. Excuse me, I have to go."

"Suit yourself, but you'll only make him more lame. When he's limping tomorrow, remember that I told you so." He stepped aside to let her ride out and join her group.

Lindsey cast a look back at the rude man who seemed to think he had some say in what she did. He was a little above medium height and slender, but not skinny. His gray eyes were piercing and a perfect match to the leaden sky overhead. Nicely dressed in a gray tweed sport coat over a blue button-down oxford shirt and gray slacks, he wasn't a bad-looking guy. She might even have said he was kind of cute except for his personality. *Arrogant* wasn't a strong enough word to describe him.

Dismissing the man's brusque words, Lindsey forced herself to concentrate as the unit lined up for their first maneuver. Today they would begin the exhibition by riding two by two and taking four low hurdles as a column while their bugler blew "To the Gallop." It was a sure crowd-pleaser.

Lindsey patted Dakota's neck while they waited. They were the first horse and rider in a line of three. During his warm-up, he hadn't seemed as eager as usual, but they had been training hard the past few days and they were both tired. Still, he certainly hadn't been favoring either front leg.

"We'll take a few days' rest after today, fella. How does that sound?"

Actually, it sounded like a really good idea. She hadn't realized how tired she was until her conversation with the grumpy guy.

She glanced back once more. He was watching her from the picket line. The wind blew his shaggy blond hair this way and that. The frown on his face made him look intimidating. He was rubbing his right thigh until he saw her looking. He stopped and straightened. Still scowling, he walked down the sidelines in front of the stands. She couldn't help wondering why he needed the cane. Was it a recent injury?

Perhaps the last woman he had tried to bully had kicked him in the shin. The image made Lindsey smile until she realized how unkind it was. The man had only been trying to help.

Beside them, the bugle sounded and Lindsey leaned forward as they began at a walk, then advanced to a trot and then into a gallop down the football field. Making a turn in tight formation, the horses thundered toward a row of jumps set up on the fifty yard line. As they approached the first obstacle, she felt Dakota hesitate then jump off stride. With another horse close behind them, there was no room for error.

Something was wrong. Before she could pull out of line they were on the second jump. Dakota launched forward, and she relaxed. This jump was good. He was fine.

Only he wasn't. His knees buckled when his front feet hit the ground. He fell, catapulting her forward. Lindsey threw out her arms and tried to kick free of the stirrups. She had an instant to breathe a prayer for help before she felt the impact of her body hitting the ground, followed by Dakota's weight rolling over her.

Chapter Two

Brian watched in horror as the woman and her horse went down directly in front of him. The next rider was so close behind that he couldn't turn aside and his horse fell on top of the downed pair. In a split second the precision-riding exhibition had turned into a melee.

Brian hurried toward the pileup even as the other members of the team leaped from their horses to race toward their fallen comrades. One horse scrambled to his feet and limped a few feet away. His rider sat on the ground looking dazed, with blood oozing from a cut on his forehead. The first horse that had gone down was struggling to rise but couldn't gain his feet because the rails and the pillar of the jump were tangled with his legs.

Brian didn't see the woman until he reached the horse's head, but he heard her bloodcurdling scream. She was lying facedown with her right arm pinned beneath her mount. He grabbed the horse's bridle and spoke softly. "Easy boy. Miss, lie still."

She dug the fingers of her free hand into the thick turf. "Get…him…off!"

Each word sounded as if it was being torn from her throat by unbearable pain.

Brian sank to one knee, his stiff leg stretched awkwardly out in front of him and pulled the frightened horse's head into his lap. He knew the animal's struggles could inflict more injury on the trapped rider. He stroked the gelding's cheek until he quieted. "I can't move him yet. Help is coming."

"Is he hurt?" Her voice was muffled, but her concern was unmistakable.

"I can't tell."

She raised her head to look at him. Her hat had come off. Bright auburn curls framed her oval face in stark contrast to her frightening pallor. One cheek was smeared with dirt and scratches. When she met his gaze, her eyes gleamed with anguish and unshed tears.

"Why…isn't he…getting up?" She moaned, then bit her lip.

"His legs are caught in the jump pillar. Don't try to move. We'll get you both free in a minute."

Brian saw with relief that medical personnel were swarming onto the field. A soldier from her unit dropped to his knees beside her. "Lie still, Lindsey. How badly are you hurt?"

Lindsey dropped her head back onto the turf and sucked in a series of quick breaths. The scent of trampled grass and loamy dirt filled her nostrils. Dakota's weight was crushing her arm. Trying not to scream, she gritted her teeth and dug her fingers into the thick grass again. Screaming would only frighten the horse and make him struggle.

"I think my arm is broken."

"We'll get you free in a minute."

Please, God, let them hurry.

She felt Shane take her hand and she gripped it tightly. Don't scream, she thought, be brave. Act like a soldier. She squeezed her eyes shut and tried to stay calm. Only it was so hard. It hurt so much.

Through clenched teeth, she managed to say, "We tripped Avery…and Socks. Are they okay?"

Shane said, "Socks is up. Avery looks a little shaken, but I think he's okay. Hold on, kid."

"Dakota is all right, isn't he, Shane?" She panted, trying to block out the merciless agony. "Please, tell me he's all right."

"I'll check him over once we get you free." She recognized the voice as the grouchy vet who had suggested Dakota wasn't sound. If only she had heeded him instead of resenting his interference.

Pride goeth before a fall. Dear, Lord, why did I have to find that out the hard way?

She raised her head once more to look at him. "This is my fault. I should have listened to you."

Two men in EMS uniforms reached her, saving Brian from having to reply. For that, he was thankful. As they attended to Lindsey, soldiers from the unit quickly dismantled the jump and pillar, making room to move the stricken horse. With their help, Brian coaxed Dakota to roll off his side and onto his stomach, but kept the horse from rising. The move freed Lindsey's arm, but tore a scream from her that ripped into his heart.

While the medics worked on her, she kept asking about her horse. Others offered her reassurances, but Brian remained silent and avoided her pleading eyes.

When she was finally placed on a stretcher and taken off the field, he breathed a sigh of relief. She obviously cared a great deal for the animal. The last thing he wanted was to have her see the brave fellow put down.

For the horse was being brave. Brian's admiration of the bay gelding grew as the big fellow remained still in spite of the activity going on around him. Even though his eyes were wide, with the whites showing all around indicating pain and fear, he didn't struggle or thrash the way most horses would have.

When the area had been cleared, Brian gave up his position to a color guard member and rose awkwardly to his feet. He leaned heavily on his cane until he was sure he could take a step without falling on his face. He then moved to check out the horse's leg. There was already serious swelling below the delicate ankle joint. It didn't look good.

Several of the football officials in black-and-white striped shirts approached the group. One of them asked, "How soon can you get him off the field? We have a game to play."

"Your game will have to wait." Brian didn't bother to hide his ire.

The man Lindsey had called Shane remained crouched beside Dakota, keeping him still with a hand on the horse's neck. He ignored the officials completely. "Should we let him try to get up?"

Brian shook his head. "Not with the way that leg is swelling. We don't want him to do more damage. Let me get a splint on it first. My truck is parked outside the gate next to your trailers. It's white with College of Veterinary Medicine in purple lettering on the side. I've got first-aid equipment in there."

"Private Gillis will get what you need if you'll give him your keys."

One of the soldiers stepped forward and held out his hand. After giving him a detailed list of what he wanted and where it was located, Brian waited impatiently for the private's return. It seemed to take forever, but in reality only a few minutes had passed when the breathless soldier raced back and handed Brian his kit and the supplies he had requested.

With the help of the other color guard members, Brian soon had the leg encased in a cotton wool wrap. He applied a lightweight but sturdy aluminum splint and secured it with Velcro straps.

"All right, let him try and get up, but if he doesn't make it on the first attempt, we'll need to get a lift in here."

"We'll get one, but I sure hope we don't need it. Do you think he has a fracture?"

"I do, but I can't say for sure until we get him to the clinic and X-ray the leg."

With a gentle tug on the reins and some quiet words of encouragement, Shane urged Dakota to stand. After a brief hesitation, the horse lurched awkwardly to his feet. The crowd in the stands broke into loud cheering and applause. Brian looked up in surprise. He had forgotten he had several thousand onlookers watching his every move. No doubt some of his students were in attendance. Perhaps he'd present a pop quiz on splint application on Monday to check if they had been paying attention.

"If you can get your trailer in here, I think he can be loaded. The ride to the clinic isn't far. You'll need to wedge him in securely. I don't want him moving around at all."

"Thanks, Doc. It is *doctor,* isn't it? I'm Corporal Shane Ross." He held out his hand.

Brian took it in a firm grip. "Yes, I'm Dr. Brian Cutter, Professor of Equine Surgery for the College of Veterinary Medicine here at K-State."

"Then it sounds like Dakota will be in good hands. I sure hope this isn't a serious injury. The horse belonged to Lindsey's brother. She'll never forgive herself if he has to be put down."

Lindsey endured her examination at the fort hospital in stoic silence, answering between clenched lips only the questions posed to her. The pain she could deal with, but the fact that her arm hung useless against her side had her truly frightened. She couldn't even move her fingers—they had no feeling at all. Thoughts of Danny's paralysis crowded in her head. She fought down her rising panic as she addressed the physician attending her. "Sir, why can't I move my hand?"

The gray-haired doctor sat on a stool beside her narrow bed. "Your humerus is fractured, that's the bone in your upper arm. I'm going to splint it for now and send you to see an orthopedist. This is a nasty break."

Like she needed anyone to tell her that. "I still don't understand why I can't move my fingers."

"The nerve that controls hand movement runs in a groove along the bone of the upper arm. When a break occurs the nerve is often damaged. You should recover full use of your hand in a few months."

"Months?" She couldn't believe what she was hearing.

"You'll be on restricted duty until then. I'm giving

you some pain medication. Take it regularly, don't try to tough it out. I'll write some instructions on icing the arm and have the nurse make an appointment with the specialist. Do you have any questions?"

"How soon can I ride?"

"Not for at least eight weeks, maybe longer depending on the nerve damage."

She turned her face away, not wanting him to see the distress she knew was written there. The Inauguration was only ten weeks away. Did this mean there wouldn't be a trip to Washington, D.C., for her?

No, she wouldn't accept that. She wouldn't let her chance to honor Danny and all he had stood for pass by without a fight. Besides, even if she couldn't ride, Dakota could make the trip. Danny could still watch him striding down Pennsylvania Avenue. Every recent phone conversation with her sister-in-law had been filled with stories of Danny's determination to attend the parade in person.

"You won't be able to drive," the doctor said gently. "Do you have someone who can get you home?"

She nodded. Captain Watson was waiting for her. Exactly how she was going to get back and forth from her off-post apartment to her duty station until she *could* drive was a worry she'd put aside until later.

After they applied the splint and sling and gave her some pain medication, she managed to walk out of the room under her own somewhat shaky power. She found Captain Watson perched on the edge of a chair in the waiting area. He looked nervous and ill at ease. Her heart sank.

Bracing herself to hear the worst, she asked, "How's Dakota?"

Captain Watson sprang to his feet at the sound of her voice. "I haven't heard. How are you?"

She gave a rueful glance at her big blue sling. "My arm is broken. The doctor said I'll be on restricted duty for at least eight weeks, but it may be longer than that before I regain the use of my hand."

"If you're released, I'll drive you home."

"I need to find out how Dakota is."

"Shane and Lee are with him. As soon as they know something, they'll call. You are going straight home and that's an order."

"With all due respect, sir, I need to be with him. Please?" For a moment, she thought he was going to refuse, then his shoulders slumped in defeat.

"All right. They took him to the veterinary clinic at K-State. I'll take you, but only because I want to see how he is doing myself."

"Thanks. I just need to get these prescriptions filled and then I'm ready."

Half an hour later, they pulled up to the large, white stone buildings on the outskirts of the college campus that comprised the veterinary teaching hospital. Signs at the entrance to the driveway directed them to the Large Animal Clinic at the back of the building. Lindsey's pain pills were making her woozy, but she tried to hide it. She suspected that the Captain would drive her straight home if she showed any sign of weakness. Inside the building, they found the waiting area. The long, narrow room had panels of fluorescent lights across the ceiling that seemed to glare back painfully into her eyes from the shiny, beige linoleum floor.

The far end of the room was taken up by a wide reception desk where a pretty, young blond woman was talking on the phone. An American flag stood proudly displayed near the front of the desk. Lee and Shane were seated on the one of several mauve utilitarian chairs with bare wooden arms that lined the walls. They both rose and saluted when they caught sight of their captain. They were all still dressed in their exhibition uniforms and they were gathering odd looks from the staff and clients waiting with them.

Captain Watson returned the salute. "Any word yet?"

"No, sir. The doc hasn't been out to talk to us."

"That doesn't sound good." Lindsey settled gingerly on the couch but still took a quick, indrawn hiss as pain shot through her arm and shoulder. For a second, the room spun wildly and she grabbed hold of Shane's arm.

"Easy, kid. Are you sure you're okay?"

"The pain medicine they gave me is making me light-headed, that's all."

When the room stopped spinning, she looked up to see the vet from the stadium crossing the room toward them. His thick blond hair was still mussed, but he had traded his sport jacket for a white lab coat.

He stopped in front of the group, but his gaze rested on her. Frowning, he said, "I'm surprised to see you here. How's your arm?"

The unrelenting, throbbing pain was almost unbearable. "It's broken," she snapped. "I want to hear about my horse."

Shane laid a hand on her good shoulder. "Lindsey, this is Dr. Brian Cutter. He's been looking after Dakota. Doctor, this is Sergeant Lindsey Mandel. I don't think you two managed introductions with all that happened earlier."

Lindsey realized that she must have sounded rude.

The fiery agony in her arm wasn't helping her disposition. She rose to her feet and was pleased when she stayed upright. "I'm sorry, Doctor. I'm just really worried about Dakota. How is he?"

"He has a fracture of the plantar proximal eminences of the second phalanx."

Lee glanced around the group, then said, "Do you want to try that again in English for those of us who are new to all this horsey stuff?"

Dr. Cutter looked confused by Lee's statement. "I assumed you are all expert horsemen."

Captain Watson smiled in amusement. "My soldiers come from the ranks of ordinary units assigned to Fort Riley either as volunteers or as transfers. No previous riding skill is required. The men receive instruction from manuals used by Civil War cavalrymen. Private Gillis has only been with us a few weeks."

Lee grinned. "I'd never ridden a horse before then, so I still have a lot to learn."

Dr. Cutter managed a thin smile. "I see. All right, the animal has a fracture in one of the bones in the pastern joint between his ankle and his hoof."

If Lindsey hadn't been so upset herself, the look of horror on Lee's face might have been comical when he said, "They shoot horses for that, don't they?"

Dr. Cutter frowned sharply. "We are long past the days of shooting horses here. If an animal does have to be euthanized, we use humane methods."

Lindsey sank onto the chair's edge before her legs gave out and tried to gather her scattered thoughts. "What can be done for him?"

"You have several options but the best one is surgical arthrodesis. That means we fuse the joint using special pins and a bone graft from his hip. His recovery should take about four months."

Lindsey bit her lower lip. Dakota wasn't going to Washington, D.C. It was so unfair. Why had God given her a chance to do something special for her brother only to snatch it away?

Dr. Cutter raked a hand through his hair, giving Lindsey a clue as to why it looked unkempt. "Actually, I am hoping to begin trials of a new procedure using an experimental gene therapy that will speed healing, and this type of fracture is exactly the type I'm looking to study. Unfortunately, I haven't received grant approval yet."

The captain asked, "Will Dakota be able to return to duty?"

"A horse can lead a normal life after a fusion. Some horses have even returned to being successful athletes. There are, of course, risks involved, as with any surgery."

Lindsey studied his face, hoping to see some encouragement, but there wasn't any. "What are our other options?"

"We can try and cast the injury. You will need to keep him confined to a stall to rest the leg and hope for the best. He's a calm fellow, so he may do well, but the recovery time will be much longer. The only other choice is to have him put down."

Captain Watson crossed his arms over his chest. "What will the surgery cost?"

Dr. Cutter's scowl turned into a look of sorrow. He said gently, "Around fifteen thousand dollars, depending on how well he does. Complications can raise the cost considerably. The clinic typically asks for half of the payment up front."

"That much?"

"Or more."

Lindsey's heart sank at the expression on her captain's face. She knew even before he spoke what he was going to say.

"I'm afraid the unit doesn't have a budget to cover a medical bill like that. We are just scraping by as it is."

"The costs for the cast and follow-up will be much less than the surgery. Is that the treatment you want us to use?"

Quickly, she said, "Couldn't we at least try to requisition the money?"

"Of course I will, but with the budget cuts we've had, I doubt command is going to give up that kind of money for a horse. I'm sorry, Sergeant, I know how much he means to you. Can he be transported back to the fort, Doctor?"

"I'll need to keep him here for several weeks to make sure the cast doesn't need any adjustments and monitor his condition. After that, I'm sure the fort vet can manage his care. We'll need follow up X-rays to make sure the leg is healing, but those can be done at your stable."

Captain Watson held out his hand. "Thank you, Dr. Cutter. We'll leave Dakota here until you think it's safe to move him."

Brian shook the offered hand. "Our equine services here at the Veterinarian Medical Teaching Hospital are among the finest in the world."

It was his standard line when clients were worried about leaving their animals, but this time he was the one who was worried. The young woman was so pale he thought she might pass out at any moment. The horse must mean a great deal to her if she came straight from the hospital in her condition to check on him. Brian knew how much pain a broken bone caused.

She looked up. "Can I see him?"

"I'm not sure. You look like you need to lie down."

Rising, she faced him with determination blazing in her eyes. "I'm not leaving until I see him."

He looked to her captain, but all the man did was shrug and try to hold back a grin. Brian could tell he wasn't going to get any help from that direction. He shoved one hand into his lab coat pocket and nodded toward the door. "All right, but if you pass out, you'll just lie on the floor. I don't do humans."

"What a blessing for us," she shot back.

He turned away without voicing the comment on the tip of his tongue and led the way to the door beside the reception desk. She was stubborn, irritating and yet pathetic at the same time. So, why did he find her so attractive?

It made no sense. The sooner she saw her horse, the sooner she would leave. Then maybe he could forget those beautiful eyes and the effect they seemed to have on his common sense.

He held open the door, but she stopped so close beside him that he could smell a subtle scent like peaches in her hair. He was tempted to lean closer to make sure. He didn't, when he realized how unprofessional it would appear.

"What do you think his chances are without surgery?" she asked in a low voice as she stared at him intently.

Such beautiful, sad, green eyes. How could he add

to her sorrow? This was the part of his job he dreaded most. He glanced back at the other unit members. They were watching him intently. The words he needed to say stuck in his throat. He sought to give her some hope. "Every patient is different. Only time will tell."

"If he were your horse, what would you do?"

"If he were my horse and surgery wasn't an option?"

"Yes."

"I wouldn't let him suffer. I'd spend as much time as I needed saying goodbye, then I'd have him put down."

"No! I couldn't stand that." The last bit of color leeched from her face. She turned away, and the sudden movement caused her to lose her balance. His cane clattered to the floor as he caught hold of her.

Chapter Three

"**E**asy, I've got you." Brian held the slender form of the woman against his chest and struggled to keep upright for both their sakes.

Her hair did smell like peaches. Funny, he hadn't pictured her as the type of woman to use a scented shampoo. She struck him as a soldier through and through. It was intriguing to know she had a feminine side. He steadied himself by leaning back against the wall.

"I'm fine. It's just a dizzy spell," she said quickly.

The tight grip of her hand on his lab coat lapel told him more than words how much distress she was in. If there was one thing he knew well, it was the signs of pain—in animals and in humans.

A second later her fellow soldiers reached them. Shane swept Lindsey up into his arms without a moment's hesitation and Brian had no choice but to let him. Seeing how easily and gently the man lifted her made Brian acutely aware of his own physical shortcomings. Years ago he had carried Emily just as effortlessly. He thought he had come to terms with his disability a long time ago, but obviously he hadn't.

His limp was only a small reminder of the tragedy his carelessness had brought about. In one night he had lost both his wife and their unborn child. His mistake had cost him everything he held dear and he had only himself to blame.

Lee quickly retrieved Brian's cane and handed it to him. Taking the polished wooden staff, Brian nodded his thanks and ignored his feelings of inadequacy. He extended one hand indicating a door a few steps down the hall. "My office has a sofa in it. You can lay her down in there. Do you want me to call nine-one-one?"

"No." The weak murmur came from Lindsey.

"Are you sure?" Shane asked, looking uncertain.

She nodded as if more words were beyond her.

"This way," Brian said, and moved to open his door. Inside his office, he swept up a few papers and books from the brown leather sofa to make room for her.

Shane lowered her gingerly, then stood back. None of the men seemed to know what to do next. Brian cleared his throat. "Would you like a drink of water?"

"Yes, please," she whispered. She still hadn't opened her eyes.

Brian grabbed a paper cup from the dispenser on the wall and filled it from the bottled container beside it. Moving back to her side, he settled himself on the edge of the couch. He lifted her head and held the cup to her lips. She took a sip then sighed. He lowered her head back to the cushion.

She opened one eye. "I thought you didn't do humans."

"I make exceptions for women dressed in Civil War uniforms."

For an instant a smile tugged at the edge of her lips

before she winced in pain again. "How fortunate can a girl get?"

"Are you sure you don't want me to call nine-one-one?"

"Two rides in an ambulance in one day would be more than my ego can take. I don't suppose you have some really good pain medicine handy. The pills they gave me at the hospital don't seem to be doing much."

"I've got a ton of good stuff here."

She opened both eyes. "Really?"

He nodded. "I've got drugs that will knock out a horse."

"Ha-ha. What does a girl have to do to get some?"

He was pleased to see her smile return, along with a bit more color in her cheeks. "She would need to grow two more legs and a tail."

"Are you telling me I don't measure up as one of your patients?"

"I never said anything of the kind. It's actually nice to be able to ask a patient where it hurts and get an answer."

"It hurts exactly where my horse landed on me."

"From my vantage point that looked like almost all of you."

"You are so right. If you aren't going to supply me with drugs, can you help me sit up?"

Brian didn't have a chance to help her. Her comrades were more than happy to oblige. He moved out of their way. When she was sitting upright she waved them aside. "I'm okay now. Don't hover."

The men backed up, but they didn't look ready to leave her to her own devices.

Brian filled the cup again with more water and

handed it to her. To his relief, he saw that her color was almost back to normal. "If you won't go to the hospital, at least go home and lie on your own sofa so I can have mine back."

Taking the offered drink, she sipped it and nodded. "Once I see Dakota, I'll do just that."

All of the men began to protest together, but she ignored their scolding and stood. Cradling her arm, she winced but remained steady on her feet. "Show me the way, Dr. Cutter."

"He's down the hall, through the doors at the very end and in the first stall on the left."

He felt slightly cheated as he watched her fellow unit members guide her out the door, one on each side with her captain close behind. It wasn't that he wanted her to fall into his arms again. Of course not. He simply wanted to make sure she was all right. But that was what her friends wanted, too, he reminded himself. And they certainly had more of a right to care for her than he did. He was nothing but a stranger.

The thought brought back his frown. He was more than that. He was the man who might have to put her beloved horse to sleep.

Early Monday morning, Lindsey begged a ride to the Large Animal Clinic with Shane. When they arrived, they saw Lee and Avery just going in. It seemed that all of them wanted to check on Dakota before they started their duties for the day.

As she approached Dakota's stall, Lindsey was surprised to see Captain Watson had arrived before them. He was deep in conversation with Dr. Cutter.

When her captain caught sight of them, he smiled.

"I've been talking to the doctor and he has a way to do surgery on Dakota at a reduced cost to our unit."

Lindsey's heart jumped as happiness surged through her. "How is that possible?"

Dr. Cutter cleared his throat. "Using a new surgical procedure that I've developed—I told you about it the other day. Dakota's break is exactly the sort I'm hoping to trial this repair on."

"But you said it wasn't an option." Shane frowned at the doctor.

"I received notice of my grant acceptance this morning. It is an experimental procedure. If Dakota is entered in the study, it will mean I will have total control of his care. My fees and much of his care will be covered, but that will still leave the bill for his boarding and supplies that the army will have to pay. Unfortunately, the grant isn't a large one."

"We can raise the money if we have to," Captain Watson said.

"Absolutely," Avery chimed in. "He's one of our own. We won't let him down."

"Of course not," Lindsey added. She had a little in savings. She would gladly give the money to help pay for Dakota's care. "When you say experimental, Dr. Cutter, do you mean there is a chance that this won't help him?"

"There is that chance, but I have every confidence that he will do well. If my procedure works, he could be out of his cast in as little as six weeks."

Six weeks. That meant Dakota would be able to travel to Washington, D.C., in time for the Inaugural parade. Lindsey's joy danced like a soap bubble in the wind.

Thank you, God, for giving Dakota into the care of this man.

Captain Watson turned to Brian. "You have my permission to enroll Dakota in your study."

"Excellent. There are some forms you'll need to sign. If you'll follow me to my office, we can take care of that now."

When the two men walked away, Lindsey opened the gate and stepped into the stall where Dakota stood quietly. He rested with his head lowered and his eyes half-closed. His dazed look worried her until she realized that they would be giving him pain medication and sedation to keep him quiet.

"Hey, Dakota. How's it going, fella?"

His head came up at the sound of her voice and he whinnied softly. Delighted at his responsiveness, she stepped closer and began to rub the side of his face. "Don't worry about a thing. Dr. Cutter is going to fix you up in no time."

Behind her, Avery said, "Do you think an experimental surgery using gene therapy is the best way to go?"

Shane moved up to stand beside Lindsey. Reaching out, he patted Dakota's neck. "It sounds a bit like science fiction to me."

"I have faith that it will work. I think the Lord brought us here at exactly the right time for Dakota to get this care."

Lee shoved his hands into his front pockets. "It would have been better if He had kept Dakota from breaking a leg in the first place."

Lindsey didn't answer. This, too, had to be part of

God's plan, but like Danny's injury, it was a bitter pill to swallow.

She ran her hand over Dakota's soft nose. Her faith was being tested. The words of Psalm 9:9 echoed in her mind.

The Lord is a refuge for the oppressed, a stronghold in times of trouble.

In her time of trouble, had she turned to the Lord as she should have? Perhaps that was what she was being shown. Little by little, she let go of the anger she had been holding on to.

I will try to listen with my heart for Your wisdom, Lord. Show me the path and I will do my best to travel it.

Three days later, Lindsey was struggling to use the can opener with her left hand when the doorbell rang. She stared at the container of corn that refused to fit in the opener. "We're not done. I won't be defeated by an inanimate object."

She noticed the faint smell of burning mozzarella, but the oven timer said her frozen pizza still had five minutes to go. The doorbell chimed again. Leaving the tiny kitchenette of her apartment, she crossed the living room to the front door. She opened it and stared in stunned silence.

"Surprise!" Her sister stood on the stoop with a suitcase resting beside her. Speechless, Lindsey could only stare.

Looking uncertain, Karen said, "Say something."

Shaking herself out of her stupor, Lindsey enfolded Karen in a one-armed hug. "Hello. This certainly is a surprise. What are you doing here?"

Karen returned the embrace. "I'm just visiting."

Taking a step back, Lindsey studied Karen's face. Her sister had always been the rebel in the family. Her shaggy, cropped blond hair haloed a heart-shaped face. Danny often said Karen's big brown eyes and ready smile could make men weak in the knees, but her quirky wit was her greatest gift. Karen had a smile on her face now, but it didn't erase the sadness that lurked in the depths of her gaze.

"From the look on your face I'd say this is more than just visiting. What brings you all the way from Washington, D.C. to Kansas?"

"Invite me in and I'll tell you about it. Oh, you poor woman, look at you. You're covered in bruises."

"Having a horse roll over you will do that. Honestly, Karen, why are you here? Did Dad send you to take care of me?"

"No, although I'm sure he would have thought of it in a day or two," Karen added quickly.

"You should be helping Abigail and Danny. I can take care of myself."

Karen cleared her throat. "I just needed to get away for a while. I'm sorry I didn't call. Showing up and surprising you seemed like a good idea at the time, but it wasn't, was it?"

Lindsey reached out and took her hand. "It's a wonderful idea. You know I'm always happy to see you. Come in and tell me why you're here."

Karen's face brightened. "Later. You don't happen to have some tea, do you?"

"I'll tell you what. If you can wrestle open a can of corn for me, I'll make you a whole pot."

Inside the apartment, Karen followed Lindsey into the kitchen. At the entrance to the small room decorated with rooster wallpaper and rooster border above the few white cabinets, Karen paused and stared up at the large rooster-shaped clock on the wall. The avocado-green refrigerator began its noisy rumbling and Lindsey gave it a sharp shove to silence the sound. After a moment, Karen said in a tentative murmur, "You have a…nice place."

"Don't even try to be kind. It's a rental and it's cheap. I don't care what the wallpaper looks like as long as the roosters don't crow."

"What a marvelous attitude."

"I'm easy, what can I say?"

Karen wrinkled her nose. "I think something's burning."

"Oh, that's just my lunch. Can you help me with this? I damaged a nerve when I broke my arm and my hand is completely useless. I can't feel a thing." Handing her sister the offending can, Lindsey indicated the opener with a tilt of her head.

Karen's eyes widened in alarm. "Dad never mentioned that you had no feeling in your arm. Is it permanent?"

Lindsey rushed to reassure her, knowing she was thinking about Danny's condition. "No, the specialist said in two or three months I'll be as good as new. Dad didn't say anything because I haven't told him."

"Does this mean you won't be riding in the Inaugural parade?"

"I haven't given up hope. I've got two months and then some to recover."

"Lindsey, you should let the family know you might not be there. Everyone is making plans to attend."

"By everyone, I assume you mean Danny, too?"

"It's all he talks about to the nurses and therapists who come to the house. He is so proud of you. He insists he'll be there to watch you and Dakota in person."

"Now you know why I don't have the heart to say anything yet."

"Yes, I guess I do," Karen said softly.

Lindsey hesitated. "There's more."

"What?"

"Dakota broke a bone in his front leg when we fell."

"Oh, no!"

"He's had surgery and we think he is going to be fine."

Karen pressed a hand to her forehead. "No wonder Abigail thought there was something you weren't telling us the last time you called."

"I didn't want to keep secrets, but I wanted to be sure of things one way or the other before I gave Danny that news."

"Are you sure of things now?"

"Not really."

"Lindsey, you have to tell him. Danny is stronger than you think. If you could only see the way he tackles his therapy sessions. He's able to raise his right shoulder now and he's up to almost two hours off his ventilator each day."

"He's working hard because he has a goal to reach. That is exactly why I'm not going to tell him yet. I can't risk taking away his motivation. I have faith that Dakota and I will both be in Washington, D.C., and Danny will be strong enough to be there to see it."

"I don't agree with you, but I won't say anything for now."

"That's all I'm asking. Thank you. So, are you going to open that can for me or not?"

Smiling, her sister tossed the can in the air and caught it again. "I'll give it my best shot."

Karen successfully extracted the yellow kernels from their stubborn metal prison while Lindsey put the kettle on to boil. A minute later the oven timer rang. Karen snatched up the pot holder before Lindsey could reach it and opened the oven. She pulled out a cookie sheet with a small pizza on it.

"This is your lunch?"

"That and the corn."

"Pizza and corn?"

"It's not as weird as it sounds."

"Yes, it is. You need something healthy." Karen set the cookie sheet on top of the stove.

"This is healthy."

"At least drink some milk with it." Karen pulled open the refrigerator door.

Lindsey winced. She knew there wasn't any milk. In fact, there wasn't much of anything in her fridge except a half-empty bottle of ketchup and one lonely dill pickle in a jar. "I haven't had a chance to get to the commissary."

Karen shut the door and frowned at Lindsey. "Since when?"

"Since before the accident."

"Obviously, it's a good thing I stopped by. Eat while I have a cup of tea and then I'll drive you to wherever you need to go."

Lindsey used a spatula to transfer her overly crisp pizza to a plate and then set the plate on the table. "You don't have to run errands for me."

"I can see that no one else is. Where are the tea bags?"

The kettle began to whistle. After finding a cup and filling it with hot water, Karen joined Lindsey at the table. Waiting until after her sister had fixed the tea, Lindsey asked, "Are you going to tell me why you're here?"

Karen raised her cup to her lips and blew on the steaming brew. She took a sip and set the cup down. "This is very good tea. What kind did you say it was?"

"Earl Grey, and don't change the subject."

Taking a deep breath, Karen closed her eyes and said, "It's Dad."

"I don't understand."

Karen leaned her elbows on the table. "He won't stop fixing me up. I'm only twenty-one but all of the sudden he acts like I'm the only chance he'll ever have for grandchildren. There has been a steady parade of guys who just *happen* to stop by our apartment. He's driving me crazy."

"I'm sure Dad—like the rest of us—is having a hard time adjusting to Danny's condition. Do you want me to talk to him?" Lindsey took one bite of her pizza, then pushed the unappetizing concoction to the side.

"Thanks for the offer," Karen said gently. "But I'm hoping a little separation will be good for both of us. That's why I'm at your door begging to stay and nurse you through this injury. And before you say no, I did discuss this with Abigail. She can do without me for a few weeks. Please, can I stay?"

Lindsey patted the orthopedic brace and sling the specialist had fitted her with. "I don't need a nurse, but a roommate who can grocery shop and run the can opener will be a welcome addition until I'm out of this contraption."

"Honey, that sounds great." Karen's relief was evident.

"Don't be too sure. This is a one-bedroom apartment and that means *you* get the sofa."

Karen's tinkling laughter was music to Lindsey's ears. During their frequent and lengthy phone conversations, the sound of happiness had been sadly lacking in her sister's voice. Danny's injury had affected everyone. They were all trying to find a new "normal" for the family.

Picking up her teacup, Karen said, "Roommates pay rent. What's space on a lumpy couch going to cost me?"

"The use of two good arms and your skill as a chauffeur. If you really don't mind driving me, I'm dying to get over to the university to see how Dakota is doing. But what about school? Can you afford to take the time off?"

Setting the white cup down, Karen picked up her spoon and began to stir. "I had already decided to take a semester off. I couldn't concentrate in class. There was no use flunking out on top of everything else."

Seeing Karen's grief made Lindsey acutely aware that her baby sister was dealing with a lot more than their father's matchmaking. "I wish I was closer so that I could help, too."

Rising, she carried her plate to the counter. After dumping the remains of her uneaten lunch in the trash, she laid the dish in the sink and turned on the water. It was then that she felt Karen's hands on her shoulders turning her around.

Tears blurred Lindsey's vision and she loathed the

fact. She had tried so hard not to cry. "I hate that this has happened to him."

"I know." Karen's voice was low and brimming with emotion. "But Danny believed that protecting his country was more than a job. It was something that he knew in his heart he had to do."

Lindsey squeezed her eyes shut against the pain that swallowed her heart and made it hard to breathe. "But the price…was too high. He is the best…and the brightest…and this seems so cruel." The words, when she finally managed them, were ragged and broken between her sobs.

"I know you love him. He knows it, too."

"I haven't told him that often enough."

"You don't have to. He sees it. I wish I could hug you, but I'm afraid I'll hurt you."

"My left side is fine," she hiccuped. To prove it, she embraced Karen with one arm and the two of them clung together as they wept.

From the corner of his eye, Brian caught the fugitive movement. Without looking up from the grant application on his desk, he said, "Isabella, don't chew on that pencil."

The culprit ignored him.

He tried injecting more menace into his tone. "Isabella, I said, no!"

The oversize brown lop-eared rabbit perched on the corner of his large desk chose to disregard his warning. She pulled her prize from the purple Wildcat mug he used to hold his writing utensils. Settling the yellow number two under one paw, she began to nibble it to bits.

"You little minx." He rose from his chair and scooped her up, tucking her firmly under one arm. He stuck the pencil back in the mug with numerous other scarred victims.

He drew a hand down her soft, furry body, then scratched her favorite spot behind her left ear. "Why do you always zero in on the new ones?"

Lifting his cane from the back of his chair, he crossed the office and pulled open the door. Seated at the reception desk was one of the young students who doubled as a part-time secretary for him.

"Jennifer, will you put Isabella in her outside cage, please?"

"Of course. What did you do to get banished from Dr. Cutter's desk this time?" she asked the rabbit as she took her from Brian.

"The usual," he answered.

"Ah, pencil nibbling, were we?" She, too, scratched the bunny behind the ears.

"I can't break her of the habit."

"You could try switching to pens."

"I like pencils. They let me change my mind as often as I need to."

"So does the delete key on your computer."

"It isn't the same."

Rolling her eyes, Jennifer headed for the outside door and said, "Therein lies your problem, Doctor. You have to learn to say what you mean the first time."

Brian turned back to his office. He knew how to say what he meant, but he was often accused of being too gruff. Whenever he needed to draft a letter or a grant application, he worked and reworked the words until they seemed soft and polite enough. Pencils worked best for the task. After he had the tone he wanted, he typed his work into his computer. Some might say he was making twice the work for himself, but he still preferred his tried-and-true method.

Certainly, his upcoming lecture on pastern arthrodesis for the Equine Surgical Conference in January was no exception. It was an honor to be asked to speak and he wanted his address to be perfect. He intended to rework it until he was completely satisfied. Fortunately, the college bookstore had an excellent supply of the large yellow legal pads he liked best.

Back at his desk, he put aside his work on his presentation for the moment and opened the file on Dakota. The gelding wasn't doing as well as he had hoped. The surgery itself had gone well, but the big horse seemed to be having more pain instead of less. That wasn't encouraging. A knock at his door caused him to look up. Jennifer stood in the doorway minus the rabbit.

She motioned toward the folder he held. "Is that the file on the army horse? I was wondering how he was getting along."

"I'm not happy with his progress. Even with the medication he's getting, his respiratory rate and pulse rate are higher than they should be. The staff has been reporting that he's restless and he isn't eating well."

"None of those are good signs."

A smile twitched at the corners of his mouth, but he held it back. "So you *have* been paying attention in class. Will wonders never cease?"

She blushed and looked chagrined. "Is there anything else you need, Doctor? If not, I'm going to take off."

He hadn't meant to offend her, but before he could form the right words to apologize, she was out the door.

Of all the females he had known in his life, only Isabella never seemed to care what tone he chose or how gruff his words sounded. If only more women had her tolerance, his life would be a lot easier.

Before he had a chance to dwell on the current poor state of his interpersonal skills, Jennifer opened the door again. "Doctor, Sergeant Mandel is here to see you."

The sudden rush of pleasure he felt at hearing her name unnerved him. He tried unsuccessfully to stifle his excitement.

"Show her in."

"Yes, Doctor."

She nodded but before she could close the door, he said, "Jennifer, I was teasing earlier when I made that remark about you paying attention in class."

"You were?"

"Of course. I think you have an excellent future in the surgical field."

She looked doubtful. "You do?"

"I do."

She flipped her long blond hair back over one shoulder. "Wow! Okay, but next time you're kidding someone, Doc, you should smile."

"I'll certainly try to do so."

Chapter Four

Jennifer held open the door so that Lindsey and another young woman could enter Brian's office. Lindsey appeared much more rested today, he noticed when she walked in. To his surprise, she looked even prettier than he remembered. She radiated an energy that seemed to warm a place inside him that he had almost forgotten existed. Like the dancing flames of a campfire on a cold night in the mountains, she left him longing to draw closer to the warmth.

Wearing a camouflage shirt and matching pants with black boots, she looked every inch the soldier—except for the blue sling on her arm. She certainly wasn't the type of woman that normally would have interested him. Since his wife's death he couldn't think of a single woman he had been this attracted to, but there was something about this woman that intrigued him. He didn't care for the sensation. When he realized he was staring, he shook off the fanciful notion and rose to his feet. "Please come in, Sergeant Mandel. Have a seat."

Her smile flashed briefly and was gone. She appeared hesitant as she sat on the sofa. "Thank you for seeing us. This is my sister, Karen Mandel."

He nodded to the woman dressed in jeans and a tailored navy shirt. "I'm pleased to meet you."

Addressing the two of them, he said, "As you may know, Dakota's surgery went very well. He's tolerating his cast, which is always a good thing. In two to three weeks he'll go back to surgery to have the pins removed and a new cast applied."

"Yes, Captain Watson has been keeping us informed," Karen said softly.

"Captain Watson is the reason we're here," Lindsey began. "Because of this arm, I've been reassigned to light duty. My orders are to oversee Dakota's care."

"I don't understand."

"I'll be doing what I can to help here. Karen has asked to be involved, as well, and Captain Watson has agreed. Providing we're not in the way, of course."

"Are you sure you're fit to work?"

"I can do whatever is needed, within reason."

"Working around sick and injured horses can be dangerous."

She leaned toward him, her smile changing from hesitant to forced. "I know that, Doctor."

Of course she did. She was the one with the broken arm. Retreating into his most professional demeanor, he said tersely, "That is something you can't forget when you are here. Given your injury, I'm not sure what you will be able to do."

Her smile disappeared. Did he only imagine the room grew a few degrees cooler?

"I've been taking care of the unit's animals for over a year, Doctor. All sixteen horses plus the two mules.

I'm sure I can manage to be of some help to you and your staff, even if all I do is muck out the stall. I know how to follow orders."

He sat back in his chair, registering her annoyed tone. She was upset, but he didn't know why. "Very well. I'll let the staff know that you'll be…assisting here until the horse is fit to return to the army's stables."

"Thank you," she snapped back.

"May I see Dakota now?" Karen asked, glancing between Lindsey and himself with an odd gleam in her eyes.

"Certainly. He is through the double doors at the end of the hallway. His stall is the first one on the left down the first aisle. I need to speak with my secretary and then I'll join you at his stall in case you have any questions."

Brian tucked the file under his arm and escaped from his office. Fortunately, Jennifer had already left for the evening. He laid the file down and raked his fingers through his hair as he tried to gather his scattered thoughts.

The idea of having Lindsey in the clinic every day was a disturbing one. Without understanding exactly why, he knew she would interfere with his work. She would be a distraction he didn't need, but he couldn't see how to prevent her from coming.

Her request wasn't all that unusual. Animal owners occasionally spent long hours with their pets and he'd rarely had to forbid access. Besides, she had her orders. There wasn't much he could do about it except try to avoid her.

Even as the thought occurred to him, he knew that avoiding Lindsey wasn't what he really wanted.

* * *

"Take a deep breath, Lindsey," Karen said after Dr. Cutter had left the room.

Lindsey tried to swallow her irritation with the man. "I'm a soldier in the United States Army. I've been trained to do my duty no matter what the circumstances. A broken arm is no treat, but I've been assigned to Dakota's care and I'll follow my orders. It doesn't matter if he thinks I can or not."

"He's only trying to be kind."

"I didn't hear a lick of kindness in his tone."

"Maybe not in his tone, but I certainly saw it in the way he was looking at you."

Lindsey turned to Karen in stunned surprise. "You've got to be kidding."

"I don't blame you for being interested in him. He's attractive and he loves animals—what's not to like?"

"I certainly don't see the same thing you do. Come on, I'll show you where they're keeping Dakota."

Leaving his office, Lindsey glanced toward the reception area. Dr. Cutter was standing at the desk, but his cute young secretary was nowhere to be seen. Not that it mattered what his hired help looked like. It certainly didn't matter. Not to her, Lindsey decided.

Leading Karen toward the recovery stalls, Lindsey waited until they were through the door before she spoke her mind.

"The man is rude and he's arrogant and I am certainly not interested in him."

"I'll admit he needs a little fine-tuning, but he has potential."

"Potential for what? No, don't tell me or you'll sound like Danny. He never lets up with the 'When are you

going to settle down?' speech. Once he got married, all
he could think about was how I needed to find someone, too."

Being in love had made him forget the painful scenes
from their childhood, but Lindsey never forgot them.
She knew better than to believe she could make an army
career and a marriage work. Her own parents had been
perfect examples of how wrong it could get. The endless fights, the recriminations, the tears and the broken
promises she had witnessed as a child were things she
couldn't forget. As far as she was concerned, it was better not to have children than to subject them to the kind
of childhood she'd had.

Marriage was hard enough without adding frequent
reassignment, long separations and dangerous duty to
the mix. Danny had been willing to take the chance that
he could make it work with Abigail, and maybe they
would be one of the blessed ones, but Lindsey wasn't
willing to open her heart up to that kind of pain.

At Dakota's stall, Karen leaned through the rails
and ran a hand down the big bay's nose. "Whatever
made you think I was talking about settling down?"
she quipped. The sly smile she cast Lindsey over her
shoulder made Lindsey want to shake her.

Leaning on the gate beside her sister, Lindsey decided to set her straight. "For your information, I have
no intention of starting a relationship. The army is my
life. I love moving to new posts, seeing new places,
meeting new people."

"Why? I hated it as a kid."

"I guess the good Lord gave me the wanderlust gene.
Our father had it and the next generation of Mandels
will probably have it, too."

"Except that there won't be a next generation of Mandels." Karen's soft words brought the extent of their loss into sharp focus.

Lindsey slipped her good arm over Karen's shoulders. "I'm sorry. That was a thoughtless comment on my part. We can pray that Danny and Abigail may still be blessed with a child."

"I guess we can't spend our lives trying not to say or do something that will remind us of Danny's condition. I think it has been hardest on Dad. He really wanted to see the traditions of the family carried on."

"I know. That's my duty now. I'm going to carry on and serve with distinction."

"Why? Hasn't our family given this country enough?"

"You don't mean that."

"I've often wondered if you aren't trying to live the life you think Dad wanted without finding out what kind of life you wanted for yourself."

"This *is* the life I want," Lindsey insisted.

Karen sighed in defeat. "As long as that's true then I'm going to be happy for you, but you don't have to do it alone. Sharing life's burdens is part of the reason God made it so that two could become one."

Reaching out, Lindsey tweaked her sister's nose. "When did you get so wise?"

"I think it was in Philosophy 101 my freshman year."

Lindsey smiled at her joke. The door to the hallway opened and Brian walked over to join them. "Do you have any questions, ladies?"

Lindsey turned to study Dakota. The cast extended from above his knee to below his hoof. It was wrapped in bright blue cloth.

"As you can see," Brian began, "he is wearing special shoes on his other feet to accommodate the height of the cast and keep him standing level."

"Why is that important?" Karen stepped over to make room for Brian to stand between herself and Lindsey.

"It will help prevent undue stress on his other legs. Horses carry most of their weight on their front legs. Unlike dogs or cats, they can't stand three legged for long. We want him standing evenly, but not moving around much."

"I expected to see him hanging from a sling."

"We do use slings if we have to, but usually that is for bone breaks in the upper legs."

Lindsey drew her hand down Dakota's neck. "He doesn't look as if he feels well. Is he in pain?"

Brian flipped through the chart that was wired to the front of the stall. "I've ordered pain medication. He's been receiving regular doses. His X-rays show the pins are in excellent position. He should recover full use of the leg."

Lindsey finally voiced the question she had been afraid to ask until now. "Do you believe Dakota could be healed enough to walk three miles with a rider by late January?"

"It might be possible, but I can't give you a guarantee."

"He has to be fit by then. If it's possible, then that's good enough for me. If you do your best for him, prayer will take us the rest of the way."

"I'm sorry, but why does he have to be fit by late January?"

She turned to face him. "Because the Commanding

General's Mounted Color Guard will be participating in the Inaugural Parade in Washington, D.C., on January twentieth and Dakota has to be there."

Brian shook his head. "That's only ten weeks away."

"But is it possible?"

"If this new treatment works as well as I hope, perhaps, but you certainly can't count on it."

"He'll make it. I know he will. I have faith."

"Unrealistic expectations will only lead to disappointment, Sergeant Mandel."

"Aren't you a man of faith?" Karen asked.

"I'm a man of science, especially when I'm in this building. Dakota's progress will be carefully documented and analyzed to help gauge the success or failure of this therapy. I believe in what can be documented. I believe in results that I can quantify."

Lindsey studied his face and noticed again the stormy gray color of his eyes. Was he always so serious, she wondered? What did he do for fun? Was he married? She glanced at his hand. He didn't wear a ring.

The direction her speculations were heading surprised her. She forced herself to stick to the important topic at hand. "Has this therapy been tried before?"

"In small animals like rabbits and dogs, but surgical repairs on horses are very different. Their weight is the biggest issue. The stress load on the healing break can be very high. That can lead to repair failures, especially if the horse is high-strung and doesn't remain quiet."

"Dakota isn't high-strung, but he loves to work. I'm not sure how he'll take being confined."

"He has been quiet for us."

Lindsey ran a hand down Dakota's back. "I still think

he is in pain. Isn't there something else you can do for him?"

"I don't want to add additional medications unless I have to. If he is having pain, I'm sure it will decrease soon."

Lindsey noticed that Brian seemed ill at ease. He didn't make eye contact with her. He kept a tight grip on the chart as if it was some type of shield. His superior manner began to irritate her. Either he wasn't really concerned about the horse or he didn't think she knew what she was talking about. Why did everything this man said rub her the wrong way?

"It isn't fair that Dakota has to suffer because you don't want to mess up your study."

"I assure you we don't let our patients suffer needlessly."

"How can I be sure of that?"

His eyebrows shot up in surprise. "Are you questioning my judgment?"

"Of course not, Dr. Cutter," Karen interjected calmly. "I'm sure Dakota is getting the best of care."

"He is. If you intend to make yourself useful, Sergeant, I suggest you see my secretary first thing in the morning. She will supply you with a list of duties and the times we have set up for Dakota's treatments. I'm sure she'll be able to find something you can manage with one arm."

With that, he left the two women and exited through an outside door.

Lindsey cast a sideways glance at Karen. "You're right, he has potential. He has the potential to annoy me to no end. He isn't the only one who knows about horses. There's more than one way to treat pain in an animal."

"You aren't giving him a chance, Lindsey."

Maybe Karen was right. "I know, but something about him gets to me."

"Why?"

"Maybe it's because he never smiles. When he's talking to me, I get the feeling that he'd rather be somewhere else. Maybe I just don't like that he was right and I was wrong the day Dakota fell."

Karen studied Lindsey for a long moment. "I think there is more to your feeling than dislike. You know, I think I'm going to enjoy watching the two of you butt heads."

As he pulled into the driveway of his home, Brian decided he had wasted enough time thinking about Lindsey Mandel. Why should he care if she didn't trust his judgment? Except that he did care.

Stepping out of his pickup, he opened the small carrier on the front seat that Isabella rode in and lifted her out. "Come on, girl, we're home. Let's see what the mailman left for us."

With Isabella tucked under one arm, he made his way up the walk to a small white cottage with dark blue shutters. The house stood on a tall hilltop overlooking the Kansas River as it wound its way eastward out of the plains and through the rolling hills of eastern Kansas before it emptied into the wider Missouri River near Kansas City.

The view was one of the reasons he'd purchased the place. It reminded him a little of the view from his parents' home in Montana. Although the Kansas hills didn't compare to the foothills of the Bighorn Range, the view and the smell of the tall cedars and pine trees beside the front door always took him back to the mountains—back to where he and Emily had been so happy together. He let the grief pour out now that he was alone. The ache in his heart had become a part of him. It never left.

From the brass mailbox, he extracted a handful of envelopes and flyers. "Looks like you're in luck, Isabella. There's lots of junk mail."

He tucked his mail under his chin as he struggled to unlock the door without dropping the rabbit, the correspondences or his cane. Once inside, he closed the door, then set his pet on the floor. She scampered to a box beside his chair and hopped in.

Brian crossed the hardwood floor and sank with a sigh of relief into his recliner. He rubbed his thigh for a minute before leaning back and raising the leg cushion. From the table beside him, he picked up a silver-framed photo. In it his wife, Emily, smiled sweetly back at him. He had taken the picture of her when they were on their honeymoon. It had been her favorite.

"You wouldn't believe the day I've had," he began. "My newest patient has the most irritating owner."

He often told Emily about the challenges of his job, but tonight he found he didn't want to tell her about Lindsey. It didn't seem right.

The silence of the house closed in, filling him with an aching sense of loss that never faded. He didn't deserve to have it fade. He had killed the woman he loved and nothing would ever change that fact.

He set the picture aside and picked up his mail. Sorting through it with Isabella was also a nightly ritual.

The flyers from the local grocery stores he tossed into the box with the rabbit. She instantly began to shred them into pieces. Next to nibbling pencils, paper shredding was her favorite pastime and one he allowed her to indulge in only in her special plastic bin.

It hadn't taken him long to learn that a bored rabbit could be very destructive. He'd had to replace the wooden handle on his recliner twice during the first year Isabella lived with him. Fortunately, he had discovered the cure before any other items of furniture had to be replaced. If he gave her something fun to do, she was as good as gold.

He turned over the first envelope. "Hey, we might have won ten million dollars. It says all we have to do is enter to win. Like that will happen."

He crumpled the envelope and contents and tossed it into the box. Isabella attacked the new paper with glee. The next two envelopes were bills. He considered tossing them in with the rabbit, but decided against it. Telling the electric company that his rabbit had ripped up the bill wasn't likely to keep the lights on if he missed a payment. The third envelope bore the logo of the United Jockey Club Research Foundation. Knowing the UJC Research Foundation had donated nearly one million dollars in grants the previous year, he quickly tore open the letter.

"Listen to this, Isabella. They are interested in my new study. They're calling it groundbreaking work and their grant committee is interested in learning more. They plan on sending a representative to hear my presentation and review my data at the Equine Surgical Conference in January."

Brian glanced at his pet, but she was only interested

in her game. Picking up Emily's picture, he studied the face he knew so well.

"Do you know what this means, honey? If they back my project, I won't have to beg money and cut corners to make ends meet at the clinic for years."

Things were falling into place for his work. The conference would bring the best and brightest equine surgeons in North America to hear him, along with a dozen other speakers. If he could persuade Equine Equipment to have one of their ambulances on display he might be able to convince the college advisory board to actively pursue purchasing one for the clinic. Just the thought of the horses who could be saved by being safely transported to the clinic brought a lump to his throat.

He held Emily's picture close to his heart. "I wish you were here to share this with me."

After a while, the unshed tears stopped stinging the back of his eyes. Little by little, the silence of the house lulled him into sleep. As he did almost every night, he fell asleep in the chair with Emily's face pressed to his chest and her presence filling his dreams.

Sometime later, Brian awoke with a start. He had been dreaming, but not about his wife. The woman he saw riding toward him on a bay horse had had red hair and green eyes. Disgusted with himself for letting Lindsey intrude into his personal life, he got up and put Isabella in her cage before making his way to his bedroom.

Sleep was a long time in coming. When it did arrive, he dreamed about his childhood—about lying on his back and looking up through the green aspen leaves and feeling the whole world was full of promise. Green leaves that were the same color as Lindsey's beguiling eyes.

* * *

Early the next morning, Brian walked into the entrance of the Large Animal Clinic with a half-formed plan for the day. Isabella lay firmly tucked in the crook of his arm. He hadn't slept well and he was sure it showed. Thoughts of Lindsey had kept him up until long into the night.

Why on earth he couldn't stop thinking about her was something he couldn't understand. And she was going to be here again today. The plan he had come up with for dealing with her was to make rounds as early as possible and then barricade himself in his office. It wasn't much of a plan, but it was all he could come up with at three-thirty in the morning. Looking up, he was surprised to see Jennifer crossing the room quickly to meet him.

"Good morning, Dr. Cutter. Let me take Isabella outside for you."

"Thank you, but I'd like to have her with me in the office today." He had a feeling he was going to need her comforting presence to help keep him on track and not think about Lindsey. Sergeant Mandel, he corrected himself.

Jennifer gave him a tight smile and took Isabella out of his arms. "I'm just going to take her anyway. You know how loud voices upset her."

"Not that I've ever noticed." Puzzled, he tried to make sense of Jennifer's tense demeanor. "Are you planning on yelling at me? Whatever I did, I apologize."

Gathering the oversize rabbit into her arms, Jennifer said, "It's not something *you* did."

"I'm glad to hear that. Oh, before I forget, Sergeant

Mandel is going to be in today. Give her a list of her horse's treatments and let her do what she can to help."

Jennifer's look held a trace of pity. "She's already here. I'm just going to be outside with Isabella for a while."

With the rabbit in her arms, Jennifer hurried out the door.

Shrugging off her peculiar behavior, Brian limped toward his office. So Lindsey was here already. That shot down the first stage of his plan. He would certainly encounter her when he made rounds. As he was unlocking his door, two of the fourth-year students came down the hall from the holding area. They stopped short at the sight of him, then hurried past with their heads down. He glanced after them with a puzzled frown. What was going on? Whatever it was, he wasn't ready to face it until he had at least one cup of coffee.

Inside his office, he set out the carpet-covered boxes Isabella used as steps to reach the top of his desk and her favorite spot—an old towel in a shallow tray at the far corner. After starting the coffee, he held his cup under the brewer until it was full, then slipped in the pot. The first sip of the scalding hot, dark brew was exactly what he needed. Taking a second sip, he set the cup on his desk, put on his lab coat and headed down the hall to check on his patients.

The first thing he noticed when he entered the stall area was the large group of students clustered outside Dakota's stall. He hurried forward. If something had gone wrong and he hadn't been called, heads were going to roll.

Chapter Five

"What's going on here?" Brian's irate bellow caused the students hovering outside Dakota's stall to part like the waters of the Red Sea.

Lindsey winked at the elderly woman inserting hair-fine acupuncture needles along the horse's neck and turned to face the oncoming battle. She even managed to put on her sweetest smile. "Good morning, Dr. Cutter."

"What is the meaning of this?"

"Allow me to introduce Mia Chang. She is a horse acupuncturist."

"I can see that. What is she doing with my patient?"

"I am relieving his pain and the great stress he is suffering from," Mia said with a slight bow in Brian's direction before turning her attention back to Dakota.

"It's quite remarkable, actually," one of the students ventured. "His pulse and respirations are back to normal and he has a brighter look in his eyes after only twenty minutes of therapy."

"Yes, he is feeling much better. This will help strengthen the healing bones." Mia pulled a handful of pellets from her pocket and held them under Dakota's nose. He nibbled them up with relish.

"What is that?" another student asked.

"My special blend of healing herbs with a little honey to sweeten the taste. I can give you the recipe if you like."

Lindsey didn't think Brian's scowl could get any deeper, but it did. He leaned forward on his cane. "Ms. Mandel, may I speak to you privately in my office?"

His cold, clipped words told Lindsey not to expect a thank-you. He turned and left without waiting for her answer. She followed him down the hall, fully prepared to fight for Dakota's well-being. It was obvious that the horse was feeling better and she wasn't about to let Dr. Grumpy change that.

Inside his office, he indicated she should take a seat. She preferred to stand, but the thought that he might be uncomfortable or in pain standing made her hasten to sit on the sofa. She wondered what the carpeted boxes stacked up beside his desk were for but decided not to ask.

Brian sat with a tiny sigh of relief that made her glad she hadn't insisted on confronting him while he was on his feet. Knowing that the best defense was a good offence, she launched into her prepared speech. "I'm sure you're happy Dakota is obviously in less pain. I'm certainly glad Miss Chang was able to come on such short notice."

"Sergeant Mandel—"

"Her techniques have worked wonders with some of our other horses. My father was stationed in South Korea when I was ten and I saw firsthand the value of their nontraditional medicine."

"I appreciate your desire to help your horse, but—"

"I knew you would. That's why I asked her to come. She is also a trained veterinary assistant."

"Miss Mandel—"

"Her fee will be covered by me personally, so you don't need to worry about that."

"Lindsey, please."

The husky way he said her first name sent an unexpected shiver along her nerve endings and blotted all other comments from her mind. She waited in silence for his next words. For a heartbeat he simply stared into her eyes and she wondered what he was thinking.

He looked down and took a deep breath. When he looked up again he didn't appear angry, just tired. She had the craziest urge to take his hand and offer him comfort or at least a cup of hot tea.

"Lindsey, do you know how many horses are put down each year in this country for a simple fracture of the leg? I don't mean just the expensive racehorses or show horses, but horses that belong to ordinary people who love them?"

"No."

"Hundreds. Maybe even thousands. I've euthanized far too many of them myself. Do you know why I put most of them down?"

"Because the breaks can't be healed?"

He shook his head. "No. It would be easier to take if that were true. Money is the single biggest reason a horse gets put to sleep. The average person simply can't afford to spend fifteen thousand dollars on an animal's medical care. But what if that cost could be cut in half?"

"More horses could be saved?" she ventured, feeling less in the right with each passing minute.

"Maybe hundreds more each year. That is what I'm trying to do with the study Dakota is in. I'm trying to prove this therapy will cut healing time and therefore the cost of a break significantly. But to do that I have to have absolute hard facts. Facts that can be reproduced in other horses time after time. Facts that can be published in a reputable journal."

She listened to him with a sinking sensation. "You're trying to tell me I've altered the study."

"I'm trying to make you understand how important this work is. I don't want to see your horse in pain any more than you do. But I have to know that what I give him to help won't interfere with what I'm trying to accomplish."

"I don't see how simple acupuncture can interfere with your gene therapy."

"In all likelihood it won't. But what if he begins to run a fever? What if the herbs he ate today react with the antibiotics I have to give him? Just because a substance is a natural remedy doesn't mean it can't have side effects. The fewer variables I have to deal with, the better."

"I understand what you're saying. I wasn't thinking about how important Dakota's recovery will be for others. I was only thinking of how important it is for me. I'm sorry if I've interfered with your work."

She looked so contrite that Brian was tempted to smile. "I want your help and input. All I'm asking is that you discuss your ideas with me first. Can I have your promise on that?"

Nodding, she said, "Of course."

"Good. This is a teaching hospital and acupuncture is gaining ground as a legitimate treatment for pain and lameness in horses. The students seemed quite interested in Miss Chang's techniques. I may see about including her in our guest lecture series next semester."

"She would like that."

The sudden silence between them seemed weighted with tension and expectation.

"Will you be staying long today?" he asked, not wanting to see her leave in spite of his earlier plan.

"I have to get back to the post. Karen and I are helping organize a fund-raiser for the cost of Dakota's care that isn't going to be covered by your grant. The men and women at the fort have been overwhelming in their offers of support. We've already raised nearly a thousand dollars just with donations from the troops and their families."

"That's amazing."

"Dakota is an army horse. He's no different than any other injured soldier. We take care of our own."

"I'll see you tomorrow then."

"Tomorrow our unit is traveling to Medicine Falls for their centennial celebration. I'm on restricted duty so I won't be riding, but I'm going along to help the ground crew and do the PR part of the job."

"PR?"

"People are always curious about the unit. We are ambassadors for the army, as well as a living history exhibition. We put on a really good show if you ever get the chance to see it."

She rose to her feet. Brian headed for the door and held it open for her. "If you need any help with the fund-raising, please don't hesitate to call me."

Brian could hardly believe what he heard himself saying. The words were out of his mouth before he even had a chance to consider the ramifications. He didn't get involved in the lives of the people who brought their animals to him. He certainly had no intention of getting involved with someone as impulsive and outspoken as this woman. His life was quiet and orderly. It was exactly the way he wanted it. At least it had been until he arrived at work this morning.

Lindsey cocked her head to the side and grinned at him. "Thank you. I may take you up on that offer."

As she walked out the door, he realized with a sinking sensation that she might do just that.

Ten minutes later he looked up from his work at the sound of a timid knock. The door opened and Jennifer peeked in. "Is it safe to bring Isabella in?"

"For her, but maybe not for you."

She pushed the door open and stepped in with his pet draped over her arm. "Why? What did I do?"

"You took off faster than the proverbial rabbit at the first sign of trouble. I'd like to remind you that you work for me. The next time there's trouble brewing in this office, I expect you to be the first one to inform me of it."

"Was there trouble this morning?" she asked, giving him a wide-eyed innocent stare.

He glared back at her, but she simply put Isabella on the floor. The rabbit made a beeline for the steps he'd set out and quickly climbed to his desk. She paused in front of him long enough to have her head stroked, then she hopped to the far corner and settled herself in her favorite spot.

"I like Sergeant Mandel, don't you?" Jennifer asked, still lounging in the doorway.

He felt the heat of a blush creeping up his neck. "I haven't given it much thought."

"You spent a long time with her in here this morning."

"We were discussing Dakota's plan of care."

"I just noticed that the two of you seem to be getting along rather well when she left."

"Because we weren't shouting at each other?"

"That was my first clue, but I think it was your offer to help with fund-raising that clinched the deal. Is she married?"

"That is none of our business. She is a client."

"She's a cute client, even if she does wear combat boots. Don't you think so?"

Exasperated with her prying, he said, "Is there something you wanted, Jennifer?"

"Oh, right. The people who make that horse ambulance are on line one. I knew you'd been waiting for their call."

He picked up his phone, but hesitated before pressing the blinking button. It was his hope that he could convince Equine Enterprises to allow the school the use of one of their new ambulances for an extended period of time. The need to transport injured horses safely was no different than the need to transport people. He wanted to raise awareness of the issue and hopefully convince the school's board to purchase one. His first challenge would be to persuade Equine Enterprises to loan him the vehicle, only *his* PR skills weren't the best.

The image of Lindsey pressing his case popped into his mind. *She* was a persuasive person. She would be hard to stop when she had her mind set on something.

"Do you need anything else, Doctor?" Jennifer asked.

"No, thank you. Oh, wait. How far away is Medicine Falls?"

"It's about an hour northwest of here."

"Can you pull up a map on your computer?"

"Yes," she drawled. "But why would you want to go to Medicine Falls?"

That was a very good question, and one he wasn't sure he knew the answer to, except that Lindsey would be there.

"I have Saturday off. I heard they were having their centennial celebration. I thought I might take a drive up that way."

As answers went it was pretty weak, but it was the best he could do on the spur of the moment.

The look she gave him said louder than words that she wasn't fooled. "If you don't want to give me a straight answer, I can take a hint."

"Fine." He waved his hand in dismissal before she could probe deeper into his motives—motives he didn't understand himself. He picked up the phone and, with renewed determination, launched into his plea for the loan of an ambulance.

When he finished his call, he had the satisfaction of knowing the company was at least considering his proposal. He had begun putting away his papers and shutting down his computer when Jennifer came in and held out a thick manila folder.

He scowled at her. "What's this?"

"The map you asked for and the file on the Shetland pony you did hip surgery on last spring. Remember fat Dolly? The family was from Medicine Falls. I thought since you were going out that way, you could do a follow-up visit to see how they're getting along. Besides, it's a better excuse than saying you thought you'd take a drive. The whole, 'I just happened to be in the neighborhood' line is kind of lame, but this way you can back up your story with a straight face."

"I don't need an excuse to go for a drive. This is a free country."

"I believe Sergeant Mandel will agree with you when you see her in Medicine Falls. Did you know they're putting on a performance tomorrow?"

"And how do you know that?" Had she been eavesdropping on his conversation with Lindsey?

"Avery told me. He drove Lindsey out here this morning. Isn't his accent the cutest thing?"

"I hadn't noticed."

She smiled. "Don't lose that map."

Brian opened his mouth to tell her he had changed his mind about going, but instead found himself saying, "Jennifer, I'm beginning to see you in a whole new light."

"Finally. I've worked here, what, two years? And this is the first time you've noticed that I'm a genius?"

"I was going to say I've begun to notice that you're rather devious."

"Oh. Well—only when I know it will help."

"Will help what?"

With a long-suffering sigh, she said, "Never mind. You'll figure it out.

Lindsey watched from the running board of the unit's candy-apple-red pickup as eight other members of her unit led their horses out of the matching red trailer emblazoned with the unit's name. The CGMCG was preparing for their last event of the season. The busy schedule of travel and performances over a five-state area would begin again in late spring. Usually by this time all the horses and riders were looking forward to a much-needed rest, but this year rest wouldn't be on the duty roster until after the trip to Washington, D.C., in late January.

All the men were looking forward to participating in the Inaugural parade with excitement and pride. The talk of late had been about little else.

Looking up, Lindsey noticed that the flawless blue sky overhead promised beautiful weather for the little town's special day. Even the relentless Kansas wind seemed to be taking a break. The flag jutting out from the ornately carved limestone post office hung quietly with barely a whisper of a breeze to ripple the Stars and Stripes. The stark branches of the trees that lined the streets radiating out from the town square were the only sign that fall had descended. The sun on Lindsey's shoulders was hot enough to make her glad she was wearing the unit's red T-shirt and not one of the dark wool uniforms.

"Lindsey!" Avery called from the rear of the truck where he was throwing a saddle on a gray gelding named Tiger. "My saber is in the back of the trailer. Can you get it for me?"

"Sure thing." She stood and moved toward the trailer, taking the time to speak softly so that all the horses knew she was passing behind them. In the trailer, she opened the door of the storage compartment and pulled out Avery's sword.

"Is that real?" a small voice asked behind her.

She turned to smile at two young boys who were obviously brothers. They boasted the exact same shade of ash-blond hair and identical pairs of bright blue eyes. The oldest boy looked to be about ten years old. She pegged the younger one at six or seven.

"Yes, this is a real saber. It's a replica of the type used by the U.S. Cavalry back in the Civil War. If your parents take you over to the rodeo arena after the parade, you can see how they are used."

"Wow," said the littlest, wide-eyed youngster.

"Told you it was real," his brother said smugly.

"But soldiers don't ride horses anymore. They drive jeeps and tanks," the younger one stated with a glare at his older sibling.

Lindsey vividly remembered arguing with Danny over silly things when they were kids. Her memories of him were good ones, she realized. For the first time since his injury, those memories didn't bring pain, but rather a quiet joy.

"You're right," she said. "Modern soldiers do drive jeeps and tanks, but there are special units like mine that are keeping the traditions of the Old West cavalry alive. We are real soldiers and this is our job."

"Cool."

"Way cool. Can I hold the sword?"

She shook her head. "I'm afraid not."

Clearly disappointed, the young pair took off back into the crowd forming along one side of the town's main street.

Lindsey carried the saber to Avery. He tipped his head in the direction to the boys. "New recruits?"

"Maybe. The little one would have been more impressed if you had a tank instead of a horse."

"Boys and their toys."

"You know that's true," Lee Gillis said as he led

his horse over to stand beside them. "How's the arm, Lindsey?"

"Not painful as long as I don't bump it, but I still can't feel my fingers or use my hand. I won't be riding for a while. Who gets to stay behind with me?" Lindsey asked, looking over the line of saddled horses.

"Captain said to leave Socks with you. He's been a little nervous since the fall and we don't want him acting up in the parade. The Captain is riding Tiger."

"That's fine. Tiger will be happy he doesn't have to wait here while the rest of the boys run off and have fun."

Having one of the horses waiting beside the trailer was a good way to get people to stop and visit. Tiger, as the oldest and most calm four-legged member of the unit, usually had that honor.

Lee frowned as he looked toward the gray gelding standing alert at the end of the picket line. "I heard Captain Watson telling someone that it was time to retire Tiger."

If that was true, Lindsey was happy Tiger would be able to participate today. "He's been with the unit for more than fifteen years. That's a long time."

"What will happen to him?" Lee asked.

Shane patted his shoulder. "Don't worry. We'll find a good home for him."

Once the unit was mounted and ready to proceed, the grand marshal, who was also the mayor and the local grocery-store owner, fired a starter pistol into the air and the small-town parade began. The floats might have been put together on hay wagons, but they had been decorated with as much care and pride as any Rose Bowl entry.

All along the street people rose from lawn chairs and curbsides to stand as the unit rode past with the flag unfurled and the horses' hooves clattering in unison. Farmers, mill workers and townsfolk alike took off their hats. Most placed a hand over their heart and, beside them, their children did the same. Here and there in the crowd, a few men saluted and Lindsey knew with certainty that those proud few knew exactly what price freedom asked.

As the parade moved away, Lindsey waited beside the pickup prepared to answer questions from people who were interested in military history, who were horse lovers, or who were simply curious about the unit. It was a part of her job that she truly enjoyed. Once the last float left the staging area, she didn't have to wait long before a few people began to gather around and venture close enough to pose inquiries.

It always touched and humbled her when people came up just to say they were proud of America's military or to say thank you for serving their country.

Lindsey had just finished telling several high-school-aged girls about what it was like to serve in the army when she spied a familiar figure walking toward her. Her heart gave a funny little leap. "Dr. Cutter, what a surprise. What are you doing here?"

"I was in the neighborhood…what I mean is…"

Lindsey thought she detected a blush on his tanned cheeks.

He cleared his throat and began again. "I was doing a follow-up visit on one of my patients and I remembered that you mentioned your unit would be here today. I thought I would see firsthand what type of work your horses do. It will help me better evaluate when Dakota will be fit to return to duty. I had a glimpse of what you do the day you fell, but I'd like to see the whole thing minus the pileup."

"I'd be delighted to have you attend our exhibition. When the men return from the parade route, we'll travel over to the rodeo arena and set up there."

"Great, I'll see you later."

"I'll look for you."

Brian found the rodeo arena without difficulty. It wasn't long before the parade ended and those planning on attending the Little Britches rodeo began filling the seats. Sitting on the wooden planks of the grandstands, he watched for Lindsey. He spotted her along with the other unit members when they rode into the arena on the back of a flatbed truck loaded with rails and jump pillars. Dressed in red shirts and matching red ball caps, they went into action with military precision.

Lindsey was in charge of carefully measuring the distance between jumps and directing their setup down the middle of the course. As she was doing that, other men marked off and placed a series of upright poles along one side. Yet another soldier walked onto the field carrying a huge bunch of red, white and blue balloons. Soon they were divided up and secured to the jump pillars.

Once they were finished, the truck pulled out of the gates and Lindsey, breathless and bright eyed, joined Brian in the stands.

"Are you ready to be amazed and awed by fabulous feats of skill and daring?"

"I'm ready." The words were barely out of his mouth before rock music began blaring from the loudspeaker.

The gates opened and eight horses and riders thundered in and circled the enclosure at a gallop. By the time they had made their second pass around the area, Brian was entranced.

Dressed in blue period uniforms and with banners waving, the detachment looked exactly like a piece of Western history come to life.

At a shouted command that he couldn't quite understand, the group came to a halt, head to tail. A second shout of orders had the horses wheeling into a single line. Like the sweep hand of his watch, they all turned in tight formation. The inside horse was actually prancing backward as they kept a straight line until a full circle had been made.

"Pretty good, huh?" Lindsey leaned forward and grinned at him.

"Very impressive."

"You ain't seen nothing yet."

She was right. The line broke apart and reformed into a column of twos, then charged down the course flying over each balloon decorated jump. At the end, they split apart and galloped back to the start where they formed into twos again.

A unit member on foot walked into the arena. He carried a red-painted milk jug in one hand. Stopping near the center, he turned to face the mounted men and held up the jug in his hand.

Lindsey leaned toward Brian. "In the old days they used melons to practice this."

All the soldiers drew their sabers. Suddenly, the first horse exploded off the line and charged toward the man on foot. With precision that Brian couldn't believe, the rider impaled the jug off the man's hand and bore it aloft

like a trophy until he reached the far end of the arena.
Wheeling his horse around he held his saber and the jug
out to his side and raced back. A second horse and rider
charged down the field and speared the jug from the
extended saber as they flew past each other. All eight
riders repeated the maneuver, transferring the jug from
sword to sword at a full gallop without a single miss.

Brian looked at the small woman seated beside him.
"Can you do that?"

"Sure. Piece of cake."

"Now *that* is amazing."

"There are about seven historical mounted color
guards in the United States military, but we are one of
the few that train in combat techniques. Here, there is
no distinction between women and men and the jobs
we perform."

"Did you know that the equestrian sports are the
only Olympic event in which men and women com-
pete as equals?"

"I did. Do you know that we have our own cavalry
competitions?"

He shook his head. "No, but after watching this, I'd
like to see one."

"You'll have to wait until next September. I forgot
to ask, how is your other patient doing?"

He looked momentarily perplexed. "My other patient?"

"The one you came here to see?"

"Oh, right, that patient. Dolly is getting along very
well. Her owners say she is doing everything she was
doing prior to surgery and more. That consists mainly of
eating a lot and giving rides to their grandchildren when

they visit on the weekends. I've advised them on a better diet for her and stressed the need for more exercise."

"Like having the grandkids over twice a week?"

"Three times a week would be better."

She laughed. "It was never hard to convince me to ride a pony when I was a kid. Hopefully, Dolly's family is the same way. Do you have any children?"

The smile that had been lurking in his eyes vanished. His face turned stone cold so quickly that Lindsey was taken aback.

"My wife and our unborn child died in a car accident several years ago."

His voice held the hard edge she had noticed the first time she had spoken to him. Back then, she had wondered if his leg was giving him pain. Now, she knew his suffering went much deeper than that.

She laid a hand on his arm. "I'm sorry for your loss."

He stood up. "Thank you. If you'll forgive me, I just remembered that I have to get back to the clinic."

Surprised, she said, "Aren't you going to stay for the rest of our performance?"

"Another time, perhaps. Good day, Sergeant Mandel." He made his way out of the grandstands, leaning heavily on his cane.

Lindsey watched him walk away and couldn't help but think that he looked like a very lonely man, even with the festive crowd milling around him.

Chapter Six

"Do we have everything?" Karen pushed a cardboard box in on top of a stack already filling the front passenger's seat of the Jeep nearly to the roof. The backseat was equally loaded.

"If you don't, that's too bad," Shane said, holding open the door for her. "Nothing else will fit in here."

"There's still room for a few more things," Karen insisted. Dressed in faded jeans and a pink cable-knit sweater with her blond hair pulled back in a ponytail, she looked much younger than twenty-one.

"Only because I'm not sitting in the driver's seat yet. Once I'm in, we won't have room for a toothpick. I may have to eat a box or two of cookies just to reach the gearshift."

She thrust her hands on her hips. "Don't you dare eat anything unless you pay for it, soldier."

"Yes, ma'am," he replied with a good-natured grin.

Lindsey listened to the exchange with a little smile playing on the edge of her lips. It didn't require mind-reading skills to see that Shane had taken a liking to her little sister. She wasn't sure how Karen felt about him, but she hoped nothing serious was forming.

She knew she was getting ahead of herself. A few smiles and jokes didn't make a relationship. They'd only known each other for a few weeks.

Almost exactly the same amount of time that she had known Brian.

Giving herself a mental shake, she dismissed the idea that Karen was interested in Shane. Knowing Karen's dislike of the military, and after seeing what had happened to Danny, Lindsey was sure her sister wouldn't want to become involved with a serviceman. Perhaps she should mention as much to Shane. He was a friend and she didn't want his feelings hurt.

"Are you sure you know where to take this stuff?" Karen asked as she moved aside and let Shane shut the door.

He didn't exactly roll his eyes, but he came close. "The east entrance of the K-State football field."

"Good. We'll meet you there. Lindsey, are you ready to go?"

"I am. Thanks for doing this, Shane."

"Anything to help, Lindsey. You know the whole unit is rooting for Dakota. The Captain said his second surgery went well yesterday."

"According to Dr. Cutter, he removed the pins and replaced the cast without any problems."

The curt postoperative report yesterday had been the longest amount of time Brian had spent in her company since that day at Medicine Falls. He was obviously a busy man with a heavy surgery schedule, lectures to prepare and students to teach. Each time Lindsey saw him he seemed to be heading somewhere else. All week she had wondered if he was deliberately avoiding her.

Shrugging off the hurt that idea caused, she glanced into the packed vehicle. "You'd better get going. We'll meet you there."

Once Shane pulled away from the curb, Karen's liveliness visibly deflated, causing Lindsey to take a closer look. Karen seemed pale and there were dark circles under her eyes that she had tried to disguise with makeup. Without a word, Karen climbed into her blue sedan. It was then that Lindsey remembered her cell phone was still sitting in the charger in the living room. "I'll be with you in one second, Karen."

She dashed into the apartment, snatched up the phone and raced back down the steps. As she hurried around the front of the car to the passenger's side, she saw that Karen was resting her forehead on her hands at the top of the steering wheel. Opening the door, Lindsey slid into the seat. "Are you okay?"

Looking up, she gave Lindsey a wan smile. "I have a headache, that's all. I guess I stayed up too late baking last night."

"You've been baking for three days nonstop. I told you we would have enough. Just look at how much food the people on post donated. You didn't have to try and do it all by yourself."

"I wanted to do my part."

"You've done more than your part. You've been my driver, my cook, my nurse and my constant companion for the past two weeks. Why don't you stay here and lie down? I can catch a ride with someone else."

"Don't be silly, I'll be fine."

Lindsey wanted to believe her, but an hour later she

could see that Karen truly wasn't feeling well. Once the tables and home-baked goodies had been set up outside the stadium, Shane returned to post, leaving the two women to hopefully sell all of their baked goods to hungry college football fans.

The day couldn't have been much better for a football game or for a bake sale, Lindsey decided. The temperature wasn't bad as long as she stayed in the sunshine. The bright rays kept the breeze from feeling cold until one of the white clouds with a flat gray bottom blocked the sun as it drifted past. Then, it wasn't hard to imagine that Thanksgiving was less than a week away.

Before long, they were doing a brisk business, but Lindsey kept one eye on her little sister. When they had a break in customers, she insisted Karen sit down and put a cool cloth on her forehead.

"That feels good. I'm sorry to be a drag, Lindsey. I don't get these headaches often, but when I do, they really take it out of me."

"You should go home and rest."

"I can't leave you to sell all this by yourself. Besides, how would you get home?"

"I could drive her."

Lindsey looked up in surprise to see Brian standing with a loaf of homemade bread in his hand. He wore a long-sleeved, pale yellow shirt tucked into khaki chino pants. The perpetual frown was missing from his face as he smiled at her.

After the way he had been avoiding her, she hadn't expected to see him today.

"How much for this bread?" he asked, holding out a loaf.

"Two dollars," Lindsey answered, willing her suddenly erratic pulse to calm down and her voice to sound casual. He shouldn't have this effect on her, but every time she laid eyes on him, it was the same.

"Are you sure you don't mind driving Lindsey home, Dr. Cutter?"

"Please call me Brian. Of course I don't mind giving her a lift." He handed over the bills.

"But it's out of your way," Lindsey protested as she took his money. She wasn't prepared to deal with the emotions his sudden appearance evoked. She needed more distance between them, not less.

"I don't mind."

"Good, it's settled then," Karen cut in quickly. "You're an answer to my prayers."

If Lindsey didn't know better, she might have suspected that Karen was doing a little matchmaking. But because she knew her sister really wasn't feeling well, she swallowed any further protests.

"Go home and lie down, Karen. I can handle the sales by myself."

"You won't be by yourself. I can stay and help."

Brian's offer caught her off guard. "That's all right, I can manage."

"I'm sure you can, but I'm going to help anyway." He came around to her side of the table. With him close beside her, she noticed the crisp, spicy scent of his aftershave. All her senses suddenly seemed heightened. He began rolling up his sleeves and she took note of the tanned muscles on his forearms. His fingers were long and well manicured. He had the gentle but strong hands of a surgeon.

She looked up to find him watching her in return. Sunlight glinted off his blond hair. He didn't look the least bit grumpy. *Handsome* was the word that came to mind. Her breath caught in her throat. He definitely was good-looking when he wasn't scowling. So why did he want to spend time with her?

The flattering notion that he might enjoy her company as much as she enjoyed his was quickly discarded. She wasn't looking for a man in her life, handsome or otherwise.

Once Karen had gathered up her belongings and left for her car, Lindsey turned to Brian. "You don't have to stay or give me a ride. I can call one of my friends on post and have them come get me."

"I don't mind helping. Besides, you're going to be overrun with customers in a few minutes."

"Why do you say that?"

"My secretary saw your flyer about this sale and suggested I have an announcement made during the game. A lot of these kids saw your fall and I'm sure they'll want to help."

"That was very kind of you."

"Don't give me too much credit. It was Jennifer's idea."

"I'll have to remember to thank her tomorrow."

"You can, but don't overdo it. The woman already has a high opinion of herself."

Before Lindsey could think of something else to talk about, his prediction came true. The football game ended and they were swamped with fans eager to buy cookies, cakes and brownies for a good cause. A few people even made donations without buying anything.

Brian sat at the cash box making change while Lindsey stayed busy answering questions about Dakota and visiting with the customers. Whenever he had a free moment, he spent it studying her. Having one arm in a sling didn't appear to hamper her as she boxed up the requested items. She was a true people person with a ready smile and an easy laugh that everyone around her responded to. It was no wonder he found her attractive.

For the first time he admitted the truth of those feelings, but that didn't change the fact that she wasn't for him. She deserved someone with a whole heart to give her. He wasn't a whole man in body or in soul.

Thrusting aside his somber thoughts, he resolved to keep a tight rein on his feelings. He would be foolish to allow something other than a professional relationship to start between them.

Before long, the last bag of chocolate fudge was bought and paid for and Lindsey dropped into a folding chair beside him.

"I can't believe we sold everything."

"Everything except these cookies." He pushed the plastic bag with a dozen dark brown oatmeal cookies toward her.

Lindsey opened the Ziploc top and offered him one. "Please accept this humble payment in return for your help today."

He took the cookie and bit into it. "I see why they didn't sell. They're kind of burnt."

"I know." She zipped the bag shut and tossed it into a box at her feet.

He indicated the bare tables. "What do we do with these?"

"They belong to the college. We just rented them for the afternoon. They can stay here."

"Are you ready to leave then?"

"I guess I am. Hey, didn't you have a loaf of bread in your hand earlier?"

He checked around. "It must have been sold out from under me."

"I'm sorry."

"Don't worry about it."

"I'll have Sergeant Link's wife bake you another one."

"You didn't bake it yourself?"

A bark of laughter escaped from her before she pressed her hand to her lips. "I made those oatmeal cookies. Baking is not one of my strengths as you can plainly taste."

He grinned. She didn't seem the least bit embarrassed to confess her shortcomings. He admired that. "What is one of your strengths?"

Wrinkling her brow, she considered his question. "Adaptability. That's my strength. I lived in five states and four countries before I turned twenty. I'm not even sure how many schools I attended as a kid."

"That must have been hard."

"It might have been worse if I hadn't had Danny and Karen. Having Danny looking out for us made it easier to always be the new kids. That and the riding schools. No matter where Dad was stationed he always enrolled us in riding classes."

"Where is your brother now?"

A deep sadness settled over her features. "He lives in Washington, D.C., but I wish he lived closer. Danny was wounded in action last summer. He's a quadriplegic, now. He's finally at home, but he still requires around-the-clock nursing care."

"I'm sorry."

"Thank you."

"So, do you ever get tired of moving around?"

She tilted her head to the side. "No. Karen hated it when she was little, but Danny and I did okay. Maybe someday I'll find a place that will make me want to settle down, but for now the army is my home."

He rose and grasped his cane. "That must be my cue to return you to your post."

She rose, too, and finished stuffing several empty boxes in a nearby trash barrel. "Are you sure you don't mind?"

"Not at all. I'm parked over there." He pointed across the emptying parking lot to his white truck.

Lindsey fell into step beside him, adjusting to his slower pace without any sign of impatience. The silence lengthened between them, but he didn't find it uncomfortable. At his truck, he unlocked the vehicle with his remote key. She moved without hesitation to the passenger side, not waiting for him. He tried to hurry and open the door for her. She realized what he was doing when their hands closed over the handle at the same time.

The softness of her skin caught him by surprise. The bones of her hand felt delicate and dainty beneath his palm. A warmth stole over him that had nothing to do with the sunshine beating down on them.

She gave him a chiding look. "Oh, puleeze. I can get my own door."

At least she seemed unaware of the effect she had on him. He strove to keep his voice neutral. "Perhaps, but my mother raised me to be a gentleman."

"And my father raised me to be a grunt."

"A what?"

"That's slang for a foot soldier."

"It's not a very nice term."

"It's not always a nice job."

"In a test of wills, I'll match my mother against your father any day of the week. They don't make them any tougher than she is. Please allow me." He nodded toward the door.

Slowly, she pulled her hand out from beneath his. "You win. This time."

"Duly noted." He pulled open the door and waited while she climbed in.

Lindsey watched Brian move around to the driver's side and took a few quick breaths to calm her racing heart. Never had the touch of a man's hand unnerved her the way Brian's touch did. The idea that she might be attracted to him was something she didn't want to contemplate. Falling for him was a sure road to heartbreak.

"Please, Lord. More heartache is the last thing I need," she whispered under her breath before Brian opened his door.

He stowed his cane on a rack in the rear window and started the ignition without a word. The silence that had seemed so comfortable only a few minutes before now seemed tense. They were only a few blocks from the stadium when his cell phone rang. He pulled it from his shirt pocket. Lindsey listened to the terse conversation with interest. After a few questions, he gave brisk instructions to the person on the other end of the line and then snapped his phone closed.

"I'm sorry, Lindsey, but I have to get back to the clinic. I have an emergency coming."

"Don't worry, I totally understand. I'll call a cab or get a friend to pick me up at the hospital."

"Are you sure?"

"Absolutely. It will give me a chance to spend a little time with Dakota."

He pulled onto a side street to turn around and in a few minutes they were heading back the way they had come. At the clinic, he hurried inside and met with several young men and one young woman. Lindsey knew they were the senior students on call for that day. As they walked toward the surgical suites, Lindsey found herself standing in the reception area where a young girl in a colorful Western costume sat with an older man dressed in jeans and boots. His cowboy hat rested on the chair beside him. The young girl was sniffling into a tissue. The man put his arm around her shaking shoulders and spoke to her softly. Lindsey couldn't hear what they were saying, but it was obvious that these were the people with the injured horse.

Pulling her cell phone from her back pocket, Lindsey punched in Shane's number. If he wasn't free to give her a ride, she'd try Avery next. Shane answered on the third ring. She could hear the sounds of laughter and cheering in the background. "It sounds like you're having a party."

"I'm watching a football game with some of the guys. What's up?"

"I'm looking for someone to give me a ride back to post."

"I thought Karen was driving you."

"She had a nasty headache so I sent her home early. I thought I had a ride, but it fell through."

"Bummer." He groaned loudly. A chorus of groans from his friends was followed by one lone cheer.

"What was that about?" she asked.

"Lee's team just made the tying touchdown. If they make this extra point, they'll move ahead at the half."

"Are Avery and Lee both there?"

"Yup."

"All right, never mind. I'll find another way back."

"Are you sure? Wow! Did you see that block? That's the way we Texas boys play ball!"

"Thanks, Shane. Enjoy your game." She hung up without waiting for his reply. It was obvious she was going to have to take a cab.

She walked up to the reception desk and asked the young man seated there for the use of a phone book. He had just handed it to her when Brian came back into the room. His face looked grimmer than she had ever seen it.

He walked up to the tearful young girl and sat down beside her. Lindsey tried not to listen in, but she couldn't help overhearing his words.

"I'm sorry. There isn't anything we can do for Storm. He is suffering a lot of pain. The kindest thing we can do is to put him to sleep."

The young girl's heartfelt cry tore at Lindsey's heart. Tears of sympathy pricked her eyes.

Brian awkwardly patted the weeping girl's shoulder, then rose to his feet. "You can come and say goodbye first, if you like."

As the pair went down the hallway, Brian stopped beside Lindsey. "Is someone coming to pick you up?"

"I was just about to call a cab."

"If you don't mind waiting a few more minutes, I can take you. I won't be needed here, after all."

"I'm so sorry."

"Thanks. Why don't you wait in my office?"

"I think I'd rather visit with Dakota. Whenever you're ready. Don't hurry on my account."

"This is the one part of my job I hate." He turned away and followed Storm's grieving family.

Lindsey walked down the hall and out into the large room that housed Dakota's stall along with eight others. Opening the gate, she slipped in and circled his neck with her good arm. He swung his head around and nuzzled her side briefly before lowering his head and closing his eyes. Leaning against his warm coat, she breathed deeply, drawing solace from his familiar scent.

"Dear Lord, offer Your comfort to those people and to Brian at this sad time. Let them know that You will wash away every tear and heal every heart."

She wasn't sure how long she stood there before she heard Brian's voice behind her. "There's something about the smell of a horse that makes you think of hot summer days and shady rests under the spreading branches of a tall cottonwood tree."

"I love the feel of them," she said softly, not looking up. "They feel like living silk over powerful muscles."

With each breath Dakota took, she listened to air rushing and rattling in and out of his lungs. His heartbeat was like a muffled drum, steady and strong, and yet so vulnerable.

Brian stepped closer. As if he were reading her mind, he said, "They are so powerful. It's always a shock when we see one get hurt."

She turned her face to look at him without letting go of Dakota. "Is it over?"

Brian nodded. "He was a four-year-old quarter horse and according to his young owner, he had the makings of a barrel-racing champion. It was such a shame."

"What happened to him?"

Brian moved up beside her and began to stroke Dakota's face. "He suffered a fracture of the pastern much like this fellow's. We see a lot of breaks like that in horses who make quick turns and sliding stops."

"Why couldn't you do surgery on him?"

"He started out with a simple break, but by the time the family got him here, he had done so much damage to the leg trying to stand in the trailer that we couldn't do anything for him."

"I don't understand."

"There was irreparable damage done to the soft tissue and blood supply by the broken bone fragments. If he could have been brought to us in an equine ambulance, we might have been able to save him."

"Do you have one?"

"Not at present, but I haven't given up hope. For the most part, you'll only see them at big racetracks like Belmont Park or Santa Anita. However, I'm trying to persuade the company that makes them to loan us one to have on display during our conference here on January twenty-first."

"I remember seeing one on television when that Kentucky Derby winner broke his leg."

"They're quite expensive. It seems that the board forgot to add the money for one to my budget," he joked.

"We could hold another bake sale. I would contribute more cookies."

"Another burnt offering?"

Delighted to see the ghost of a smile on his face, she grinned. "I don't always singe them. The oven in my apartment is fickle. Some days it gets hotter than others."

"I'm sure that is totally true."

"Speaking of hot things, Dakota feels warm to me."

"Now that you mention it, he does. I see that he hasn't eaten much today. There's still feed in his bucket."

"That's not like him. He's always ready to eat. Do you think he's sick?"

Dakota coughed deeply. Alarm raced through Lindsey's body and her gaze shot to Brian's face. He pulled his stethoscope from the pocket of his lab coat and moved to examine the animal. After listening to the horse's chest, he stepped back. The frown she hated seeing was etched between his brows.

"What is it? What's wrong?"

"I'll need an X-ray to confirm, but I'm afraid he's developed pneumonia."

"That's bad, isn't it?" She knew it was a stupid question the second the words were out of her mouth. Of course it was bad. Brian's look of deep concern only confirmed it.

Chapter Seven

Over the next days Dakota's life hung in a delicate balance. With his head held low he wheezed and coughed until Brian thought he couldn't possibly draw another ragged breath. It hurt just to watch him try. Brian knew minimizing the animal's distress was just as important as keeping him warm and well hydrated. Lindsey rarely left his side. Her presence seemed to bring the horse comfort. Somehow, her presence was a comfort to Brian, as well.

On the second night, a traffic accident with an overturned horse trailer brought in three more injured horses and the hospital's staff was stretched to the limit. With Brian's permission, Shane and Avery brought in a cot and placed it in an empty adjacent stall. All the unit members, Karen and numerous students took turns staying to help care for the animal. Their dedicated presence seemed to be all that was keeping the tired horse from slipping away.

Brian gave up going home and slept fitfully on the sofa in his office at night. During the daylight hours, the clinic operated normally and his surgery and teaching schedule kept him busy. At night, he rose every two hours to take vital signs and temperature readings looking for the least sign of improvement in Dakota. He could have left the horse's care to the senior students on duty, but he didn't. Dakota had become a special patient. Every four hours he gave the horse pain medication and every six hours he gave the massive doses of antibiotics needed to help stem the infection. In spite of all they were doing for him, Brian knew that it was Dakota's will to live that would ultimately be the deciding factor.

By the middle of the third night, he had given up urging Lindsey to rest. Instead, they worked side by side. While he administered the intravenous drugs, Lindsey held an inhaler over Dakota's nose to make sure he breathed in all the medicine designed to ease his labored respirations.

A few hours before dawn on the fourth night, Brian stifled a yawn as he leaned on the gate to Dakota's stall.

"You should go and rest," Lindsey suggested as she came to stand beside him.

"I'm all right, but I think your sister is out for the count." He nodded toward the cot in the next stall.

Lindsey looked over to see Karen had fallen asleep. "I can't say that I blame her. I feel like taking a nap myself."

"You're welcome to use the couch in my office."

"I may when I'm sure Dakota is doing better. What is his temperature now?"

Brian entered the stall and took a quick reading. "A hundred and five down from one hundred and six point five. His fever looks like it's breaking."

"Still, it isn't normal."

"No, it's not a hundred and one, but it's a definite improvement."

"Thanks to you." She entered the stall and held out a slice of apple. She was happy to see Dakota nibble it up.

"You're the one who has managed to coax him to eat. Nutrition is really important when a horse runs a fever." He gave a weary sigh as he sank onto a bale of straw in the corner.

"He's just used to me, that's all. Besides, apples are his favorite treat."

"I've noticed you slipping in horse chow and vitamins along with those slices."

"Do you think he is out of the woods?" She came over and sat on the bale beside him.

"In my professional opinion, I think he is."

"Are you ever wrong?" she asked.

"Frequently when it comes to people, but rarely about horses."

She managed a tired smile. "Are you saying you lack people skills?"

He called up a smile to match hers. "Why do you think I'm a vet?"

"You have been a blessing for us, that's for sure. I hate to think of Danny facing Dakota's loss on top of everything else he has been through."

Brian heard the catch in her voice and saw such pain on her face that he hesitated to ask any more questions. As if sensing his scrutiny, she glanced up and gave him a sad, sweet smile.

He reached out and covered her hand with his own. "Do you want to talk about it?"

"Danny was wounded while serving in Afghanistan. He singled-handedly saved the lives of two men in his unit when they were ambushed in a roadside attack. He risked heavy fire to pull those men to safety. Then, when a mortar exploded nearby, a piece of shrapnel hit him in the back of the neck and severed his spine."

"He sounds like a very brave man."

She looked toward the ceiling. "He is very brave. He's facing his disability with a determination that's amazing."

"It's all about having the will to live."

She studied him for a moment and then asked, "What happened to your wife?"

The question caught him off guard. He had never told anyone the details of the accident. For years he had kept those terrible hours and days locked away in his mind. He met Lindsey's gaze and saw only compassion looking back at him.

Sitting beside her in the dim building, he discovered a need to share his pain and his loss. "I had been working a lot of long hours that winter. I had only been out of school a year and I was intent on building up my practice. The Sunday before Valentine's Day, Emily planned to go visit her family. She wanted to share the news about the baby in person. I should have let her go alone. I was dead tired. If only I had let her drive..." His voice trailed off into silence.

"What happened?"

"While we were visiting her parents, the weather started to turn bad. She wanted to spend the night, but I wanted to get back. I thought my practice couldn't do without me for another day. I insisted we leave." He grew silent as the memory of the terrible night fanned the guilt he always carried.

"You don't have to tell me about it if you don't want to."

"I don't remember much about the accident itself. I do remember how hard it was to keep my eyes open looking into the snow. I must have fallen asleep at the wheel."

He patted his leg. "When I woke up rescue workers were cutting me out of what was left of our car. I reached for Emily. I found her hand in the darkness and then I felt her leave me. I felt her spirit touch mine and then she was gone."

"I'm so sorry."

Instead of answering, Brian rose and took another temperature reading on his patient. He had exposed enough of his soul for one night. "The fever is definitely going down."

"Thank the Lord for answering our prayers."

"I would say it is thanks to modern medicine."

"Perhaps the Lord's plan called for both medicine and prayers."

"I doubt it. I'm sorry. It's just that I gave up praying a long time ago."

"Because of Emily?"

He wanted to say yes, but he wasn't sure the words would make it past the lump in his throat.

She laid a hand on his arm. "It's okay. God will be there when you are ready to pray again."

"I don't think much of a God who allows terrible things to happen to good people."

"The Lord never promised that we wouldn't suffer. He did promise that He will always be with us."

"You surprise me."

"Why?"

"Religion and a military life don't seem to go together."

She smiled slightly. "Maybe not to you, but to most of us serving our country, it makes perfect sense. If I'm called to put my life on the line, I know that God has my back."

"Didn't your brother's injury leave you with doubts about that?"

"My brother's injury left me with the same anger and grief that everyone feels at a time like that. What God gives me is comfort, and the sure and certain knowledge that He is with me. My strength comes from Him."

Deciding it was time to change the subject, he asked, "Whatever possessed a woman like you to enlist in the army in the first place?"

She looked at him askew. "Why shouldn't a woman join the army?"

"I not saying a woman can't do the job. I'm just wondering why a woman would want to. You could be sent into a combat zone."

"You mean people might shoot at me?"

"Well, yes."

"Here's a news flash. I've been trained to shoot back. I even have a gun."

"Would you? Shoot back, I mean?"

"Yes. Does that make me a bad person in your eyes?"

"Of course not. Do you plan to make it a career?"

Leaning against the wall, she stretched her legs out and stared at her feet. "You have to understand that I come from a military family. The Mandels have served with distinction since the Civil War. Growing up, I always knew that I would enlist when I was old enough. I don't think my father would have approved of any other choice. He certainly wasn't happy when Karen started talking about becoming a teacher instead of a soldier."

"Teaching is an admirable profession."

"Not for a Mandel."

"So will Karen enlist, too?"

"Not for all the tea in China. She has stated categorically that she has no interest in wearing fatigues or taking orders from strangers."

"What does your mother think about your career choice?"

It was the first time Brian had seen uncertainty and regret in her eyes. She looked down and plucked a piece of straw from the bale. "My mother doesn't care one way or the other."

Brian sat down beside her. "What makes you say that?"

Fighting back ugly memories, Lindsey wrapped the piece of straw around her finger like a wedding ring. When she realized what she was doing, she pulled it off and threw it aside. "My mother left my father when I was ten. Two days before my birthday, actually. We never heard from her again."

"That must have been rough," he said gently.

"We managed." Only because she, Danny and Karen had had each other. Their father had retreated into his work, the work their mother had hated. He spent long hours away from home, and it wasn't long before he was transferred to a new post. After that, Lindsey gave up watching for her mother to come back.

It was at the new post that they met a wonderful man by the name of Chaplain Carson. A kind and generous man, he always made time for the lonely kids who lived next door. In more ways than one, he helped all of them through that terrible time as he taught them about God's love.

"Does your father still feel the same way about the service after your brother was wounded?"

Brian's question jerked Lindsey out of the past. "I'm sure my father suffers as any man must suffer to see his son injured and hurting. But Dad is as proud as I am of what Danny did."

"Of course. I just thought that he might want you out of harm's way."

"He worries, but he knows I'll do my duty. It's up to me to carry on the family tradition. My father doesn't have to tell me that. It's understood."

"What would you do if there wasn't an army?"

She scowled at him. "What kind of question is that? There will always be an army. 'The price of freedom is eternal vigilance.' Thomas Jefferson said that and he was right."

"But what if you couldn't stay in the service for some reason? What would you do?"

The question was so foreign that Lindsey wasn't sure how to answer it. It had always been the army or nothing.

"Come on," he coaxed. "Think outside the box."

"I honestly don't know."

"What did your father do after he retired?"

"Drove us nuts."

Brian chuckled and Lindsey found to her surprise that she adored the sound. Still, she wanted to change the subject, so she asked, "What do your parents do?"

"They're ranchers. My family owns a spread outside of Missoula, Montana. They both still work as hard as they ever did, according to my older brother. He ranches with them."

"Why didn't you stay in the family business?"

"That's a long story."

She glanced at her watch. "Looks like I have time to listen."

"Okay. Long story short. As a kid, I was reckless. I thought more about impressing my friends than my own safety. One day, on a dare, I tried to ride my horse down the side of a steep embankment the way they do in the movies. We fell. How I wasn't killed outright I'll never know, but my mare broke both her front legs. When my friends brought my father to the scene, Dad gave me the rifle and told me to put her down because it was obvious her life didn't mean anything to me."

"What a cruel thing to say."

"Maybe it was, but he was right."

"Did you do it?"

"I couldn't, so my father did. But that day I vowed I'd never be the cause of another horse's suffering. I knew then that I'd be a vet."

"And you never wanted to be anything else?"

"Occasionally, I have this recurring desire to work in a movie theater and make popcorn."

"You're kidding, right?" She stared at him in amazement.

"Think about it. The smell of buttery popcorn all day long. Can't you just imagine it?"

Lindsey closed her eyes. "The sound of the popper and the sight of fluffy white kernels pouring out from under a silver lid."

"Can you think of a better job?"

"Driving a tank," she stated without hesitation.

"You'd never be caught in another traffic jam. You could roll over anything in your way."

"Parking on campus might be a problem, though."

"Not a bit. Find the space you want and park on top of the car that's there." She glanced at him trying to control the laughter building inside. "After all, who is going to argue with a woman in a tank?"

"Good point. Can I rent one from you?"

She giggled and he began to laugh outright. His laugh had a wonderful, deep timbre. One she wanted to hear over and over again.

His smile slowly faded. "Since it looks like Dakota is through the worst of it, I'd better get home for a few hours and make up with Isabella."

The name was like a douse of cold water on Lindsey's joy. Did he have another woman in his life? The thought was a sobering one. Then the realization hit her. It mattered. It mattered more than she cared to admit. She swallowed hard. "Who is Isabella?"

"My bunny."

She wasn't quite sure she'd heard him correctly. "Your bunny. As in rabbit?"

He looked at her sharply. "Yes. Why is that so odd?"

She grinned, almost giddy with relief. "I'm not sure. I guess I pictured you as the kind of guy who kept a bulldog or maybe a python."

"Sorry to disappoint you. All I have is a domineering French Lop."

"I sense a story."

He glanced at his watch. "One that will have to wait for another day. I'll be back in a few hours. I have a surgery scheduled for eight o'clock this morning. You have my beeper number if you need me. I only live about ten minutes away."

"Dakota seems much better. I'm sure we'll be fine on our own for a few hours."

"There is always a student on duty if you need anything. I'll see you later."

"Good night, Brian."

He stood and she rose to face him. The air between them suddenly seemed charged with electricity. She longed to reach out and smooth his rumpled shirt. She wanted to comb her fingers through his tousled hair and coax it into some kind of order. Instead, she stuffed her hand into the hip pocket of her jeans and took a step back.

For a long moment, he simply stared into her eyes, then with a nod, he walked away. It wasn't until then that she remembered to breathe.

A few hours later, Dakota's temperature had fallen to a normal level. His appetite returned with a vengeance and he made short work of any apple slices that came within range. When Lindsey turned away to pull another piece of fruit from the brown paper bag by the cot, he whinnied loudly, waking Karen.

She sat up rubbing her eyes. "That sounds like he's feeling better."

"Much better."

"What time is it? Or maybe I should ask what day is it?"

Lindsey glanced at her watch. "It's the day before Thanksgiving and it's after nine."

"Why did you let me sleep so long?"

"You looked so peaceful that I didn't have the heart to wake you."

Tipping her head first to the right and then to the left, Karen winced. "My neck would have been happier if you had. Where is Brian?"

"He had a surgery this morning."

"You two seemed to be getting along rather well last night."

"I thought you were asleep?"

"I was—most of the time. What did you and he find to talk about until the wee hours of the morning?"

"This and that. You know how it is. Small talk mostly."

"Small talk?" Something in Karen's expression told Lindsey that she wasn't buying that line.

"All right, if you want me to admit that I'm beginning to like the guy, I will."

"I thought so." She folded her arms over her chest and looked smug.

Lindsey turned away and began to toss flakes of hay into Dakota's stall. "Just because I like him doesn't mean anything except that it will be easier to keep working with him."

"I wouldn't be too sure about that. I sense more than a casual interest."

"I'm not looking for love, Karen, if that's where this is going. I have plans to make the army my career. Marriage and the military don't mix. Not for me, anyway."

"You're thinking about Mother. Just because our parents couldn't make their marriage work isn't any reason to believe you can't make a relationship work. I don't remember much about Mom because I was only six when she left, but from all that Danny has told me, I can see you are a much stronger woman than she was. You have a good heart and a strong faith. Why not trust that God will bring the right man into your life?"

She glanced at Karen. "What makes you think Brian is the right man?"

Karen stepped up and took her by the shoulder. Giving her a gentle shake, she said, "Girlfriend, what makes you so sure he isn't?"

Chapter Eight

The Monday after the holiday weekend, Brian sat in his office trying to concentrate on drafting a letter of appeal for funds to buy an ambulance when he noticed Isabella creeping toward his Wildcat mug. He knew that look in her eye. Picking her up before she could snatch one of his freshly sharpened pencils and chew it into splinters, he scolded softly, "I see what you're trying to do. I've got to get this letter done, so that means you have to go outside."

Outside was one of her favorite words. She loved racing up and down the long fenced area he'd had built beside the building and nibbling on the fresh grass.

He needed a break anyway. The words on his yellow legal pad weren't anywhere near the tone he wanted to convey. Instead of fine-tuning his letter, all he had done that morning was think about Lindsey.

Rising, he picked up his cane from where it leaned against his desk and made his way toward the door. As he pulled it open, Isabella suddenly leaped out of his arms and took off toward the stall area. He hurried after her, knowing she could easily be hurt if she ran into one of the occupied pens. Fortunately, he saw the double doors at the end of the hall were closed.

He was only a step away from his pet when one of the doors opened and two students came through. It was all the opportunity Isabella needed.

"Catch her," he called out.

By the time the befuddled students realized what he was talking about, the rabbit had darted between them and through the doorway.

"Isabella, come back here!" His shout did nothing to stem her headlong flight.

Running past the students, Brian entered the stall area and scanned the large enclosure for any sign of his fleeing pet. Checking each pen as he hurried past, he didn't see Private Barnes until he almost ran into him.

"Whoa, there, Doc. What's the rush?"

"Did you see a rabbit come this way?"

"A what?"

"Isabella is loose?" The familiar female voice made Brian looked past the young soldier. Jennifer was sitting on a folding chair beside the army cot, but she jumped to her feet, a look of alarm on her face.

Happy to have an ally who understood what was needed, Brian nodded. "Make sure all the outside doors are closed."

She grabbed the soldier's arm. "Of course. Avery, you go that way and I'll make sure everything on this end is shut. Give a shout if you see her."

"What sort of rabbit am I looking for?"

She rolled her eyes and gave him a shove. "The fuzzy kind that hops. Now hurry, but don't scare the horses."

Brian retraced his steps and began searching more slowly. There were numerous bales of hay and bags of feed stacked along the center of the wide aisles. She could be behind any of them or under the wooden pallets they rested on.

He'd only finished checking a small area when Jennifer returned. "None of the outside doors are open. I've left Avery in charge of seeing that no one goes in or out."

Brian stared around the large building. "Why would she suddenly decide she wanted to come in here? She loves going outside. I distinctly told her she was going outside."

"That may be my fault," Jennifer admitted with a pained look. "I brought her out here with me yesterday."

"And why were you out here instead of at the desk?"

"Avery…that is…Private Barnes asked for some help with the thermal thermometer."

His scowl prompted her to add quickly, "I held on to Isabella the whole time. I didn't let her run loose. She wasn't even frightened by the horse when he came over to check her out."

Brian sighed, trying to hide his vexation. "All right, we'll talk about this after we find her. You take that aisle and I'll take this one. Check everywhere."

"We don't have to. There she is."

He turned to see Jennifer pointing toward Dakota's stall. The big horse was lying down with his legs tucked under him. His neck was arched as he sniffed the bunny cuddled up against his chest. Brian approached the stall slowly. He didn't want to startle Dakota into lunging to his feet. One misstep and the little rabbit could be seriously injured, or worse.

"Come here, Isabella," he called softly. Dakota looked up at the sound of his voice, but the rabbit didn't move. Brian didn't see any choice. He would have to go in and get her.

"All right, big fella, you just stay relaxed." Brian opened the gate slowly and stepped inside the stall. Dakota threw his head up as if he was about to rise.

"Stay down, Dakota." The command came from behind Brian. He shot a quick look over his shoulder. Lindsey stood at the gate.

"He'll stay still now. It's okay," she assured him.

"How can you be so certain?"

"It's what he's been trained to do. He has to follow orders just like the rest of us."

Trusting her word, Brian walked to the pair and scooped up Isabella. She squirmed and tried to get down again, but he held on tightly.

Lindsey arrived beside them and squatted to pat Dakota's neck. "They look so cute together. Why don't you leave her here. She certainly seems to make him happy."

"It would be too risky." Brian ran his hand down Isabella's long, soft ears. "Lindsey, allow me to introduce you to Isabella the Terrible."

Rising, Lindsey stroked the rabbit's small round head. "You don't look very terrible to me."

"Reserve judgment until you know her better," Jennifer suggested. "Shall I take her outside?"

Brian shook his head. "No, I'll take her and then you and I are going to have a talk in my office."

"Yes, Doctor." She turned away meekly and left the building.

"I can't believe it," he said in astonishment.

"What?"

"She always has some sort of snappy comeback."

"Maybe she's saving it until you're alone."

"That's a scary thought." He made a mental note to be gentle with his secretary when he took her to task for neglecting her duties.

He glanced at the woman beside him.

Thoughts of Lindsey kept him from sleeping, kept him from working, and, worst of all, they kept him from thinking about Emily. It certainly wasn't Lindsey's fault, but he had decided it would be best if he didn't see as much of her in the future. During the past two days, he had accomplished his goal with difficulty. Like today, she always seemed to turn up when he least expected her.

Determined to put some distance between them now, he said curtly, "I have to put Isabella away. Excuse me."

Lindsey watched his abrupt retreat and wondered why he always seemed to be rushing out the door as she came in. After their exchange of confidences during Dakota's illness, she felt she had gained a better understanding of the man, perhaps even made a friend. Obviously, she had been mistaken. Brian couldn't have made it plainer that he didn't need or want her friendship.

"Not a very sociable chap, is he?" Avery said, coming to stand beside her.

She felt compelled to defend Brian in spite of his recent attitude. "He can be."

"I'll take your word for it."

"Where have you been?"

"Jenny had me guarding the doors to keep the rabbit from getting away. She stopped by to tell me the rodent has been recovered. Where was she?"

"Making nice with Dakota."

"No joke? I didn't know horses and rabbits got along."

"I've seen horses that weren't happy unless they had a stall mate. Usually it's a pony, but I've seen them adopt goats or dogs, so why not a rabbit?" Lindsey said.

"If it helps Dakota get better, I'll buy him a whole herd of rabbits."

"I'll second that. Speaking of Dakota, how is he today?"

"Relaxed, eating and drinking well. I'd say he's much improved. And how are you? You saw the doctor again today, didn't you?"

"The bone is mending, but I still don't have feeling in my fingers or my hand."

"How much longer does he think that will last?"

"You know doctors. It could be a week, it could be a month. Time will tell."

"Bummer."

"No kidding. It sure would be nice to be able to drive myself again and not have to depend on everyone to get me places. Karen is a doll, but I think even she is tired of being my chauffeur."

"Is your car a stick?"

"No, why?"

"Because if it isn't a stick, then you only need one arm to drive. Get a spinner for your steering wheel."

"What's that?"

"A kind of doorknob that attaches to the wheel and allows you to steer with one hand."

"Isn't that only for handicapped people?"

"Have you looked in the mirror? You *are* handicapped even if it's temporary. But no, they aren't only for the people with disabilities. I've got one on my sports car."

"Don't tell me, let me guess. So you can keep one arm around a girl while you're driving your Jag?"

"Exactly."

"How did a guy like you end up in the army?"

"You mean how did one of Boston's most eligible bachelors find himself enlisted as a private?"

"Yes. I've been wondering about that."

"So have I. My grandfather has some explaining to do when I get home. And for the record, the evils of alcohol cannot be overstated."

"You got drunk and ended up enlisted?"

"I'm ashamed to admit that I was so plastered I don't remember, but even my grandfather's lawyer couldn't get me out of Uncle Sam's contract. If he actually tried."

"Why wouldn't he?"

"I've done a lot of dumb things in my life. I was careless and selfish because I thought money fixed everything. My grandfather was at his wit's end with me. Maybe he thought the army could straighten me out."

"I think he was right."

A half smile pulled at one corner of his mouth. "It's nice of you to say so. At least I've given up drinking anything stronger than soda."

Lindsey patted his shoulder. "The Lord moves in mysterious ways."

"So does my grandfather," he grumbled.

"The spinner is a good idea. Would you be able to put one on my car if I gave you the money to buy one?"

"It would be my pleasure. But before you get behind the wheel, I insist you let me take you to an empty parking lot for some practice before you try it alone."

"You've got a deal. Thanks, Avery. Now, you're relieved. Is there anything I need to know about Dakota?"

"The Doc wants us to keep checking the cast for hot spots with the thermal thermometer at least once every four hours."

"Any signs of pressure sores?"

"No, his leg is as cool as a cucumber, but he is getting up and down more and that could cause problems. Are you taking leave for Christmas?"

"I hadn't planned on it. I don't want to desert Dakota after his close call." Voicing her excuse out loud didn't lessen the nagging guilt she had been saddled with since her conversation with Karen that morning.

"What about your family?"

"Karen has decided to spend the holidays with my brother since I won't be going home."

She dreaded the coming holidays. It was hard to think about celebrating Christmas with Danny's injury looming like a dark cloud over everyone's mood. "What about you?"

"I'll be here. Maybe we should have our own Christmas party."

"That's a good idea. I'll talk to the Captain about it."

After Avery left, Lindsey walked into the stall and sat down beside Dakota. He nuzzled her shoulder briefly, then began nipping at her pocket.

"Okay, I do have a few alfalfa treats in there, but don't get greedy. You're not the only horse in this place. See that little pinto across the way?" She pointed to a pony across the aisle. Dakota ignored her extended arm.

"He likes alfalfa, too, so you'll have to share." She pulled a handful of green pellets from her pocket and held them out for him. He lipped them up quickly.

After visiting with the horse for half an hour, Lindsey rose and began walking between the pens, stopping to visit with several other inmates. At the end of the building she glanced out the window and saw Isabella racing back and forth in a wire run.

Slipping out the door, Lindsey stopped beside the rabbit's kennel and knelt down to put her fingers through the chain links. Isabella stopped running long enough to investigate the potential new playmate. "Have you been banished from his office?"

She glanced toward the front of the building. "Care to share any secrets about your owner? Do you know why he's treating me like a plague victim?"

Isabella sniffed at Lindsey's fingers then dashed away. "I can see you aren't going to be any help."

From inside the barn, Lindsey heard Dakota's whinny. Rising, she headed back into the building. With only horses and rabbits to talk to, it promised to be a long day. Mainly because the one creature she really wished to spend time with had retreated to his office and she couldn't think of a good reason to follow him.

It was late afternoon and Lindsey had just closed the book she was reading when the sound of raised voices reached her.

Brian stormed through the doorway. A deep frown etched a groove between his eyebrows.

Jennifer was hard on his heels. "I didn't take her out of her pen, honest."

"Is she in here?" he demanded, stopping in front of Lindsey.

Not a word all day and now he had the nerve to behave like this? He wasn't the only one capable of pretending indifference. "More rabbit troubles, Doctor?" she drawled.

"Isabella has never run away before. You want me to believe she's done it twice in one day?"

"Dakota and I haven't seen hide nor hair of her, have we, boy? How much trouble is it to keep track of one bunny?" She rose from the cot where she was sitting and looked toward her horse. He stood in the corner of his pen with his head down. She assumed he had been sleeping. It was then she noticed the small bundle of fur beneath his nose.

Brian spotted his pet at the same time. "She *is* here."

Taken aback, Lindsey turned to him. "I'm sorry. I never saw her come in. I was outside by her pen for a little while, but I didn't take her out. She was inside her run when I left."

"I seriously doubt a six-pound rabbit could open a kennel door and then a barn door all by herself."

"I wouldn't put it past her," Jennifer muttered.

Brian glared at her but didn't allow himself to be diverted. "It isn't safe to let her in with Dakota no matter how cute you think it is."

Lindsey opened her mouth and closed it again. Anger at his accusation momentarily robbed her of speech. She took a step toward him.

"Are you saying you think I took your precious rabbit out of her cage and put her in with my lame horse just because I thought they looked cute together?" Resentment lent a steely edge to her words.

"You go, girl." Jennifer crossed her arms and looked smug.

Brian took a step back. Lindsey could see the indecision wavering in his eyes. "If this is another one of your harebrained ideas for stress reduction…"

"I have no idea how your rodent found her way out of her pen and into here, but I had nothing to do with it."

"Rabbits aren't rodents, they're lagomorphs," Jennifer supplied with a bright smile.

"My horse doesn't need a lop-eared fur ball to reduce his stress and keep him company. He has me. Perhaps if you paid more attention to *your* pet, she wouldn't be looking for love in all the wrong places."

"Lagomorphs have four upper incisors. The second pair is peglike and posterior to the first. Rodents only have two upper incisors."

Both Lindsey and Brian turned to stare at Jennifer.

"Well, it's true. A rabbit *isn't* a rodent. I can't believe the pair of you. There's absolutely nothing wrong with a hare's brain and don't ever say *rodent* like it's a bad word."

Brushing between Brian and Lindsey, Jennifer slipped through the gate into the stall and picked up Isabella. Slipping out again, she paused and looked from Brian to Lindsey and back. "Any more name-calling and someone is going to find their mouth washed out with soap. Apologies are in order, and I mean now."

Lindsey watched Brian's secretary exit through the main doors with the squirming rabbit under her arm. Dakota whinnied frantically as his new friend was carried away.

Without taking her eyes off the doorway, Lindsey asked, "Did she mean it?"

He stood beside her looking in the same direction. "I'm not sure, but I'm not taking any chances. I'm sorry I suggested you were harebrained."

"I've been told there's nothing wrong with a hare's brain, so apology accepted. I'm sorry I called Isabella a rodent."

"You're forgiven."

"She's kind of a weird woman," Lindsey ventured.

"I had no idea until recently just how strange she is," he acknowledged.

Glancing at Brian from the corner of her eye, Lindsey suddenly found herself overcome with giggles. Brian shot her a dour look but couldn't keep the smile off his face. A second later he was chuckling, too.

By the middle of the following week, Dakota's condition had improved enough to allow him to be transferred back to the fort stables. With the unit members providing around-the-clock care, Brian knew there wasn't any reason to keep the horse at the clinic. Except that it meant he wouldn't be seeing Lindsey anymore.

The day after the big bay left it suddenly became a much quieter building. At least twice before noon Brian found himself standing beside the empty stall and staring into the space. He should be wondering how Dakota was getting along, but he had confidence that Lindsey and the men would follow his instructions to the letter. What he found himself wondering was how Lindsey was getting along. What was she doing? Was she resting her arm the way she should, or would she be trying to do too much?

Jennifer came up beside Brian and propped her chin on the rail. "I miss him already."

"He'll get the best care possible and he'll be happier in his own stall with the other horses he knows."

She sighed. "I know the horse will be happier, but I'm not sure the rest of us will be."

Puzzled at her depressed tone, he looked at her closely. "You're not taking about missing the horse, are you?"

"Duh? I'm talking about that gorgeous hunk."

"Forgive me if I seem a little slow, but which hunk would that be?"

"Private Avery Barnes. That Boston accent of his was to die for. Can't you think of some reason to send me out to the fort?"

"Jennifer, if Private Barnes is interested in seeing you again, he'll call."

"Oh, like you're going to call Lindsey?"

"That's neither here nor there."

"Which means, no." She shook her head as she walked away muttering, "Men are *so* not bright."

At the doorway, she stopped and looked back. "How is it that so many of you are in charge of stuff?"

Brian watched her walk out without replying. He had no intention of seeing Lindsey unless it was in an official capacity. He liked her, but it would never be more than that. The love of his life was dead and he knew there would never be another.

Yet, he did miss Lindsey.

He rested his arms atop the cool metal bar of the gate. The hay bale where they had shared bits and pieces of their lives still sat in the corner of the stall. In those hectic hours when Dakota had been so ill, Brian had learned a lot about Lindsey Mandel.

She was dedicated and tireless when it came to doing her duty. She was witty and funny, often when he least expected it. The mental image of her parking a tank outside the clinic made him smile even now. She was sure of her place in the world and that place was in the army. Yet she didn't believe in mixing marriage with her career.

It was a shame, really. She had so much to offer. She was more than a pretty face. She was a woman with a heart and a soul. Her faith in God seemed unshakable in spite of being abandoned by her mother as a child and her brother's devastating injury. She would make some man a fine wife if he didn't mind her going off to war.

Like most Americans, he listened to news and saw almost daily the way brave young men and women sacrificed everything for the freedom he took so much for granted. He was ashamed to admit that he had thought of them as foolishly brave. But there was nothing foolish about Lindsey or about her love of country.

Emily would have liked her.

Pushing away from the gate, he made his way back to his office. He had a mound of paperwork waiting for him. The extra work would be good. It would help keep his mind off the void that had formed in his life. Lindsey and her horse were gone. Now his life could finally get back to normal.

But was that what he really wanted?

Chapter Nine

Lindsey ran the flat brush from Dakota's withers to his rump and worked down his side until his coat held a high shine. Inside the cavernous limestone stable that had been built in 1889, she listened to the sounds of other horses being led out for their morning exercise. Their shod feet clattered noisily on the uneven cobblestone floor. The cool interior smelled of old wood, horses, hay and oiled leather. It was a scent she had come to love in the sixteen months that she had been assigned to the unit.

The repetitive motion of brushing Dakota didn't require much thought, leaving her mind free to wander. The place it chose to go was back to the Large Animal Clinic.

Had Isabella managed another escape only to find Dakota gone? What was Brian doing today, Lindsey wondered? Was he thinking about her?

"A penny for your thoughts?"

She turned to see Shane leaning on the lower half of the wooden stall door and looking bored now that their season was over.

"They aren't worth that much," she replied, picking up a mane and tail comb.

"Need some help?" he offered.

"Sure. Trying to comb a tail one-handed is harder than it looks."

"How's the arm doing?"

"It hurts, it itches, and the fact that I can't use my hand is driving me nuts—other than that, it's fine."

"At least you don't have to stand on it." He motioned to the cast on Dakota's leg.

"I know. Poor boy, I can't imagine being uncomfortable and not being able to tell anyone."

"He'll tell us, just not with words."

"He has been nipping at the wrap today."

"See what I mean?"

Lindsey ducked under Dakota's neck and began grooming his other side. Shane spoke softly and patted the big bay's rump before pulling his tail to one side to comb it.

Lindsey glanced at him and her hand stilled.

"What?" he asked when he noticed her staring.

"Danny and I were doing this very thing the last time I saw him before he was wounded. It was only a few days before he shipped out. Neither one of us wanted to say goodbye, so we worked side by side grooming Dakota without saying a word. Danny loves this horse. I thought he was crazy to pay boarding fees and buy feed on an enlisted man's salary, but he vowed he would trailer Dakota to any post in the U.S., including Alaska, rather than sell him. I think he would have taken him overseas if he thought it was safe."

"Karen said the same thing."

It was just the opening she had been looking for to

ask Shane about his feelings for Karen, yet was it really any of her business? Because she cared for both of them, she took the plunge. "Shane, about Karen—"

"Rest easy." He cut her off before she got any further. "Karen is a wonderful person and as sweet as they come, but there isn't anything between us."

"I only wanted to say that I wouldn't object if there were. I think you're a great guy."

"I think I am, too," he agreed loudly. "Feel free to fix me up with any of your friends. This down-home Texas boy will show 'em a good time."

"I beg to differ," Avery said from the doorway. "If any of your friends want to be treated like a lady, they need to go out with a gentleman like myself, not a hayseed cowboy."

Lindsey chuckled at their good-natured teasing. "I want to keep my friends, so I won't let them go out with either of you."

Avery wrinkled his brow. "Ouch."

Shane looked at him. "Did she just insult us?"

"Yes, but she did it with a smile. It makes me wonder if I should show her our new toy?"

Glancing between the two of them, she pressed her lips together, then said, "Okay, I'll bite. What toy?"

Avery held up a small gray case the size of a camcorder. "Our new thermal-imaging recorder. This way we can keep an infrared eye on Dakota's leg and report any hot spots or inflammation in his other legs before they get serious."

She ducked under Dakota's neck and came over to examine the camera. "This is great. Did Brian send it over?"

Shane shook his head. "No, your boyfriend didn't splurge on this. This is army issue."

"He isn't my boyfriend. How does it work?"

"I'll show you." Avery flipped up the screen, pointed the camera at Dakota and a multicolored image of a horse appeared.

"What do the colors mean?" Lindsey pointed to the screen.

"Blue is cool. The warmer an object is, the closer to red it appears on the screen. See how the floor and walls show up as blue. Dakota is warmer than the floor. He shows up as greens and yellows."

"Except for that spot on his cast," she pointed out.

Avery moved closer. "Yes, he has quite a bit of heat coming from the lower portion of his leg."

"Does that mean there's a problem?"

"It means I'm going to give your boyfriend a call and have him check it out."

"Stop it. I told you he isn't my boyfriend."

Avery closed the camera and winked at Shane. "Methinks the lady doth protest too much."

Brian finished rewrapping Dakota's new cast with a bright blue elastic webbing designed to help prevent the horse from chewing on it.

"That was a good call, Captain. If the rub had gotten much worse we could have had a real problem with a pressure sore."

"Private Barnes is the one who found it."

"Your men have done a good job of looking after this fella." Rising from the short three-legged stool he used when he was out in the field, Brian patted Dakota's shoulder.

"We want to see him well and back on active duty."

"I hope that happens, Captain." Putting his supplies back into his case, Brian tried to sound casual. "Where is Sergeant Mandel today? When Dakota was at the clinic she stuck to him like a burr."

"She had to report for physical therapy up at the hospital."

"Her arm isn't worse, is it?"

"No, but there is some concern about the damage to the nerve. It's too bad, really. She and Dakota were to carry the U.S. flag in the upcoming Inaugural parade.

"She mentioned that Dakota needed to be healed enough to walk three miles with a rider by January twentieth."

"Do you think he'll be able to do it?"

"Six weeks in a cast would leave four weeks for rehabilitation and strengthening. He might be ready by then, but it's a big if."

"This ride is very important to Lindsey."

"Keep doing what you're doing and he may improve enough to go. I'll have some of our students check back in a couple of days to see how he's doing."

The two men shook hands and Captain Watson walked back to his office. Brian began repacking his bag and supplies into the special compartments built into the bed of his truck. He had just closed and locked the tool chest when a dark blue sedan pulled up beside him. The door opened and Lindsey got out. It was as if the sun had come out from behind the clouds.

"Hi," she said as she walked up to him.

"Hi." He couldn't think of anything else to say. Oddly enough, she seemed at a loss for words, as well.

He gestured toward her car. "I didn't think you could drive."

"Avery suggested I get a spinner for my steering wheel. It works great, but I still overcorrect a little. How's Dakota?"

"Fitted with a new cast and doing fine." The silence lengthened again. He closed the truck door.

"So, how is Isabella getting along?" Lindsey asked quickly.

"She's good."

"Not making any more escapes?"

"Not a one."

"Glad to hear it."

"I guess I'd better be going."

"Oh, sure. I didn't mean to keep you." She took a step back, uncertainty clouding her eyes.

"I'll be back the day after tomorrow to check on Dakota. Maybe I'll see you then?" He knew he should send some of his fourth-year students, but he found he wanted the excuse to come back and spend time with Lindsey.

"Great. I'll look for you." Her bright smile tugged at his heartstrings.

He climbed into his truck and drove away. Glancing in his side mirror, he saw her watching him from the edge of the roadway. Resisting the urge to turn around and go back was the hardest thing he had done in a long time.

A week later, Lindsey was leaning against Dakota's stall door when she heard halting footsteps on the cobblestones behind her. She knew who it was without turning around and her heart gave a happy leap. Brian had been out to check on Dakota twice during the past week, but at the last visit, he had pronounced Dakota well on the way to recovery. Since there wasn't any problem with the horse, had he come to see her?

"Good morning, Lindsey." The sound of Brian's voice sent a sparkle of happiness shooting through her veins. She turned to face him, hoping her delight didn't show. "Good morning, Brian."

"How's my patient doing?"

"Getting better every day."

"I'm glad to hear it."

He stopped close beside her, his arm just brushing hers. She didn't pull away as she realized how much she had missed his company and how right it felt to be with him. "What are you doing here?"

"I want to take a few X-rays to document the bone's healing progress."

Of course he hadn't come just to see her. Lindsey pushed aside the tiny disappointment she felt and resolved to be content with his company no matter why he had chosen to come. "Do you need any help?"

"I will if you aren't busy."

"I'm afraid I have a tour due any minute. I'll get one of the other men to help."

"I'm not in any rush. What sort of tour?"

"It's a group of schoolchildren from Topeka."

"Is that why you're dressed in your itchy-looking blues?"

She brushed at the shoulder of her short cavalry jacket with one hand, then tugged the hem down as she stood up straight. "How do I look? Notice anything different about me?"

"Is this a trick question?"

"No, I got my cast off yesterday."

"I see that now. Good for you, but you still have the sling."

"I don't have much feeling in my hand or arm yet. This way it isn't dangling against my side."

"Nerves heal slowly. Give it some time. Even with the sling, I think you look very nineteenth century."

"That's the idea." She dusted the top of her knee-high black riding boots by rubbing them on the back of each pant leg.

At the sound of a vehicle, she looked toward the parking lot and saw a small yellow school bus pulling up. She settled her cap snuggly on her head. "Pardon me while I see to our visitors."

Lindsey was proud of the CGMCG and she especially enjoyed giving tours to the dozens of Scout troops, grade-school classes and veterans' groups that visited the post each year.

Brian asked, "Is there any reason I can't join the tour? I'd like to know more about your unit."

"I'd be delighted to have you, provided you help keep the kids in line. I've found that the boys especially tend to get rowdy when no one is looking."

She put on her best welcoming smile and walked outside. In the courtyard, she noticed a wheelchair lift being lowered to the ground at the back of the bus. A middle-aged man waved to her and instructed the group of ten-year-old boys next to the van to stop horsing around. The girls, standing off to one side, were giggling and whispering to one another.

"Good afternoon, and welcome to the Commanding General's Mounted Color Guard stables."

"Hey, you're a girl." The biggest boy in the group smirked. "Girls can't be in the army."

"Actually, women serve in many units in today's military. But during the period when this stable was built, women were not allowed to enlist."

"Didn't a few women serve in the Union Army during the Civil War?" Brian asked.

She shot him a grateful look. "That's correct. Both the Union and Confederate Armies had women who fought disguised as men. It goes to show that women can be good soldiers and as brave as men in battle. If you'll come this way, we'll start our tour with the barn."

She paused inside the large double doors where a life-size model horse stood before a wall displaying photographs of cavalry horses in action.

"Please watch your step. These old cobblestones can be treacherous." She gestured toward the uneven floor.

"Wouldn't it be better for the horses to have these torn up or paved over," Brian suggested.

She wrinkled her nose. "Don't think we haven't asked. Unfortunately, this is a historical building and can't be altered. This is the last remaining original stable building. It was constructed of native limestone and timber in 1889. It originally housed sixty mounts. At one time it was converted into a pistol range before being returned to its original function when our unit was formed. Before we get started, I'd like to have each one of you sign our guest book."

One by one, the children signed their names in a ledger on a podium until only the boy in the wheelchair was left. Brian took the book and handed it down to the youngster. The boy shyly smiled his thanks.

"As you can see," Lindsey continued, "our model

horse, Stick and Stone, carries everything a cavalry horse would have been equipped with in the 1880s. The saddle is called a McClellen and has the unique feature of an open split down the center and a rawhide seat. Would anyone like to guess why?"

The boy in the wheelchair raised his hand. Lindsey pointed to him. "Yes?"

"It allowed air to circulate and help keep the horse's back from getting sore?"

"That's right."

"Brainiac," one of the group muttered.

"The only thing he knows about riding a horse is what he reads in a book," the big boy scoffed.

As Lindsey led the group down farther into the barn, Brian replaced the visitors log and waited while the boy in the wheelchair struggled to maneuver his chair down the wide aisle.

"Do you need a hand?" Brian offered when it was obvious that the boy's wheels weren't rolling well over the uneven stones. He put his hands on the handles of the chair.

"No, I can manage," the kid said defensively, pushing harder.

"I'm sure you can. I only offered because…please don't tell anyone…but walking on a rough surface like this makes me afraid of falling."

The child looked back at him. "It does?"

"Would you mind if I just held on to the back of your chair to steady myself?"

Sitting up straighter, the boy shrugged. "I guess that would be okay."

"We'd better catch up with the group or we'll miss the tour."

"I'm not really interested in it anyway."

"You don't like horses?"

"They're okay."

"Their big size can make them scary." Brian tipped the wheelchair backward slightly freeing the front wheels.

"I'm not scared of them."

"You're not? That's good. My name is Brian. What's your name?"

"Mark."

"It's nice to meet you, Mark."

"How'd you hurt your leg?"

Taken aback, Brian hesitated before answering. He'd forgotten how forthright children could be. "I hurt it in a car accident."

Mark's eyes widened. "Me, too. Was it a drunk driver?"

"No, it was my own fault."

"Will you get better?"

"I'm afraid this is as good as I'm going to get. I'll always need a cane."

"I got hit by a drunk driver when I was riding my bike home from school. Do you like horses?"

"I like them very much." Brian followed the abrupt change of subject easily.

"Does anyone make fun of you because you can't ride?" Mark's dejected tone told Brian how much the earlier gibe had hurt.

Brian let the group move farther ahead. "I don't pay any attention to them if they do. Besides, being handicapped doesn't mean you can't ride a horse."

Catching Lindsey's eye, he motioned for her to continue with her tour. She nodded and began walking.

"All our tack repairs are done here in the leather shop. This is Corporal Shane Ross. He's going to explain the different types of leather we use and show you how we repair our harnesses," Lindsey said.

Lindsey stepped aside as the group crowded into the small room where Shane sat behind a large sewing machine. She walked back to where Brian had stopped pushing Mark.

Looking up with a mixture of disbelief and interest, Mark asked, "How can someone like me ride a horse?"

"I have a friend who runs a riding stable just for kids with disabilities. She has special saddles that will hold you strapped in place. Her horses are very gentle. All kinds of kids learn to ride there."

"Is it far away?" Mark's tone was wistful.

"It's only a half-hour drive from here. Why don't I give you my card. Have your parents call me and I'll tell them all about it."

"I don't know. Mom is funny about me doing stuff."

"Tell her that it's a very safe place and they have trained therapists there."

"Okay."

Lindsey dropped to one knee beside the boy. "How would you like to meet one of our horses up close and personal?"

He nodded eagerly. "That would be totally sweet."

"Good." She sent a questioning look at Brian. He nodded his approval.

"Right this way." Standing, she led them to Dakota's stall and opened the door.

Brian maneuvered the chair into the stall and Lindsey closed the door, shutting him and the boy inside.

Dakota limped a few steps forward to investigate his visitors.

Mark held out one hand. "Come here, fella."

Lowering his head, Dakota sniffed at the boy's hand and then took another step closer so that Mark could pet the side of his face.

"What's wrong with him?" Mark gestured toward the cast.

"He broke his ankle and Dr. Brian fixed it for him," Lindsey said from the doorway.

Mark looked up with interest. "You're a horse doctor?"

Brian nodded. "I'm a veterinary surgeon and I specialize in horses."

"That's tight, dude."

Brian glanced back at Lindsey. She grinned. "That means he thinks you have a cool job."

"Oh."

"We should get on with the tour," she said, holding open the door.

"Aw, do we have to?"

"I think we should." Brian waited until the boy said goodbye to Dakota and then pushed his chair out of the stall.

Outside the leather shop, he waited until the rest of the children came out and then followed the group and listened intently as Lindsey talked about the unit's job, their performances and the history of Fort Riley. It was obvious by the way she answered the children's questions that she enjoyed sharing her knowledge.

It wasn't until the last child was herded onto the bus and the vehicle pulled away that he saw her sag with relief and rub her arm.

"Are you hurting?"

"A little. Tell me more about the riding stable for disabled children." They began walking back into the barn.

"It isn't just for children. Hearts and Horses is run by a woman I met when I treated one of her horses for colic. What she does is called hippotherapy."

"What is that exactly?"

"Hippotherapy uses the movement of the horse as a treatment in physical, occupational and speech therapy for people living with disabilities. It has been shown to improve their muscle tone, balance, coordination and motor development, as well as emotional well-being."

"That sounds like you have some firsthand experience."

"I volunteer at Hearts and Horses on the last Saturday of each month. It's a great way to spend an afternoon."

"I've heard of places like that, but I didn't know there were any near here."

"Actually, there are a half dozen such stables in the eastern part of Kansas. Some are members of the American Hippotherapy Association. Others belong to NARHA, the North American Riding for the Handicapped Association."

"I wonder if something like that would help my brother?"

"Every case is different, but didn't you say he lived in Washington, D.C.? I know they have a center that works with veterans."

"I'll tell my sister-in-law to look into it. I think it would do Danny a world of good to be around horses again.

"Places like that would need very calm horses. We

have a horse named Tiger who is getting ready to retire. I'll mention your friend's place to the Captain. Tiger might be a good fit for that kind of work."

"They also need trained volunteers to work with the children. Unfortunately, both good horses and volunteers are in short supply."

"That's a shame. I could see how eager Mark was to ride and yet how guarded he was about expressing his desire. I know it was because he was afraid of being disappointed."

"You should have children of your own," Brian said.

The second the words were out of his mouth he knew it was the wrong thing to say. It was a very personal comment. He glanced at her to see her reaction. Other than looking bemused, she didn't seem upset by his odd statement.

"I'm afraid children aren't on my agenda for quite a few more years."

Not exactly sure why he felt compelled to press the issue, he said, "Agendas can change."

"Yes, they can, but I don't have a reason to change mine."

"I forgot. The army is your life. Is that enough?"

She cast a sideways glance at him. "I've always thought it would be."

He decided to change the subject. "I haven't seen Karen for a while. How is she?"

"Karen's fine. She's gone home for the holidays, but she is actually thinking of moving here and attending college next semester. She wants to become a grief counselor."

Brian looked down and used the tip of his cane to draw circles in the dirt. His family in Montana had tried to get him to see a grief counselor after Emily's death, but he had refused. He deserved the pain his grief brought. "What do you think of the idea?"

"Karen has a good heart and a great faith in God. I think she is taking my brother's tragedy and turning it into something positive. I really respect her for that."

He considered the idea that he hadn't allowed anything positive to come from Emily's death. He had wanted to stay wrapped up in his grief, but was he doing an injustice to Emily's memory?

He cocked his head to one side as he studied the woman who seemed so in control of her life.

"You did a good job with those kids today. Keeping a bunch of ten-year-olds interested in history for an hour is no easy feat."

She patted the holster at her side. "I wouldn't attempt it if I wasn't armed."

"I don't believe that for a minute."

She held up her free hand in a gesture of surrender. "Okay, you've found me out. I like kids. Arrest me."

Her smile was so adorable that he leaned in and kissed her.

Chapter Ten

Lindsey was so startled by Brian's kiss that she froze for an instant. Her next thought was how right it felt.

Abruptly, he took a step back. He looked as surprised as she was. She smiled shyly and touched her fingers to her lips.

Without a word, he began walking again. Not understanding exactly what was going on, she followed, perplexed by his silence.

"Brian, wait. Would you like to talk about what just happened?"

He stopped and faced her. "I'm sorry, I don't know what came over me."

Disappointment followed close on the heels of his words. "That is not exactly what a woman likes to hear after a man kisses her."

"You're a very attractive woman, but that isn't any excuse. I was way out of line. It won't happen again."

"So I guess we're clear on that?" About as clear as mud, she decided.

"Absolutely clear. I value your friendship and I admire you as a person. I hope my lapse won't affect how we work together."

"Of course not." She had no idea what else to say.

"Good. That's good," he muttered.

At the barn door, Shane stood waiting for them. "I heard you needed some help with your X-ray equipment."

Brian nodded. "If you'll come with me, I'll show you what I need." The two of them walked to Brian's truck.

Lindsey entered the barn and walked into Dakota's stall. She began rubbing his cheek. Glancing around to make sure she was alone, she leaned forward and whispered in the horse's ear. "Brian just kissed me."

A happy glow swelled from within and she couldn't keep her smile contained any longer.

"As kisses go, it was pretty nice until he opened his mouth and began apologizing."

Her glow dimmed by several watts. He had certainly backpedaled quickly enough. Obviously she shouldn't read more into it, but she wouldn't mind if it happened again. She had begun to care a lot for Brian, but it was foolhardy to think that anything could come of those feelings. No, the best thing would be to put the episode firmly out of her mind.

If only it hadn't been such a nice kiss.

In a few minutes, Shane came in carrying several black cases. He and Brian were laughing about something and her heart quivered at the sound. Putting his kiss out of her mind wouldn't be easy.

Brian produced a tall block of wood from one case. "Lindsey, can you put this under his hoof, please?"

He was all business again. She did as he asked and tried to be as professional as possible. "Yes, sir."

"Now that Dakota is doing so well, you'll be seeing less of me. Once a week should be often enough for follow-up visits. My students can handle those."

"We've gotten kinda used to your company, Doc," Shane drawled from the stable door.

Lindsey realized with sudden clarity that Brian might simply fade out of her life the way numerous other friends had done over the years. Dakota was the reason they had spent so many hours together. When the horse was healed, their paths might never cross again. The happy glow she had been basking in went out like the flip of a switch.

Brian soon had his portable X-ray machine set up. By positioning Dakota's hoof on a block of wood to raise it off the ground, they were able to get the views Brian wanted while Lindsey kept the horse still by talking to him and scratching him behind his ear.

Shane watched from outside the stall. "Do you have big plans for Christmas, Doc?"

"No. I usually take call so that the other staff with families can have the day off."

"You're welcome to join us for dinner," Lindsey offered, and then thought of slapping her forehead with her hand. Would he think she was desperately trying to hold on to the relationship?

"Sure," Shane chimed in. "We're on duty, too. We usually get together in the ready room and bring in all the fixings."

Brian slanted a look at Lindsey. "Will you be doing the cooking?"

Her heart lightened at the sight of the humor glinting in his eyes. He was thinking about her burnt cookies.

She grinned back. "No, my contribution will be two pumpkins pies from the commissary—already baked."

"I don't know. I hate to intrude on your party."

"You won't be intruding, Doc," Shane assured him. "After all you've done for Dakota, you're practically a member of the unit yourself."

"Thanks, I'll think about it."

"You could bring Isabella along," Lindsey suggested with a cheeky grin. "Dakota has been missing her."

Now that was desperate, but if it enticed him to come to dinner, she didn't care.

"I think she's been missing him, too. At least, she has been pouting about something."

"Who's Isabella?" Shane asked.

Lindsey winked at Brian. "She's Dakota's new friend, and she's as cute as a bunny."

Shane looked interested. "Is she that pretty blond secretary at the clinic?"

Brian shook his head. "She's much cuter than Jennifer."

Sending him a chiding look, Lindsey said, "Oh, I'm going to tell Jennifer you said that."

His eyes widened in mock alarm. "Please don't. I shudder to think what she might do to me."

"All right, I won't squeal on you if you promise to join us for dinner on Christmas Day."

"Barring the need for my services at the clinic, I promise to try."

"We plan on eating about six, and don't feel that you have to bring something. We'll have more than enough."

"I'll keep that in mind."

Lindsey grinned as she rubbed Dakota's neck. Suddenly, this holiday had become something special to look forward to, and Brian was the reason.

Christmas morning dawned bright and clear with just enough bite to the cold air to remind Brian that winter had arrived. As he scraped the frost from his truck's windshield, he still hadn't decided whether to accept Lindsey's invitation to dinner.

He tried telling himself that she had only offered out of kindness. It certainly couldn't be construed as a date even if it was a dinner invitation. After all, a half dozen other men would be there, too. He would go, and he would give her the present he had found for her. The trinket had caught his eye in the window of a gift shop downtown. The moment he saw it, he knew Lindsey would love it.

On the drive to the clinic with Isabella beside him, he passed one of the local churches. The tall white spire silhouetted against the clear blue sky looked Christmas-card perfect. The parking lot was already filling with early worshippers.

Lindsey would be at the fort chapel this morning.

He envied her certainty, her belief in God's love above all else. Brian knew his heart was made of weaker clay. He had turned his back on God after Emily's death. He didn't expect his feelings would change anytime soon. He drove past the church without stopping, but the image of Lindsey bowing her head to pray stayed with him. That and the memory of their kiss.

Suddenly, he began to think of all the reasons he shouldn't go to Christmas dinner. One by one they crowded into his mind. He didn't belong to their group. He was an outsider invited out of charity. His presence would put a damper on their camaraderie and fun. His gift would seem too personal. The more he thought about it, the more certain he became—he wouldn't go.

Although the clinic was officially closed and he could have taken call from home, he decided to go in to catch up on some work. No holiday was complete without someone needing a vet in a hurry. If he was at the clinic already, it would speed up his response time. Throughout the day he glanced frequently at the clock. By noon he hadn't seen a single patient or taken a single call. His conference presentation had been worked and reworked until he couldn't stand looking at the numbers and slides another minute.

Around two o'clock he decided there wasn't any reason his holiday should turn into a total waste. He could enjoy a meal that wasn't takeout or warmed up in a microwave for a change. He didn't have to stay long and make small talk. He would go.

As the afternoon dragged on, he finished reviewing a stack of odds and ends of paperwork, checked the clock, and then his watch a half dozen times. Isabella did nothing but nap in her box so he didn't even have her antics to help pass the time. After sharpening all his pencils and straightening his desk, he checked the clock again. It was four-fifteen and he finally made up his mind.

He wasn't going.

At five-thirty he closed the clinic doors and carried Isabella to his truck. Setting her in her carrier, he climbed in and shut the door. With his hands on the steering wheel, he sat in his parking space without starting the engine. It had turned colder outside. Gray clouds had moved in and occasional snowflakes drifted earthward to vanish as soon as they touched anything.

It might be snowing, but the forecast was only calling for a trace of the white stuff.

"We should get going," he told Isabella. But he didn't move. The thought of heading home to an empty house tonight left him feeling forlorn.

I don't have to be alone tonight.

He had spent so much time avoiding people that he wasn't sure he knew how to interact in a purely social situation. Especially with a woman as lovely and lively as Lindsey. The last thing he wanted to do was to stir up feelings that were better left buried.

Who was he kidding? Those feelings had been coming to life since the first day he met Lindsey Mandel— and it scared him half to death.

Lindsey's anticipation slowly seeped away as six o'clock, then six-thirty slipped past. She tried to enjoy the feast brought together by the men, but disappointment made even the cranberry salad taste bland.

Why hadn't Brian come?

Maybe he'd had an emergency surgery. If she knew that for certain she might be able to enjoy what was left of the day, but something told her he wasn't tied up at work. Some small part of her knew that Brian didn't want to see her. He had kissed her, but it had meant nothing to him. If only it had meant nothing to her, too.

"How about some dessert, Lindsey?" Lee held out a paper plate loaded with a huge slice of pie and mounds of whipped cream.

She held up her hand. "No, thanks. I'm full."

"Full? You hardly touched a bite of the Captain's smoked turkey."

"I ate my share. Just because I can't put away as

much chow as you do is no reason to imply that I'm finicky."

"Leave her alone," Shane said as he snagged the plate from Lee's hand. "She has to watch her girlish figure."

He forked a piece into his mouth as he whirled away from Lee's attempt to grab the plate back. "Hey, fix your own!"

Lindsey smiled at their foolishness but didn't feel like joining in as they returned to the folding chairs positioned in front of the small portable TV Avery had provided for the evening. Instead, she began to gather up the dirty paper plates and toss them in the trash.

"Is something wrong, Lindsey?" Captain Watson moved to help her clean up.

"No, sir."

"I thought maybe your arm was hurting."

"It aches, especially with the weather turning colder."

"Are you getting any feeling back in your hand?"

"A little, but I still don't have any kind of grip."

"Dakota looks like he's doing well."

"I think so, too. How are you doing, sir?" She had heard through the grapevine that he and his wife had separated.

He looked at her sharply. "You mean on my first major holiday as a divorced man?"

"Something like that. Not that I want to pry."

"It's okay. No, it's been rough."

"Do you have kids?"

"Two. My son is fifteen and my daughter just turned thirteen. I've been gone for so many holidays during my career that I doubt they even miss me tonight."

"I'm sure that isn't true."

"Maybe not, but I wasn't there much for my kids

when they were little. I can't blame them if they ignore me now."

"Don't let them. Nothing is more important than your family. Pick up the phone and give them a call. Let them know you care."

Indecision crossed his face, followed by a growing look of determination. "Thanks, I think I will."

As he walked away to his office, Lindsey thought back to all the times her father had been gone when she was little. He had missed more than his share of Christmas days even after their mother left. That had left Lindsey, Danny and Karen to fend for themselves. They had worked hard at making presents for each other and even harder at sneaking around to fill stockings when no one was looking. They had made the holidays something special for one another.

Did her father regret those missed opportunities the way Captain Watson did? She wanted to believe that was true. There was really only one way to find out. Talking to her father wouldn't change the past, but it might make the future brighter for both of them.

Pulling out her cell phone, she walked into the hall away from the noise and laughter and dialed her father's number. The least she could do was follow the advice she gave out so freely.

He answered on the second ring. "Hello?"

"Dad, it's Lindsey."

"Lindsey, honey, it's so good to hear your voice."

She relaxed at the sound of his genuine happiness. "It's good to hear you, too. I wanted to wish you a Merry Christmas, only…it doesn't feel right to be celebrating."

"I know." His voice became choked with emotion. "But life goes on."

"Yes, it does." She wanted to cry away the pain she had been holding inside. She wanted to feel the comfort of her father's arms around her.

After a long pause, he asked, "How's your arm?" His voice sounded more in control.

"I got my cast off last week, but my arm is still pretty weak and I can't use my hand much. Will you be coming to the parade?" she asked quickly.

"Of course. You'll still be riding, won't you?"

"Yes, Dakota and I will be there."

"So the horse is doing better?"

"Karen told you?"

"She did. I agree with you. As long as things look like they're going to work out, I don't think we should tell Danny. The last thing he needs is to start fretting about the animal. Are things looking good? Because if they aren't, I can't keep that from him."

"Dr. Cutter says Dakota may get his cast off in a few days."

"That's good, but you won't be carrying the flag if you can't use your hand."

"I haven't given up. I still have time to get better. I do my exercises, and I'm as determined as Danny to get in shape for the big day."

"That's my girl. Make your old man proud and show the world what we Mandels are made of. I know Danny is looking forward to seeing the pair of you."

"I won't disappoint him or you."

"Have you talked to him lately?"

"I called them last night, why?"

"Did he tell you that with his tracheotomy capped off, he can stay off his ventilator for eight hours?"

"Yes, Abigail mentioned it."

"He's getting stronger every day and we have you to thank for that."

"Danny is doing the work, Dad."

"Yes, but Abigail and I both think you and that horse are the reason he's found the focus he needs. We both thank God that you have done this for him."

"He's my brother. I'd do anything for him."

"I know you would, honey."

She finished talking to her father and talked briefly with Karen, then ended the call. Stuffing her phone back in her pocket, she stared at the ceiling.

Please, Lord, let Dakota be healed enough to travel and let me be strong enough to hold the flag. I couldn't bear it if I had to let Danny down.

She had started to rejoin the men in front of the TV when a knock sounded at the front door. Hope sprang up in her heart. She pulled open the door and saw Brian standing in front of her. The darkness behind him was filled with soft, feathery snowflakes drifting down. It was a perfect Christmas evening.

Thank You, Lord, for bringing him here tonight.

"Merry Christmas," she said, knowing she had to be grinning from ear to ear.

"Merry Christmas." He held out a small red box with a silver bow. "This is for you."

She took the gift and clutched it close to her chest. She had a present for him, too, but it could wait until later. "Thank you. Come in. The guys are watching TV in the other room."

"Did I miss dinner?"

"I saved you a plate."

"Good, because I'm starved."

She looked behind him toward his truck. "Where is Isabella?"

He motioned with his head toward the stables. "I put her in with Dakota in his stall. I couldn't believe how excited she was to see him."

"The horse and the holiday hare. There's a children's story in that somewhere." Lindsey stepped back and allowed him to come inside.

Brian shook the snow from his black overcoat and hung it on an empty peg behind the door. He couldn't get over the way Lindsey stood watching him with that adorable, kissable smile on her face.

He smiled back. "Aren't you going to open your present?"

"Not yet. After you've had your dinner."

"All right, lead the way." He followed her into the crowded room where other members of the unit were gathered around the television set.

Shane noticed him first. "Hey, look who decided to join us. Have a seat, Doc. The game's tied and Baltimore has the ball on the six-yard line."

Lindsey pulled him by the arm toward a table set up in the opposite corner of the room. "After he gets a plate. Turkey or ham, Brian?"

"Both."

"Help yourself, we have plenty left."

After loading his plate, Brian took the seat Shane offered. Lindsey sat crossed-legged on the floor in front of him and it wasn't long until they were all engrossed in the football game.

The rapid-fire banter and good-natured teasing going on around him reminded Brian of his own family gatherings when he was a kid. Oddly enough, he didn't feel like an outsider amongst these people. They were all far from their families and homes. They were strangers joined together by the special bond of military service. He relaxed and joined in the chatter, adding his own armchair-coaching comments and rooting for the team opposite the one Lindsey urged on.

In the end, his team lost, but he didn't care. Watching Lindsey's brief victory jig was enough of a reward.

As the evening grew late, one by one the men left until only Shane, Avery and Lindsey remained. Brian wished them all good-night and was headed toward the door and his coat when Lindsey rushed up beside him.

"I'll go with you to fetch Isabella."

"It may take two of us to pry her away from Dakota. Let me help you with your coat."

"Thanks." She turned around and slipped one arm into the heavy military-issue jacket he held. The other sleeve hung empty as he covered her sling.

"You need to button up. You'll catch cold running around like that." He pulled her jacket closed and began doing up the snaps.

"I can manage," she protested.

"So can I," he countered, and continued until he had the last one snapped beneath her chin. In the sudden stillness, he gazed down at her in wonder. His heart had been bound by grief for so long that he wasn't certain what he was feeling. He was only certain that this woman had somehow managed to work her way past that barrier and plant seeds of kindness and friendship. What, if anything, might grow from those seeds he had no way of knowing, but he was willing to wait and see.

He stepped back and opened the door. "It's getting late. I don't want to keep you up past your bedtime."

She wrinkled her nose. "Duty call does come early. Oh, wait a minute, I forgot something."

Hurrying down the hall, she vanished around the corner and reappeared a few seconds later with a bulge in one pocket. "Okay. Let's go round up the rabbit."

Outside, the air had turned colder and the snow had begun to accumulate on the cars. A light dusting covered the ground, as well. Brian leaned on his cane heavily as they crossed the asphalt parking lot made slippery by the still-falling snow. Lindsey hurried on ahead. Brian was thankful she didn't seem to notice his difficult progress. He really disliked walking on slick surfaces. He hated knowing one slip might leave him unable to rise unaided.

Once inside the barn, he breathed a sigh of relief. Lindsey, a few yards down the aisle, was turning on the lights at Dakota's end of the stable. The commotion woke the other horses, who moved to hang their heads out the stall doors and check out their nighttime visitors.

Brian stopped to pet the onlookers as he made his way slowly over the rough cobblestones. "Merry Christmas, Trooper. Merry Christmas, Socks. Merry Christmas, Tiger."

"They all wish you a Merry Christmas, too," Lindsey said when he reached her side.

She nodded toward Dakota's stall. "You won't believe where your rabbit has decided to take a nap."

"Where?" He leaned over the half door to look inside. Dakota lay at the back of the stall with his legs folded under him. Isabella lay perched on his broad back sound asleep with her head pillowed on her front paws and her long ears draped on either side of them.

Brian glanced at Lindsey and they both began to

laugh. "You are right," he said. "This really has the makings of a great children's story."

"Before you go, I want you to have this." She pulled a black box from her pocket. "It's actually from all of us, including Dakota, but I picked it out."

"Thank you, but you didn't have to get me anything. The turkey and dressing was more than enough." He took the box from her and opened it. Inside lay a gold pocket watch engraved with a U.S. flag.

She leaned forward eagerly. "Turn it over and read the inscription."

He did as she suggested. "'To Dr. Cutter with endless gratitude. The CGMCG.'"

"I hope you don't mind the initials. Writing out the Commanding General's Mounted Color Guard would take up most of a large wall clock."

"This is beautiful. Thank you."

"I'm glad you like it."

"I do. This makes two terrific presents this year."

"What was your other one?"

"The equine ambulance company called the day before yesterday. They're loaning us their newest model for our conference."

"Brian, that's great. I know how much it means to you."

"True, but I'm still a little disappointed."

She cocked her head to one side. "Why?"

"I didn't get to see you open your gift."

With a saucy smile, she pulled his box from the depth of her pocket. "I didn't want to open it in front of the guys."

"Open it now," he suggested quietly.

"I can't get the ribbon off one-handed, and I'm sure you don't want to watch me try to do it with my teeth."

"Let me help." He hung his cane over the stall door and took the gift from her. Carefully, he worked off the silver satin ribbon and bow without breaking it, then held out the box.

She lifted the top and gasped with delight. "Brian, it's beautiful."

With the utmost care, she lifted out a small delicate snow globe. Inside the glass dome a bay horse pranced between snow-laden pine trees. She shook it and sent the glittering snowflakes whirling about him. "It looks just like Dakota!"

"There are fifteen bays in the stable. How can you tell that it looks like Dakota?"

"Because it's my present and I say it's Dakota." She shook it again and the snow whirled faster.

"I'm glad you like it."

"It will always remind me that your presence with us tonight was a special Christmas blessing."

More than anything, he wanted to kiss her again, but something held him back. Some part of him didn't trust the new emotions churning inside him the way her miniature blizzard swirled inside the glass bubble.

He said, "It's getting late. I should get going."

"Of course." Did she look disappointed? She turned away before he could read her face.

He opened the stall door and stepped inside. Lindsey followed him and spoke softly to Dakota. She squatted by his head while Brian plucked his pet from her perch and cradled her in his arm.

"I'll be back the day after tomorrow without the rabbit. If Dakota's X-rays look good, we'll get his cast off."

She stood and shoved her free hand in her coat pocket. "Once that's done, will you still need to see him?"

"I'll need monthly follow-ups for at least six months to document his recovery."

"And after that?"

"You won't see me ever again." He tried to make it sound like a joke, but his words fell flat.

She stepped close and he didn't move away. She pulled her hand from her pocket and laid it on his chest as she gazed into his eyes. "I hope that isn't true, because I would miss you."

Raising on tiptoe, she brushed her lips softly against his.

Chapter Eleven

For the next day and a half, Brian couldn't put Lindsey's kiss out of his head. The scene played over and over in his mind and left him wondering constantly what he should have done or said differently. Anything might have been better than standing like a mute statue while every trace of common sense and logic evaporated from his brain, leaving nothing but the yearning to gather her close in his arms.

At least he hadn't done that. Instead, she left him without a word, but her shy smile and knowing glance made it pretty obvious that the next move would be up to him.

So exactly what would he say to her today?

Packing his equipment into his truck, he prepared to go and take another set of X-rays of Dakota. In spite of the setbacks, the horse's recovery had progressed much better than he had hoped. His combination of arthrodesis and bone-growth-gene therapy certainly looked like a success. The first draft of his report on the procedure sat on his desk. Having serial X-rays and a sound horse to back up his hypothesis would certainly make for a more interesting presentation at the conference.

He should be happy that the horse's recovery was almost complete, but he wasn't. Once Dakota's cast was off, Brian knew he wouldn't be seeing Lindsey unless he decided to become involved in a relationship with her.

Shoving an awkward piece of equipment into place, he tried not to think about her—about the softness of her lips or about the way she made him feel. He didn't have time for a relationship. The more he tried to convince himself that was true, the more often thoughts of Lindsey intruded into his working day. When he was alone, it was even worse.

He stowed the last X-ray cassette in the truck and closed the door. He knew by the tenderness of her kiss that Lindsey had grown very fond of him. He wanted to be fair to her. She needed to understand that he couldn't give her more than friendship. Not even if he found himself wondering exactly where *more* would take them.

He moved to the driver's side and yanked open the door. It was with mixed emotions that he headed toward the Fort Riley stables.

Lindsey coasted through her morning duties on the same cushion of air that had held her up since Christmas night. Everything seemed right with the world and she couldn't stop smiling. She was in love with Brian Cutter.

She hadn't planned it. She still didn't know how they could make their different situations work, but she knew that he was the man of her heart.

It was a secret she hadn't told anyone. Karen had returned from Washington the night before, but the feeling was just too new and special to share.

Humming her favorite Christmas tune, she carried a bucket of grain to each of the horses and the mules in the barn and made sure that they all had water. The sprinkling of snow that had helped to make Christmas night so special had quickly melted. Today's bright sunshine would soon dry the lingering mud. On one hand, Lindsey would have liked the Christmas white to last a little longer, but the horses were eager to get out into the open pastures and she didn't relish the idea of brushing down a muddy herd when they came back in.

As she worked, she kept glancing out the stable doors toward the parking lot. Brian should be here soon.

Dakota whinnied loudly and she turned to him with a chuckle. "Are you anxious to see Brian, too?"

Shane came down the aisle pushing a wheelbarrow loaded with straw. He set down his load and rubbed Dakota's forehead. "I think he's anxious to get his cast off."

"I know exactly how he feels. I couldn't wait to get mine off, but I hope he does better than I did."

"You're getting better."

She massaged her hand in the sling. "I can move my fingers a little, but my arm is still weak. I have a doctor's appointment at four o'clock. I'm hoping he'll let me out of this thing."

"Hey, your boyfriend just pulled up."

She spun around to peer out into the bright sunshine. "Brian's here? Where?"

Shane lifted the handles of the wheelbarrow and pushed it past her. "No denials today? Do I hear wedding bells, Sergeant?"

Grinning back at him, she shook her head. "Don't be silly. We haven't even had a first date."

"If he doesn't snap you up, he's a fool."

"What a nice thing to say. Thank you, Shane."

"I mean it. Morning, Doc," he called out.

"Good morning, Corporal." Lindsey watched Brian make his way toward them and she drank in the sight of him. He was dressed in a dark maroon sweater over faded jeans and his hair looked as unruly as ever. She resisted the urge to comb it out with her fingers. He stopped a few feet away from her. She wondered if he was as delighted to see her as she was to see him.

Shane glanced at the two of them, then chuckled as he pushed his burden outside. "I'll be back to give you a hand with Dakota in five minutes."

Brian looked down at the cobblestone floor. "How are you?"

"I'm good. How are you?"

"Fine. Lindsey, I'd like to speak to you in private."

"I'd like that, too." Avery and Lee walked by a second later. She tried to look nonchalant as she smiled and nodded at them.

Once they were out of earshot, Lindsey said, "It seems privacy is hard to come by around here, today."

Brian seemed ill at ease, too, and she found that adorable. Love left her feeling shy but happy to be in his company.

Just then two soldiers came in with their saddles headed for the leather shop. Any hopes she had of finding time alone with Brian vanished. Knowing that they could be overheard, she said, "I mentioned your friend's place, Hearts and Horses, to Captain Watson as a possible retirement place for Tiger."

"What did he think?"

"He's interested. He wants to talk to you about it and perhaps have us visit the facility. I know you said you volunteered there on the last Saturday of each month, but will you be going out there this Saturday?"

"They'll be closed because of the holidays, but I did promise my friend that I would be there next Saturday. I should stay home and work on my lecture, but I really hate to disappoint any of the kids. Do you remember Mark, the boy in the wheelchair from your tour group?"

"Of course."

"My friend told me his mother enrolled him as a Christmas present."

"That's great. I know he's going to love it."

Shane came back into the barn followed by a dozen unit members. "I brought the cheering section, Doc."

"Then let's get started."

With the help of Shane and another soldier, Brian soon had his X-ray machine in place. That left Lindsey free to watch him work. He didn't allow his stiff leg to hamper his job. Instead, he seemed to accomplish things with a minimum of motion, as if he had learned to make every move count.

"It will take a few minutes to print these," he said as he exited the stall and headed for his truck. More of the men from the unit had gathered in the barn.

When Brian walked back in, Captain Watson was with him. As they stopped in front of the group, Brian held the black-and-white film aloft. "The cast can come off."

A cheer went up and everyone began pounding each other on the back, shaking hands with Brian and giving Lindsey heartfelt hugs.

The Captain was the one who asked the question they all were wondering about. "Does this mean Dakota can travel to Washington, D.C.?"

"No, it means he can begin his rehabilitation. He'll need to be hand walked for short periods only. I'll give you a schedule of times to start with and then we'll see how he progresses. I want to be notified at the first sign of any lameness."

Lindsey clasped her hands together in front of her. "But there's still hope that he'll be able to make the trip, isn't there?"

"A slim hope, I'm afraid."

"That's good enough for us, isn't it?" Lindsey asked the men around her. They responded with resounding affirmatives.

"We have faith in you and in Dakota, Dr. Cutter," Lindsey said. "He's going."

Brian studied the determined and hopeful faces around him and decided not to press the issue. No one here would endanger the horse by insisting he make the long trip if he wasn't ready when the time came.

"Before I remove his cast, he'll need new shoes put on. The ones he has on now will be too tall and I don't want him to experience an uneven gait."

"We have our farrier standing by, Doctor," Captain Watson assured him. "It shouldn't take long to change them."

Once the new shoes were in place, Dakota stood quiet and calm as his cast was removed. Brian stepped back and asked Lindsey to lead him around the stall. At first, Dakota balked, but with some easy coaxing, he finally took his first steps. Without the weight of the cast, he raised his newly freed leg higher than the others several times but soon seemed to realize he didn't need to.

"He has a slight limp, but I think he's going to

do fine," Brian said to Captain Watson as both men watched the horse closely.

"You've done great work and the army is grateful."

"I'm the one who is grateful, Captain. You allowed me to enroll him as my first patient in my clinical trials. His success will certainly add weight to my upcoming conference presentation. He may even make more funding available for the study. I can't tell you how important that is to me."

"We wish you all the best."

"Thank you, sir."

The Captain crossed his arms over his chest. "I wonder if we might ask one more favor of you?"

"Certainly, if I can."

"Sergeant Mandel mentioned you know of a riding stable for handicapped children that might be interested in Tiger. He's extremely well trained, as are all our horses, but I'd like your opinion on his suitability before I officially ask for his release from service."

"I'll be happy to look him over and make sure he's sound, but the only way to tell how he'll do is to expose him to the new environment. We'll need to see how he reacts to wheelchairs, noisy children, unsteady riders, any number of unexpected occurrences. Hearts and Horses has an evaluation program and I know they would welcome the opportunity to see if Tiger would be right for them."

"We can do that. Sergeant Mandel, assign a detail to arrange transport for Tiger to the Hearts and Horses facility. At the facility's convenience, of course. We'll go ahead with his evaluation, but make sure they know that he won't be available until our return from Washington, D.C. I don't want our senior member to miss this

Inaugural parade. Fifteen years of service has earned him the right to participate."

"Yes, sir."

Brian felt the sensation of his beeper vibrating on his belt. He pulled it from his clip and read the message. He was wanted back at the hospital, but he still hadn't had a chance to speak to Lindsey in private. He looked around and saw she was talking to Shane and Avery. It seemed that he wasn't going to get a chance today.

Maybe it was for the best. Now that they wouldn't be seeing each other so often they could simply allow the relationship to fade. Besides, what if he had read more into her kiss than she meant?

No, he decided, not speaking to her was taking the coward's way out. He walked up beside her. "Lindsey, I've got to go."

"Now?" She couldn't have looked more disappointed if she had tried.

"I'm needed back at the clinic. Is there any way I could see you later this afternoon? I need to talk to you."

"Sure. I have to go into Manhattan tonight. Why don't I stop by the clinic later."

"That would be fine. If I'm not in surgery, we can get a cup of coffee or something." He wasn't happy with the way that sounded. It was too much like asking her for a date, but he had no way to change his words. Why couldn't a guy buy a verbal eraser?

"I'd like that. I'll drop by about five-thirty. Is that too late?"

"Five-thirty will be fine. See you then."

His emergency turned out to be a horse with a severe cut to its left hind leg. It took less than an hour to supervise while his fourth-year student stitched up the patient and another twenty minutes to update the owners and outline a plan of care. He had just finished his paperwork and was handing it to Jennifer to be filed at the front desk when he saw Lindsey coming in the front doors. His breath froze in his chest.

She paused inside the doorway and slipped off her tan coat, then draped it over her arm. It was then that he noticed she wasn't wearing her sling. Smiling, she waved when she saw him.

She wore a dark green blouse with tiny flowers embroidered around the gathered neckline and on the short puff sleeves. A full black-and-green print skirt flared about her slim legs as she walked toward him. Dainty, high-heeled black shoes made those legs look even longer.

Jennifer pulled the file folder from his slack hand. "Wow. That is a big improvement over combat boots."

He couldn't have agreed more.

Lindsey stopped in front of him. Her bright smile turned his insides to pudding.

She said, "Hi. Am I too early? I can wait if you aren't finished with your work."

He found his voice and tried for a professional tone. "Ah, no, your timing is good. Why don't we just step into my office?"

"Okay."

He turned to his secretary. "Jennifer, hold my calls please."

"With pleasure." She winked.

He wanted to strangle her. Instead, he said, "Sergeant Mandel and I won't be long."

He allowed Lindsey to precede him down the hall.

As he opened the door for her, he spied his rabbit in the middle of his desk engaged in her forbidden activity.

"Isabella, put down that pencil!" Brian strode to the desk and pulled the prize from between her paws. He picked her up and sent Lindsey a defeated look.

"I've tried everything and I can't break her of getting into these."

He raised Isabella to eye level and scowled at her. "You are a bad bunny. Do not chew on my pencils."

Then, as if regretting his harsh words, he tucked her under his arm and stroked her head. Walking to the door, he opened it and called for Jennifer. She arrived and took one look at Isabella and the yellow paint flakes on her face and feet.

"Pencils again?"

"Will you put her in her outside kennel for me, please?"

"Of course. Come here, you naughty little girl," she cooed as she took the bunny from him. Ruffling the rabbit's fur, Jennifer continued to talk baby talk as she carried the offender away.

Lindsey watched the whole exchange, then raised one eyebrow. "Do you treat her that harshly each time she chews up a pencil?"

"I didn't think I was too harsh."

"You picked her up, petted her, gave her to Jennifer so that she could pet her and then sent her to the place she most likes to go—outside. In spite of all that she won't stop chewing your pencils. Will wonders never cease?"

Walking to the desk, she picked up his pencil cup, opened the deep drawer on the right-hand side of his desk and set the cup in it.

"Have you tried this?" She stared at him as she closed the drawer.

Brian pursed his lips searching for a good reply. None came to him. Feeling sheepish, he stepped closer. "Is your advice to simply remove the temptation?"

Oh, what a temptation this woman presented. Her bright eyes were brimming with mirth. The subtle scent of her perfume filled him with a desire to hold her close and breathe in the freshness she brought to his life just by being near.

"You're the animal specialist." Her sassy tone was almost too much. Calling on every ounce of self-control that he possessed, he resisted the urge to take her in his arms and kiss her. He didn't deserve to love another woman, but somehow Lindsey had a way of making him forget that fact.

Could that be the reason their paths had crossed? Was it time for him to move past the grief that had controlled his life until now?

He pulled open the drawer and set his cup back in its place in the center of his desk. "I like my pencils where they're easy to reach."

She grabbed a new one out of his cup and tapped it gently against her cheek. "I see."

He knew he was in trouble the moment he saw the mischievous glint in her eyes.

"So, is this what a girl has to do to get some attention from you?" She grinned and placed the pencil between her teeth.

Her playfulness melted the last of the icy barrier that enclosed his heart. Reaching up, he took the pencil from her and dropped it onto his desk, then he took her by the shoulders and drew her into his arms. She stepped into his embrace and lifted her face. Lowering his mouth to hers, he tasted again the poignant sweetness that was so uniquely her.

After a long second, he pulled away. Tucking her head under his chin, he drew a ragged breath. "I've been thinking about doing that all day."

"If I had known, I would have come sooner. Just don't start apologizing again."

"I won't."

"Good. You could give a girl a complex that way."

"Somehow, I don't see that happening to you. You're much too sure of yourself and your place in the world."

Resting in the comfort of his arms, Lindsey knew Brian was mistaken about that. She might sound sure of her plans, but more and more she had begun to question what she really wanted out of life. She had dismissed the idea of having a husband and children because she had seen how badly her parents had mismanaged their marriage. She never wanted to subject a child to that kind of pain. Only now, being held by Brian, she wondered if she had been wrong.

She drew back, determined to regroup her scattered wits. "I believe you asked me here for a reason. We seemed to have gotten sidetracked."

"It wasn't anything important, but I do owe you a cup of coffee."

"Yes, you do." She reluctantly stepped out of his embrace.

"We can make some here or we can go out to one of those trendy coffee shops that have sprung up all over town."

"Yours will be fine. It can't be worse than what Shane makes for us at the office."

"Don't be too sure about that. But you're all dressed up. Are you certain you don't want to go out?"

"I'm dressed up because I have a Bible-study class in about half an hour."

"Is it on post?" He busied himself with filling the coffeemaker and adding heaping scoops of grounds to the filter.

"No, it's at Grayson Community Christian Church." She sat down on the sofa, remembering the gentle way he had cared for her the first time she had been in his office. So much about Brian Cutter was a contradiction. He often sounded gruff and uncaring, but the more she came to know him, the more certain she was that he was a man with a tender heart.

"I know that church. It's on the road that leads to my house."

"Is that where you worship?"

He paused in the act of pouring water into the coffeemaker. "I haven't been to church since my wife died."

"Did the two of you attend before that?"

"Emily was really involved with our church back home. She sang in the choir and helped out in the nursery. She even edited the newsletter for the pastor. She had such boundless energy. I attended when I could, but animals get sick and injured as much on Sunday as any other day. At least, that was the excuse I used."

"Why haven't you been back?"

"I blamed God for her death. I blamed myself. I can't get past the anger."

"Forgiveness is such a large part of our faith, Brian. You can't truly love someone else unless you first love yourself. And you can't truly forgive someone else unless you first forgive yourself."

He didn't answer her. He finished pouring in the water and pressed the on switch. She rose from the sofa and crossed to his side. Linking her arm through his, she laid her head on his shoulder. "Come with me tonight."

"To Bible-study class?"

"Yes."

"I don't know."

"Brian, we all struggle to find where we fit into God's plan, but if you aren't looking, you'll never find the answer."

"How can you be so sure that God *is* the answer?"

She straightened and cupped his cheek with her hand. "We use our head to make a lot of decisions in life, but some decisions have to be made with the heart. This is one of them. Do what your heart tells you is right."

He covered her hand with his own. "My heart is telling me that kissing you again is the right thing to do."

"See, your heart knows best," she whispered as she leaned toward him. Their lips met and the kiss was everything she had dreamed it would be. After a long moment, she pulled away and placed her palm over his lips.

"Okay, my head is telling me that I'm going to be late for class."

He kissed her palm, then drew her hand away from his mouth. "Smart, as well as beautiful. I never thought I could feel this way about someone again. I'm not sure this is real."

"It's real enough for me. I care for you deeply, Brian."

"And I care for you, so where exactly does this leave us?"

"I'm not sure." There were so many things to consider, but with happiness zinging through her veins, she couldn't think of anything but how wonderful it felt to be in his arms.

"Lindsey, I want to keep seeing you."

Smiling softly, she said, "That sounds like an excellent start."

"I want to know everything there is to know about you."

"Everything?"

He pulled her close and kissed the tip of her nose. "Everything," he whispered.

"I'm just an ordinary girl."

"Who happens to be a sergeant in the U.S. Army."

"Is that a problem?" She held her breath, hoping he didn't see her career as a roadblock to this budding relationship.

"I don't know. Have you thought about leaving the service?"

She frowned and leaned back to study his face. "Are you asking me to do that?"

"I'm asking if you have considered it."

"I will admit that I've been toying with the idea, but it's something I would have to give a lot of thought."

"Of course. I don't want to rush you or pressure you into making a decision you'll regret."

"Thank you."

"I know that I want to see more of you. I want to be a part of your life."

"My life includes church, Brian. Can you accept that?"

"I'll try. I can't promise anything more than that."

A small voice in the back of her mind pointed out

that he hadn't mentioned the word *love*. She ignored it by telling herself that things were happening too fast, for both of them.

Chapter Twelve

Lindsey let herself into her apartment a little after ten-thirty that night. She tried to be quiet, but Karen was a light sleeper.

"Lindsey, is that you?" she asked from the sofa.

"Yes, I'm home. Go back to sleep."

"I will, but I'm supposed to give you a message. Dad wants you to call him."

"Tonight?"

Karen sat up and stretched. "He said whenever you got home. You know how he likes to watch the late shows. He'll be up."

"Did he say what he wanted? Is something wrong?"

"I don't think so. I got the feeling he wanted to discuss your next duty station."

"Great. After years of ignoring me, he suddenly wants to pick my career moves." She tossed her purse on the overstuffed chair in the corner and hung her coat in the closet.

"He's trying to be a better father, Lindsey. Danny's injury was a wake-up call for Dad. He knows he hasn't always been there for you. Give him a chance."

"You're right, I'm sorry. It's just that he was always so eager to hear about what Danny was doing, but I got the feeling that he thought my duties weren't important."

"You've been invited to participate in the Inaugural Parade. How many people ever get the chance to do something like that?"

"I know. I'm thankful for the opportunity, but it's not because of anything I've done. Don't get me wrong. I'm delighted to be able to honor Danny and all the other men and women who have given so much for us, but it isn't like I've done anything special."

"It's because of you that Danny is working so hard in rehab. It's only because of you that the army accepted Dakota. Don't sell yourself short. What you do counts for a lot."

"Thanks."

"You're home late—did your class run over?"

Lindsey settled on the sofa beside Karen. She needed to share her happiness with someone. "Brian went with me to Bible study tonight. Afterward, we stopped and had a cup of coffee together."

"That's wonderful! Did he like it? What did he say?"

"He said, 'Double-chocolate latte, no foam.' Or something like that, and he really seemed to enjoy it."

Karen growled as she punched Lindsey's shoulder. "I don't mean what did he say about the coffee. I meant, what did he say about the class?"

Lindsey rubbed the tender spot. "Careful. That's my only good arm."

"It won't be good for long unless you tell me everything."

"He said it gave him a lot to think about."

"That's great. I'll pray that he finds his way back to God."

"I'm praying for that, too."

"And I'll add a special request that he ask you out on another date."

"It wasn't exactly a date."

"Close enough. Oh, I can't wait until Danny meets Brian. I think they'll like each other."

Lindsey took her sister's hand and squeezed it. "They will, won't they? I'm so in love. Does it show?"

"Yes. Oh, girl, I'm so happy for you." She enveloped Lindsey in a quick, hard hug.

Lindsey returned the hug. "Thanks, sis."

Karen drew back. "Now go call Dad and let me get back to sleep."

Lindsey wanted to talk about Brian all night long, but she kept the rest of her happiness in check. "All right. Good night, kid."

Alone in her bedroom, Lindsey sat on the side of her bed and dialed her father's number. He picked up on the first ring.

"Hi, Dad. It's me. Did I wake you?"

"No, I was up."

"What did you need?"

"Nothing really. I just wanted you to know that we plan to be in front of the Hoover Building so you'll know where to look for us."

"I'm glad you're going to be there."

"I wouldn't miss it. My daughter in the Inaugural parade. Makes me mighty proud just to think about it."

She had longed to hear those words from him for so many years that she could barely speak. "Thanks, Dad. How is Danny?"

"He's making good progress. How's the arm?"

"I'm out of my sling. I can make a fist now, but my grip is still weak. I don't know if I'll be able to hold a flag."

"You'll be ready. I know you will. Say, your enlistment will be up soon, won't it?"

"I've got two months left."

"How long are you reenlisting for?"

It was the question she least wanted to hear. "I'm not sure."

"If you give them eight years you can just about pick any billet you want. I've got friends here in Washington. A Pentagon job isn't out of the question. That way you'd be close to Danny."

Eight years—it sounded like an eternity. For the first time she gave voice to the thought that had been roaming around in the back of her mind. "There isn't anything that says I have to reenlist."

"What? Mandels have always been soldiers. It's in our blood." He sounded appalled that she would even suggest not reenlisting.

"It was just a thought."

"I know you've taken Danny's injury hard, but think how he would feel if you quit because of him. You're not going to leave the service. Not my daughter. I raised you better than that."

"Karen isn't in the service." Lindsey felt a fleeting touch of envy for the way Karen had always stood her ground on the issue.

"No, that one takes after her mother's side of the family for sure, but I haven't given up on her. You, on the other hand, take after me. You'd be lost in civilian life."

Maybe he was right. She had wanted to be a soldier

all her life. Just as she had wanted to earn her father's respect all her life, she thought with sudden clarity. The two issues were so closely intertwined she wasn't sure she could tell which was which, not that it mattered. But he was right about one thing—she couldn't have Danny thinking she left the service because of him.

"It was just a thought, Dad. I'm sorry I said anything."

"That's more like it. You had me worried."

"If you had left the army, would it have made a difference with you and Mom?"

He was silent for a few seconds, then he said, "There were a lot of things wrong with our marriage, Lindsey. Being in the service was only part of it. Your mother was miserable in our situation, and I knew I would be miserable if I got out of the army. In the end, we did what made us both less miserable. I'm sorry you kids were caught in the middle."

"You did your best, Dad."

"And it must have been good enough. Two of my children joined up and followed in my footsteps. A man couldn't ask for more than that." His obvious pride came shining through in his words.

"I'll give some thought to working in Washington, D.C."

"You do that. Wherever you decide to go, I know you'll make me proud."

Tears pricked her eyelids. "Thanks, Dad."

"The army will take you places, kid. It's a great life."

The army had already taken her to the far-flung corners of the earth. Would it be so bad to stay in one place?

Not if it was the right place.

As she hung up the phone, she realized that the right place for her had nothing to do with a physical location. The right place would be where she could make a home and a life with Brian.

Were his feelings as strong? She simply wasn't sure. He liked her, she could tell that, but his guilt over his wife's death had a strong hold on his heart. She prayed she could help him find the forgiveness he needed.

Over the next week, Brian managed to make time to see Lindsey almost every day. One night they enjoyed quiet conversation over a delectable dinner at a small romantic café. On New Year's Eve, he joined both Lindsey and Karen for dinner at their apartment. Lindsey freely gave Karen credit for the hearty cooking he sampled. While the sisters laughed together over stories of previous cooking failures, he was free to admire how beautiful Lindsey's face looked when she was happy and carefree.

The following Friday night he took her to see the latest blockbuster action movie. The place was nearly empty with most of the students gone for the holiday break. Holding Lindsey's hand in a dark theater, he paid little attention to the story unfolding on the screen. What he saw was a new chapter unfolding in his own life and he liked what he saw. He knew it was too soon to talk about marriage, but the idea took hold in the back of his mind and wouldn't leave.

When he took her home that evening, they stood for a short while on her front porch and shared another sweet kiss full of promise and hope. Unbidden, the words, "I love you," rose from his heart and crossed his lips.

Her luminous eyes widened and filled with joy. "Oh, Brian, I love you, too."

"I could stand to hear those words every day of my life."

"It would be easy to say them every day," she said with quiet sincerity.

He wanted to say more, but found he didn't yet have the courage. For now, it was enough to know that she loved him. In time, they would talk about what the future might hold for them together.

On Saturday morning, Brian was determined to enjoy a few quiet hours at home after his evening with Lindsey. The trouble was, he couldn't stop thinking about her. In the light of day, it all seemed unreal. Had she really said that she loved him? Could they have a future together? The new year seemed to hold so much promise. Just thinking about it scared him witless.

All he wanted to do was to be with Lindsey. He wanted to see her eyes light up when they met his. He wanted to hold her in his arms and kiss her soft lips. He wanted to feel this happy every day of his life.

Their evening at the Bible-study class had given him a lot of food for thought. He wasn't certain that he was willing to accept Lindsey's version of a loving and caring God, but he was willing to listen and learn more from the energetic young pastor he had met.

Deciding it was better to work than to moon over a woman, he took out his seminar speech and began practicing it aloud. An hour later, Isabella went scampering through the living room past his chair toward the front entrance. She slid into the door panel then began to hop up and down.

He listened carefully and heard the faint clank of

the mailbox closing. Limping to the door, he scooped up the excited rabbit and held on to her as he opened the door and fetched his mail. The grocery store flyers were exactly the kind of paper Isabella delighted in shredding. Back inside the house, he closed the door firmly before putting her down. Her recent escapes at work had made him much more cautious about keeping an eye on her.

Once she was on the floor, she darted to her special box, hopped in and then stood on her hind legs to peer at him over the rim. Her anticipation was obvious.

Sitting in his recliner, he quickly tossed the discount ads in with her. As the crackle and ripping of paper replaced the quiet of the house, he grinned and began to look through the rest of his mail. A small, pale blue envelope caught his attention. A painful spasm clenched his stomach when he read the return address. He glanced at his wife's face in the photo on the table beside him.

"It's from your mother."

His in-laws had spoken to him only once after Emily's death. Three days after the accident, his father-in-law had come to Brian's hospital room to tell him they had arranged to have the funeral in their hometown sixty miles away the following day. Groggy from pain medication and still in traction for his shattered hip, Brian had begged him to wait until he could attend, but Emily's father had walked out of the room without saying anything else.

No words could have conveyed more strongly the blame they placed on Brian for their beloved daughter's death. He tried phoning, but they never took his calls. The few letters he wrote came back unopened.

Now, after all this time, the note in his hand was the first contact he'd had from them.

Irritation battled with his curiosity. He had loved Emily and she had loved him. If her parents had offered even the slightest sign of forgiveness, perhaps he could have found a way to forgive himself, too.

He held the unopened letter over Isabella's box, but he didn't drop it. Instead, he tore open the envelope and pulled out a single sheet of pale blue stationery.

Brian,

This coming February will mark the fifth anniversary of Emily's death, as I'm sure you are aware. Her father and I have planned a memorial service for the occasion. As the passing years have dulled our grief, we have come to regret the way we excluded you from our lives. You were Emily's one true love and we know that you never meant to hurt her. Our excuse is that our lives ended with the death of our only child. Our grief and anger needed an outlet and it was easy to blame you.

I hope you will accept our invitation to attend her memorial service. Perhaps in this way we can begin to make amends for the way we treated you. Please join us as our family and friends come together to celebrate Emily's life.

Grace and Emit Todd

Tears blurred his vision as he glanced to his wife's face smiling at him from the silver frame. She would be happy to know her parents were making an attempt to repair their relationship with him. Noticing a thin coat of dust on the glass, he realized that he hadn't held her picture close in weeks. Guilt cut deep in his heart.

He picked up the photo and wiped the front with his sleeve then pressed it to his chest. "I've been forgetting you. How could I do that? I'm sorry, sweetheart. I'm sorry about everything."

It was because of Lindsey. Lindsey had turned his life upside down and made him dream about happiness again. How could he be happy when he had ruined the lives of so many people? Her life, their child's life. Her parents were suffering still. What right did he have to any happiness in the face of so much sorrow?

The clock on the wall chimed twelve times. Today was his day to volunteer at Hearts and Horses. He was scheduled to be there at two o'clock. For a second, he considered calling to say he couldn't make it, but that would only place more of a burden on his friend. He would go, but first he would answer the letter from Emily's parents and tell them he would join them in February.

Later in the afternoon, Brian stepped out of his truck in front of the Hearts and Horses stable. He turned up the collar of his black overcoat against the chilling wind, then pulled his cane out from behind the front seat. As he made his way across the gravel driveway to the office door beside the barn, he glanced around at the well-groomed farm.

White rail fences bordered the road and enclosed several corrals. The old two-story house was also painted white, but bright blue shutters kept it from looking austere. An American flag fluttered in the breeze from its holder on one of the porch's tall square columns. In the spring and summer, Brian knew the green lawns were bordered with colorful flower beds, but winter had put an end to their bright displays weeks ago.

He stopped at the office door, but Patience Duncan opened it before he had a chance to knock. Patience's erect bearing and boundless energy belied her sixty-odd years. Her salt-and-pepper gray hair was cut in a simple bob. Her worn jeans were tucked into tall black rubber boots and her green hooded parka had a hole in one elbow where an occasional down feather found its way to freedom.

"Brian, thank you for coming." She threw her arms around him in a hearty hug.

"I'm always happy to help." He was glad now that he had come. He needed to get away from his somber thoughts.

Patience stepped back. "Come in out of the wind. It sure turned cold fast. Makes me doubly glad our indoor arena is finished."

Brian followed her inside the office. A second door connected the cluttered room to the larger pole barn. "Are my pupils here yet?"

"I'm only expecting one child today. The boy you referred to us."

"Mark? Is this his first time?"

"It is. He was disappointed when I told him he wouldn't actually be riding today, just getting to know Sprite and learning to take of her. His mother seemed very relieved. I think she needs this therapy more than her son does."

"You may be right."

"I'm happy for the light schedule because the army is sending out one of their horses for evaluation today."

His heart sank. The last thing he wanted to do was

face Lindsey today. Perhaps she wouldn't be one of the people who brought Tiger. He could only hope. "I've seen the horse in action. I think he'll be great for you."

"I hope so. Speaking of the army, I think that must be them." Patience stepped to the office window and drew the blue-and-white-checked curtain aside.

Brian moved to stand beside her. The red pickup and matching red trailer rumbling into the circle driveway were unmistakable. His heart jumped into overdrive when he noticed Lindsey in the front seat between Avery and Shane.

Patience let the curtain fall back into place. "Why don't you show them where to take their horse."

"Mark and his mother are waiting. I should get started with them."

"All right. I've set up the arena so that you can have the back third. I'll go meet the troops." Patience gave him an odd look as she walked past.

Lindsey had noticed Brian's truck in the driveway as soon as they pulled in. Excitement and delight raced through her, leaving her giddy with joy.

Resisting the urge to run and find him and fling herself into his arms took a fair measure of her resolve. There would be time for that later. Today, she was under orders to assess this facility as a possible home for a valued member of their unit. She didn't take her assignment lightly.

A middle-aged woman came out of the office and walked toward them. "Hello, and welcome to Hearts and Horses. Call me Patience. You'll never meet anyone so misnamed." The woman flashed a broad friendly smile that put Lindsey instantly at ease.

"Good afternoon, ma'am. I'm Sergeant Mandel and this is Corporal Ross and Private Barnes."

"It's a pleasure to meet you. Well, let's get a look at your horse, shall we?" Patience strode to the rear of the trailer without waiting for anyone. "How old did you say he was?" she called over her shoulder.

"Eighteen," Shane answered as he hurried to keep up with her.

"A good age for horses and for men. How old are you, sonny?"

Lindsey smiled at Avery. "I like her already."

A clang signaled the rear gate of the trailer opening. Lindsey and Avery followed as Shane and Patience led Tiger into the barn. Across the arena, Lindsey saw Brian introducing Mark to a small black mare with two white stockings and a star on her forehead. Mark's grin told Lindsey exactly what he thought of his new friend. When Brian looked their way, Lindsey smiled and waved. He nodded in acknowledgment, but continued to give his attention to the boy. Puzzled by his less-than-enthusiastic greeting, she worried that she had done something to upset him. The idea was ridiculous. He had seemed fine when they parted company last night, but she couldn't shake the feeling that something was wrong.

Patience quickly began a series of tests for Tiger. First, she rode him bareback around a small section of the barn to get the animal used to her and his surroundings. Next, she asked Shane to walk him on a loose lead and guide him beside a long ramp. Once alongside the platform, Patience turned around backward and had Shane continue to lead the horse while she shifted her weight numerous times. It was obvious that Tiger was surprised by the activity, but he remained calm and composed. Patience dismounted and pushed a wheelchair up to Tiger. He sniffed it over, then proceeded to ignore it as she pushed it close beside him, even bumping into him slightly.

While Tiger and the men got a workout with Patience, Lindsey had time to watch Brian's interaction with Mark and the horse. His quiet confidence and gentle encouragement soon had the boy and his mother brushing the mare's coat and feeding her treats. A few minutes later, Brian took them over to show them the special saddle Mark would be using. It was fastened to a stand with handrails around it and Brian had Mark practice transferring on and off until he seemed satisfied the boy could do it without difficulty.

After a half hour, Mark and his mother left. Brian began walking toward the door just as Patience declared an end to her test. She told Shane to tie up Tiger and follow her. Dusting off her hands, she came to stand beside Lindsey. "I think he's a keeper. He's cool, calm and collected and he seems readily adaptable. That's exactly the kind of horse we need. My thanks to the army for thinking of us."

"It was Brian's idea." Lindsey was happy to give him credit.

"Then my thanks to you, Brian," Patience called out. He stopped as the group led by Patience closed the distance between them.

"I have tea and coffee in the office and a dozen oatmeal cookies that I don't want going to my waist—so you are instructed to go in and enjoy them. Let me put Sprite up and then I'll give you the grand tour afterward so you can see if my stable meets your requirements. No arguments. Brian, show them the way."

"I really should be going."

"Nonsense. I've never known you to pass up one of my cookies. What's wrong with you?"

"Nothing's wrong with me," he said defensively.

"Well, then, go show my guests a little hospitality until I get back," she muttered as she tromped off.

Lindsey studied Brian, but he wouldn't look at her. Something was definitely wrong.

Avery settled his cap more tightly on his head. "Nobody has to tell me twice to eat oatmeal cookies."

They all began walking toward the office. "She would have done well in the military," Shane said as he held open the door for the others.

"She certainly enjoys giving orders," Avery agreed.

Shane patted Brian on the shoulder. "I've found most women do, especially women sergeants. Have you sent in your reenlistment papers yet, Lindsey?"

"They're filled out, but I haven't turned them in."

"You're still planning to reenlist?" Brian asked, a scowl on his face as he looked at her for the first time.

The disapproval in his tone cut her to the quick. "Brian, the army is my career."

He glared at her. "I thought things had changed."

"Have they? I don't recall being asked anything except to consider it."

Shane cleared his throat. "I'm going to go load Tiger. Avery, come help me." He grabbed two cookies and pushed Avery toward the door back into the barn.

Lindsey crossed her arms over her chest. "I thought you understood my feelings."

"Yes, you always made them clear."

"I hope I have." She couldn't help the defensive tone in her voice. "I plan to ask for an assignment at Fort Riley."

"But you can't guarantee they'll give you that assignment, can you?"

"Of course not."

"For you it's the army, your country, your family, your horse and then Lindsey somewhere way at the back of the line."

"Brian, what's wrong? Why are you so angry?"

"I thought we had something good between us."

"I thought so, too."

"Then where do I fit in your list, Lindsey? After the army but before the horse?"

"That's not fair." The hurt his tone caused went deeper than she had ever imagined.

"Life isn't fair and you didn't answer my question."

"How can I give you an answer when we've never talked about it?"

Shaking his head, he walked to the door and pulled it open. "The same way you made your decision to re-enlist without talking to me about it."

He slammed the door behind him, leaving her staring after him with no idea what had just happened.

Chapter Thirteen

Lindsey tried to pretend that everything was okay. She went to work and to her physical therapy sessions, but her arm seemed to be getting weaker instead of stronger. She spent long hours walking Dakota, first around the small pen beside the stable and later on longer trips through the pastures and along the less traveled roads of the fort. When it was only the big horse walking beside her, she didn't have to pretend, and the tears that she tried to hold in check would slip out.

Shane, Avery and Lee offered a few times to go with her, but she politely refused. After a few days they seemed to realize that solitude was exactly what she wanted and needed. Captain Watson made sure that the unit ran smoothly as preparations got underway for their trip to Washington, D.C. All the horses were out-fitted with the special shoes that were required, uniforms were pressed and boots were buffed to a high gloss. Lindsey went through the motions without thinking about them.

When the first heavy snowfall blanketed the fort, she tried not to remember how happy she had been with

Brian in the snow on Christmas night. Her heart might be broken, but it would heal in time the way her arm and Dakota's leg had healed. Breaks were excruciatingly painful in the beginning, but with time the pain would fade to a dull ache. If she could just find a way to get through it until then.

When anyone asked about Brian, she would smile and say he was too busy to come out to the fort. She thought she had convinced the rest of the unit that she was fine. It was her sister she couldn't fool.

A week after the trip to Hearts and Horses, Karen confronted Lindsey in the kitchen of their apartment.

"All right. What is going on?" Karen demanded, standing in the doorway with her hands propped on her hips.

"I'm not sure I know what you mean. I'm setting the table for dinner."

"You know exactly what I mean. What happened between you and Brian?"

"Nothing happened." She lined up the spoons beside the knives.

"One night you float in here telling me how in love you are and the next night I hear you crying yourself to sleep. Okay, call me crazy, but I think something is going on."

"It didn't work out. What do you want me to say?"

"A little more than that."

Stepping up to her sister, Lindsey laid her hand on Karen's shoulder. "It didn't work out. That's all there is to it. Now can we please talk about something else?"

"Do I need to have Shane go punch his lights out?"

Lindsey managed a weak smile. "As satisfying as that may sound, it won't help."

"I didn't think so. Oh, honey, I'm so sorry."

"Thanks, but it's better to find out now than after we've spent seventeen years together the way Mom and Dad did."

"I think it's better to fall in love and stay in love."

"That isn't the path God has chosen for me."

"You shouldn't give up so easily. You love the guy. Take my advice and go talk to him. Isn't he worth fighting for?"

He was, but she didn't know how or who to fight. Brian had made the choice to end their relationship before it truly began. She strongly suspected his motives had more to do with his guilt over his wife's death than her career choice, but she didn't know how to make him see that. Tonight, she was too tired to search for answers.

"I've got a more important battle to win. I have to get Dakota fit to go to the Inauguration. I'm not going to disappoint Danny when he has worked so hard. After Washington, D.C., maybe I'll go and see Brian. Until then, can we please not talk about him anymore?"

Karen reluctantly agreed and Lindsey was almost sorry she did.

Lindsey threw a saddle up on Dakota for the first time since their fall. It proved to be difficult with her weak arm, but she managed. It had been three weeks since his cast had come off. He was up to walking five miles a day without problems. To her eye, he looked as sound as a dollar, but the real test would be to see if he could carry her weight.

The company horses were due to depart for Washington, D.C., in two days. The decision whether or not to take Dakota had to be made within the next forty-eight hours.

In the small enclosed riding pen beside the stable, she spoke softly to him and stepped into the stirrup. He stood motionless as she swung up onto his back.

"Good boy. Let's try a walk, okay?" She nudged him with her heels and he began walking with a smooth stride that gladdened her heart.

After ten circuits of the area without any sign of lameness, she pulled him to a halt.

"How does he feel, Sergeant?" Captain Watson asked from the stable doorway.

"As good as he looks, sir." She patted Dakota's neck.

"Excellent. All we need now is Dr. Cutter's okay and Dakota is on his way with the rest of the herd."

Just the mention of Brian's name was enough to make her want to cry, but she didn't give in to the urge. Once more she'd had it pounded into her head that a military life and romance didn't mix. This time she had learned her lesson for good.

"I don't see any reason Dr. Cutter won't release him. His walk is sound."

Captain Watson stepped out of the stable and came to stand beside her. Under one arm he carried the unit's banner.

Lindsey's heart sank. Her grip wasn't strong in spite of the physical therapy that she had been doing religiously.

"Are you ready to try this?" he asked, nodding toward the staff in his hand.

"Yes, sir." Lindsey was happy her voice sounded calm even if she was quaking inside.

Please, dear Lord. I need Your help now. Lend me the strength I need to do this for my brother.

Captain Watson handed up the banner. As soon as her fingers closed around the staff, she knew she couldn't hold it. The flag slipped out of her grasp. He caught it before it hit the ground.

He didn't say anything. He didn't have to. She dismounted and spent a long moment staring at her boots before she looked up and met his sympathetic gaze. The choking pain in her chest made it almost impossible to speak, but she did. "I respectfully request that you appoint another soldier to carry the flag, sir."

"Lindsey, I'm sorry."

"Don't be sorry. It never was about me. It's about honoring men and women like Danny—people who have given everything, including their lives, to protect and defend our flag. The last thing I want to do is disrespect their sacrifice by dropping the colors."

"Do you feel that you can hold a saber in salute?"

Oh, how she wanted to say she could, but the truth came out instead. "I doubt it."

"I see."

"Does this mean that I'll stay behind as part of the rear detachment?"

"No. Your family will be there and so should you. As you know, normally flag bearing goes by rank."

"Yes, sir. Highest-ranking soldier carries the U.S. flag, next highest rank carries the army flag and so on."

"That means Corporal Ross will carry the American flag in your place."

"Sir, my concern is that Shane's weight will be too much for Dakota."

"I agree. I'll leave it to you to decide who will ride

Dakota in your place. At least he will be in the parade to represent your family if Dr. Cutter okays the trip."

"Yes, sir. I know Danny will be honored to have any one of our unit members ride Dakota."

"Thank you, Sergeant. You're dismissed for the day. Let me know who your choice is tomorrow morning."

Trying hard to maintain control, Lindsey saluted smartly, then watched the Captain walk away. When he was out of sight, she buried her face in Dakota's mane and gave in to her tears.

Brian pulled up the most recent digital X-rays of Dakota's leg on the computer in his office. They weren't the best-quality films. The fourth-year students he had sent to the post to take the X-rays that morning hadn't done as good a job as he would have liked. He should have gone himself, but he hadn't wanted to risk running into Lindsey.

He leaned forward to examine the pictures more closely. He couldn't be sure if the faint line extending into the second phalanx bone was artifact or new trouble brewing for Dakota.

He looked up at the sound of a knock on his door. Jennifer opened it and said, "Doctor, Captain Watson and Sergeant Mandel are here to see you."

His heart sank. So much for avoiding Lindsey. He steeled his heart against the pain he knew was coming. "Send them in."

He rose and extended his hand as Captain Watson entered. The Captain took it in a firm grip. Lindsey came in and stood quietly behind her commander.

"We've come to get a travel release for Dakota."

"I'm afraid I have some concerns about that."

Captain Watson frowned. "What type of concerns?"

"His last X-ray shows a small area that has me worried. I'd like to repeat the films tomorrow."

"I'm sorry, Doctor, but the horses are due to ship out tomorrow morning and my men will be flying out the following afternoon. The custom hauler the army has hired will be at the stable at ten sharp. If you need more films you'll have to get them today."

"You're using a custom hauler? I thought your men would be taking the horses."

"Army regulations make that difficult. If we haul the horses ourselves, we would have to stop every eight hours and rest the animals. The trip would take days. By hiring an outside firm, the horses can be transported straight through to Washington, D.C."

Brian frowned. "You're talking about almost twenty-four hours without a break."

"That's correct."

"I'm afraid I can't release Dakota to travel under such conditions."

"Why not?" Lindsey demanded, looking at him for the first time.

"Standing in a moving trailer and being jostled in amongst other animals for so many hours would place entirely too much stress on his leg. I'm sorry, but I won't grant his release under such circumstances."

Captain Watson glanced at Lindsey. "I'm certainly disappointed to hear that. This is a very important event for my men. They've worked hard to get Dakota fit and ready to go."

"I understand that, but the risk to the animal's welfare is simply too great."

"I can't take the horse without a release." He looked

back and forth between Brian and Lindsey as if waiting for more to be said. When neither of them spoke, he drew a deep breath. "That's it then. Thank you for your time, Dr. Cutter."

Lindsey waited until Captain Watson left the room. When he closed the door behind him, she swung around to face Brian. "How can you do this to me? You know how important this is!"

"I'm not doing anything *to* you. I'm doing this *for* Dakota."

Lindsey stared at Brian in growing disbelief. "He's healed."

"And I intend to see that he stays that way."

"Brian, you know how important it is that he be in the parade, how important it is to my brother."

"I know you want Dakota there to honor your brother, but what good will it do if Dakota's leg fails on the trailer ride and he has to be destroyed? I know you don't want that."

"He can make the trip. He's strong enough."

"Maybe he is and maybe he isn't. As his vet, this is my call. I can't let you risk his life for a few minutes of fame."

"You mean you won't risk letting the world see that your wonderful new procedure doesn't work." Disappointment gave her words a bitter edge.

"It did work. Dakota was out of his cast in record time."

"But his leg isn't strong enough to stand the trip to Washington, D.C.? How is that a success? Why not let us at least try using a sling or some way to support him?"

"I might agree to that if I knew the trip could be

made in easy stages, but you heard Captain Watson. The horses are going nonstop by commercial hauler. That means hours of being shaken and jarred and crowded in with fifteen other animals. The risk is too much. Especially after all it took to save him in the first place."

"But to not even try?"

"You're upset. I don't think this discussion needs to go any further."

"I thought you understood what was at stake. My brother is going to be at that parade. How am I going to tell him Dakota won't be?"

"Lindsey, I'm sorry."

"I wanted to carry the flag for him, but I can't. My arm isn't strong enough. So, I want Dakota there because he was an important part of Danny's life. When my brother gave Dakota to the army, it was his last piece of freedom, his last ounce of pride. He had nothing left to give his country and now you're going to say that sacrifice means nothing."

"Do you honestly think your brother would want you to risk Dakota's life?"

At his question, the fight went out of Lindsey. "No."

He stepped close. If only he would take her in his arms the way he had before. How could the feelings between them have changed so quickly?

"Go to Washington, D.C., Lindsey. Ride beside the flag with your unit. Honor your brother's sacrifice, even if it isn't in the fashion you had hoped."

She pulled away from his touch. "I want to thank you for all you have done for Dakota, Dr. Cutter. You have the gratitude of the U.S. Army. I can see myself out."

As she walked out the door of his office, Brian knew with a sinking heart that she was walking out of his life.

He started to go after her, but stopped with his hand on the doorknob. It was for the best. He didn't have a heart to give her. He had buried it with his wife and child.

If I don't have a heart, then what is breaking inside me?

Chapter Fourteen

Work had always been Brian's answer to keeping his innermost pain locked away. Today should have been no different, except nothing helped erase the memory of the disappointment on Lindsey's face when she had walked out of his office two days ago.

He glanced at the clock above his desk. It was only a few minutes after nine. The unit's horses would be almost to Washington, D.C., by now. Except for Dakota. Lindsey and the other soldiers would be flying out in a few hours. The Inaugural parade would take place tomorrow at noon.

"And my conference is less than forty-eight hours away," he muttered.

What he needed now was to concentrate on his presentation, to make sure he had enough hard facts to impress the United Jockey Club representatives and ensure substantial grant monies for his research. He needed to focus. Reaching for a pencil, he paused with it in his hand. The memory of Lindsey grinning at him with one between her teeth made him smile. Remembering the kiss he had shared with her in this office erased all thoughts of work from him mind.

"You're a fool, Brian Cutter," he stated forcefully. "What right did you have to fall in love again?"

It was a question to which he already knew the answer. He had no right to love another woman. His carelessness had cost Emily her life. She had loved him with all her heart and trusted him to care for her always. He never should have survived the crash. He should have died with her and the baby.

Passing through what was left of his days without love had seemed a fitting punishment for living. Until Lindsey.

Lindsey had made him think about a future and not about the past.

He heard a timid knock at the door. An irrational hope rose that it might be her, but it was quickly dashed when Jennifer peeked in.

"I thought I made it plain that I didn't want to be disturbed." He turned away before she could read the disappointment he knew must be written on his face.

"Someone is in a sour mood today."

"What do you want?"

"Wow, the list is so long. A new car, a diamond tennis bracelet, a trip to Jamaica…"

"If you think you can get all of those things with your first unemployment check, keep making jokes."

The sudden silence told him he had made his point. After a moment, she cleared her throat and said meekly, "I wanted to inform you that your ambulance has arrived."

"Thank you, I've been informed. Is that all?" When she didn't reply, he turned around. She was standing in the doorway tapping her cheek with one finger as she stared at the ceiling. She sighed as if she had come to an important decision.

"The unemployment check might make a down payment on the tennis bracelet, so I'm going to go ahead and tell you that you are an abject idiot."

The last thing he needed was one of her scoldings. "Jen, please. Not today."

"You let your friend down. Even if there was nothing romantic between you and Lindsey, and I don't believe that for a minute, but even if there wasn't, she was your friend."

"I had no way of proving that Dakota's leg would be strong enough for the journey."

"You mean you don't have enough data to make that assumption."

He threw his hands up. "Exactly. Finally, someone understands."

"But you believe in your work, don't you?"

"Of course I do. Dakota will be as sound as ever."

She crossed her arms and asked, "How much proof would you need?"

"I don't understand."

"How much proof of his soundness would you need to let him go to Washington?"

"Perhaps another month without any signs of lameness."

"Was he sound before?"

"Before the accident? I assume so."

"He was sound and he broke his pastern anyway."

"Jennifer, what are you getting at?"

She stepped forward and laid a hand on his arm. "What I'm getting at is that we never get a guarantee in life. All we get are opportunities. In life and in love there are no guarantees. We get hurt, we lose, we cry and then we get up and keep going because God made us this way. The only guarantee of failure is in not trying."

Why did what she was saying suddenly make so much sense?

She crossed her arms over her chest again and stared at him. Arching one eyebrow, she asked, "So, am I fired?"

Her cheeky question pulled a wry smile from him. "I'll let you know by the end of the day."

"I'd like to know now. Stylish Gems jewelry shop is having a sale. My bracelet is twenty percent off if I put it on layaway by noon."

"You aren't fired."

She sighed. "It's just as well. I never learned to play tennis. Okay, come outside and show me your new toy."

It beat trying to work surrounded by memories he couldn't forget. The horses had already left. Even if he did change his decision it wouldn't change the outcome for Dakota. Grabbing his cane, he accompanied Jennifer out the main doors.

In the parking lot beside the clinic, the equine ambulance sat looking like a white, overly tall and extrawide horse trailer.

"This is it? This is what you've been begging for?" Jennifer didn't look impressed.

"Don't let its unassuming exterior fool you. This is the best they make." Brian had spent long hours poring over the features of this particular model. He pressed a switch on the front. A muffled hiss filled the air as the hydraulic system allowed the entire trailer to sink to ground level.

A second switch lowered one whole wall of the vehicle and turned it into a gentle ramp. "This will keep an injured horse from having to step up."

"Cool." Apparently intrigued, she ventured closer. "What's that?" She pointed inside.

"Those are hydraulic padded sides that move in and hold the animal still so he doesn't have to shift his weight. There is a sling, too, if one is needed, and a winch to pull the horse in if it can't stand."

"So a horse could ride in this thing and never put a hoof on the floor?"

"I guess that's true."

"If the army had something like this, then Dakota could travel to Washington, D.C., and not risk injuring his leg."

"The Army doesn't have anything like this, believe me."

"No, because we have it. For how long?"

"Two weeks."

She patted his shoulder. "I knew you'd think of something."

He followed her sudden shift in logic way too easily. "No. No! I'm not giving this vehicle to the army."

"Loan, not give. Loan for a few days. Calm down."

He rubbed his chin as he considered what she was suggesting. It was crazy. Unthinkable. "The unit is leaving today. There isn't time to get over there."

"Avery said they aren't leaving until noon. It's only ten-thirty. You've got plenty of time."

"This is insane. They wouldn't even know how to operate it."

"You know how."

"Me? I can't go to Washington, D.C. I've got to present a lecture at the conference the day after tomorrow."

"What will you lose by missing one lecture?"

"Funding, respect, a chance to prove my work is making a difference."

"Fair enough. What will you gain by missing it?"

What would he gain? A chance to make things right with Lindsey? A chance to make amends for his cruel behavior? A chance to let a brave man see that his sacrifice meant something to this nation?

He turned to walk away. "No. I'll get fired."

She raced to stand in front of him, blocking his retreat. "You have tenure. They won't fire you."

He stepped to the side, but she moved to match him. "I'll end up teaching the first year's bone lab."

"So what? You'll be great at it."

He shook his head. "No, I can't do it."

"Dr. Cutter, look at me." When he did, she said quietly. "Tell me that you don't love her."

The words couldn't come out of his mouth, because he knew they weren't true. He did love Lindsey. He would always love her. God had blessed him and he had turned his back on that blessing. He had been too scared of coming alive again, of risking more heartache, and because of that he had pushed Lindsey away. Would this wild scheme give him another chance? Or was it already too late?

Like a gentle whisper in his ear, he heard Lindsey's voice saying, "We use our head to make a lot of decisions in life, but some decisions have to be made with the heart. This is one of them. Do what your heart tells you is right."

Lord, I know it's been a long time since You've heard a prayer from me, but please let this be the right decision.

Lindsey stood apart from the rest of the unit as they waited beside the barn for the bus that would take them to the airport. She didn't want to dampen the excitement of the others. Attired in their sharply pressed dress uniforms, the men were laughing and joking and bursting with pride. This was the most prestigious event many of them would ever attend in their entire lives. Tomorrow, families from across the nation would be glued to their televisions hoping for a glimpse of their sons, grandsons or fathers as this unit rode proudly down Pennsylvania Avenue—without her.

Lindsey blew on her hands and wished she hadn't packed her gloves away. The air was cold and crisp enough to frost the windows of the office with lacy patterns. Karen sat beside her on an overstuffed suitcase bundled up to her ears with a thick red-white-and-blue scarf over her heavy quilted blue parka. The Captain had managed to secure a seat for her on the military flight and for that Lindsey was grateful. When the bus rolled into sight at last, Lindsey said, "I'm just going to run in and say goodbye to Dakota. I know he wonders why he was left behind."

Karen pulled down her scarf enough to say, "I won't let them leave without you."

"I almost wish they would."

"No, you don't. Danny, Abigail and Dad all want to see you."

"I let them down. I let Danny down."

"Did he take it badly when you called last night?"

"It almost broke my heart to tell him that Dakota and

I were going to have to sit this one out." Her heart was already in so many pieces that Lindsey wondered if it would ever be whole again.

"I'm sure he understands that it wasn't your fault."

"He tried to be cheerful and upbeat, but I could tell he was so disappointed."

"Our brother is a strong guy."

"He is. He tried to make me feel better by telling me he was glad he didn't have to get out in the cold tomorrow. I let him down. I don't know how I'm going to face him."

"You did your best. You can feel sorry for yourself all you want, but your family still loves you, so get over it." She covered her nose again.

Lindsey couldn't help but smile. "When we were little I used to ask God over and over again why He gave me such a pain in the neck for a sister. Little did I know what a favor He did me and how much I would come to cherish you."

"What a sweet thing to say. But for the record, I thought you were a pain in the neck, too," came her muffled reply.

Lindsey's giggles mingled with her sister's. It felt good to laugh again.

The bus pulled into the parking lot, but a second vehicle pulled in behind it. Lindsey looked on in amazement as Brian got out of his truck and started toward her. The laughter and voices of the men grew silent as they watched him approach. Shane, Lee and Avery stepped in front of her, blocking Brian's way.

Facing the men with their arms crossed over their chests and scowls on their faces, Brian knew it wouldn't be easy to persuade Lindsey's friends to let him speak to her.

Captain Watson stepped out in front of the group. "Dr. Cutter, what brings you here today?"

Brian decided his best chance would be to make this offer seem professional instead of personal. "I've come to put a proposal to you, Captain."

"What type of proposal?"

"I'd like to transport Dakota to Washington for you."

He saw Lindsey's eyes widen in surprise. A murmur ran through the group until the Captain held up his hand for silence. "I don't think I understand. You said it wouldn't be safe for him to make such a long trailer ride."

"I now have a special ambulance that can transport Dakota in complete safety without placing any undue stress on his leg. I'm willing to take him if I can have another man go with me to share the driving."

Lindsey spoke at last. "I thought the ambulance was going to be on display for the conference. How did you get permission to take it across the country?"

Since he didn't exactly have permission, he chose his words carefully. "The vehicle is on loan to the clinic for two weeks. There is no stipulation that it stays in our parking lot. In fact, we especially asked that we be allowed to use it for patient transports." He shrugged. "No mention was made about how far those transports might be."

He watched as the possibility of seeing her dream come true brightened her eyes, replacing the coolness she had regarded him with. He hoped she could read the regret on his face as easily as he read her growing excitement.

The Captain looked at his watch. "You would be cutting it close to make D.C. by assembly time tomorrow."

"I know that."

"I wouldn't feel right sending one of my men with you knowing they might miss riding in the parade."

Lindsey stepped between her friends and addressed Captain Watson. "Sir, I respectfully request that I be allowed to accompany Dakota since I won't be riding."

"Me, too," Karen added, wiggling between Shane and Lee.

Captain Watson rubbed a hand over his jaw. "This is highly irregular, but I do have orders for *all* our horses to travel to Washington, D.C., by independent contractor."

Karen looked around. "Does that mean he can go?"

"Corporal Ross," the Captain barked.

"Sir." Shane stepped forward.

"Get the forge fired up and get those special shoes on Dakota."

"Yes, sir." He replied with a bright grin.

Karen's shriek of joy was echoed in Brian's heart. Now he would have twenty-four hours to try to set things right with Lindsey.

With the help of all the unit members, they soon had Dakota shod and secured in the trailer along with enough feed and water to last the trip. Lindsey and Karen stowed their suitcases behind the seat of the truck and then came to stand beside Brian.

He said, "There's a jump seat in the trailer. One of us should ride back here and keep an eye on him. There's a walkie-talkie by the seat and one in the truck cab so we can keep in touch."

"I'll ride with him," Lindsey said, and moved to climb in.

Karen caught her by the arm. "Oh, no you don't. I'm taking the first turn with Dakota." She pushed past her sister to stand in the open doorway at the rear of the trailer.

Brian could have kissed her. He walked to the front of the truck and waited beside the passenger door.

"Karen, you're riding in the truck and that's an order." Lindsey's low tone brooked no argument.

"I'm not in the military. I don't take orders. Stop being a coward and go get in the truck or we'll never get there."

Lindsey considered jerking her sister out of the trailer, but decided she didn't want to look that undignified in front of her men. Instead, she slammed the rear door shut, walked up beside Brian and climbed into the cab.

Moments later, he got in behind the wheel, started the engine and pulled out onto the road. Long minutes passed as they drove through the fort on the winding, narrow road. She didn't say anything and neither did he.

It wasn't until he pulled out onto Interstate 70 fifteen minutes later that she gave in and spoke first.

"I thought your big conference was the day after tomorrow?"

"It is."

"You'll never make it back from D.C. unless you plan to fly."

"I can't fly. I have to drive this trailer back."

She looked at him in surprise. "What about your presentation? What about the bigwigs with money wʰ will fund your research if you wow them?"

"They won't be wowed by me. Hopefully, my research will speak for itself when I publish the study later on."

Lindsey couldn't quite get her mind around the idea that he had given up a chance for peer recognition and substantial additional funding...for her. A slim thread of hope began to bind up the shattered pieces of her heart. "Why are you doing this?"

He looked over at her. "Because my head said this was a crazy idea, but my heart said it was the right thing to do."

His eyes, so intense and full of sincerity, begged her to believe him. A whirlwind of emotions swirled through her mind. "I don't know what to say."

"Then let me start by saying I'm sorry that I treated you so badly that day at Hearts and Horses. I know I have some explaining to do."

She settled back in the seat and crossed her arms over her chest. "Yes, you do."

"Until I met you, I had kept the pain of my wife's death very much alive. The accident was my fault and I wanted—no, I needed—some kind of punishment for being the one to live."

"Survivor's guilt."

"Is that what they call it?"

"Yes. That still doesn't explain why you were so angry about my reenlistment."

"I wasn't angry about that. I was angry because I had ⸀llowed myself to fall in love with you. Your reenlist- ⸀t was just an excuse to push you away. I would have ⸀me other reason to stop seeing you. I didn't be- ⸀deserved to be loved."

She wasn't sure she was ready to accept what he had to say at face value.

"You really hurt me."

"What can I do to make you forgive me?"

"Groveling might be good," she suggested.

He managed a small smile. "I'll do that the first chance I get."

"Telling the truth is always a winner, too."

"All right, the truth. I have been afraid since the first moment I saw you."

"Afraid of what?"

"Of living and loving and perhaps losing that love. I couldn't face those risks, but I couldn't forget about you, either, and that scared me witless."

"All of life is a risk, Brian. Only God knows what lies in store for us."

"I'm trying to accept that, but it's hard to have faith in something I can't see or touch."

She reached across and laid her hand on his arm. "You can't see or touch love, yet you still believe in it, don't you?"

"Yes, I do believe love exists."

"Then so does God. God *is* love."

"Is it really that simple?"

"It really is."

"Have I told you how beautiful and wise you are?"

"No, but I may allow you to do so for the next thousand miles."

He chuckled, but quickly sobered. He took one hand off the wheel to clasp hers tightly. "Lindsey, I need to know that I haven't ruined what we had between us."

Her hand felt so small and snug in his grip. When she was eighty years old, would she still want to hold this man's hand? "My feelings for you haven't changed, Brian. I don't expect that they ever will."

"If I wasn't driving seventy miles an hour I would kiss you, darling. I love you so much it hurts."

"I love you, too, and we're going to have to stop for gas sometime."

He laughed out loud and squeezed her hand. "I promise to make up for lost time at our first pit stop. Sergeant Lindsey Mandel, will you marry me?"

In the sudden and telling silence, Brian glanced at Lindsey in concern. A second later his newfound bubble of happiness nose-dived toward the floor. "What? What's wrong?"

"Oh, talk about being scared. Brian, my family have always been good soldiers, but we make lousy spouses."

He sought for the words to reassure her. "You make your own decisions, Lindsey. What your parents or grandparents did doesn't automatically determine what you will do. I don't need an answer now. Think about it—that's all I'm asking."

"I will."

He managed a smile and tried to recapture their easy banter. "Do I still get a kiss when we stop for gas?"

A grin pulled at the corner of her lips. "I'll think about that, too."

Brian settled back in his seat. There were a lot of miles to go and nothing to do but look at the passing winter scenery and think. Her decision was much too important to risk pressing her for an answer. Instead, he said, "Why don't you call your brother and tell him that Dakota is on his way to the parade."

The walkie-talkie crackled on the dash as Karen's

voice came over it. "I've already called him. He's as excited as a five-year-old on Christmas morning."

Brian chuckled as Lindsey grabbed the radio and demanded. "Karen, have you been listening this whole time?"

"I heard someone mention stopping for gas and that was all. I just turned this talkie thing on to report that Dakota seems happy as a clam in his snug, padded… holder thing."

Lindsey looked as if she wasn't certain she believed her sibling. "All right. I'll trade places with you when we make our first stop."

"How long will that be?"

Brian checked the gas gauge. "About three hours."

"That long?"

"Yes, little miss busybody. Try taking a nap," Lindsey suggested.

"Back here with a smelly horse? I don't think so."

Brian listened to their chatter and drew a deep breath. He had three hours to wait until he could collect his kiss. Three hours alone with the woman he loved. He looked down the long four-lane highway and smiled. He was determined to make the most of every minute God had given him.

For the next few hours, he talked about Emily, about Isabella and about his early years on the ranch. He listened to Lindsey's stories of her childhood as an army brat and her worries about her brother and about Karen. When they finally stopped, he was rewarded with a kiss that was pleasant but far too brief.

After Lindsey took her turn in the trailer, he received a very different version of their youthful experiences from Karen. It was obvious that Lindsey found the military lifestyle to her liking while Karen didn't. He tolerated some not too gentle grilling by Karen about his intentions and listened to some hopefully useful advice about Lindsey, as well. Every four hours they took a short break to let Dakota stretch his legs and let the women change places.

East of St. Louis, Brian finally gave up the wheel to Lindsey, and just outside of Cincinnati, Karen took over for a few hours while Brian rode with Dakota. It wasn't until they were heading into Wheeling, West Virginia, that the weather began to turn bad. Brian didn't know about the growing storm until they stopped to switch drivers at a roadside rest stop. As Karen walked the horse for a few minutes, Brian took Lindsey aside.

"This could slow us down."

She looked up through the flakes that filled the night sky. "How much farther do we have to go?"

"A little over three hundred miles. Five, maybe six hours."

She tilted her watch to see it better in the vehicle's headlights. "We need to be at the staging area by ten at the latest. That's six and a half hours from now."

"We'll make this Dakota's last exercise stop. We go straight through from here. I'll drive next. Dakota has been as quiet as a lamb so far. I think both you girls can ride in the truck from here on out."

For the next hour, he drove into the swirling whiteness as Lindsey and Karen leaned against each other and tried to sleep. The excitement of the trip had worn off hours ago, and Brian struggled to stay awake. He couldn't stop. He had promised Lindsey that Dakota would reach Washington, D.C., in time. He glanced at the clock on the dash and saw it was nearly five-thirty in the morning. They were falling behind schedule. From the radio forecast bulletins he figured they should be driving out of the worst of it soon. If the weathermen were right for a change.

Forcing himself to concentrate, he peered into the snow. After a few more minutes, he found himself blinking repeatedly. The thick flakes flying into his headlights were mesmerizing. He rubbed his face with one hand. The glare reflecting back from the snow was making it hard to focus. If only he wasn't so tired. He closed his heavy eyes for just a second....

Chapter Fifteen

The sickening lurch of the truck woke Lindsey from her doze. She sat up abruptly, instinctively throwing her arm across Karen.

"Ouch! What was that for?" Karen said, pushing her sister's arm aside and sitting upright.

"I'm sorry." Brian's voice sounded weary and defeated. "I hit a drift pulling over. We have to stop. The storm is making it too dangerous. I'm not risking your lives in this weather."

He leaned forward and turned on the emergency flashers then leaned back with a deep sigh. Thinking of what he had told her about his wife's death, Lindsey leaned toward him and took his hand between her own. "It's okay. We tried. No one is faulting you."

He looked at Lindsey and reached out to cup her cheek with his free hand. "I wish I could have gotten you there."

"I know you do and I love you for that."

She raised her face and met his kiss with only gladness in her heart.

Karen cleared her throat. "At least you two won't

freeze to death. The temperature on your side of the truck is rising fast."

Brian slipped his arm behind Lindsey's shoulders and jerked Karen closer by the sleeve of her jacket. "I'll do my best to keep both of you warm."

Tightly sandwiched between them, Lindsey enjoyed a feeling of rightness. She was disappointed they wouldn't make it to Washington, D.C., but she was so very glad they had taken this trip.

She said, "Don't worry about freezing, Karen. I've had survival training."

"Can you make fire with two sticks?" Brian asked, his amusement clear.

"Doing it with two sticks is hard. I'd rather wait until the sun comes up and use a soda can and a chocolate bar."

"What?" the other two said in unison.

"It can be done. I'll show you someday. For now, I think we could all use a little sleep."

"I know I could," Brian said, leaning his head back.

Lindsey settled herself against his shoulder and drew Karen into the same position against her. This was where she truly wanted to be, held safe in Brian's arms while the storm outside raged on. This was the one place that was the right place for her. She knew it in her soul.

Thank You, Lord, for bringing this man into my life.

Sometime later, she opened her eyes at the sound of a large truck rumbling past them. She looked at the clock. It was a quarter till seven. Brian sat up and pulled his arm from behind her. Flexing it, he grimaced.

"What was that?" Karen mumbled, sitting up and rubbing her eyes.

Brian turned on the windshield wipers and the white blanket enclosing them was swept aside. The first faint light of dawn tinged the sky to the east of them.

"Hey, it stopped snowing," Karen said in delight.

Brian reached down and started the engine. "Yes, it has, and that was a pair of snowplows." He looked at Lindsey. "What do you think?"

"I think we are closer to Washington, D.C., than to Kansas. Let's finish the trip."

He leaned forward. "Karen?"

"Finish what we started. Maybe we'll get to see the tail end of the parade."

"All right. I'm going to check on Dakota and then we'll get back on the road."

He stepped out of the truck and used his cane to find firm footing. When he closed the door, Karen jerked on Lindsey's arm. "Well, what is your answer going to be?"

"I said let's go to D.C."

"Not that. Your answer to his marriage proposal."

"You were listening in!"

"I promise you I wasn't listening on purpose. I was trying to find a way to turn the silly thing off."

"Right. Like the dial on the side that says Off is so very hard to find."

"It was dark in the trailer, but never mind that. What's your answer?"

"You'll be the second—no, the fourth—person I'll tell after I make my decision."

"Fourth? I'm your only sister."

"You're a pain in the neck."

Karen sat back with a huff. "I think you should say yes."

"I'll take that under advisement."

Karen opened her mouth to say something else, but by that time Brian had returned. Thankfully, she kept what she wanted to say to herself.

Once they were back on the road, their spirits revived. Within an hour they had driven out of the snow-covered area and onto dry roads. Brian pushed the speed limit trying to make up some of their lost time.

It was eleven o'clock when they reached downtown D.C. and passed through the first of the security stops. It was then they got their first bit of good news.

The marine handing back their papers said, "The start of the parade has been delayed. It's set to go for one o'clock."

"Do you know why?" Brian asked as he took the forms.

"No, sir."

Rolling up his window, Brian said, "Lindsey, call your Captain and tell him we're almost there."

"They aren't going to wait for us."

"Just call them and let them know we're close."

She dialed the number with hands that shook. "Lord, please don't let him have turned off his cell phone yet."

He answered on the third ring. "It's about time you called, Sergeant."

"Sorry, sir. I knew you would be busy."

"Where are you?"

"We just passed the first checkpoint."

"Okay. All I can say is hurry. We aren't going to be able to wait if we get the order to go."

"I understand, sir."

At the next checkpoint, they waited as a police officer with a bomb-sniffing dog made a circuit through the trailer. Dakota lowered his head to check out the four-legged visitor, but the German shepherd gave him only a cursory glance before moving on.

Karen shifted from one foot to the other as she stood beside Lindsey. "Why won't they hurry up?"

"They are doing their job."

"They could do it a little faster."

Lindsey turned from watching the search to face her sister. She put both hands on Karen's shoulders. "It doesn't matter if we don't make it. Danny will still get a chance to see Dakota after the parade and he'll get to meet Brian. That's reward enough for me."

"Oh, you're just happy because you're in love. Are you guys done yet?" She called over Lindsey's shoulder. "The President is waiting on us."

"Karen!"

"He might be," she said defensively. "You don't know why the start was delayed."

"You're all clear," the officer said.

"Thank you," Karen called sweetly, then hurried to climb in the cab.

Fifteen minutes later they pulled into the staging area and located Lindsey's unit. They were all mounted except for the Captain. A drill team from a high school in Iowa was just stepping out, while their marching band was hurrying to form up behind them. The Commanding General's Mounted Color Guard was next in line. Shane and Avery dismounted and hurried toward the trailer.

Captain Watson motioned for them to hurry and then turned to speak to a parade official. Brian had already opened the door and was backing Dakota out of the trailer. He handed the horse's lead rope to Shane. Avery grabbed the tack and began to saddle the big bay.

Brian moved to speak with Captain Watson then accompanied him back to Lindsey. She stood gazing at Dakota with tears of joy in her eyes. "Wait until Danny sees you. You behave yourself out there and make him proud."

"Sergeant Mandel, you're out of uniform." Captain Watson stood scowling at her.

She looked down at her rumpled dress uniform in confusion.

"You heard me, change into the unit's performance gear ASAP."

"But I'm not riding."

"Oh, yes you are." Brian pushed her toward the trailer. "Is your uniform in your suitcase?"

"I've got it," Karen cried as she hefted it into the back of the trailer. "Come on, I'll help you."

Captain Watson grinned. "Sergeant, you didn't think you came all this way just to stand on the sidelines, did you?"

"Sort of."

"No. Get dressed. That's an order, soldier."

Brian watched as a Lindsey snapped to attention. She saluted smartly and climbed into the trailer with her sister.

A few minutes later she emerged in period uniform as she pulled on a pair of white gloves. She walked up to Captain Watson.

"Sergeant Mandel reporting as ordered."

"Give the order to mount up, Sergeant."

"Sir, yes, sir."

She barked out the command, mounted Dakota and rode out into the street. At the order to unfurl the colors, three flags were taken from their covers. Captain Watson took the American flag and handed it to Brian. "As a way to say thank-you for all you have done for this unit, would you please present this flag to First Sergeant Mandel."

"It would be my honor, sir."

Brian looked to where Lindsey sat and read the fear in her eyes.

Lindsey called on every ounce of inner strength that she possessed when Brian handed her the symbol of her country—the country her brother and so many other brave young men and women had given so much to defend.

She closed her hand around the staff, but her grip failed and the wind pulled it from her grasp. Brian caught it before it hit the ground.

"I can't do it." Tears sprang up in her eyes, blurring her vision.

"You can do it, honey. God didn't bring you and Dakota this far to fail you now. Have faith, Lindsey. I have faith in you. Give me your hand."

He placed the end of the rod into the metal cup on her stirrup and folded her fingers around the staff. "Which color in our flag stands for courage?"

"The colors have no official meaning, but to me, all of them stand for courage."

"Show me that courage now."

She closed her eyes and willed her grip to strengthen. An instant later, she heard the sound of tearing cloth and looked down. With the flag braced against his shoulder,

Brian ripped a piece of tape from a wide, white roll and made a quick loop around her wrist.

"Open your fingers."

She did and he made two quick passes around the staff and then back around her wrist. The tape blended with her white gloves. When she closed her fingers, it didn't show on the pole.

"Now you don't have to be afraid. You couldn't drop it if you tried."

"Brian, you're a genius."

"Be sure and tell Jennifer that when we get back."

"I haven't turned in my reenlistment papers," she said quickly.

"Why not? I hope it wasn't because of anything I said."

"I love the service, but maybe it's time for *me* to make a change in my life."

"Whatever you decide to do, I'm behind you 100 percent. If you want to remain in the army, we'll find a way to make it work for both of us."

"What about your research? You love your work."

"I do, but I love you more. If we are meant to be together, the Lord will show us the path."

"Proverbs 16:9, A man's heart plans his way, But the Lord directs his steps."

Grinning, he patted Dakota's neck. "He certainly directed my steps to you."

Looking into his love-filled eyes, Lindsey smiled. "Yes, he did. And the answer to your question is yes."

"Yes, what?"

"Yes, I'll marry you."

"You will? But I can't kiss you up on that horse. Lean down here."

"Meet me after the parade," she suggested with a wink. "I love you, Brian Cutter."

"I love you, too. Now, go make me proud."

Nodding, she touched her spurs to Dakota's sides and rode to the head of the column.

"This is for you, Danny," Lindsey whispered.

Suddenly she knew she wasn't alone. The wind died away to a gentle breeze and a deep warmth surrounded her. An inner strength filled her and her grip on the flag's staff tightened. This had all been a part of His plan.

Thank You, Lord, for giving me this day.

Captain Watson gave the command to move out. The Commanding General's Mounted Color Guard left the staging area and rode out to take their place on Pennsylvania Avenue.

As Brian watched her ride away, his heart was filled with more happiness than he had ever expected to know again. A second later, Karen was pulling at his sleeve.

"Come on. If we hurry, we can find Dad and Danny before Lindsey passes by. They're going to be in front of the Hoover Building. It's only a couple of blocks."

Following her, he tried to hurry, but she soon disappeared into the crowd. Looking up at the tall, imposing structures lining the street, he wondered if he would recognize the Hoover Building when he saw it.

Just when he had decided to rest and watch the presidential detail passing by, Karen appeared at his side. "They're right over here. Come on."

"Right over here" turned out to be another block. He was gritting his teeth against the pain in his hip by the time Karen announced, "There they are."

He slowed down to catch his breath. Karen hurried

toward a man in a wheelchair stationed at the curbside and threw her arms around him. When the man didn't hug her in return, Brian realized what a high price Danny Mandel had paid for the idea of freedom in a country half the world away. Karen knelt beside him and motioned to Brian.

Stepping closer, Brian nodded to the man about his own age held strapped upright in a specially designed chair. Karen quickly made the introductions to Danny, his wife and to Lindsey's father.

Danny grinned. "So you're the rabbit guy Lindsey is always talking about."

"I've been called worse."

Abigail extended her hand. "Dr. Cutter, I want to thank you for the information you sent about hippotherapy. We found out that the Old Guard has a program here. We're looking into it."

"That's great." Brian shook her hand then turned to the senior Mandel. Lindsey's father was an imposing man. Brian could only hope he wouldn't object to a civilian marrying his daughter. With his gray hair still short in a military buzz, he looked quite capable of holding his own in any kind of a fight.

"Thanks for getting my daughter and my boy's horse here. It means a lot to us."

"I'm glad I could help."

"Oh, look, here they come." Karen pushed Danny's chair closer to the curb. Marching in a straight line, Lindsey's unit passed by, pride evident in everyone's ramrod-straight bearing. Lindsey was looking straight ahead, but Dakota swung his head toward them and whinnied loudly.

Karen dropped to her brother's side. "He remembers you."

"He did, didn't he? But he never broke stride. He's a trouper. I'm glad he made it into Lindsey's unit. I'm so proud of both of them."

"Not half as proud as Lindsey is of you," Brian said, laying a hand on Danny's shoulder.

On the other side of them, a young man with a press badge stepped closer. "Excuse me, do you have family in the parade?"

Karen rose, smiling at the young man. "My sister."

"Would you mind if I asked you a few questions about her? The magazine I work for is looking for a common-man angle to the Inauguration."

"There's nothing common about my family," Mr. Mandel declared, turning back to the parade.

Karen wrinkled her nose and stepped closer to the reporter. "Don't mind my dad. But he is right. This is no common family. My sister is a sergeant in the army, my brother here, Danny, was also in the army until he was wounded in action. After that, he selflessly donated his beloved horse to my sister's unit at Fort Riley. Then what happened? The horse fell and broke his leg."

She paused to catch her breath. The reporter was quickly making notes.

She looked at Brian and winked. "That's when Dr. Brian *Cutter,* that's Cutter with a *C,* came to our rescue. He used a new gene therapy to heal Dakota's leg in record time."

Looking around at her family, a mischievous glint brightened her eyes. "Did I mention to everyone that he's going to marry Lindsey?"

* * *

Hours later, when the parade was finished and the crowds had dispersed, Brian waited beside the equine ambulance while Lindsey visited with her family. Still dressed in her turn-of-the-century uniform, the woman Brian loved with his whole heart finally made her way to his side. He slipped his arm across her shoulders as she slid her arm around his waist and leaned against him. Standing together, they drew comfort and happiness from each other. He looked down at her but she was watching Danny and Dakota.

It was obvious that Danny was tired but just as obvious that he wasn't ready to go home. Joy radiated from his expression. Dakota stood beside his wheelchair nuzzling his former master's face and searching his pockets in hopes of hidden treats. The smile that Abigail flashed at Brian made every minute of the long trip worthwhile.

"Thank you," Lindsey whispered.

"It was nothing," he answered softly.

"Oh, it was certainly something, Dr. Brian Cutter. How can I ever repay you?"

He looked down at her and smiled. "I'm sure I can think of something, darling."

Her soft laughter in response was all he needed to make this day and every day of his life—complete.

* * * * *

Dear Reader,

I hope you enjoyed Lindsey and Brian's journey toward love. The story of *The Color of Courage* was inspired by an actual event. I first met members of a mounted color guard when a detachment led the parade that opened the county fair near my hometown in Abilene, Kansas, in 2005. I assumed the young men dressed in 1860s period cavalry uniforms were local reenactors. I soon learned that they were active duty soldiers from Fort Irwin, California. The men, some recently returned from Iraq, were proud to share information about their unit and others like it. From them I learned about the Commanding General's Mounted Color Guard at Fort Riley, Kansas.

I knew I wanted to do a story about such a unit, but I wasn't sure where to start so I turned to the internet for some research. It was online that I first read about a horse named Ike from the CGMCG who suffered a fractured pastern and how the Kansas State College of Veterinary Medicine teamed up with the army to save his life. Ike was still in recovery when the rest of his unit went to Washington, D.C., for the 2005 Inaugural parade. When I read that bit of information, my story was born.

I had the privilege of visiting with the men and women of the Commanding General's Mounted Color Guard and I witnessed firsthand their feats of horsemanship. While their skill is truly extraordinary, it is their pride in serving their country and preserving a part of our history that impressed me the most. My words cannot do justice to their sacrifices and dedication.

Innumerable people helped with the research that went into writing this story. I'd like to thank Patrice Scott, media relations at K-Sate; Dr. James Lillich, DVM, MS associate professor, Equine Ortho and General Surgery at K-State; the department of public relations at Fort Riley; former unit commander Shane Pruente; and the men and women currently serving at Fort Riley. Any mistakes I made in writing this book are entirely my own fault.

Patricia Davids

Questions for Discussion

1. Brian had never been able to move past his guilt over his wife's death. Why do you believe he couldn't?

2. Should women in the army be allowed to serve in combat units? Why or why not?

3. Lindsey kept Dakota's condition from her brother until the very last minute. Was she right to do so? Why?

4. Hippotherapy is gaining recognition as a valuable form of rehabilitation. Is there a program in your area? How can you find out?

5. What two characters were most instrumental in getting Lindsey and Brian together?

6. Brian found it hard to believe that faith in God and military service go hand in hand. Do you believe that they do? Why or why not?

7. What lesson did Lindsey have to learn before she was ready to fall in love? How was that expressed in the story?

8. How did the humor in the story add to its enjoyment?

9. Did any element in the story affect how you view military service? Why?

10. Was Lindsey's decision to leave the army the right one? Why or why not?

Love Inspired
CLASSICS

Four sweet, heartfelt stories from fan-favorite
Love Inspired® authors!

HIS BUNDLE OF LOVE and
THE COLOR OF COURAGE
by Patricia Davids

HIS WINTER ROSE and
APPLE BLOSSOM BRIDE
by Lois Richer

Get two happily-ever-afters for the price of one!

Available in April 2013 wherever books are sold.

www.LoveInspiredBooks.com

LIC65159

REQUEST YOUR FREE BOOKS!

2 FREE INSPIRATIONAL NOVELS
PLUS 2
FREE
MYSTERY GIFTS

Love Inspired®

YES! Please send me 2 FREE Love Inspired® novels and my 2 FREE mystery gifts (gifts are worth about $10). After receiving them, if I don't wish to receive any more books, I can return the shipping statement marked "cancel." If I don't cancel, I will receive 6 brand-new novels every month and be billed just $4.49 per book in the U.S. or $4.99 per book in Canada. That's a saving of at least 22% off the cover price. It's quite a bargain! Shipping and handling is just 50¢ per book in the U.S. and 75¢ per book in Canada.* I understand that accepting the 2 free books and gifts places me under no obligation to buy anything. I can always return a shipment and cancel at any time. Even if I never buy another book, the two free books and gifts are mine to keep forever.

105/305 IDN FVV7

Name _____ (PLEASE PRINT) _____

Address _____ Apt. #

City _____ State/Prov. _____ Zip/Postal Code

Signature (if under 18, a parent or guardian must sign)

Mail to the Harlequin® Reader Service:
IN U.S.A.: P.O. Box 1867, Buffalo, NY 14240-1867
IN CANADA: P.O. Box 609, Fort Erie, Ontario L2A 5X3

Are you a subscriber to Love Inspired books
and want to receive the larger-print edition?
Call 1-800-873-8635 or visit www.ReaderService.com.

* Terms and prices subject to change without notice. Prices do not include applicable taxes. Sales tax applicable in N.Y. Canadian residents will be charged applicable taxes. Offer not valid in Quebec. This offer is limited to one order per household. Not valid for current subscribers to Love Inspired books. All orders subject to credit approval. Credit or debit balances in a customer's account(s) may be offset by any other outstanding balance owed by or to the customer. Please allow 4 to 6 weeks for delivery. Offer available while quantities last.

Your Privacy—The Harlequin® Reader Service is committed to protecting your privacy. Our Privacy Policy is available online at www.ReaderService.com or upon request from the Harlequin Reader Service.

We make a portion of our mailing list available to reputable third parties that offer products we believe may interest you. If you prefer that we not exchange your name with third parties, or if you wish to clarify or modify your communication preferences, please visit us at www.ReaderService.com/consumerchoice or write to us at Harlequin Reader Service Preference Service, P.O. Box 9062, Buffalo, NY 14269. Include your complete name and address.

LI13

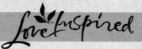
*Jolie Sheridan gets more than she bargained for
when she arrives at Sunrise Ranch for a teaching job.*

**Read on for a preview of
HER UNFORGETTABLE COWBOY by Debra Clopton.**

Jolie followed Morgan outside. There was a large gnarled oak tree still bent over as it had been all those years ago. She didn't stop until she reached it, turning his way only after they were beneath the wide expanse of limbs.

Morgan crossed his arms and studied the tree. "I remember having to climb up this tree and talk you down after you scrambled up to the top and froze."

She hadn't expected him to bring up old memories—it caught her a little off guard. "I remember how mad you were at having to rescue the silly little new girl."

A hint of a smile teased his lips, fraying Jolie's nerves at the edges. It had been a long time since she'd seen that smile.

"I got used to it, though," he said, his voice warming.

Electricity hummed between them as they stared at each other. Jolie sucked in a wobbly breath. Then the hardness in Morgan's tone matched the accusation in his eyes.

"What are you doing here, Jolie? Why aren't you taming rapids in some far-off place?"

"I…I'm—" She stumbled over her words. "I'm taking a leave from competition for a little while. I had a bad run in Virginia." She couldn't bring herself to say that she'd almost died. "Your dad offered me this teaching opportunity."

"I heard about the accident and I'm real sorry about that, Jolie," Morgan said. "But why come here after all this time?"

"This is my *home.*"

Jolie saw anger in Morgan's eyes. Well, he had a right to it, and more than a right to point it straight at her.

But she'd thought she'd prepared for it.

She was wrong.

"Morgan," Jolie said, almost as a whisper. "I'd hoped we could forget the past and move forward."

Heart pounding, she reached across the space between them and placed her hand on his arm. It was just a touch, but the feeling of connecting with Morgan McDermott again after so much time rocked her straight to her core, and suddenly she wasn't so sure coming home had been the right thing to do after all.

*Will Morgan ever allow Jolie back into
his life—and his heart?*

*Pick up HER UNFORGETTABLE COWBOY
from Love Inspired Books.*

Detective Melody Zachary halted abruptly at the sight of her office door of the Sagebrush Youth Center cracked open. Unease slithered down her spine. She'd locked the door last night when she left the center.

Pushing back her suit jacket, she withdrew her weapon. She pushed the door wide with the toe of her boot. Stepping inside the room, she reached for the overhead light switch and froze.

A shadow moved.

Not a shadow. A man.

Dressed from head to toe in black. Black gloves, black ski mask....

Palming her piece in both hands, she aimed her weapon. "Halt! Police!"

The intruder dove straight at her. She didn't have time to react, before he slammed into her chest, knocking her backward against the wall. Her head smacked hard, sending pain slicing through her brain.

The man bolted through the open doorway and disappeared.

Melody pushed away from the wall. For a moment her off-balance equilibrium sent the world spinning.

The exit door at the end of the hall banged shut. He was escaping.

Melody chased after the intruder. Out on the sidewalk, she searched for the trespasser. Sagebrush Boulevard was empty.

Holstering her piece and pulling her jacket closed, she retraced her steps and entered Sagebrush Youth Center's single-story brick building.

She stopped in her office doorway. The place had been ransacked. The filing cabinet had been emptied, the files strewn all over. The pictures of her family had been knocked off the desk.

A sense of violation cramped her chest. She was used to investigating this sort of vandalism, not being the victim herself.

Yanking her cell phone out of her purse, she dialed the Sagebrush police dispatch and reported the crime.

For the past several years, a crime wave had terrorized the citizens of Sagebrush. The mastermind behind the crime syndicate was a faceless, nameless entity that even the thugs who worked for "The Boss" feared.

A short time later, the center's front door opened. A small dog with his black nose pressed to the ground entered. Melody recognized the beagle as Sherlock, part of the K-9 unit. A harness attached to a leash led to the handsome man at the other end. Melody blinked.

What were narcotics detective Parker Adams and his K-9 partner doing here?

To find out, pick up SCENT OF DANGER
wherever Love Inspired Suspense books are sold.
Available May 2013

Love Inspired

Will You Marry Me?

Bold widow Johanna Yoder stuns Roland Byler when she asks him to be her husband. To Johanna, it seems very sensible that they marry. She has two children, he has a son. Why shouldn't their families become one? But the widower has never forgotten his long-ago love for her; it was his foolish mistake that split them apart. This could be a fresh start for both of them—until she reveals she wants a marriage of convenience only. It's up to Roland to woo the stubborn Johanna and convince her to accept him as her groom in her home and in her heart.

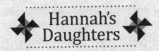

Hannah's Daughters

Johanna's Bridegroom

by

Emma Miller

Available May 2013

www.LoveInspiredBooks.com

LI87811

Love Inspired HISTORICAL

In the fan-favorite miniseries
Cowboys of Eden Valley

LINDA FORD

presents

The Cowboy's Convenient Proposal

Second Chance Ranch

She is a woman in need of protection. But trust is the one thing feisty Grace "Red" Henderson is sure she'll never give any man again—not even the cowboy who rescued her. Still, Ward Walker longs to protect the wary beauty and her little sister—in all the ways he couldn't safeguard his own family.

Red desperately wants to put her tarnished past behind her. Little by little, Ward is persuading her to take a chance on Eden Valley, and on him. Yet turning his practical proposal into a real marriage means a leap of faith for both…toward a future filled with the promise of love.

Available May 2013